"While you are here, I expect you to conduct yourself wisely and in a ladylike fashion," Eddie said.

Linette's nostrils flared. "You mean play the lady of the manor."

He had his doubts as to whether she even knew how a lady conducted herself. Like his father said, the Edwards family didn't fit in. Softly he asked, "How do you see your role here?"

She ducked her head so he was unable to see her expression. "I suppose I thought you meant to marry me." She lifted her head and faced him with her eyes flashing courage and challenge. "I will make a good pioneer wife."

"I never got your letter, or I could have warned you I'm not desperate for a wife. Besides, you can't simply substitute one woman for another as if they are nothing more than horses."

"Why not? Are you madly in love with Margaret?"

Love? There was no such thing as love in an arrangement like theirs. "We suited each other."

"She doesn't seem to share your view of suitability."

Linda Ford

The Cowboy's
Surprise Bride
&
The Cowboy's
Unexpected Family

LOVE INSPIRED
INSPIRATIONAL ROMANCE

Recycling programs
for this product may
not exist in your area.

ISBN-13: 978-1-335-97196-8

The Cowboy's Surprise Bride & The Cowboy's Unexpected Family

Copyright © 2021 by Harlequin Books S.A.

The Cowboy's Surprise Bride
First published in 2013. This edition published in 2021.
Copyright © 2013 by Linda Ford

The Cowboy's Unexpected Family
First published in 2013. This edition published in 2021.
Copyright © 2013 by Linda Ford

This edition published by arrangement with Harlequin Books S.A.

For questions and comments about the quality of this book, please contact us at CustomerService@Harlequin.com.

Love Inspired
22 Adelaide St. West, 40th Floor
Toronto, Ontario M5H 4E3, Canada
www.Harlequin.com

Printed in U.S.A.

CONTENTS

Linda Ford lives on a ranch in Alberta, Canada, near enough to the Rocky Mountains that she can enjoy them on a daily basis. She and her husband raised fourteen children—four homemade, ten adopted. She currently shares her home and life with her husband, a grown son, a live-in paraplegic client, and a continual (and welcome) stream of kids, kids-in-law, grandkids, and assorted friends and relatives.

Books by Linda Ford

Love Inspired Historical

Big Sky Country

Visit the Author Profile page
at Harlequin.com for more titles.

THE COWBOY'S
SURPRISE BRIDE

I have set before thee an open door,
and no man can shut it.
—*Revelation* 3:8

Chapter One

North-west Territories, Canada
October 1881

For the first time she was about to meet Eddie Gardiner. The man she intended to marry. The answer to her prayers.

Linette Edwards parted the curtains on the stagecoach—meant to keep out the dust and cold. The first few days of their trip, dust had filtered through them, and now cold with the bite of a wild beast filled every inch of the tiny coach. Four adults and a child huddled against the elements.

"You're letting in the cold," her traveling companion complained.

"I fear we are in for an early snowstorm," one of the male passengers said.

Linette murmured an apology but she managed to see the rolling hills and the majestic mountains before she dropped the curtain back in place. Since they'd left Fort Benton, headed for the ranch lands of the Northwest Territories of Canada, she'd peered out as much as she could. The mountains, jagged and bold, grew larger and larger. A song filled her heart and soul each time she saw them. This was a new country. She could start over. Be a different person than she'd been forced to be in England. Here she would be allowed to prove she had value as a person. She ignored the ache at how her parents viewed her—as a commodity to be traded for business favors.

She shifted her thoughts to the letter of invitation hidden safely in the cavernous pocket of the coat she'd acquired in Fort Benton. She longed to pull it out and read it again though she had memorized every word. *Come before winter.*

"I expect more than a shack," her friend Margaret had fumed when she'd read an earlier letter from the same writer. "After all, he comes from a very respectable family." With bitterness edging each word, Margaret read the letters describing the cabin Eddie assured her was only temporary quarters. "Temporary? I'm sure he doesn't know the meaning of the word. A year and a half he's been there and he still lives in this hovel."

"It sounds like an adventure." Linette could imagine a woman working side by side with her man, being a necessary asset to establishing a home in the new world. It sounded a lot more appealing to her than sitting and smiling vacantly as a female spectator. She'd been raised to be the lady of the manor but she wanted more. So much more.

Margaret had sniffed with such disdain that Linette giggled.

"I have made up my mind," Margaret said. "I cannot marry him and join him in the wilds of the Canadian

West. I expected far more when he asked for my hand before he left to start a Gardiner ranch out in that—" she fluttered her hand weakly "—in that savage land." Her shudder was delicate and likely deliberate.

"Oh, Margaret, surely you don't mean it."

"Indeed I do. I've written this letter."

Seated in the overstuffed parlor of Margaret's family home in London, Linette had read each word kindly but firmly informing Eddie that Margaret had changed her mind and would not be joining him now or anytime in the future. *I expect it makes me sound small and selfish, but I can't imagine living in a tiny house, nor being a woman of the West.*

"But what about your feelings for him? His for you?"

Margaret had given her a smile smacking of pity. "I enjoyed his company. He was a suitable candidate for marriage. There are plenty other suitable men."

How often she'd envied Margaret the opportunity to head to a new world with so much possibility simply for the eager taking of it. "But he's counting on you. Why would you want to stay here when the whole world beckons?" Wouldn't he be dreadfully hurt by Margaret's rejection?

"You should marry him. You're the one who thinks it would be a lark." Margaret was clearly annoyed with Linette's enthusiasm. "In fact, write him and I'll enclose your letter with mine."

"Write him? And say what?"

"That you're willing to be his wife."

"I don't know him." A trickle of something that felt suspiciously like excitement hurried up her limbs to her heart. But it couldn't be. It wasn't possible. "My father would never allow it."

Margaret laughed. "I think the Gardiner name would make even your father consider it a good idea. And would it not provide an escape from the marriage your father has planned?"

Linette shuddered. "I will not marry that old—" Her father had chosen a man in his fifties with a jangling purse of money and a drooling leer. His look made Linette feel soiled. She would do anything to avoid such a fate. She'd been praying for a reprieve. Perhaps this was an answer to her heartfelt petition.

Yes, the Gardiners were an old family, well respected, with a great estate and vaults of money, as her father so often said with utmost reverence in his voice.

"Of course," Margaret started, considering her with a mocking smile, "if you're dreaming of love and romance—"

Linette jerked back. "All I'm thinking of is escape." Love did not enter into a suitable marriage, which was fine with her. She fully intended to keep her feelings out of the picture. A trembling in the depths of her heart warned her that love would make her weak, vulnerable, ready to give up her personal goals. Not something she intended to let happen. She grabbed a piece of paper. "I'm going to do it. Anything is better than what my parents have in mind." Being a rancher's wife in the new world suited her fine. She was weary of the social restrictions her parents insisted on and not at all loath to living the kind of life she'd heard existed in the new world. There, women marched side by side with their men. They were even allowed to own land! Doubtlessly they'd be allowed to get their hands dirty and be involved.

Before she could change her mind, she'd penned a

short letter. *A marriage of convenience if it suits you. Please reply to Margaret's address.* She knew her father would read any letter that came to the house. Much better to know she had a positive answer from Mr. Gardiner before confronting her father. If she had to be part of a business deal, it would be on her terms. She'd say who and where.

She clasped her fingers on the answering letter that had carried two tickets—one for herself and one for a traveling companion. The missive was brief. Not much more than an invitation to come. Her heart had danced for joy. Margaret was right; her father had glowed at an invitation from a Gardiner.

The stagecoach swayed to a stop. "Hello, the house." The driver's call shivered up and down Linette's spine. They'd arrived at Eden Valley Ranch.

It wasn't as if Eddie were a *total* stranger. She'd read his letters to Margaret. He sounded like a strong man, an independent thinker. She had no trouble imagining herself sharing his life. Yet her insides clenched in trepidation.

She squeezed right back in protest. She would not let nerves weaken her resolve. She'd prayed for such an escape and God had generously provided. *Hitherto hath the Lord helped me.* Renewed faith filled her, driving away any doubts and fears.

One of the two men who also rode in the coach flicked aside a curtain. "Looks like a fine establishment."

Linette parted the curtains again and peeked outside. The coach had drawn up before a log cabin with only a narrow door and small window in the wall facing them. This must be where the man lived. She pressed her tongue to the roof of her mouth and refused to think how small it looked. Hardly big enough for all of them. Never mind. Nothing could deter her now. She'd prayed her way from London, over the Atlantic Ocean, and across most of the North American continent. The rooms she'd had on the trip had left barely enough space for stretching. Although vastly different from the spacious home she'd grown up in, she'd gotten used to it readily enough. This cabin would be no different.

The door of the cabin opened and Linette took a deep breath. A man stepped forth, ducking as he crossed the threshold. This had to be Eddie Gardiner. She'd seen his likeness in pictures, but they failed to do the man justice. Despite the chill in the air, he hadn't bothered to grab a coat or hat and in the bright sunshine his brown hair shone. He dressed like a range hand—dark denim trousers, a blue shirt that had faded almost colorless on the sleeves with dark remnants of the color in the seams, and a leather vest that looked worn and friendly.

Her heart jumped to her throat. She hadn't expected to feel anything for him. Surely it was only excitement, combined with a touch of nerves. After all, despite the letters, he was a stranger. She wanted nothing more or less from him than a marriage of convenience.

His gaze sought the parted curtains and his dark eyes narrowed as he tried to make out the face in the dim interior.

She flicked the curtain closed and turned to her traveling companion. "You keep the child while I meet him." The boy would remain a secret for now. Seeing her intention, one of the gentlemen stepped down and held out a hand to assist her. She murmured her thanks as Eddie strode forward.

He slid his gaze over her as if she were invisible and looked toward the stagecoach. "Is Margaret inside?"

Linette shook her head trying to make sense of his question. Surely he'd mistakenly spoken her name out of habit.

"Is she at Fort Benton? If so I'll go for her immediately." He glanced at the sky as if already trying to outrace the weather.

Her mouth felt like yesterday's dust as she realized what he meant. "You're expecting Margaret?" It took every ounce of her stubborn nature not to stammer.

"Any day. I sent tickets for her and a chaperone to come before winter."

Come before winter. She remembered the words well. They'd bubbled through her heart. But she thought they were meant for her. "Did you not get the letter?"

At that the driver jumped down. "'Spect any letters you'd be wanting are in here." He waved a small bundle. "Seems you haven't picked up your mail for some time, so I brought it."

Cold trickled across Linette's neck, dug bony fingers into her spine and sent a faint sense of nausea up her throat. She swallowed it back with determination. If he hadn't received her letter, then the tickets he'd sent hadn't been meant for her. He didn't know she was coming. He wasn't prepared to welcome her and accept her as a suitable helpmate on the frontier. Now what?

She stiffened her shoulders. She had not crossed an ocean and a vast continent to be turned back now. Her prayers for escape had been fervent. God held her in the palm of His hand now as He had on the journey. This was her answer. She nailed her fears to the thought. Besides, nothing had changed. Not really. Margaret still wasn't coming and he still needed a wife. Didn't he? She sought her memories but could not remember that he'd ever said so in clear, unmistakable terms. Had she read more into his missives than was meant?

Eddie took the bundle of mail and untied the strings. He flicked through the correspondence.

Recognizing Margaret's handwriting, she touched the envelope. "That one." Her own message lay inside, unseen by the man she thought had invited her to join him. She sucked moisture from the corners of her mouth and swallowed hard.

He slit the envelope and pulled out the pages in which she'd offered to take Margaret Sear's place. *I look forward to being part of the new West.* He read her letter then Margaret's, his fingers tightening on the paper as he understood the message. A flash of pain crossed his face before he covered it with a harsh expression.

Her heart twisted. He expected Margaret and instead got his hopes and dreams shattered. If only she'd known. But what could she do about it now? Except prove she was better suited to be a woman of the West.

Thankfully he did not read the letter aloud, which would have added to her growing embarrassment as the three men listened intently—one peering from the inside of the coach, one standing at its side where he remained after helping her alight, the other pretending to check on the horses though he made certain he could hear what was said. Even so, her face burned at their curiosity about an obvious misunderstanding of mammoth proportions.

Eddie jammed the pages back in the envelope. "This is unacceptable."

Her muscles turned to warm butter. It took concentrated effort to hold herself upright, to keep her face rigid. She would not let him guess that the ground threatened to rise up and clout her in the face.

One hand clasping the mail bundle, he jammed his fists to his hips and turned to the driver. "You can return her to the fort."

The man tipped his hat back on his head and shook his head. "Ain't goin' a mile more'n I have to. It's about to snow."

The wind bit at Linette's cheeks but the cold encasing her heart was not from the wintery weather. She could not, would not, go back to London and her father's plans.

The coach driver went on in his leisurely way of speaking. "I'm taking these two gentlemen to the OK Ranch then I'd hoped to make it back to Fort Benton where I intend to hole up for the winter. I don't fancy being stuck in Edendale." He made a rattling noise in the back of his throat. "But it looks like I'll be stuck at the OK for the time being."

Linette cared not whether the man was returning to the tiny cluster of huts bravely named Edendale or back to Fort Benton. She wasn't going anywhere.

The gentleman who'd helped her down still stood at the steps, waiting and watching. "The girl is strong. Tough. Takes a special kind of lady to take care of travel arrangements and her traveling companions. Not a lot of young women are prepared and able to do that. You could do worse than have her at your side in this brave new frontier."

Linette gave the man a fleeting smile of appreciation then turned back to Eddie.

Eddie met her gaze. He must have read her determination though she hoped he hadn't seen her desperation. "We need to talk." He grabbed her arm and marched her around the side of the house, out of sight and hopefully out of earshot of the others, where he released her to glare hotly at her.

She tipped her chin and met his gaze without flinching even though her insides had begun to tremble. Where would she go if he sent her away? Not back to the marriage her father had arranged. Perhaps money would convince him. "I have a dowry."

"Keep your money. I have no need of it."

"I came in good faith. I thought you'd received my letter." *Come before winter.* The words had seemed so welcoming. She'd made preparations as quickly as she could. How was she to know he didn't respond to her letter? Hadn't even received it. She stood motionless. She wouldn't let so much as one muscle quiver.

"Obviously I hadn't." He stared at the bundle in his hand, sounding every bit as confused as she felt. A contrast to the anger her parents had expressed when she'd informed them she would not marry the man of their choosing and meant to go West. Only after she showed her father the letter from Eddie and only because the Gardiners were a well-respected family had he agreed. With many constraints. Her father knew her too well. Knew she would avoid this marriage, too, if she had the means to strike out on her own. Knew she would not flinch before the dangers nor shirk from the challenges. That's why he'd allowed her barely enough money to keep from starving to death on the journey and made sure her dowry would be held until he had proof she was married. He'd made her understand he would allow her only enough time for the necessary documents to cross the ocean. Should they not arrive in a reasonable time he would send one of his henchmen to bring her back. She'd used the limited funds he'd provided caring for the sick and destitute she'd crossed paths with. She had not so much as a penny to her name.

She shuddered as she imagined one of her father's cruel servants poised and ready to pursue her.

There was no escape from her father's plans apart from this marriage.

She understood Eddie's shock. It couldn't feel good to realize Margaret had refused to come, refused his offer of marriage. She swallowed back a swell of sympathy, and resisted an urge to pat his arm. She brought her thoughts back to her own predicament. "I'm prepared to care for your home." As soon as she and Margaret agreed Linette should take her place, Margaret had reluctantly arranged for their cook to teach Linette to prepare food and run a house. She hadn't dared to ask for such instructions at home. Her father had often enough said they were rich and had servants to do menial work. Only the death of some distant relative of her mother's who'd made a fortune in India had changed the family circumstances from penniless to well off before Linette's birth. Father wanted everyone to believe they were landed gentry, but she often wondered how much of the inheritance still existed and suspected her father's plans for her were meant to add to the coffers. But how much was enough to satisfy her father? She wondered if enough existed.

"He should have servants to do those things," Margaret had fumed when Linette badgered her to arrange instruction.

"It will be an adventure to do something useful."

Unless Eddie changed his mind, her lessons seemed destined to be useless. She stiffened her spine. Failure was not an option.

Eddie turned his gaze back to her then with a great sigh eased toward the stagecoach.

She followed at his heels. "I'm a hard worker." She would press her point but she wouldn't beg.

The driver stood at his horses, staring at the horizon and shifting from one foot to the other. "Eddie boy, the wind has a bite to it. Winter is likely to clutch us by the throat any moment."

She'd wondered at the earliness of the snow, but the man in the coach had explained it was due to being in high country. "Snow can come early and stay or leave again. There's no predicting it."

Eddie turned to speak over his shoulder. "I'm to be stuck with you then. But only until the weather moderates then I'll send you back."

"Stuck? Seems you're getting the better part of this bargain." She had no intention of staying one day more than she must, but she silently prayed the winter would set in early and be long and cold, preventing travel. That would give her sufficient time to persuade Eddie to change his mind.

She would not—under any circumstances—return to her father and his despicable plan for her.

Despite her lack of funds, she considered setting off on her own but she must acknowledge the facts—her father would not let her escape his clutches. He had ways and means of tracking her wherever she went. And he wouldn't hesitate to use them. She knew she couldn't hide from him even if she found a means of surviving on her own.

Eddie still provided the only answer to avoiding her father's plans. Winter provided a reprieve. She would use the time to prove to him she was the ideal pioneer wife. She would make him want to keep her. He'd beg her to stay.

Eddie ground to a halt and turned to face her.

She blinked back her silent arguments lest he guess at her thoughts.

He edged forward, forcing her to retreat until they were again out of sight and hearing of the interested party waiting at the stagecoach. "You might want to reconsider this rash decision of yours. It's wild out here. There are no luxuries. No chaperones."

"I brought my own chaperone." If he found her arrival a burden, he was not going to like her next announcement. She tipped her chin and faced him squarely. Not for all the roses in her mother's garden would she reveal so much as a hint of trepidation. "And a child."

"A child?"

"Yes, I brought a child."

He swallowed hard enough to lose his Adam's apple. "You have a child?"

He thought the child was hers? Embarrassment, laced with a heavy dose of amusement, raced through her at the shock on his face. Her amusement could not be contained and she laughed delicately, feeling her eyes dance with merriment. "He's not mine."

"Then why do you have him?"

"I met his mother on the boat. She died in the crossing and asked me to take the child to his father."

"I'm not his father." The poor man almost choked at the thought.

She laughed again, thoroughly enjoying his discomfort. "I didn't mean to imply you were. His father met us in Montreal and when he heard his wife had expired, refused to take his son." A dreadful scene had ensued as Linette tried to convince the man of his duty. "I had little choice but to bring him along."

Eddie choked again.

Maybe she would have to thump him between the shoulders, and found the idea rather satisfying. With every passing moment, he proved more and more annoying. She'd expected a welcome of some sort, guarded perhaps, or even perfunctory. She assumed he would have made arrangements to have someone present to perform their emotionless union. But never in her many far-flung imaginings had she considered this possibility.

He cleared his throat. "I think a place the size of Montreal would have a foundling home. I think the nuns have—"

"Are you suggesting I should have abandoned him to strangers?"

"It's not called abandon—" He must have read the challenge in her eyes for he stopped short. "Seems to me that's what a sensible woman would have done. Besides, wouldn't he be better off there with schools and playmates?"

She pulled herself as tall as she could, annoyed she still had to tip her head to glare at him. "We better get something straight right here and now. I have no tol-

erance for the pharisaical affectations of our society. I
refuse to stand by and not offer help to someone when
it is within my power to give more than an empty blessing. I could not, nor would I, turn my back on a small
child." Helping others was one of the many things she
and her father had warred about. She expected things
to be different in the British Territories of Canada.

She planned to make sure they were.

Eddie stared at her then scrubbed at the back of
his neck. "All I have is a small cabin. Only one bed."

She had gained a small victory. No need to push for
more at this point. "We'll take the bed."

"And I'm to what?"

"I understand from your letters to Margaret that
there is a bunkhouse for men who work for you."

"I will not sleep with them."

His words had a familiar, unwelcome ring to them.
"Does it offend your sensibilities to share quarters with
the men who work for you?"

"Not at all, but it would be awkward for them. I'm
the boss. They deserve a chance to relax without thinking I'm watching them."

His reply both surprised and pleased her. She admired a man who thought of others. But her admiration did not solve what he perceived to be a quandary.
She didn't see a problem. "I believe the cabin has two
rooms. You can sleep on the floor in the other room."

"You are too generous." The look on his face made
her want to laugh, but she sensed he did not share her
amusement.

"Eddie boy," the driver called. "I'd like to get on my
way before nightfall."

Eddie and Linette did silent duel with their eyes. Although their weapons were invisible she understood her life and her future hung on the outcome of this battle. Finally he sighed. "Come along. Let's get your things."

"There's something I better tell you first."

"You mean there are more surprises? Let me guess. Another child? A brother or sister? A—"

"My chaperone is a woman I met in Montreal. Her husband died and she has no family."

"You traveled from England without a chaperone?"

She flicked him an impatient glance. It was easy to see that rules meant a lot to him. She'd prayed he wasn't like her father. Now he seemed frighteningly so. "Of course not, but Miss Snodgrass was eager to return, and when she saw I intended for Cassie to accompany me, she got on the next boat home."

He waited, aware there was more.

"Cassie is a little…well, I suppose you could say she's having trouble dealing with her grief."

"Trouble? In what way?"

Words came quickly to her mind, but none of them seemed the sort to make him kindly disposed toward Cassie. Perhaps the less she said the better. "Let's just say she's a bit sharp." She hastened to add, "I'm sure she'll settle down once the edge of her grief has passed."

He scrubbed at his neck again. "Let's see what you have."

She hurried past him, fearing if he thrust his head in the door and ordered the pair out, the ensuing reaction would give them all cause for regret. The kind gentleman who had assisted her from the coach watched for her return, doubtless listening with ears cocked. She wondered how much he'd heard. Not that it mattered.

He'd already managed to get most of the story from her as they bounced along for several days with nothing to do but stare at each other. He held the door for her and with a quirk of his eyebrows silently asked if things had gone well.

She gave a quick nod, grateful for his kindly interest, then turned to the other occupants. "Cassie, we're here. Come out. Grady, come here." She reached to take the four-year-old from Cassie's lap

Grady seemed to shrivel into himself. Only at Cassie's gentle insistence did he let Linette take his hand and lift him to the ground. He took one look at Eddie and buried his face in her skirts. She knew he would stay there until she pried him free.

Cassie grabbed her small travel valise and paused in the open doorway. The look she gave Eddie blazed with anger.

Please, God. Keep her from saying something that will give him a reason to put us on the stage again without any regard for where we'll end.

"He's passable, I suppose."

Linette's breath stuck halfway to her lungs. She stole a glance at Eddie. Surprise flashed in his eyes and then he grinned. He had a nice face when he smiled, but more than that, his smile made her feel he would be patient with Cassie, who often expressed her pain in meanness. Relief poured through Linette like a warming drink.

"Thanks," Eddie said.

"Wasn't meant as a compliment," Cassie murmured.

"I've been told worse." He held his hand out to assist Cassie, but she pointedly ignored him and accepted help from their traveling companion.

Linette's attention was diverted as the driver handed down the two trunks she'd brought. Grady had only a grip bag.

Eddie whistled sharply, causing Grady to sob. Two men stepped from the building across the way.

"Yeah, boss?" one called.

"Boys, take these trunks to my house."

Linette watched the two cross the roadway in long, rolling strides. Their gait reminded her of the sailors on the ship. They had on Stetson hats, worn and rolled, unlike the new, uniformly shaped ones she'd studied back at the trading post in Fort Benton where she'd exchanged her fine English silks and bustles for frocks she considered more appropriate for living in the wilds—simple-cut dresses of calico or wool. She'd procured a dress for Cassie too but the woman refused to wear it. "I am who I am and I'm not about to pretend otherwise," she'd said. Linette hadn't pressed the point. Sooner or later the old garment Cassie wore would fall apart and then she'd be glad for what Linette offered.

She glanced at her own dress. A little the worse for wear after crossing the prairie. She'd clean up once they got settled in case Eddie took note of her rumpled state.

As they walked, the men jingled from the spurs on their boots. They yanked their hats off and squirmed inside their buffalo coats. "Ma'am." They nodded to Linette and Cassie.

"Miss Edwards, may I present two of my men, Slim—" he indicated the taller, thinner man. "And Roper." The other man was heavier built. Solid. Younger. And he watched Cassie with guarded interest.

Linette realized she hadn't introduced her companion and did so. "Cassie Godfrey." Then she indicated the boy half-buried in her skirts. "This is Grady Farris. He's four years old." He shivered enough to make her leg vibrate.

The men nodded then jammed their hats back on and took the trunks into the house.

Eddie spoke privately to the driver who then swung up to his seat and drove from the yard. Linette stared after the coach, knowing she now had no escape. She was at Eddie's mercy. Her resolve hardened. Only so far as she chose to be. She'd be no man's slave. Nor his chattel. Any arrangement between them would be based on mutual benefit. No emotions involved to turn her weak.

The stagecoach no longer blocked her view and she saw, on the hill overlooking the ranch, a big two-story house, gleaming in its newness. It had the unfinished look of raw lumber and naked windows. They must be expecting neighbors. People who put more value in their abode than Eddie. When would these people finish the house and move in?

"I suppose you would like to see your quarters." Eddie indicated they should step toward the low dwelling.

She turned from studying the house on the hill to closer inspection of the cabin. It looked even smaller than she expected. But she didn't care. She'd escaped her father's plans and the future beckoned.

Eddie resisted the urge to squeeze his neck. It was tight enough to withstand a hanging. He'd expected the mail would contain a message to meet Margaret. He'd planned to marry her at the fort before bringing her to his home. He'd thought of her every day as he worked on the new house. He'd counted the days until she joined him.

Margaret was the ideal young lady for him. He remembered many a pleasant afternoon sharing her company in her family home in London before he'd left for the British Territories. He'd grown quite fond of her and she of him. Or so he thought. In time their affection would grow. He anticipated the day she would arrive and marry him. Margaret would grace the big house he would have completed by now except for the necessity of making sure the breeding stock he'd had shipped from Chicago was herded safely from Fort Benton to the nearby pens.

Instead, a ragamuffin of a woman stood before him in a black woolen coat that practically swallowed her. As it flapped open he saw a crude dress much like those he'd seen worn by wives on hopeful dirt farms and the half-breed women in the forts. She looked ready to live in a tepee or log hut, which was likely a good thing because the latter was all he had to offer her.

The cold wind reminded him he'd hurried outside without a coat. "We might as well go indoors."

How Linette managed to make her way to the house with the boy clinging to her side like a giant burr amazed him.

She was an Edwards daughter if he believed what she said. He wasn't prepared to believe anything about her at the moment. How had he ended up in such an awkward position? And with an Edwards woman! His father had had some business dealings with Mr. Edwards years ago and had expressed distaste for the other man. "A churlish man," he'd said. "Thinks because he inherited money through his wife it makes him an aristocrat, but he lacks any sense of decorum or decency. I vow I will never have business dealings with him again and I intend to avoid any social contact." Eddie couldn't think the Edwards daughter would warrant any better opinion from his father.

Slim and Roper hurried out and jogged back to work. Not, he noted, without a backward glance at the women. They'd be filled with curiosity for sure and spend the rest of the day speculating about this turn of events.

Eddie had always done his best to live up to his father's expectations. After all, he owed the man so much. Coming West and starting a ranch to add to the Gardiner holdings, establishing a home that would make his father proud provided him an opportunity to repay his father for giving him the Gardiner name. Randolph Gardiner had married Eddie's mother when Eddie was an infant. If not for that, Eddie would have been an outcast bastard child and his mother would have lived in shame and disgrace.

He held the door for the ladies and Linette stepped inside first. The sigh that whistled from her lips drove back the gall in his throat and made him grin. Had she been expecting something fancy? No doubt this crude cabin shocked her. It was only temporary and then would serve as quarters for a foreman. If the man was married and had a family, Eddie would add on to it but had not seen any need for that now. It had solid walls. It was warm and dry. It served as a place to put his feet up and have a cup of coffee and somewhere to catch a comfortable night's sleep. Not much else.

The letter clutched in his fist crackled. Margaret had

changed her mind. As if he didn't measure up. His insides twisted in a familiar, unwelcome way.

He studied the woman he was stuck with. Linette was almost plain. Her eyes too direct. Her lips too narrow and stubborn, almost challenging. Her hair was light in color. Neither brown nor blond and coiled in a braid about her face. Her eyes were so pale they didn't deserve to be called brown. She was too small. Built like a struggling sapling out on the prairie. In fact, everything about her was wrong. Quite the opposite of Margaret. No way would she fit into his plans. His father's instructions were clear. "Find suitable land and build a house. A replica of our home and life back here in England." Eddie had been surprised his father had entrusted him with the task and vowed he would make his father proud.

Linette Edwards could not be allowed to ruin his plans.

But he couldn't send her away with the weather threatening to turn nasty. He'd shelter her until it moderated…which likely meant for the winter. Then, under armed escort if necessary, he would see her returned to England or wherever she might have a mind to go… just so long as it wasn't here.

Trouble was, she wasn't alone. Not that she should be. But the woman she'd brought along looked as if she'd been rescued from the gutter. Her clothes barely missed being called rags. Her untidy black hair and scowling face indicated she was not happy to be here. He snorted silently. At least they shared that. He wasn't happy to have any of them here.

Then there was the boy with a flash of blue eyes and a mat of blond hair sticking out from under his cap.

He often thought of children to fill the rooms in the big house, but children bred with a woman like Margaret. Not waifs.

Cassie hesitated at the doorway. The noise that escaped her mouth was full of anger and discontent. "I had more room back in Montreal."

Linette laughed softly—a merry sound full of pleasure. She didn't seem the least bit distressed about the conditions.

"You slept in the train station after your husband died and left you stranded in a strange city," she said to Cassie. "Of course it was bigger. But it wasn't home. This will be home." The word was full of promise and warmth.

He figured he better make sure she remembered it was temporary. "Until better weather." Silently, he again acknowledged that might not be before spring and the thought made his neck muscles spasm. "Then you're headed back to your father."

"There's many a slip between the cup and the lip."

Her disregard of his warning made him chomp on his back teeth. It took an effort to release the tension so he could speak. "There'll be no slips here."

Cassie edged forward into the room and stood with her arms crossed. He figured her eyes would be crossed, too, and full of displeasure. Good. If both women found the situation intolerable… But it was a long time until spring. A crowded house with two women dripping discontent would be miserable for everyone.

What had he done to deserve this?

Margaret's letter said she didn't think she could face the challenges of frontier life nor live in small quarters.

He'd meant the big house to be a surprise. Now he saw keeping it a secret had been cause for her to think she'd be confined to some sort of settler's shack. His mind kicked into salvage thoughts. Miss Edwards would see the house. She'd realize it was almost finished. She could report its fineness to Margaret. Margaret would change her mind. She'd be pleased to join him. Tension drained from him so quickly his limbs twitched.

He realized the interior of the little house lacked warmth and closed the door behind him. He'd been about to leave the cabin and had let the fire die to embers. "I'll get some heat in here." Deftly, he added wood, and in minutes welcoming flames sprang to life. Now he'd have to plan on heating the house all day. He'd have to get more firewood chopped. These women and the boy were going to be a nuisance as well as a threat.

"I didn't realize how cold I'd grown," Linette said, holding her hands toward the stove. "Is it usually this cold in October?"

"Snow comes early this close to the mountains, though I hope it holds off for a time yet. The cows are still up in the higher pastures."

"And you would prefer to have them where? Down here?"

"Yes. Down in the lower meadows where they'll be able to get to the grass."

"You don't feed them?"

She sure was full of questions. "Do you know anything about ranching?"

"A cousin raised cattle. He always kept them in barns and pens in the winter and fed them hay."

He chuckled. "Hard to build a barn big enough for

a thousand head or more." The way she widened her eyes in surprise gave him a moment's victory then he wished he'd kept the fact to himself. If she was a gold digger he'd provided her with more to dig for. "I have some hay. Most ranchers don't think it's necessary, but one of the first men I talked to when I came out here was Kootenai Brown. He's lived in the mountains for years and says only a buffalo can survive without hay. They dig through the grass like a horse. He told me if I want to succeed in this venture I should plan to have hay available." Why was he telling her all this? Surely she didn't care. But her pale brown eyes flashed with intelligent interest. Not the fake batting of eyelashes he'd seen from women who seemed to think any sign of intelligence would frighten off a man.

"Kootenai Brown? Isn't Kootenai the name of an Indian tribe?"

He couldn't hide his surprise. Didn't even try. "How do you know that?"

"I've read everything I could find about the Northwest."

He turned his attention to stoking the fire to conceal his reluctant admiration.

Cassie groaned. "And she likes to talk about it all day long." She moved marginally closer to the stove as if reluctant to allow herself any comfort her circumstances might provide.

Linette laughed softly. "I didn't realize I was boring you."

"You and that gentleman from the coach. Did he say he was going to another ranch?"

"Yes. I believe he said he was an investor with the

OK Ranch and intended to check on its operation."
She turned back to Eddie. "Would that be correct?"

"Could be. Good thing if it's true. The OK bunch
has run into some trouble."

"What sort? Wild animals? Rustlers?" She practically quivered with excitement.

He studied her more closely. Was she the sort to be
bounding into trouble just because it sounded adventuresome? He did not need that sort of aggravation. He
answered her question first. "They lost cows by driving
them north too hard. The rest of the herd is weakened.
If they don't see them properly fed I fear they will lose
the works." He intended to make sure she wasn't about
to turn his life inside out and upside down and put his
peace and security at risk—any more than she had already. "You don't find trouble to be exciting, do you?"

"If you think I'd be happy to hear of a herd of cows
suffering—" Her eyes snapped with anger.

"I was thinking you seem overly anxious to think
there might be wild animals or rustlers. I warn you I
won't tolerate anyone deliberately putting themselves
or others at risk simply for an exciting experience."

"What will you tolerate?" Linette demanded.

They studied each other with wariness. And a startling sense of shared determination that shifted his
opinion of this woman. Of course, they shared that.
Only in different directions. He was determined to
carry out his original plan to marry Margaret and establish a home he could be proud of. She meant to upset
his plans. "While you are here, I expect you to conduct
yourself wisely and in a ladylike fashion."

Her nostrils flared. "You mean play the lady of the
manor."

Behind her, Cassie snorted.

She'd no doubt been raised as such. Why didn't she offer to be so here? Not that it made any difference. He wasn't about to toss Margaret aside over a misunderstanding. Softly, he asked, "What do you see your role as here?"

She ducked her head so he was unable to see her expression. "I suppose I thought you meant to marry me." She lifted her head and faced him with her eyes flashing courage and challenge. "I will make a good pioneer wife."

"I never got your letter or I could have warned you I'm not desperate for a wife. Besides, you can't simply substitute one woman for another as if they are nothing more than horses."

"Why not? Are you madly in love with Margaret?"

Love? There was no such thing as love in an arrangement like theirs. "We suited each other."

"She doesn't seem to share your view of suitability."

He guessed she meant if she had, Margaret would be here instead of her. He pointed toward the window. "I mean to correct that. Did you see that house out there?"

She nodded.

"I built it for Margaret."

Linette's eyes widened. "But she said…" She looked about at the tiny quarters and shook her head. "I don't understand."

"I wanted it to be a surprise. I see now I should have informed her about the house. But you can write and tell her how special it is. Once she knows, she'll reconsider and come."

She fixed him with a direct stare. "You really believe that's all there is to her refusal to come?" Her gaze demanded honesty.

His neck knotted and he squeezed the back of it. He thought Margaret wanted to share his life. He still believed it. Surely what he had to offer was acceptable to Margaret. She only objected to meager quarters and that would soon be a thing of the past. He looked about the small room. "I obviously don't need help running this place. And I don't need or want a pioneer wife. My wife will have a cook and housekeeper to help her run the big house." He returned to confront her demanding look. "But with winter coming on—"

"You'll tolerate our presence until spring?" Her voice carried a low note of something he couldn't quite put his thumb on. Warning? Challenge?

He scrubbed the back of his neck again, wondering how much more tension it could take before something snapped. Most of his time was spent with animals who had little to say but *moo* and with cowboys known to be laconic. It didn't much prepare him to pick up on subtle nuances of social communication, but even a dolt would understand her question was more than mere conversation. "I expect we'll have to tolerate each other, crowded as we'll be in these quarters."

Cassie spun away to stare at the door. "I should have stayed in Montreal."

Linette gave her a tight smile. "You weren't exactly happy there, if I recall."

"Seems happiness is too much to hope for."

Linette hurried to her side and wrapped an arm around the woman's waist. "Of course it's not. We'll be happy here. About as happy as we make up our minds to be. All of us." The look she sent Eddie warned him to disagree or make it impossible. "Isn't that right, Mr. Gardiner?"

"I'm sure we can be civilized. After all, we're adults." Except for young Grady, and all eyes turned toward him. "I expect he's the only one we need to be concerned about." The child had been abandoned then put into the care of strangers. Which made Eddie that much more grateful to his father for the life he'd been given.

Seeing everyone watching him, Grady started to whimper. The boy's fears vibrated through the room.

Eddie thought of stroking the child's head to calm him but knew it would only upset him further. He was at a loss to know how to comfort the boy.

Linette knelt to face Grady squarely. "You're safe here. We'll take care of you."

"I want my mama," he wailed loudly.

Linette dropped to the floor, pulled the boy to her lap and crooned as she rocked him. "Mr. Gardiner, I believe Grady is hungry. Can you direct me to the food supplies and I'll gladly make us tea."

Food? He had no food to speak of in the cabin. "I've been taking my meals over at the cookhouse." Would they like to go to the cookhouse, too?

Grady wailed louder, as if Eddie had announced they were all about to starve. Seems Grady had answered the question. He would not be comfortable among so many strangers. Best to let them eat here. "I'll rustle up some supplies right away." Grateful for an excuse to escape the cabin, crowded as it was with bodies and feelings, he grabbed his coat and hat and headed across the yard.

Dare he hope the weather would moderate long

enough for the stagecoach driver to decide to venture back to Edendale or Fort Benton? If so, he would have that trio on their way.

But he knew that scenario was about as likely as finding a satchel full of money on the ground before him.

Another thought sprang to life. After less than an hour his nerves were strung tight as a drum. How would he endure months of this?

Chapter Two

Eddie told Cookie the whole story as he waited for her to put together supplies for the unwelcome guests. "I intend to rectify the situation just as soon as the snow goes." With any favor from the Lord above, that would be sooner rather than later. Until then, he would simply make the best of it.

"She ugly?" Cookie demanded.

"She's passable."

"Cross-eyed?"

"No. Can you get things together a little faster?"

"I'm goin' as fast as these old legs will go."

Eddie let out a long, exasperated sigh. Cookie wasn't old except when it pleased her to be so. The rest of the time she kept up a pace that would wear out a horse.

"Then she's got those horrible teeth so many women have." Cookie did a marvelous imitation of a beaver with protruding upper front teeth.

"Didn't notice any such teeth when she smiled." Though he did note how she carried herself with such grace. She hadn't been raised to be a pioneer woman. Why would she choose it? "Now, how about some tea?

You got lots or do I need to run to the supply shed?"
Provisions for the winter months were stored in a tight
outbuilding lined with tin to keep rodents out.

"I got tea enough to spare. Smile, did you say? So
she has a pleasant nature?"

"Look, Cookie. I've spent only a few minutes in
her company. It's not enough time for me to form an
evaluation of her personality." Except to note she had
a cheerful laugh and—it seemed at first meeting—an
equally cheerful nature. Matched by a dreadfully stubborn attitude.

Cookie laughed boisterously and clapped him on
the shoulder hard enough to set him forward a step.
"Guess you won't be able to say that after a winter together in that tiny shack."

Her husband, Bertie, came in with a load of wood
for the big stove. "Bertie," Cookie roared. "There's two
women and a little boy in Eddie's shack."

Eddie groaned at the blatant pleasure wreathing
Bertie's face.

"Well, I'll be hornswoggled and hog-tied. This is
turning into a real homey sit'ation. Eddie, lad, you've
surprised us real good."

Cookie and Bertie grinned at each other like a pair
of silly children.

"It's all a mistake, as I told Cookie. They'll go home
come spring. I'd send them now only the stagecoach
isn't running, and with winter—"

"Eddie, lad, I'm thinking this opportunity is a rare
one. Don't be letting it slip through your fingers." Bertie nodded and grinned.

"I'm of like mind, my love. I'm of like mind."
Cookie clapped her husband hard on the back.

Eddie wasn't a bit sorry for the other man when he shifted under his wife's hearty affections. "It's temporary. Why can't you accept that?" He grabbed the sack and stomped across the yard, their laughter echoing at his heels.

"He's not happy to have us here." Cassie's observation was almost laughable.

Linette simply smiled. "Then it's up to us to convince him otherwise." She had not come this far and prayed this hard to give up at the first sign of resistance. Though she hadn't expected to be resisted. No doubt his initial reaction was fueled by pain. It couldn't be pleasant to know he'd been rejected.

Cassie snorted. "Don't expect me to try to sweeten him up. If you ask me, I'd say the man is as stubborn as he is high."

Yes, he was a tall man. And well built. And he had a smile that drove the clouds from her mind. None of which mattered as much as a single gray hair. All that mattered was she had the winter—God willing and the cold weather continued—to convince him a marriage of convenience suited him. She saw no other way out of her predicament. "I'd say he has high ideals. That could serve us well."

Cassie stared as if Linette had suggested something underhand.

Linette sighed. Cassie seemed bent on seeing everything in some dreadful fashion. "I only mean that a man with honor can be trusted."

"No man is completely honest and honorable. Take it from me. They'll take your heart and treat it with total disregard."

Linette had no desire to know the details behind such a statement, so she ignored it. She had no intention of giving her heart to a man. Her only interest in a marriage to Eddie was escaping from her father's plans and gaining the right to act according to her conscience.

She turned her attention to the room. It was small. The stove was the tiniest she'd ever seen. It was nothing like the one Tilly, Margaret's cook, had taught her on. For a moment, she doubted her ability to prepare food despite all her reading. Everything was so different from what she'd practiced on or imagined. She stiffened her spine. She would do whatever needed doing, do it well and without complaint. A tiny table, one wooden chair and a small bookcase crowded with papers and books completed the furnishings. She longed to explore the book titles, but first things first.

"Help me get organized," she told Cassie. She hung her coat by the door and rubbed her hands together. "At least the table has wings." Flipped up, they would all be able to crowd around for their meals, assuming they had more chairs.

"We'll have to take turns lifting a fork to our mouths," Cassie predicted.

"It's perfectly adequate. Now let's organize the bedroom. I want to put Grady's things where I can get at them." She took the boy's hand and stepped into the tiny bedroom. With the two trunks beside the bed there was barely enough room to stand. The bed was narrow. Two would be cozy. Three crowded.

Cassie pointed out the fact. "We'll have to take turns sleeping."

Linette reached down and touched the fur covering. "It's as soft as down. We'll be just fine so long as we're prepared to manage." She faced Cassie squarely. "I seem to recall you complaining about not being able to sleep for fear someone would steal your bag. Or worse."

Cassie shuddered. "But at least it was warm and roomy."

"But here it's safe." She shoved the narrow dresser hard against the corner. There were nails driven into the logs across the end wall. She bundled Eddie's belongings onto one hook, freeing up the others. The scent of leather, horseflesh and something subtle, bringing to mind grassy slopes and warm sunshine, assailed her senses. A tremor of anticipation scooted up her throat. She dismissed the sensation and hung some of Grady's things. She placed her smaller items on top of her trunk.

Cassie stood in the doorway. "I don't see how we're all going to fit in here. A person will have to step outside just to change their mind."

Linette chuckled. "We'll simply have to make sure we don't all try to change our minds at the same time." She'd hoped for a small smile from Cassie but got nothing but a sigh of displeasure. "Come on, Cassie. Look on the bright side."

"I don't see that there is one. I'm a widow in a big country. A man's country, I might add. Need I point out that we are at the mercy of Mr. Gardiner? And if it wasn't him, it would be another man."

Linette hated the thought of being at his mercy, but it was true. But only to the degree she allowed it to be. "Then let's be grateful he appears to be honorable." At least he hadn't left them out in the cold.

They stepped back into the other room. It took only two dozen steps to circle the whole house, but as Linette pointed out, it was safe and Eddie was an honorable man so far as she knew. *Lord, keep us secure and help Cassie find peace. And help Eddie to change his mind before spring.* She had no doubt it could happen. Didn't the Word say "with God all things are possible"?

Grady shuffled toward the stove and stared at the black surface.

Cassie studied Linette with narrowed eyes. "Were you really prepared to marry Mr. Gardiner, a complete stranger?"

"Yes."

"Why?"

Before she could reply, a cold draft shivered across the floor and up Linette's shins. She turned to see Eddie standing in the doorway, three chairs dangling from one arm and a bulging gunnysack from the other. He kicked the door closed with his foot and stared at Linette.

"I'd like to hear the answer to that." His gaze burned a trail across her skin, making her cheeks burn.

She ignored the question and her reaction to his look, grabbed a chair and planted it beside the stove for Grady. Simply by turning it about, she could pull him up to the table.

Eddie dropped the other chairs and indicated the women should sit then turned the last chair to the heat.

At his approach, Grady pressed to Linette's side and whimpered. She wrapped her arm around his tiny shoulders. "Hush, child. You're safe here. Nice and warm."

Eddie dug in his pocket and withdrew six perfectly round stones and an assortment of interestingly shaped pieces of wood. Two were round knots. Four resembled crude animals and the other two were smooth lengths. "Grady, here's some things you can play with."

Grady buried his face against Linette's shoulder and wailed.

"It's not personal. He's feeling lost. He'll soon enough realize he's safe." It was her daily prayer. The boy had been inconsolable since his mother's death. She reached for the objects. Eddie dumped them into her palms. They were warm from his touch and her throat pinched tight. She told herself it meant nothing and she dropped them to her lap. "Look, Grady. This one looks like a cow."

The boy wasn't interested.

"Perhaps later." She turned away knowing natural curiosity and abject boredom would overcome fear in short order. "Thanks for bringing the chairs."

"There's food and other things I figured you might need in order to survive." He indicated the sack he'd dropped on the floor.

"Thank you." She started to edge away from Grady's grip. "I'll see to tea." *Please let there be something in that sack I can prepare.*

Eddie signaled her to remain seated. "First, I'd like to hear the answer to Mrs. Godfrey's question."

Linette shook her head and did her best to look confused, as if she didn't recall.

The way Eddie quirked one eyebrow she knew she hadn't fooled him. Nevertheless, he repeated Cassie's question. "Why would you cross the ocean and most of North America to marry a stranger? Surely there are interested men in England."

Linette's shudder was sincere. "Of course, and my

father made sure all the men I met were suitable in his estimation." She tried to keep her voice strong but suspected everyone heard the tremor that came from the pit of her stomach. She swallowed hard and forced back her revulsion. "He agreed to a marriage between myself and a distant relative who to all accounts is rich in land and money." She clamped her teeth together to keep from revealing how disgusting she found the idea then released them to speak again. "He is a fat old man."

"How old?" Eddie's voice rang with doubt.

"He's fifty-one." Did he think she'd made up the age difference? Even that wouldn't have been so bad. It was the way the man looked at her, his eyes undressing her as he licked his lips like a hungry dog. Realizing she clutched at her upper arms as if to protect herself, she lowered her hands to her lap.

"How old are you?" He still sounded unconvinced.

"I'm twenty." She tipped her chin proudly. "Some might think I'm old enough to welcome any sort of a marriage, but I'll never be that old."

Eddie chuckled.

"You wouldn't find it amusing if you were in my position."

Cassie sniffed. "Men are never in that position."

Eddie sobered though his eyes continued to spark amusement. "I'm trying to guess what you said or did to convince your father to let you travel West."

"Your good name and your letter were enough." She ducked her head. "I also pointed out the nearness of a convent where I knew I could find shelter and protection." Her father had vowed all kinds of damage to the convent if she had actually gone there, so it wasn't really an option.

Grady edged a hand to Linette's lap and gingerly explored the largest rock.

"Do you know my age?"

She returned her gaze to Eddie. "Margaret said you're twenty-five." How must Eddie feel to be turned down by the woman he expected to become his wife? It hurt to think about it. "I'm sorry for your disappointment."

He held her gaze for a heartbeat. She read a distant hurt, then he blinked and let only his disapproval reveal itself. She would assuredly make a far better rancher's wife than Margaret ever would. But of course, the heart did not always see what the head knew was best.

"I was married at sixteen," Cassie said, rocking slowly, pulling Linette's attention to her. She wished she could erase the pain from the woman's expression. "We worked hard to save enough money for our passage. Then we worked in Ontario. I wanted to stay there. We had a nice house, but George heard there was good land along the North Saskatchewan River. He saved enough to buy an outfit and settle in the Northwest. We sold everything. But George got sick in Montreal." Her voice fell to a whisper. "I thought I'd die when he died. I used the last of our savings to have him buried," she moaned. "He deserved far better."

So did Cassie, but Linette didn't say so, knowing far too well the woman was given to bouts of discouragement and defeat.

Cassie gave the stove a bleak look. "Here I am not yet twenty-five, a widow. I'll be alone the rest of my life."

"God has a plan for your life. He says His thoughts toward us are of peace, and not of evil." She spoke of a verse she thought to be in Jeremiah.

"I've seen little reason to believe God wants to do me good." Cassie's voice shook. "Until I see otherwise, I think I'll trust my own resources."

"What is your opinion?" Linette asked Eddie. Even if he'd received her letter and agreed to a marriage of convenience, she'd made up her mind not to marry until she was certain of his convictions. He'd expressed his faith in his letters, but she wanted to hear it firsthand. She still wanted to hear it, though marriage now seemed but a distant possibility. But no, she would not abandon hope that God could work a miracle over the winter.

He gave his answer some consideration. "I believe God honors those who honor Him."

"Yes. I agree."

"And how do you suggest we do that?" Cassie demanded.

"I can't answer for everyone," Eddie said. "For me, it means doing my duty. Honoring my father and mother. Being charitable."

A man of honor, just as she'd guessed from the first. Surely she stood a chance of finding favor in his eyes. She tried to signal her relief to Cassie. But the other woman only stared at Eddie.

"So you think if we do what is right, God will treat us fairly?"

"That's my belief."

"So what did I do wrong to lose a husband and two babies? They were born beautiful and whole but never drew breath."

"I can't say. That's between you and God."

"Oh, no," Linette protested. His words sounded condemning, as if Cassie harbored secret sins. Linette found such reasoning to be flawed. "You can't reduce God to human intelligence and emotions. There are circumstances we aren't aware of. We don't see the big picture, but God does. That's where trust comes in."

Cassie made a sound of raw disbelief. "When you've lost everything, then you can talk to me about trust. Until then, it's only childish wishing."

Linette ached for Cassie's pain, but the woman was stronger than she realized to have survived such hardship. However, Linette couldn't imagine enduring such tragedies without God's help. "Whatever happens I will trust God." She wondered what Eddie thought and met his gaze, felt a jolt in her lungs at the way he studied her.

"I hope you never have occasion to believe in anything but the goodness of God." Did he sound just a little doubtful? As if he considered it possible? This situation was about as bad as things could get. And her faith had not faltered.

"'He will never leave me nor forsake me.' Now I'm going to make tea." She clapped her hands to her knees, startling Grady, who whimpered and buried his face against her shoulder. She put the toys on the floor, took his hand and drew him after her toward the sack.

Eddie jumped to his feet and accompanied her. "Cookie wasn't sure what you would want. She says if you need anything, just trot on over to the cookhouse."

"There's another woman on the place?"

Eddie chuckled at her delighted surprise. "Yup. Cookie."

Linette stepped past the sack to peer out the window. "Which is the cookhouse?"

Eddie stood close to her, bending a little so he could see out the window. "Can't miss it. It's the two-story building right across the road. Cookie—Miz Liza Mc-Cormick—and her husband, Bertie, live on the upper floor, but mostly you'll find both of them cooking and feeding the crew."

"Liza? Pretty name. How many are in your crew?"

"During the summer, there's twelve men, give or take, plus me and the McCormicks. Less once winter sets in. Six or eight men. Right now most of them are up in the hills, edging the cattle down. And best call her Cookie."

"Another woman. Isn't that nice, Cassie?"

Cassie showed marginal interest. But it didn't dampen Linette's relief. The place suddenly seemed a lot more civilized and friendly. She studied the building across the wide expanse Eddie had called a road. As soon as possible, she'd pay Liza—or Cookie, if she preferred—a visit. Eager to get on with this new life, Linette spun away from the window and almost pressed her cheek to his chest.

His eyes widened.

Something quivered in the pit of her stomach.

Their gazes held for a moment of nervous awareness at the realization they were going to be sharing these tight quarters for several months.

She ducked her head, lest he guess at the way her heart had come unsettled. She could expect such encounters throughout the winter. She must prepare herself. Learn how to keep her emotions under lock and key. She would not be controlled by feelings.

The winter...only a few months...but more than long enough for God to work a change in Eddie's heart. In the meantime, she had to prove to him how nice it was to have her around.

"Let's see what Cookie sent over." He hadn't meant to be drawn into questions about Linette's personal life. What did it matter to him if her father had chosen a marriage partner she didn't welcome? Yet the idea made his muscles tighten. He'd seen the way she held herself and knew she didn't make up her fears. It couldn't be pleasant to be controlled by a father who didn't take her feelings into consideration.

He could only hope something would change on her behalf before spring when he'd send her back to her father.

Linette tried to extract herself from Grady's clutches. "Look, Grady. Play with these things and I'll make you something to eat, but I can't work with you hanging from my arm."

Grady poked his face around Linette enough to expose one eye. He saw Eddie and with a loud cry burrowed into Linette's skirts.

Eddie backed off, carefully avoiding looking directly at the boy.

Grady waited until Eddie picked up the sack and carried it to the table before he untangled himself from Linette's side and hurried back to the stove, where he squatted to examine the objects that would have to pass as toys until something better could be found or fashioned. Grady made sure to keep his face toward Eddie as if he had to know where the enemy stood.

Linette edged to Eddie's side. "Thank you for being patient with him."

He pulled flour and sugar from the sack as he considered her words. Why should she care, when she had no connection to this child? Yet it made him realize even more how generous his father had been in taking in himself and his mother and giving them his name. He redoubled his vow to live a life that would honor that gift. "He's not a lot different than a scared animal. Here's a slab of bacon and other things Cookie thought you could use. Lots of women wouldn't give an orphaned child a second glance." In his case, his father and mother had married. Eddie was part of the union. But Linette had no connection to this boy. "Why do you?" He kept his voice low so Grady wouldn't hear.

She shifted the supplies around, examining them and lining them up. "We need a shelf for these."

Just when he thought she intended to ignore his question, she faced him.

"I simply cannot walk by someone in need and pretend I don't see them or can't help them." Her eyes flashed some kind of challenge as if she'd had to defend her views before.

"I'm guessing your feelings haven't met with approval."

Her sigh puffed out her cheeks. "According to my parents, ladies don't soil their hands with such matters. They say there are people whose calling is to do such things. People of the church. Not regular people." All the while she talked she held his gaze. Her compassion and conviction poured from her like hot tea.

"You've rescued an orphan boy and a widowed woman. I'd say you've done your share."

Her eyes turned to cold amber. "Are you warning me?"

"Miss Edwards, sometimes practical matters must be considered. And propriety. This cabin won't hold any more charity cases."

"Propriety?" She kept her voice low, but still managed to make the word ring with distaste. "It will never stop me from following my heart and conscience."

Eddie stopped removing items from the sack. "Are you informing me you will have no regard for how you conduct yourself? I warn you, so long as you are under my roof and living with the protection of my good name, I expect you to live in a way that will not bring dishonor to it." Why couldn't Margaret have chosen to follow through on their agreement? She had proven an agreeable companion. Was this all some colossal joke played by the universe? Until this moment, he would have said God had a hand in all the events of his life. Now he wasn't sure. Seems Linette was a stubborn, headstrong woman. If people acted contrary to God's directions, how could they still be under His control?

His jaw ached and he forced it to unlock. He would not let any of these people bring disgrace to the Gardiner name.

Linette regarded him, her face set in hard lines and flat disapproval. "I have always lived in an honorable fashion. I simply refuse to live by silly social expectations, especially if they require I go against the teaching of my Lord and Savior."

He squeezed the back of his neck, feeling the muscles corded like thick rope. "I certainly wouldn't ask that of you. Honoring God is first in life." Right along with honoring his father and mother.

"Good. Then we are agreed." She reached into the sack and pulled out a fry pan and pot. "I'll soon have something for tea."

Eddie didn't feel nearly as satisfied that they understood each other. Somehow he expected she would agree to his terms only if they suited her. How was he going to make sure she didn't turn this into a disaster for him and his family?

She smiled across the table. "Mr. Gardiner, you have nothing to fear from me. I promise I will do all in my power to make this a most pleasant winter. In fact, you might decide you want us to stay."

"Only until it's safe for you to travel."

She ducked her head, but not before he glimpsed the self-assured satisfaction in her expression.

What did she have in mind? Whatever it was, he could tell her she could do nothing to make him change his decision.

Besides, Margaret would reconsider becoming his wife when she heard about the fine house.

He glanced at Cassie, who sat staring at the stove. She had the look of someone lost in her thoughts. The woman was supposed to be Linette's chaperone. As such, shouldn't she be the one preparing the meal? Seems Linette couldn't see when she was being taken advantage of. Allowing a father to thrust a child into her care, allowing a widow woman to sit idle while she did the chores.

If Cassie had been one of the cowboys, he would have whistled and tipped his head toward the work.

How did one order a woman to do her share?

Linette stood at the table, turning the hunk of bacon over and over. He watched her, wondering what her problem was.

She set aside the meat and lifted the towel from the bowl of cooked potatoes Cookie had sent over. She poked them with one finger. Her brow furrowed. Was she unfamiliar with basic cooking? His stomach growled at the thought.

Thanks to Cookie's generosity, there were baking powder biscuits and some cold roast beef. Linette set the latter two out on a plate and put out butter and syrup, along with the tea she had made. She set the table carefully, arranging each piece of silverware as exactly as if she used a ruler. "It's ready," she said, indicating they should sit at the table.

Eddie pulled himself from the wall where he'd been alternately observing the newly arrived occupants of his house and studying the darkening sky out the window. He should be with the men, bringing the cows down from the hills, but the unexpected guests had delayed him and now the sun dipped toward the horizon. It would soon disappear behind the distant mountains.

Heavy clouds hung from the sky. It would be good if the snow held off a few more days. A few more weeks would be even better, but he didn't like to sound greedy.

At Linette's call, Cassie sighed and pushed heavily to her feet. She wasn't as old as Eddie first judged. Life had been hard on her. He suspected a strong woman lay beneath the sharp exterior. Only a fighter would have survived what she'd been through.

The first step Eddie took had Grady scuttling toward the wall. Eddie stopped.

"I'll feed him later," Linette said.

It grated on Eddie's nerves that his presence was unwelcome in his own home. But not nearly as much as it bothered him to be the cause of Grady's fear. "We might as well start out the way we intend to continue. I eat my meals in a civilized fashion. I expect the same from my guests." He made no threatening moves as he squatted to Grady's level. "Grady, this is my house. You're welcome here, but when we eat, we sit together at the table. Think you can do that?"

Grady shook his head and whimpered. His gaze brushed past Eddie, not quite connecting but allowing Eddie to see something in the boy's eyes. Hurt. Insecurity. Rejection. He didn't understand how he knew and recognized it, but he did as surely as he knew his name. This boy was filled with consuming fear and loneliness. He had every reason to feel that way. His own father had turned his back on him.

Eddie's insides trembled and a pain shot through his jaw as he struggled to keep his expression from revealing what he thought of such a man. The boy did not deserve the hurt heaped on him by his father. No one did.

He ached to promise the boy he was safe now. But hurting and fearful animals—and little boys—needed lots of reassurance. "Aren't you hungry?"

Grady glanced toward the table then he studied Eddie hard and solemnly.

Eddie didn't move. Didn't smile. He just waited, letting the child see he meant him no harm. Finally Grady edged away, keeping as much distance between himself and Eddie as possible. He hurried to Linette's side and buried his face in her skirts.

Eddie pushed to his feet. "Grady, you will sit on

a chair to eat." Linette's glare seared, while Cassie watched with indifference.

Grady climbed to a chair and sat, giving Eddie a look of defiance. Eddie could almost read his thoughts. *I'm sitting on the outside, but I'm doing what I want on the inside.*

Eddie struggled to keep from laughing.

Linette sat down with a huff of exasperation.

Sobering instantly, he met her gaze. Did she find all rules and conventions to her dislike? "A man is ruler in his own house. Is that not from the scriptures?" At the flash in her eyes he wondered if she would defy the word of God.

The winter looked longer and colder with every passing hour.

Chapter Three

Why had God made woman to be subject to a man?

Linette knew the verse he referred to. It had mocked her on many occasions. She would never dispute God's word, but some of it was hard to swallow. It made marriage most unappealing. She would avoid it altogether except it provided her only hope of escaping her father's plans.

Eddie waited until she was settled. "I'll say the blessing."

She bowed her head. Although Eddie had insisted on Grady's obedience, he'd at least been gentle with the boy. It wouldn't be hard to be wife to a man who treated her with such kindness and respected her heart's yearnings. But she feared she wanted more than she could hope for. More and more it looked as if she would not find freedom here any more than she had in England. Still, anything was better than marrying a lumpy, lecherous old man.

She waited until everyone had taken a biscuit or several. "I'm afraid I'm not much of a cook," she murmured. "We had a cook at home who refused to let me in the kitchen."

"This is fine."

She'd done nothing but put stuff on the table. If she expected to prove her worth she would have to do much better. "I'm sure I'll manage." If only someone would explain what to do with the supplies. Surely Cassie knew. She sent the woman an imploring look. They had to learn to enjoy each other's company. "This is your second winter on the ranch, isn't it?"

Eddie looked relieved to have something to talk about. "It is."

"Tell us what it's like."

"Unpredictable."

She laughed at his tone—half regretful, half admiring. "How so?"

"It can snow four feet. The temperature can drop out of sight. Then we get a Chinook that melts the snow and makes us all foolishly think the worst is over."

Cassie perked up. "A Chinook? What's that?"

"A warm wind that blasts over the mountains. We can go from shivering under a heavy coat to working in our shirtsleeves all within an hour or less."

"It's a legend then?" Cassie said, sarcasm dripping from each word.

Linette silently prayed Eddie wouldn't be offended. Was she destined to spend her days interceding on Cassie's behalf?

Thankfully Eddie chuckled. "Part legend in that the Indians have all sorts of stories about what it is, but there's nothing remotely imaginary about what happens."

"I can hardly wait," Linette said. "It's going to be exciting to experience a wild Canadian winter."

Eddie's look challenged her before he pushed his plate away to indicate he was done. Did he think she had undertaken this trip solely for the sake of an adventure? She willingly admitted she enjoyed seeing new and exciting things. But no, the impetus behind her bold venture was twofold—escape the specter of a marriage with a man who made her skin crawl, and hopefully, God willing, find a place where she could obey the dictates of her conscience without regard to foolish social expectations.

The kettle steamed again and Linette prepared to do the washing up with the hot water. Cassie turned her chair and pushed it closer to the stove.

Eddie stood and piled up the dirty dishes. "Everyone does his share here." He glanced toward Cassie.

Linette's hands remained suspended over the washbasin. She could manage on her own and didn't mind doing the work, but Eddie gave her a warning look. She ducked her head. Seems he was intent on establishing his rules and she was helpless to do anything but cooperate. Not that she didn't think Cassie should help, but she didn't know how far he meant this rule making to go. She kept her head down as she studied him, measuring him, wondering what would happen if she refused to obey one of his directives. His expression remained patient. On the other hand, how pleasurable to share goals and dreams with such a man.

Slowly it dawned on Cassie that Eddie expected her to help. She pushed her chair back so hard it banged into the table. "Don't see how much help it will be for me to be stuck under Linette's elbow. There's not enough room for one, let alone two."

Linette pulled the basin closer and handed Cassie a towel. She took it silently and dried the few dishes.

Eddie strode outside.

"He's lord and master here, that's for sure," Cassie grumbled. "I'm sick of men controlling everything. Why don't we pack up and leave?"

"Cassie, where would we go?" She'd gladly leave if she could find an alternative that wouldn't bring her father's wrath about her head. Except—an errant thought surfaced—this was where she wanted to be. She'd dreamed of it for weeks as she prepared to leave home and as she crossed the ocean and the country. She pictured herself sharing life with a man who honored her heart's desire, and the dream refused to die in spite of Eddie's insistence that she go back home. She forced her mind back to Cassie's question. "It's not like there are hundreds of homes around here that would welcome us."

"What about that ranch where those men were going? They seemed like nice gentlemen."

"They were very polite but no doubt would expect to rule their home as well."

"I'm sure we could throw ourselves on their mercy."

Linette grabbed Cassie by the shoulders. "I don't intend to beg any man to keep me." She'd prove her worth to Eddie. She'd make him want her to stay. "Wherever I go, whatever happens, I will do my share. In return, I will expect freedom to make a few decisions on my own."

Cassie shook Linette's hands off. "Mr. Gardiner told you he expects obedience."

"Surely a woman can please a man and still be allowed to express her opinion and choices."

Cassie rocked her head back and forth. "He could make life miserable for us."

"I pray it won't be so."

"You were prepared to marry him."

"I thought I knew a bit about him from Margaret's letters." Now she wasn't so sure. In fact, nothing seemed so simple anymore.

Cassie plucked at her sleeve. "He could take advantage of us if he wants. Both of us. Look at how small this place is. We have no hope of escaping him."

Linette smiled. "The closeness is our protection. If you feel threatened, you only have to call out. But I think we have nothing to fear from him. Does he not strike you as a man of strong morals?" He seemed intent on doing things the right way. Just how far that went, they would no doubt see in the following weeks as they shared this tiny cabin.

Eddie strode through the door with a length of lumber and a hammer in hand.

Cassie watched with undisguised wariness as he fastened a shelf across one side of the room.

"This should serve as a pantry for now."

"Thank you." Linette truly appreciated his efforts. She hoped it meant he intended to make the best of the situation—a thought that buoyed her heart.

Now that she'd finished the clean-up, Linette called Grady to her and washed him in preparation for the night. "Cassie, do you want to put Grady to bed?"

Cassie jerked her gaze away from studying Eddie, relief filling her eyes. "I'll lie down with him." Linette understood she was grateful for escape from the close quarters.

Linette soon had the shelf neatly organized with their kitchen supplies. Cassie and Grady were only a few steps away in the bedroom, but suddenly she was alone with Eddie. Neither of them spoke and the quietness crowded every corner of the room.

"Tell me about Grady."

His question shattered the stillness and made her nerves twitch. Then she drew in a deep breath, grateful he had initiated conversation. "You mean besides the fact he is an orphan?"

"He has a father, so technically he is not an orphan. No other relatives?"

Was he hoping he could send the child away? "Apparently not."

"And what if the father changes his mind and wants him back?"

"It would be wonderful if he did. I pray he will."

"In the meantime, you have his care, but who is his legal guardian?"

"I am."

"By whose authority?"

"His father signed the papers naming me such."

Eddie quirked an eyebrow, perhaps in disbelief. "It surprises me he cared enough to do so."

"He didn't. I asked him to do it."

Both his eyebrows rose and Linette allowed herself a little smugness at having surprised him.

"You seem to have thought this through."

"You might be surprised at how carefully I consider my choices."

His pause filled the air with quivering tension. "And yet you still do them."

She ignored the slight sarcasm.

"Cassie has no family she could appeal to?"

"What is this? Trying to find alternate arrangements for your guests?"

He looked at her with annoyance. "No need to be rude. I'm only trying to learn as much as I can."

For a moment she silently challenged him. But he was right. The man deserved to be treated better. "I'm sorry. I didn't mean to be rude. To answer your question, Cassie has no family she's willing to admit to. I know she complains a lot and Grady is still afraid of everything, but I promise I will do my best to—"

"I'm not trying to get rid of you. I said you're welcome until spring. Rest assured, I won't withdraw my word."

She wondered when the deadline had shifted from improved weather to spring but wasn't about to question God's good favor. "It's good to know I can count on it." There was so much more she wanted to say. How much she'd enjoyed seeing the vast plains of the Northwest. How she'd felt free for the first time in her life. How she didn't mind the crowded conditions of the cabin because it felt cozy. How she couldn't keep from wanting to help those in distress. Instead, she turned the conversation to less controversial topics. "You said you met Kootenai Brown. He sounds like an interesting man. Tell me about him."

Eddie relaxed, stretching his legs out and angling back in the chair. "Kootenai Brown has been in the western territories for twenty years or more. In that time, he has established quite a reputation, if one were to believe all the stories told about him. Soldier, gold miner, police constable, wolfer, whiskey trader. Tales say that he was captured by Sitting Bull and escaped. Another says he murdered a man in Fort Benton. Still another claims he was shot in the back by a Blackfoot arrow, pulled it out himself and treated the wound with turpentine."

Linette watched Eddie as he spun tale after tale of a man larger than life. Some of the stories were undoubtedly exaggerated. Eddie's eyes flashed with humor as he talked. His mouth gentled and his voice carried a rich timbre. And as she listened, she came to a firm conviction. "I can't go back."

Eddie blinked and seemed to pull his thoughts toward her words. "Are you really Linette Edwards?"

Her chin came up and her eyes stung with defiant challenge. "Of course I am Linette Edwards. Why would you doubt it? Who do you think I am?"

He took his time answering. "You aren't dressed like the daughter of wealthy man."

She laughed. She'd managed to confound him and it pleased her to no end. "I traded my fine dresses for practical ones at Fort Benton."

He didn't seem to care that his eyes revealed doubt.

She smiled. "I'm grateful for the few months I'll be able to enjoy this vast country."

The door rattled as if a person sought entrance.

She turned. "Is someone there?"

Eddie chuckled. "You might have cause to hate the country before the winter is out. That, Miss Edwards, is the wind knocking at the door."

He looked a totally different man when he relaxed and smiled. Handsome, kindly and appealing. She caught her thoughts and pushed them into submission. Yet one lingered long enough to be heard. Sharing his company throughout the winter might be pleasant enough.

His smile deepened and his eyes darkened.

She ducked away, pretending to examine an imaginary spot on her skirt.

"Hear the snow against the window?" he asked.

Glad to leave the awkward moment, she turned toward the window. Wet white flakes plopped against the glass with a definite *platt* sound.

"Come have a look." Eddie pulled himself into action with the grace of a young kitten.

She followed him to the door. When he slipped a coat over his shoulders, she did the same. As they stepped out into the night air, she was glad she'd traded her gold locket for the heavy coat even though it was too large. She pulled it tight around her neck and waited for her eyes to adjust to the darkness. Large flakes of snow, driven by the wind, stuck to the side of the cabin. She lifted her face and let flakes land on her cheeks. Cold and refreshing. She put out her tongue and laughed at how the snow tasted.

Eddie chuckled.

She closed her mouth and swallowed. "It's so clean and fresh."

"If it keeps up all night, it will be deep and dangerous."

"But we are safe and warm."

"My cattle aren't."

"I'm sorry. I didn't mean to be selfish. What will happen to them?"

"The wind will drive them, hopefully, into a place

of shelter. Then we'll have to find them and push them out."

"Why can't you leave them there?"

"We can if the snow isn't deep, but if it is, cattle can't dig through it. They'll starve. We've been moving them down, but this snow is earlier than expected."

"Then I will pray you'll be able to get your cows to a safe place."

"I will pray the same."

It made her feel as if he valued her offer. It made her feel as if they were partners in some small way. Linette wished she could see him better and gauge if he felt even a fraction of the same connection.

"It's cold. We better go inside."

His words were her answer. He obviously did not wish to prolong the moment.

Eddie rolled up in his buffalo robe and got comfortable on the floor. He'd slept on the ground many times, often out in the cold. In comparison, this was warm and pleasant. If the temperature dropped too low, he would put more wood on the fire during the night.

He lay on his back listening to the women murmur. He could make out enough to follow their conversation.

"Where did you go?" Cassie's voice carried its perennial sharpness.

"Just outside the door."

"What for? You two got secrets?"

Eddie groaned. Cassie seemed bent on seeing evil and inconvenience at every turn. He wondered if Linette would scold her.

But Linette laughed softly. "I wanted to see the snow."

"You're twenty years old. Surely you've seen snow before."

"Not like this. It was so quiet you could hear each flake hit the ground. And the wind sighed as if carrying the snow had become too much of an effort."

Eddie clasped his hands under his head and listened unashamedly. Linette made it sound magical. Perhaps it was. He hadn't put it into words, but there was something about the country. Maybe its newness. How many times did he wonder if he was the first white man to set foot on a certain spot?

"I told Eddie I would pray his cows are safe."

Eddie. She said his name as if it was as special as the new-falling snow. Yet face-to-face, he was Mr. Gardiner, all formal and stiff. But then, that was proper.

Somehow *proper* didn't sound as pleasant as *Eddie*.

"Who cares about cows?" Cassie obviously didn't. "I don't know how I'm going to endure this for an entire winter."

Linette chuckled again.

Eddie smiled just hearing her.

"Cassie, my friend, you don't have to endure. You can enjoy."

Cassie snorted so loud Grady whimpered. When she spoke again, Eddie couldn't catch her whispered words. He strained to hear Linette's response.

"God gives us each day to enjoy."

Cassie made a sound so full of doubt that Eddie choked back a chuckle.

Linette spoke into the darkness. "I had a nurse who taught me many scripture verses. One in Psalm 118 says, 'This is the day the Lord hath made... Let us rejoice and be glad in it.' She said it's a choice. An act

of our will to rejoice. And she would sing the verse."
Linette softly sang a song putting the words of the verse
to music, repeating it several times.

She'd had a privileged upbringing. Despite Mr. Edwards's dubious background, he'd expect his daughter
to be treated as aristocracy. Eddie would have to be
careful. He wouldn't give her father a chance to ruin
the Gardiner good name.

Cassie didn't say anything. Perhaps she'd fallen
asleep, comforted by the lullaby of the song.

Eddie turned to his side and listened to Linette sing.
Even after the voices in the other room had grown
quiet, the lyrics played over and over in his head. He
fell asleep to the tune.

He woke next morning, started a fire and put the
coffee to boil. It had settled in to snow seriously. He
wanted to head out and look for his cows, but doing so
would be foolhardy in this weather. He had good men,
experienced cowboys. They knew enough to circle the
cows and keep them from drifting. He didn't need to
be there helping them. Yet it was his responsibility—
and his alone—to insure the herd was safe. The future
of the ranch depended on it. But he was stuck here,
away from the action, doing nothing to protect his investment. Or more accurately, his father's investment.

Noises from the next room informed him the others were up. He slowly turned from the window and
poured a cup of coffee. He'd make sure the guests were
safe. Later, he'd head out to the barn. At least he could
check on the stock that was there.

The three other occupants of the storm-wrapped
cabin stepped into view. Cassie's expression was
enough to stop a train and send the occupants dash-

ing for safety. Grady fussed for no reason. But Linette smiled and hummed. He immediately recognized the tune. It was the same one playing over and over in his head. "'This is the day that the Lord hath made... Let us rejoice and be glad in it.'" She seemed intent on enjoying the day. She went immediately to the window. "It's beautiful. Snow covers everything like piles of whipped cream."

She turned, and her smile flattened and she frowned. "I'm sorry. This is not what you need, is it?"

"I would have preferred to have the cows closer before this hit."

She nodded, looked thoughtful a moment longer then turned to the others with a beaming smile. "Cassie, Grady, look. There's snow everywhere." She lifted Grady to the window to look out.

He laughed. "I play in it?"

Eddie stared at the boy. It was the first time he'd heard anything but a cry from his lips.

"I don't think—" Linette looked at Eddie. "It doesn't look safe out there."

"Not while it's coming down so hard." He lowered his gaze to Grady. "You'll have to wait for a little while."

In his excitement over the snow, Grady had forgotten Eddie. Now he clung to Linette's neck. His lips quivered.

Eddie sighed inwardly. He couldn't bear the idea of more fussing and crying. "If you don't cry I'll take you to see the horses as soon as it's safe. But only big boys can come."

Grady swallowed hard and blinked half a dozen times. "I not cry."

"Good boy. Now climb up to the table and let's see what Linette can find to feed us."

Grady edged around Eddie and sat as far away as the small space would allow.

Linette hadn't moved from the window. She stared at Eddie, her eyes wide.

Had he done something wrong? Did she think he was out of place telling Grady to stop crying? Or— he stifled a groan—had he offended her by calling her by her Christian name? "I'm sorry. I meant Miss Edwards."

"No, Linette is fine. Much more comfortable."

Were her words rushed and airy? He jerked his gaze away in self-disgust. Less than twenty-four hours with two women and a child in his little cabin and he was already getting fanciful. He needed the company of some cows and cowboys.

But first, breakfast.

Linette again pulled the bowl of potatoes toward her and turned the slab of bacon over and over.

Eddie grabbed the butcher knife. "I'll slice us off some pieces. You can fry them up."

"Thank you." She avoided meeting his eyes.

"I take it you've never seen bacon before."

"I'm unfamiliar with the term and the format."

He chuckled. She had a unique way of admitting she didn't have a clue. "It's the same as rashers in England."

Understanding lightened her eyes. "You mean—" She pointed to the chunk of meat and watched with keen interest as he carved off thin slices. "That's what rashers look like before they're all crispy?"

He dropped the pieces into the hot fry pan. "They'll soon be something you recognize."

She stared at the sizzling pan. A heavy sigh left her lungs. "I told you I wasn't a good cook, but I assure you I won't have to be shown twice. In no time at all I'll be creating culinary delights to warm your heart."

A man needed a good feed, especially after working out in the cold. "I could continue to take my meals over at the cookhouse."

Linette's brow furrowed. "Are you suggesting I can't manage? I'll learn. You'll see. Just give me a chance." She sucked in air and opened her mouth to start again.

"Okay. Okay." He held up his palm toward her to stop any further argument. "I'll see how things go." Besides, he could well imagine Cookie's protests if he left the ladies alone and sought his meals with the rest of the crew. No, sir, he didn't need to get a tongue-lashing from that direction. "Maybe Cookie will help you."

Her shoulders sank several inches in relief and she let out a noisy gust. "Thank you. You won't be sorry."

He kept any contrary opinion to himself, but he'd been nothing but sorry since she'd landed on his ranch. He expected he'd be sorry until the day she left.

As he waited for her to prepare breakfast he went to the window and scratched a peephole in the frost. Slim and Roper hustled toward the cookhouse. They slid their attention toward the cabin, saw him peeking through the foggy glass and nodded as if they only wanted to say good-morning when he knew they burned up with curiosity.

"Um." Linette sounded mildly worried. "Is it supposed to smoke like this?"

He spun around. The fry pan smoked like a smoldering fire. "It's too hot. Pull it to the side."

She reached for it without any protection on her hands.

"Wait. Don't touch it."

But her palm touched the hot handle and she jerked back with a gasp.

At that moment the pan caught fire.

Cassie jerked to her feet and pulled Grady after her as she retreated to the far corner, casting desperate looks at the door—their only escape route.

Linette danced about. "What do I do?" She grabbed a towel and flapped it.

"Stop. You're only making it worse. Get out of the way." He crossed the room in three strides, grabbed a nearby lid and clamped it over the pan. He snatched the towel from her hands, clutched the hot fry pan and dashed for the door. He jerked it open and tossed the sizzling pan into the snowbank. It melted down a good eight inches.

He tossed the towel to the table and grabbed her wrist. "Let me see that." He turned her palm upward. The base of her fingers was red and already forming blisters. "Put snow on it."

She seemed incapable of moving, so he pulled her to the door, grabbed a handful of snow and plastered the burnt area.

"Oh, that feels good."

He grabbed her by the shoulders. "Are you trying to burn the place down?"

She glowered back. "You could have told me this might happen."

"Told you?" He sputtered and slowed his breathing. "You said you were prepared to be a pioneer housewife. But you can't even fry bacon."

"I most certainly can and will." She marched past him and back to the house, grabbed the hunk of bacon and whacked off pieces, unmindful of the pain the burns surely gave.

Grady whimpered. Cassie pulled him close. "Shush, child."

Linette gave the boy a tight smile. "Everything is fine, Grady. Don't worry."

Eddie watched her butcher the meat. "You'll have a great time trying to fry those."

"I'll fry them." *Whack. Whack.*

"Three days from now perhaps."

She paused. "Why do you say that?"

"Because you're cutting them too thick."

"Fine." She slowed down and methodically sliced narrow strips.

He went to retrieve the fry pan, scrubbing as much of the charcoal from it as he could with snow. "Practically ruined a perfectly good pot," he muttered.

"What did you say?" she asked.

"Not a blame thing." He took the burnt pot inside and poured boiling water into it then set to scrubbing it clean.

"I can do that," she protested.

Somehow he doubted she was a fraction as capable as she tried to make him believe.

"I will make a great pioneer wife." She spit the words out like hot pebbles.

"I've yet to see any evidence supporting that claim." He held up his hand to silence her arguments. "It's a moot point. I don't need or want a pioneer wife."

"You don't know what you're missing."

"And yet I don't seem to mind." He again returned

to the window and stared out. Spring was a distant promise. If the sun came out and stayed. If a Chinook took away the snow. If the stagecoach headed back to Fort Benton or even Edendale, Miss Edwards and her entourage would be on it.

But the snow continued to fall, shutting him in the tiny cabin with Miss Edwards and her entourage.

A few minutes later, she announced breakfast was ready.

Acrid smoke still clung to the air, drowning out any enticing aroma, but still she served up a passable meal. He'd had worse. A lot worse. Some from his own hands.

Afterward, Cassie favored him with a defiant look as she helped Linette clean up.

Life had gone from simple to challenging since Linette thrust herself into his home. He shifted his chair toward the stove and pulled out a newspaper that had come in yesterday's package of mail. Linette and Cassie worked in silence and Grady huddled at the corner of the table, darting regular glances toward Eddie. The skin on the back of Eddie's neck itched. He refused to scratch it, but like the presence of the others in the room, it would not go away. The walls of the cabin pushed at his thoughts. "I'm going to check on the stock."

Grady nudged Linette and indicated he wanted to whisper in her ear.

She bent to hear his words. Her gaze slipped toward Eddie as she answered the boy. "Not yet."

She straightened and returned her attention to the dishes.

Whatever Grady said had something to do with him. "What is it?"

"Nothing," Linette replied.

He waited. He would not be ignored or dismissed in his own house.

Linette lifted one shoulder. "He wanted to know if you were taking him to see the horses." She smiled down at Grady. "It's still snowing heavily."

Eddie studied the boy. The air around him vibrated with expectation—whether in anticipation of seeing the horses or fear of being told no, Eddie couldn't be sure. Seemed the boy had every reason to expect rejection. "Grady, as soon as it's decent out I'll take you to the barn and you can visit the horses. It's a deal." He held out his hand. Perhaps the boy would trust him enough to shake, but Grady shrank back against Linette.

Eddie lowered his hand. "Well, then." He grabbed his coat and ventured out into the cold. It would take time. Trust didn't happen all at once.

The heavy wet snow reached his ankles. It would be even deeper farther up the mountains. If the men hadn't been able to hold the herd... He refused to think of a disaster. Yet how many stories had he heard of cows driven by the wind, trapped in a box canyon, found dead in the spring?

He stomped through the snow. Things were different here than back in England. The elements were more challenging, but his father would not accept that some things were out of Eddie's control. Gardiners didn't let the elements get the best of them. Gardiners conquered challenges. And his father had sent Eddie West to do exactly that. He expected regular reports at their London home informing him Eddie had dutifully fulfilled those expectations. Eddie was determined he would live up to his father's faith in him and maybe prove himself worthy of the Gardiner name.

He flung the barn door open and stepped inside. Several of the horses nickered a greeting. He breathed in the sweet smell of hay, the pungent odor of horse-flesh and sighed. He was at home here. For a few minutes he could forget his problems—the cattle needing to be brought down from the mountains and the people claiming shelter in his cabin.

But both threatened his peace of mind.

Chapter Four

Silence filled the room after Eddie left, as if everyone held their breath to see if he would return. When it appeared he wouldn't, they waited for the feeling of his presence to depart.

Grady slowly unraveled himself from Linette's skirts and edged toward the pieces of wood and rocks Eddie had given him. He sat down and sorted them. Soon he played happily, talking to himself. Perhaps before long, Linette thought, the time would come when Grady would again be a happy little boy.

Cassie grunted. Discontent seemed her constant companion.

Linette strove to keep it from affecting her own thoughts, which had been caught in a maelstrom since she practically set the place on fire. Eddie had saved them from a disaster, but the incident had done little to further her quest to prove he needed her.

"I can't imagine how we are going to survive a winter crammed together like this," Cassie said.

Linette shook off her worries and looked about. "It's really quite comfortable." She could point out that Eddie had the most reason to feel displaced, but Cassie was still too buried in her own grief to see past it. "Let's fix it up a little." Hopefully Eddie wouldn't mind.

"About the only thing that could improve this place is a fire."

"Don't even say that." Linette shuddered. "We came too close to knowing what it would be like." Thankfully, Eddie had reacted calmly when the pan caught fire. She pressed the back of her burned hand. He had taken care of her in a gentle way that brought a strange tightening in her throat. Even now there was a little jump in her heart rate at the memory. She dismissed her errant thoughts and emotions. She wanted only one thing: a businesslike marriage. No emotional involvement that would rob her of her ability to make choices and decisions on her own. "Where would we live? Out in the cold?"

"There's the big house."

Yes, there was the big house. Somehow she doubted Eddie would invite them to share it with him.

"Seems strange to me that he doesn't suggest we all live there."

"It's obviously not finished." She looked out the window toward the big structure. Snow obscured it, but she remembered the stark bareness of the windows. He'd built it for a special woman. He still hoped Margaret would change her mind and grace his big house with her refined presence. She wouldn't tell him Margaret had been relieved to let Linette take her place. It had been her idea, not Linette's as he seemed to think. She shrugged. God had given her a few months in which to prove her worth to Eddie and she meant to make the most of every minute. "I'm happy for a warm place out of the elements. Come help me." She led the way to the bedroom and knelt before one trunk. "I brought some belongings from home."

Cassie sank to the edge of the bed. "I expected things to be different."

Linette had, too. "We'll make the best of it." She pulled out two pictures and a quilt Tilly and the maids had made for her. "These will brighten the place."

Cassie trailed after her as they returned to the main room. Eddie had left the hammer and nails behind and she used those to hang the pictures. She draped the quilt over one chair. "Isn't that better?"

Cassie shrugged.

Linette refused to let the woman's indifference dampen her resolve. Brightening up the place was step number one in her plan to make Eddie see her as a beneficial addition to his life. "Cassie, you must know how to prepare meals."

"You just take the food and cook it."

"Cassie, I don't know whether to fry it, bake it or boil it. I didn't even know what to do with the bacon besides burn it to charcoal."

The other woman shrugged. "You do now."

Linette wanted to shake her. "Cassie, if I don't prove myself capable, Eddie will have no reason to ask me to stay." She fought the tightness in her jaw that made it difficult to speak. "I simply cannot return to London and marry Lyle Williamson. Will you help me or not?"

Cassie again shrugged. "I guess I could tell you whether to boil, bake or fry something."

"Good." She'd hoped for more enthusiasm, but she'd take what she could get."What can I make for lunch?"

Cassie walked to the shelf, pulled down a number of items and plunked them on the table. "Corn bread, beans and syrup." Crossing her arms across her chest, she stepped back and nodded toward the table.

"Great." One step at a time. With Cassie's help— no matter how reluctant—Linette would conquer this challenge. "Now tell me how to make corn bread and cook the beans."

The men joined Eddie in the barn. He sent two to care for the breeding stock he had in the wintering pens. Slim and Roper hung back.

"The ladies settled okay, boss?" Slim's voice was bland as if he was making idle conversation.

"Seems so." Eddie acted as if he didn't know the men were burning up with curiosity. Had they seen the smoking fry pan he'd tossed into the snowbank? Even if they hadn't, they must have smelled the blackened bacon left behind. He tucked away a smile at Linette's incompetence. It tickled him to think of her practically setting the place on fire in her determination to prove herself a pioneer woman. Seems she'd be better off trying for the position of manor wife. His smile died a sudden death as he realized where his thoughts had gone. No Edwards' woman belonged in the big house.

Roper paused from putting hay in the mangers and scratched his head. "They here to stay?"

"Only for the winter."

"Yeah? Then what?"

"Back to wherever they came from." Eddie jabbed his fork after some horse apples.

"Country could use some fine women." Slim hovered over a gate, seemingly interested in one of its hinges.

"Suppose so but not at my expense."

"Huh." Both men grunted out the sound.

The three of them returned to their chores. Silences were common when they worked, but this one carried a thousand unasked questions. Eddie paused. "I'll finish up here if you two want to go back to the bunkhouse or up to the cookhouse."

"Yeah, boss."

They sauntered out, none too anxious to be sent elsewhere. They closed the door against the snow. Silence filled the room for a moment then Eddie chuckled. They'd hoped for more information. His smile flattened. What could he tell them? That Cassie hated life and Grady hated men? On top of it, Linette couldn't cook. His stomach burned. There was an old trapper's cabin up along the river. Crude. Probably full of bedbugs. You could throw a cat through the cracks between the logs and last time he'd seen it, a corner of the roof had been ripped back. Likely by curious bears. But it held all the appeal of the finest stopping house. Maybe when the storm let up he'd hole up there for the winter.

Except he had a duty and responsibility making sure the cattle were safe and the ranch ran efficiently. He couldn't walk away.

His stomach growled. He shoveled out the rest of the pens, swept the tack room, tidied the harnesses, noted those that needed mending and generally lingered until the growing demands of his stomach made it impossible to continue hiding in the barn. Even cold potatoes would taste good.

He tromped back through the deepening snow, paused outside the door to accustom himself to the intruders before he stepped inside.

The aroma of beans, hot bread of some sort and coffee caused his mouth to flood with saliva. Had Linette suddenly learned how to cook?

He glanced about. Why did the place seem warm and welcoming? Something was different, but he couldn't quite pinpoint what it was.

"I'm hungry." He hadn't meant to sound so desperate, but it was too late to pull back his hasty words.

"Dinner is ready." Linette stood at the end of the table, her hands clasped together at her waist. "There's hot water in the kettle."

He washed up then took his place at the table where the others waited. Linette still stood. He raised an eyebrow. "Shall I say the blessing?"

"Of course." She dropped to the chair and bowed her head.

Eddie studied her a moment. Did she seem tense? Had she smiled since he stepped into the house? He couldn't remember. And why did it matter? Except it did. A man liked to find peace in his home. And as he'd said to Cookie, Linette had a pleasant smile. He forced himself to add the comment he'd tacked on for Cookie. Matched by a stubborn attitude. He bowed his head and scraped together a sense of gratitude so he could pray genuine words of thanks.

As soon as he said "Amen," Linette passed him a pan of corn bread. He dug out a generous portion, doused it with beans and syrup and lifted a forkful toward his mouth, when he realized Linette watched him. He lowered the fork. "Is something wrong?"

She laughed a little. "No, just waiting to see if you like the food."

He filled his mouth, chewed once then nodded. "It's good."

She sank deeper into her chair. The corners of her mouth lifted as if her smile came from somewhere deep in her heart.

But the second chew revised his opinion. The beans were hard pellets. He crunched bravely, hoping he wouldn't break a tooth.

She concentrated on chewing. "Are the beans supposed to be this hard?" She looked to Cassie for an answer.

Cassie shrugged. "Guess they should have cooked longer."

Eddie eyed the generous portion of beans on his plate. But after another heroic mouthful he scraped them to one side. "Cook them overnight. They'll be fine in the morning."

Suddenly the corn bread and syrup seemed far from adequate. If this kept up he'd have no choice but to throw himself on Cookie's mercy.

"I'll do better." Linette's words rang with determination. "Like I said, I'm a fast learner." Her gaze caught and held his, silently reminding him of other things she'd said. *A long time till spring. He might grow to appreciate her company.*

The words taunted him. Mocked him. He pushed from the table. Snow still fell heavily, but he must find something to do elsewhere. He grabbed his coat and left the cabin to trudge through the deepening snow to the barn. Apart from sweeping the floor again, there was nothing to do.

He considered going to the bunkhouse where the men would be gathered around the stove fixing their boots or at the table playing cards. They would welcome him, but it encroached on their spare time. He longed to go to the cookhouse and fill up on Cookie's baking, but she wouldn't give him a moment's peace. She'd demand to know why he wasn't entertaining those fine ladies while he had the chance. Even if he repeated a thousand times over that he wasn't interested in whether or not they were fine women and that he was starving, she'd never hear a word contrary to her opinion.

He stepped outside, pulled his woolen scarf around his neck and headed for the wintering pens.

Snow swirled about him, clinging to his eyelashes. The herd pressed against the wooden fences, seeking shelter. They stirred at his approach. The men had put out sufficient feed. All he accomplished by poking around was to unsettle the animals.

He retraced his steps toward the buildings. The house on the hill was barely discernible. If it didn't mean starting a fire to warm the place, he would go there even though it required marching through snow up to his knees.

His steps slowed. There was only one place for him. Back at the cabin. He squinted as he realized there was something he needed to do. No time like the present.

He reached the cabin door, stomped snow from his boots and shook it from his hat before he stepped indoors.

The room radiated warmth. He glanced about. Yes, there was a fire blazing in the small stove, but it was more. He still couldn't put his finger on it.

Cassie sat before the stove with yarn and knitting needles. Linette stood at the table chopping something and dropping the pieces into a cooking pot. He sniffed. Onions maybe.

Grady played under the table. He'd fashioned a fence of kindling and arranged the rocks and bits of wood like animals in a pen.

He chuckled. "Grady, that's how I used to play."

Grady shrank back trying to get out of sight.

Eddie didn't take offense. The child would need time to learn Eddie intended to be his friend.

Linette grabbed a cup from the shelf. "Coffee? Something to eat?"

"Coffee sounds good. Thanks."

She filled the cup and sat it before him.

"No one else is having coffee?" he asked.

Linette and Cassie exchanged glances. Cassie ducked her head, suddenly very interested in her knitting. Linette grabbed a carrot and butchered the thing, scooting the pieces into the pot. "We've had tea already, but I assumed you preferred coffee."

"Having no doubt read about the huge pots of coffee the cowboys drink while on cattle drives." His words, softly spoken, sounded dry and humorless even to himself.

Cassie snorted. "I'll venture a guess she knows more about cowboys than you."

Linette's gaze grew dark. "Of course I don't. But I did learn a lot." She looked past Eddie. If he didn't miss his guess, she looked past the walls of this cabin. "If I were a man I'd join a cattle drive." Slowly, as if realizing Eddie stared at her, she brought her attention back to the room. "Can I offer you a tea biscuit?"

"Thanks." He hoped she had a large plateful. "I kind of like tea especially on a cold wintry day."

"Why didn't you say so?" She bustled to the stove and shook the kettle, then poured in more water and moved it to the center of the stove. "I can make you tea, if you prefer it."

"Coffee will do this time. But in future wait for me and we'll have tea together." Now, why had he said that? It wasn't as if he planned to stop his work every afternoon to join them for a cup of tea and a friendly chat. No, sir. He intended to stay as far away from this place as humanly possible.

The women again exchanged looks. He couldn't begin to guess what silent signal they sent each other. Maybe they preferred to have their tea without his company.

"Unless that interferes with your plans?"

"Of course not. I'd be glad to make tea for you."

He noticed Linette did not include Cassie in her welcome. But it didn't matter. It was his house; he was the host, they the guests. Something they all needed to remember.

He savored his coffee and the biscuits. He had come indoors with a task in mind. Oh, yeah. A letter to Margaret. He pulled the writing things from the bookshelf and arranged them where they wouldn't extend into Linette's working space and get soiled. "I'm going to write Margaret. If she knows about the house I've built she'll change her mind." He bent his head and began. The first part was easy.

Dear Margaret,

How are you? I was disappointed that Miss Edwards came and not you.

I blame myself, because I planned a surprise for you. I see now that I should have told you.

He stopped writing and stared at the tabletop. How did he put his dreams and hopes into a few words and expect anyone to understand?

He'd seen men with a favorite horse share silent communication. If it were possible between man and beast, surely it was possible between a man and a woman. He and Margaret had corresponded for almost two years, and before he left London they had talked about the future. He trusted it formed a basis for understanding the message behind the words he intended to put on paper. He resumed writing.

It is true I now live in a small cabin. Hardly big enough for the four people now crowded in here for the winter. But on the hill is the surprise I planned to have ready for you before we wed. A big house. It is as fine as any house in the West. No, finer. There are six bedrooms besides the main bedroom, which has two large dressing rooms plus a nursery, so it's really a little suite in one wing of the house.

He filled a page of unsatisfying description.

I fear I am portraying this poorly. I will ask Miss Edwards to give you her own description.

The feelings filling his heart would not form as words on the page. He stared at the pen in his hand. What did he really want to say?

Margaret, my dear. I have no intention of marrying Miss Edwards. I will send her back to her home as soon as the weather permits. I hope news of the house I have built will persuade you to reconsider and come in the spring.

He blotted the ink and waited for it to dry then

folded the pages and addressed the envelope. He set the letter on top of the bookshelf in plain view. A reminder to Miss Edwards of his intention.

As soon as the weather permitted, he would give Linette a tour of the house then request she write to Margaret with a full report.

He pulled out the magazines and newspapers from yesterday's mail and returned to his chair to read. The room radiated warmth, something on the stove simmered. So far the meals had been a disappointment, but the aroma gave him hope supper might be better.

Cassie's knitting needles clicked in a steady rhythm. Underneath the table, Grady resumed play, murmuring to his toys and occasionally raising his voice as he ordered one of the pretend animals to stop or turn. Linette stirred the pot and hummed.

Eddie thought of the big house and Margaret's presence. Would she fill it with a similar sense of home and contentment? Or would they live parallel lives like so many married couples did? He only had to get through the winter to find out.

Later, they shared a tasty soup full of vegetables. The meat proved to be a little chewy but he managed. It beat starving.

Dishes finished, Cassie took Grady to bed. Linette followed shortly afterward.

For some reason he'd expected her to linger as she had last night. Not that he needed company. Of course not. He was grateful for a chance to be alone in his own house. He had plenty of reading to do. But he kept pausing to listen. He didn't hear a word and soon abandoned reading the newspapers. He unrolled his furs. As he bent to put out the lamp a flicker of color on the wall caught his eye. He straightened, lifted the lamp to a painting, ornately framed. Bluebells, yellow gorse, orange poppies and other flowers in wild abandon filled the canvas.

As he stared, winter disappeared and he imagined strolling through the spring fields of England. The warm moist air bathed his face. The scents of the flowers filled his nostrils.

Another painting hung next to the flowers. The hill country with undulating blue hills in the background and lush green pastures dotted with white sheep in the foreground. In the middle to the left, a cluster of farm buildings. To the right a large manor house. Although the buildings should have dominated the scene they instead became a mere mention in it…a flicker of interest. All that mattered was the land, the hills, the grass. He stared for a long time, as his heart drank in things he couldn't name. The artist had captured the life of the land and given it a voice.

He held the lamp closer and leaned over to see the name. There were only two initials. L.E. Linette Edwards? He drew back. Had she painted these? He looked at them again—the field of wildflowers and the pastoral scene. They both reached out to him, as if each brushstroke had the ability to talk.

He shook his head and stepped back slowly. These paintings did something to the room.

He turned and another patch of brightness caught his attention. A quilt of cheerful colors hung over one chair. When had it appeared?

He blew out the lamp and crawled into his bedroll. Had Linette painted these pictures? Who was she?

He dismissed every vestige of curiosity. It didn't matter that her paintings spoke to him. She was not the sort of woman who belonged in his home.

Or his heart.

Chapter Five

The snow fell all the next day. It piled up deeper and deeper, especially at the sides of the little cabin, like dollops of cream that had been scooped there by a huge spoon. Linette made numerous trips to the window to measure the snow with her eyes and to mentally exclaim over its beauty. The way it mounded and drifted in the wind, creating sharp edges and subtle shadows. At first, she had voiced her pleasure. "It's unbelievably beautiful."

Eddie shot her a disgusted look. "It's too early. I can't imagine how many animals we'll lose."

After that she kept her happy comments to herself and learned to take turns at the window with Eddie, who grew more and more glum, sighing heavily as he turned from the view. Then, as if searching for something he couldn't find, he poked through the bookshelf, picked up objects and put them back. After a few moments, he returned to the window. He was understandably concerned about the herd.

Linette watched with a degree of caution. Would

his worries make him harsh? *Lord, keep his cows safe. Help him trust You.*

She wanted to tell him of her prayer but feared he would not find it comforting. But to his credit, his actions did not escalate and something inside her relaxed. He was a man not only noble, but self-controlled. The winter might be pleasant enough after all. And provide ample opportunity for her to prove her worth to him.

He jerked toward the door and donned his coat. "I have to see to things outside." He ducked out into the storm.

She rushed to the window, but already the snow blocked his view. "I hope he'll be safe," she murmured. She shivered. A person could get lost in the snowstorm. She'd read about such disasters. What if he met with misfortune?

"I guess he knows what he's doing," Cassie said and resumed her knitting.

"I suppose you're right." But she couldn't see any other building from the window. How could he know where he was going? She had to find something to do to keep her worries at bay. The floor in front of the door was soiled. She prepared hot water and got down on her hands and knees to scrub it. Wouldn't he be impressed with her attention to the needs of the house—small though it was?

She finished and sat back on her heels to admire the job. The floor shone with cleanliness. A fine job indeed.

The door banged open and Eddie entered. As he stepped, his right foot skidded toward her. He windmilled his arms. His left foot went sideways. He flayed madly, but his feet continued their mad journey and he landed on his bottom with a thud that shuddered up Linette's neck.

Her breath whooshed out. She'd done this. Unintentionally but by her hand nevertheless. "I'm sorry."

He rested inches from the basin of water and looked up at her with a mixture of surprise and shock.

For a moment, time stopped as they considered each other. Again she felt an unfamiliar twinge in the region of her heart. Then his eyes burned like a smoldering fire. "Have you decided that if I won't marry you you'll kill me?"

She swallowed hard then tipped her chin. "No, sir."

"Why else would you ice the floor before the door?"

How was she to know the water would freeze rather than dry? Though if she wasn't so keen on proving how much he needed her she would no doubt have realized it. So far all her good intentions had served to give him more reason to reject her. "I don't want you dead, because unless I marry you my father will force me to return."

He sat up slowly. "Were you this vexatious to your father?"

"I fear so."

He rolled his eyes. "In that case he should pay me to take you off his hands."

"Indeed, if you recall I did offer you my dowry." She rose.

"I doubt your dowry could be enough. No matter how generous it might be." He gingerly got to his feet and rubbed his right hip.

She wanted to offer a hand but hesitated for fear

he would jerk back and perhaps fall again. "Are you okay?"

"I'll live."

If she wasn't mistaken he sucked back a groan.

How could everything she tried turn into a disaster? She pulled in air, along with a hefty dose of courage and determination. She would learn. She would get better. He would soon view her as an asset to his life. Unbidden, a deep-throated longing rose within her. She wanted to belong here.

But only as a partner, she reminded herself.

For the rest of the afternoon, she avoided meeting his gaze because every time she did, some stubborn, wayward thought reared its head pointing out that perhaps she had developed a foolish, romantic view of him while reading his letters. Over and over, she reiterated that she only wanted a way out of her constraining life in England and the marriage her father had arranged. Nothing more than a marriage of convenience.

The following morning she stepped from the bedroom and blinked at the sun streaming through the window. "It's stopped snowing."

Eddie cradled a cup of coffee as he stared out the window. "I need to get going. Can we have breakfast as soon as possible?"

"Certainly." She'd pried a few more details from Cassie about cooking and served up a decent-enough breakfast—no fire outside the stove, no raw meat and no hard beans. But did he notice or comment? No, indeed. His neglect enabled her to focus on her goal—a businesslike marriage.

He barely finished before he donned his coat. "I have to check on things." And he was gone.

She released air from her tense lungs and contemplated Cassie and Grady. who both relaxed visibly. "We'll get used to each other."

Cassie grunted. "I can't wait to get out of here." She stared out the window. "Maybe one of those miracle-working Chinooks will melt the snow. and the stagecoach will head back to Fort Benton. If it does I intend to be on it."

"Well, I don't." Linette fixed the woman with a challenging look. "Where do you plan to go?"

Cassie shrugged. "I expect I can be a housekeeper for someone at the fort."

"How would that be better than here?"

Cassie's defiance deflated. "Like I say, a woman has few opportunities in life."

Linette examined the contents of the pantry shelf wondering what to make for the noon meal. "Cassie, we make our own opportunities."

"Like your father is allowing you to do? At least George made an effort to take my feelings into consideration. Trouble was, he never thought my opinions held any weight."

Linette didn't reply, though she more than half agreed that men too seldom thought women had an opinion of any worth. She pulled down a sack and opened it to investigate the contents. Oats. Tilly had taught her how to cook porridge. A breakfast she could handle successfully. She brought her attention back to Cassie. "There's always something we can do to improve our circumstances."

Cassie laughed. "Like ice the floor so a man tumbles at your feet?"

Linette met her gaze, saw the first flash of true amusement the woman had ever revealed. "I wish it were that easy. He did fall though, didn't he?" She chuckled.

Cassie giggled. "Like a tree cut down by an ax."

They laughed until they both wiped their eyes.

She hadn't meant to create a booby trap for him. He might have been hurt. Linette tried to sober, but every time she did she'd look at Cassie and start to laugh again.

The door rattled open and her amusement fled as Eddie stepped inside. He gave them a curious look, having no doubt heard them laughing.

Cassie gave her knitting her full attention.

Grady, who had been watching them with amazement, ducked behind the table.

Eddie shook his head as if to say he wasn't interested and crossed to scoop up the roll of furs he slept on each night. "I'm going to find the cows."

"You're going overnight? Where will you sleep?"

"I've spent many a night on the ground."

"But the snow? The cold?" Her heart beat a rapid drumbeat against her ribs. She'd barely stepped from the cabin and apart from the first day when she'd met two of the cowboys, she knew no one else. She and her companions would be alone. Isolated. That was her only reason for the worry that clawed at her throat. Not, she firmly informed her wayward brain, not that she already missed Eddie and he hadn't even left.

"I thought you'd read about the cowboys. Didn't any of your books mention sleeping out in the cold?"

She'd read about how men pushed away the snow to dry ground or dug shelters in a drift, but they were nameless heroes. "What if something happens to you?" She barely managed to keep her voice calm.

He faced her. Met her gaze. She didn't care if he saw her concern. It was honest, sincere. With supreme effort she banked her worry.

"I have to check on the animals."

She nodded. "I know. I promised to pray for their safety and I have."

The air settled heavily between them, full of her unfulfilled dreams, her aching longings, her nervous worry. *In God I trust.* No need for her to be anxious. She jerked her gaze away to look at the bright window. "I pray God will keep you safe as well."

"He has in the past. But don't worry yourself. If something happens to me the men and Cookie will see you are taken care of. They'll make sure you get back to your father."

Her eyes burned. She was concerned about his safety, but he wouldn't let an opportunity pass to remind her of his intention to send her back. She gave him a look laden with every ounce of anger and denial flooding through her. "I'm quite capable of managing on my own." Never mind her temporary flight down a fear-filled path. Put it down to the unfamiliar circumstances. And thinking of Eddie being out in the wintry weather. After all, he was her means of escape from her father.

"I'm sure you are, Miss Edwards." He filled her name with resignation then ducked out of the house before she could respond.

She jerked about. "Oh, that man."

A few minutes later she heard the thud of horses' hooves riding away.

Cassie reported from her station at the window. "Eddie and three others."

Linette reached the window in time to see the snow kicked up by the departing riders. She tried to remember exactly how many men were on the place. Had he left at least one behind? Surely someone had to take care of the stock on the ranch. Would that person also check on the occupants of the cabin or were they completely on their own? The cookhouse stood across the roadway. She assured herself Cookie was there. Wasn't she? Perhaps she had left to visit someone while the men were away. Would it have hurt Eddie to give her a little reassurance?

Unable to soothe her pounding heart, she spun on her heels. Her father would be expecting a letter soon, and if he didn't receive it. . .

She shuddered. She would not let him drag her home. Any more than she would let Eddie send her back.

She yanked paper, pen and ink from the shelf. But what could she say? If her father thought Eddie didn't intend to marry her he would send someone after her, not giving any leeway for the weather. If he ordered it, he expected a man could overcome simple obstacles like snow and cold. Yet she wouldn't—couldn't—lie, and say they'd proceeded with wedding plans. In the end, she reported she'd arrived safely and didn't offer to send proof of a wedding because she couldn't.

Two days passed. She'd not seen another soul apart from the occupants of the house. With each hour

Linette's insides twisted tighter. Had Eddie abandoned them to starve and freeze? She eyed the shelf. How long would those supplies last? He'd directed her to the wood in the attached shed, but they used an alarming amount in a short time.

"Still think he's going to marry you?" Cassie asked. "If you ask me, he's left us to manage on our own for the winter. I guess we'll see if you're as good at pioneering as you think."

Cassie's words served to jolt Linette from her worry. "Cookie is across the way." Although she'd seen no evidence of it. To divert herself, she pulled out one of Grady's shirts and mended a torn seam. With each jab of the needle, annoyance at Eddie mounted. If her father heard how he'd treated her—

Heaven help them all if he did. She'd pay as dearly as Eddie. The thought only served to anger her more. She'd come in good faith. Eddie could at least allow her that.

Cassie stared out the window, as she often did. She never commented on the beauty, never saw any blessing in their situation. Linette knew she saw few blessings in her life.

Right now Linette didn't see a whole lot more. She'd forgotten to trust God. She calmed her breathing, slowed the speed of her needle.

"Someone rode into the yard." Cassie said it with resignation rather than the curiosity and anticipation Linette felt as she sprang to the window.

A man—a cowboy—with a snow-crusted buffalo-hide coat slouched low in the saddle. Eddie followed, sitting tall on his horse, his buffalo coat equally coated with snow. The others did not appear. Perhaps they'd stayed with the cattle.

He was back. Relief melted her muscles and she clutched the logs of the wall to hold her up.

He certainly looked regal. Born to rule.

He rode closer to the cabin. Despite his upright posture, his face seemed drawn. No doubt he was worn out by riding in the cold. She'd make certain he had a hot drink when he returned to the cabin. He rode by without glancing in her direction.

Hmmph. Her relief twisted into frustration. Was he too high and mighty to take note of the newcomers in his cabin? To give a thought to their comfort and security?

The pair rode to the barn.

She watched until they were out of sight. Only then did she realize she held her breath, and let it out with a gusty sound.

Cassie left Linette's side. "I expect it's bad news."

Linette strained for another glimpse. "Why do you say that?"

"Hasn't Eddie been expecting it? How many times has he told us how cows can die in deep snow? How they can't find anything to eat? Stupid animals. Buffalo are built for this land, but what happened to them? People shot them for their hides."

Linette kept her face toward the window. Buffalo coats certainly looked good hanging from the shoulders of a cowboy. "It's natural Eddie should worry. His responsibility is a heavy load."

If only he'd allow her to share the weight of his responsibility, lighten his load in any way she could.

Lord, show me how to help him.

"He's coming." She spun away and hurried to the table. She didn't want him to think she'd been staring after him. She barely found her way to a chair and picked up a shirt to mend before he flung the door open and stepped inside.

"They're safe."

Linette nodded. Her anger fled and she grinned at him. "Glad to hear it."

Their gazes connected and held. A strange feeling of accord trembled in her heart. Then Cassie made an impatient noise and diverted her gaze from Eddie's dark eyes.

He hurried to explain. "The boys had the animals all gathered and when they sensed the snow coming, got them into the shelter of a wooded area. Ward says they even had some grazing." He rubbed his hands together and looked thoroughly pleased.

"I prayed God would keep them safe and He did," Linette gently pointed out.

"So you did. Do you want me to thank you?" His voice carried a hint of teasing.

"Would it hurt you?"

He tipped his head back and laughed.

His amusement danced across her nerves until she could hardly remember what they'd been discussing. She ducked her head and returned to the mending in order to get her thoughts sorted out. In her hurry, she jabbed her finger and found the pain erased everything else from her mind. She sucked her fingertip and tried to be annoyed that he'd caused her to be so careless.

Except it rather pleased her to know he felt comfortable enough to tease her.

He stopped laughing, though he grinned so wickedly she had several errant thoughts of further enjoyment. She tried to remember that she didn't want to feel anything toward him. But he had a smile that made her forget everything else.

"Thank you for praying," he murmured, his voice thick with amusement. "Me and the boys…and the cows…appreciate your help."

Cassie rolled her eyes. "So what happens now to these wonderful cows of yours?"

"The boys will hold them there until the snow melts then ease them down. A Chinook is already blowing in. Can you feel it?"

"The wind?" Linette turned toward the window and listened. The door rattled. A sound sighed around the cabin.

"Yup. You'll soon be throwing open the door to let in some warmer air."

The room did seem warmer. Or was it only her churning emotions? She drew in a deep breath and settled her tremulous feelings. "A Chinook. How exciting." Already melted snow dripped from the eaves and she caught sight of a puddle on the road.

"It certainly makes a mournful noise." Cassie hugged her arms around her and looked about as pleased as if stung by a hornet.

Linette laughed. "Seems you have to take the bad with the good. I try to overlook the bad so I can enjoy the good."

The look Cassie shot at her held the power to curdle Linette's breakfast if Linette had a mind to let it. She didn't.

Eddie rubbed his hands together and considered the view from the window, looking as pleased as if he had personally invented sunshine. His pleasure drew her to his side.

"'Net?" Grady whispered. She turned from the window to answer Grady's insistent tug at her arm. She bent to hear his question. "I go see horses now?"

She glanced toward Eddie and met his brown eyes.

He smiled. "This change in weather makes a person want to go out and play, doesn't it, Grady?"

Grady pressed to Linette's side but nodded agreement.

The change in the weather must be the cause of her emotions swinging so wildly from worry to fear to... pleasure? Of course she was happy Eddie had returned safely. He was her means of escaping Lyle Williamson.

"We'll give it time to melt more of the snow and then I'll take you. You just be patient."

Grady nodded again and Linette's heart crowded her ribs at the way Eddie smiled at the boy. Grady needed to know not all men would look at him and dismiss him as a nuisance the way his father had. Eddie's gaze had softened as he smiled at the boy. For a moment his eyes held hers in a strong grip, as if silently promising her something she could not identify...

She managed to divert her attention to something beyond his shoulder. This was to be a marriage of convenience. Nothing more. But something inside her had shifted as she realized he was a man of his word. What he said, he would do. They could all take comfort in the fact.

Except his word to her had been that she was safe here for the winter and then he would send her back to her father.

And to Lyle Williamson with his pudgy hands and leering eyes.

She tucked in her chin and pulled herself tall and straight. Somehow between now and spring Eddie would change his mind.

From the corner of her eye she saw Eddie watching her.

She allowed herself a steady glance at him, saw what looked like concern in his eyes.

Then he blinked. "I'll take you up to the big house before it gets muddy. Then you can tell Margaret about it."

It wasn't an invitation. It was an order. Just as the "tell Margaret about it" was an order. However, she didn't care. She'd stared at the house for two days and her curiosity had built with each passing hour. She couldn't wait to see it up close. If her prayers were answered, her plan fulfilled, the house would be her home.

"I'd like to see it." She reached for her coat.

"I come?" Grady whispered.

Linette looked at Eddie for his approval.

He shook his head. "The hill will be slippery. Best you stay here with Mrs. Godfrey this time, Grady." He held the door open for Linette.

She stepped out. The wind tore at her. She pulled her collar tight and laughed as the bottom of her coat whipped about her ankles.

"Hang on to your coat." Eddie bent into the wind and headed across the yard.

She pushed after him, the wet snow heavy on her boots. Lifting her head, she sucked in air laden with promise. God had kept Eddie's cows safe. He was faithful. She trusted Him to continue to provide the ways and means for her to avoid marriage to her father's choice.

Eddie paused at the bottom of the hill. "I don't have a proper trail up to the house yet. Think you can manage the slope?"

Snow covered whatever path had been there. In most places the snow was sticky as it melted. "I'll be fine." She put a foot forward, following in Eddie's footprints, and discovered the ground was slippery where the snow had melted. She went down on one knee.

"Here." He held out his hand.

She grabbed it and straightened, tipping her head back to meet his gaze. "Thank you." Something flickered in his eyes as if seeing her for the first time. *See me,* she silently begged. *Give me a chance.*

His grasp was firm, his hand strong and reassuring. His gaze, however, warned he had only one plan in mind and that plan did not include Linette staying permanently. He turned and resumed his climb.

They reached the top and she looked back. "Oh, my. No wonder you picked this spot." She looked down on the ranch buildings, on the snow-covered river wandering through the land and past red-painted buildings, past the ridge of dark green pine trees to a white-topped mountain, purple in the distance. Strong and powerful. "I could never get tired of this view."

"I can see the whole ranch at a glance from here." He paused. "Not all the land, of course. Our lease is thousands of acres. It takes several days to ride it. Some areas are practically inaccessible on horseback." For a moment, they both took in the view.

Her breathing was ragged from the climb. His came loud and clear, matching her own. They breathed in and out in unison. She admired the landscape and knew he did as well, though he might be seeing his cows and his responsibilities while she saw the strength and beauty of God's creation. Her hope and faith drew sustenance and renewal from the sight.

They exchanged a glance of understanding then he turned away. "I'll show you the house." His brisk tone reminded her of his expectations—see the house, report on its fineness to Margaret.

The feeling of sharing something special ended with his words.

"It isn't finished yet." He sounded almost apologetic.

She couldn't imagine why. "It's a big house. No doubt it's required a great deal of work."

"Two stories." He pointed. "A balcony off the main bedroom." A stone chimney dominated the roof. Bay windows were capped by the round balcony he referred to. "Servants' quarters at the back."

Did he intentionally emphasize the word *servants* as if to remind her he didn't need or want a pioneer wife?

She would not acknowledge the possibility.

They climbed the steps to double doors and he threw them open to a large foyer. She could see through to another set of double doors at the far end with glass panes allowing light to flood through. Wide stairs rose to the second floor and curved toward a landing. Doors opened off the foyer to various rooms. Disappointment twisted through her.

"It's like…" A manor house.

"The plans were drawn up in London, a replica of the manor house on the Gardiner estate."

Linette shook her head. "This is the West. Full of possibility for change. Why would you want to replicate the old ways?"

His look was rife with disbelief. "The Gardiners are proud of their heritage."

The Gardiners? "What about you?"

"I'm a Gardiner." He seemed to think that said it all. He slid back the pocket doors to the right. "Our dining room. Those doors lead to the kitchen." He pointed to a wooden door in the far corner.

"Very convenient." Oak panels covered the walls. She could almost see a long table with heavy chairs surrounding it. But she didn't like what she saw. The room was so official and stiff. "Is there some other place for family meals?"

He led her to another pair of pocket doors and silently slid them back to reveal a smaller room filled with sunlight. The bay windows she'd admired from the outside made the room almost circular. She could easily imagine matching wing chairs in green brocade before the windows, a basket of sewing nearby and a book opened for reading. At her feet, a circular rug in burgundy and green. She stepped toward the curve of the windows and looked out at the mountains. "This is a lovely room. I expect you can see the sunset from here."

He stood at her side. "You can. It's spectacular at times. I'll bring you up some evening so you can see for yourself."

She wanted to thank him for his offer, but after a glance at the hard lines in his face she guessed he wished he hadn't spoken the words.

Again she had the peculiar feeling they breathed the same air, felt the same draw to something outside themselves, something big, inviting and exciting. Wishful thinking on her part. He would certainly deny the notion vehemently if she mentioned it.

The cattle in the wintering pens down below shuffled, sending up a cloud of steam.

"Come along. I'll show you the rest of the house so you can give Margaret a complete description."

She sighed. Of course, he was only thinking of the impossible hope of persuading Margaret to reconsider. Though a tiny doubt poked at her brain, perhaps once she learned of this manor house Margaret might indeed change her mind. Heaviness caught at Linette's limbs, so it took a great deal of effort to follow him.

He showed her the rooms on the other side of the foyer—the big parlor, a den, and the library with empty shelves. "Do you have enough books to fill these?"

"They're in crates waiting to be shipped come spring."

Come spring. Seemed everything hinged on that season.

He led her across the hall to the kitchen, stark and empty. A door from the kitchen led to small bedrooms. "For the servants." He turned from the area and led her up the wide, curving staircase with a flawless wooden banister that gleamed as if he'd spent hours polishing it.

Upstairs, to the left of the landing, he opened the door to a huge bedroom. A door with the upper half in glass gave her a view of the balcony. "Oh, what a lovely place to sit and read." She could see herself ensconced in a wicker chair, the sun warm on her face as she read her Bible and prayed. "Or draw."

"I saw the initials L.E. on those paintings in the cabin. Did you do them?"

She wished she hadn't mentioned her little hobby. "It's a pleasant way to spend a few hours."

"They're good."

Her cheeks burning with pleasure, she spun about to face him. "You think so? Really?"

"They have…" He paused, his gaze steady and unblinking. "Heart." His eyes slid away as if he was embarrassed by his comment.

She swallowed hard. "That's the nicest thing anyone has ever said about my painting. Father considers it an occupation suitable for a female. In other words, a waste of time." But he encouraged it. Found it preferable to some of the other pursuits she chose, like speaking to the people she saw on the street, or handing out coins to beggars. Which was the only reason he'd allowed her to study with one of the finest art teachers in the city.

Eddie met her look again. "The world would be a poorer place without the art of great men and women."

Surprise flared in her heart. She floundered in the depths of his gaze, got lost in his look, his words, his approval.

He jerked away, freeing her to find balance and sanity. "There's more." He crossed the room and opened the door. "The nursery."

"Ah." Thinking of babies while standing next to the man she had planned to marry filled her with hot embarrassment. But she could not stop from dreaming of little boys and girls playing noisily, happily, in this beautiful room.

She noticed three smaller rooms branching off the larger area.

"Bedrooms for children and a nurse," Eddie murmured and moved away quickly, leading her across the hall and opening the doors to a water closet and four generous bedrooms.

The size of the place awed and inspired her. She could see so many possibilities. "This is wonderful. I can see using this wing to help others. The ill. The brokenhearted."

He spun about and faced her. Any sense of connection, promise or hope fled in the anger wreathing his face. "This house is for the Gardiners. These rooms are for family." He waved toward the main suite. "My wife and children." He waved his other arm down the hallway. "These rooms are for my parents and grandfather, should they choose to visit. Or other family members and friends of the family. For company when I entertain." He indicated she precede him down the stairs. "Once Margaret learns how fine the house is, she will change her mind about coming West."

Linette's heart lay wounded and heavy. She'd momentarily imagined the house as hers. Why had she so foolishly revealed her thoughts to him?

She glanced to her right as she reached the bottom

of the stairs and fought the truth crashing in upon her. She could see he wasn't thinking pioneer wife, but rather, lady of the manor. She sucked in cold air and stiffened her resolve. She could be that, too. She'd been raised to be such. Taught to show interest in only lady-like activities, pretending no interest in the real things of life. But the idea sent shivers up and down her arms. She wanted more. She wanted to participate in life, enjoy shouldering a challenge. She wanted to be part of building a new world where women could be more than objects in a fine home.

Most of all, however, she wanted to avoid marrying Lyle Williamson and being subjected to some of the obscene things he had whispered in her ear on their last encounter.

She had only one recourse. Pray.

How foolish of her to see Eddie as her future husband before she'd even met him and given him a chance to say yea or nay. Though, in fairness to herself, she'd thought his letter meant he said yes. She wouldn't give up her dream. Not yet. With God all things were possible.

They stepped out into a warm and promising wind that caressed her face. She turned and smiled at Eddie. "I enjoyed seeing your house. It's beautiful."

The remnants of his anger fled, replaced by a look of pride. "Be sure you tell Margaret that."

She exhaled loudly. "Of course." She'd also be sure to mention the deep snow and moaning wind. Perhaps, too, the long distance to the nearest town, or what passed as a town out on the frontier. Oh, and not to forget the fact that there were only three females on the place and two of those would be leaving if Eddie insisted on sending her back to England.

Not that she had any intention of going. As she'd said the first day, there was many a slip between the cup and the lip.

Chapter Six

Eddie took Linette back to the cabin, mumbled something about returning for lunch then strode toward the wintering pens as if he had a fire to douse. Her eagerness and approval of the big house had warmed his heart, teased him into letting his guard down. For just a few minutes, he'd enjoyed her enthusiasm, seeing the place through fresh eyes, and he felt as if he'd accomplished his goal of building a house to meet his father's expectations. And then she'd said how she pictured the house—as a refuge for the ill and hurting.

He'd never heard such nonsense. He wasn't opposed to helping others. Needy people were more than welcome on the ranch, but a home was a shelter for the family.

Margaret would never have such foolish ideas. She was a refined lady. She would never sell her fashionable gowns for pioneer dresses. Or wear an over-big man's coat. She was…

He tried to bring her face to remembrance, but all he pictured was pale brown hair, direct brown eyes and a very determined expression. Linette's face! Not the one he wanted to keep in mind.

He loped onward and reached the pens where the red, white-faced cattle chowed down on the hay Roper and Slim had tossed out for them. The steam of their warm breath disappeared in the wind. Snow melted in the corrals, creating soft, mushy footing. Some of the cows jerked away at his approach, instantly alert. The younger heifers crowded around him, curious as only the young can be.

"Boss?" Slim called out.

"Just checking them over."

"Good breeding stock. You done right by bringing these in."

"Yup." His father had balked at the idea, but Eddie knew crossbreeding them with the hardier Texas stock would give him the best of both breeds.

He mucked about the yards, passing time as much as checking on things. As the sun reached its zenith, he reluctantly returned to the cabin for lunch, determined to think of nothing but his responsibilities.

He gritted his teeth. Only until spring. He could endure anything if he made up his mind to, and he had. He sat down. Linette dished up stew and kept up a steady commentary on the weather and the mountains.

Cassie grunted her displeasure. "I hate the wind. It tears at my thoughts until I feel like screaming."

Linette chuckled. "Maybe you should go outside and let it sweep your thoughts clean."

Cassie mumbled something about staying indoors until spring.

"Don't you want to see the mountains?" Linette

asked in a tone that suggested of course she would. When Cassie didn't answer, Linette continued, undeterred by the lack of response. "I told Cassie about your big house," she told Eddie.

"Too bad it wasn't finished so we wouldn't have to crowd into this place," Cassie muttered.

Grady watched Eddie. Every time Eddie met his gaze, the boy jerked away. But not before Eddie caught a glimpse of stark fear. Eddie longed to ease the boy's apprehension. "Clean up your plate." He addressed Grady. "And I'll take you to see the horses."

The boy ducked his head and scraped his plate clean.

Eddie pushed from the table, thanked the women for the meal that was finally satisfying and reached for his coat. "Get your coat, Grady."

The boy hung back at Linette's side. "'Net go."

Linette shot Eddie a look of apology then touched Grady's face and turned him toward her. "You can go by yourself, Grady. Mr. Gardiner won't hurt you."

But he only pressed himself closer to Linette.

"Looks like you'll have to come along, too." Eddie couldn't keep the reluctant note out of his voice. Bad enough the woman filled his cabin. After her visit, he feared he'd feel her presence every time he went to the big house. Now it seemed he'd be forced to have her invade the barn, too. How was he to get her face out of his mind if he couldn't get away from her?

"You're welcome to come, too, Cassie." Perhaps Cassie's presence would make the whole outing less nerve-racking.

Cassie shuddered. "No, thanks." She smiled tightly at Linette. "I'll do the dishes. So you go along."

Linette sprang into action, putting warm clothes on Grady then pulling on her own coat.

Eddie's nerves grew tauter each second as he thought of her walking at his side. Only because he feared for his safety, he silently insisted. Not because he wondered how she would see the ranch. Would she recognize its beauty? See the work he'd done? "I'm hoping you haven't any plan to do me bodily harm while we're out there." He gave a mirthless chuckle in the hopes of making her think he only teased.

She slowly faced him. "I admit I've made some mistakes. I hoped you'd put it down to inexperience."

He'd been trying to guard his own thoughts but had stumbled into bad behavior. "I apologize."

"As I said, I am a fast learner. You won't see me make the same mistake twice." She pulled on a knitted mitten and indicated she was ready.

He opened the door. "It won't change what happens when winter is over."

"Sooner or later you will change your mind." She met his gaze briefly. Long enough for him to see the hot determination in her eyes.

Her continued refusal to accept his answer made his teeth ache. But rather than continue this pointless discussion, he stepped outdoors. With relief he realized she'd successfully enabled him to consider her company with nothing more than reluctant acceptance.

Linette lifted her face to the sun and sighed. She turned full circle, pausing to look long and hard at the mountains. "Beautiful."

"The great Rockies are something to see all right." He constantly sought the view of the mountains when he was outside. The sight of them filled him with both calmness and hope. Something he needed now as never before. Having a woman show up and demand to become his wife had an unsettling effect on his normally steady thoughts.

"Reminds me of a verse," Linette said. "'I will lift mine eyes unto the hills, from whence cometh my help. My help cometh from the Lord, who made heaven and earth.'"

"Did your nurse teach you that?"

A thoughtful look came to her face. "You heard?"

He banged the heel of his hand to his forehead. "I didn't mean to let you know."

Her eyes widened and she swallowed hard as she seemed to recall what else had been said. "I hope you aren't offended by Cassie's complaining."

"I figure it's just a bad habit and nothing to do with me other than I'm handy for the moment."

She laughed. The sun caught in her eyes.

He jerked away. She was the most disconcerting female he'd ever had the misfortune of encountering. It was not yet November. Spring seemed an eternity away.

If Linette didn't give him permanent stomach problems with her cooking or maim him with her "helpfulness," she would certainly do her utmost to upset his carefully planned life with her quiet determination that he would sooner or later want to marry her.

She'd already upset his equilibrium. How would he survive? He would. Because he was a Gardiner.

Linette caught the hint of confusion in Eddie's eyes before he turned away, and she smiled. Maybe he was beginning to see her for what she was and what she could offer him as a wife.

She shaded her eyes and studied the surroundings. They stood in the center of the roadway with buildings on either side. "It's like a little town." A neat row of red buildings stood next to the cabin. To their left were a long, low building, a big red barn and a collection of corrals. The trail angled to the right where a bridge traversed the stream. Beyond that were more buildings and corrals. She could see cattle munching on feed in the pens around those more distant structures.

"Purposely designed that way for efficiency," Eddie said with a degree of pride. "Storehouses on the right. The bunkhouse to your left, close to the cookhouse." He led her past those buildings. Two men jerked open the bunkhouse door and crowded through the opening.

"Hello, boss," one called.

"Boys."

She thought Eddie intended to pass them, but he slowly ground to a halt. "You can expect to be an object of curiosity around here."

She chuckled. "It's mutual."

He shook his head. "Don't encourage them."

"Why not? Are they dangerous?"

He faced her squarely. "I wouldn't have a dangerous man on the place. But they pretend to be hard when inside they have the same hopes and dreams and desires as everyone else. It would be a mistake to take their feelings lightly."

His warning was clear as the air around them. "I don't flirt, if that's what you mean."

He studied her with unyielding eyes.

If he looked hard enough he would find truth and sincerity. He'd see her for what she was, what she could offer. *Please see me.*

"You admit you're desperate to marry. Don't toy with these men."

Before she could sputter a protest, he called, "Boys, come and meet my guests."

She wasn't desperate. At least not to marry anyone. Her father wouldn't hesitate to ignore a legal marriage if it didn't meet his purposes. Which meant marrying someone who would bring advantage to the Edwards name. Someone who met her own high standards. She quickly enumerated them—kind, noble, trustworthy, a man who would see her as a valued addition not only to his home but his life.

The two men jogged over, abused Stetsons clutched to their chests.

Eddie made formal introductions.

Blue Lyons had pale red hair and a matching mustache. His gray eyes were somber. He nodded and backed away, obviously embarrassed in the presence of a young woman.

Linette, wanting to make him feel comfortable, said it was an honor to meet the cowboys.

Blue's face grew even ruddier.

Grady shrank against her side, as uncomfortable as Blue.

Ward Walker was shorter than Eddie but solid built. He had black hair and shockingly blue eyes that smiled along with his wide mouth. He held out a hand to Grady, but when he saw how the boy retreated, he grinned. "Don't mean to scare you, young fella." He straightened to face Linette. "Pleased to meet you, ma'am. And what do you think of the country?"

"I've only just arrived, so I haven't had a chance to see much of it, but I'm looking forward to doing so."

"I'd venture to say you saw a lot of it from the stage-coach."

"For the comfort of others, the curtains remained drawn while traveling. But I saw enough. The land seems wild and free."

"And you liked that?"

"I like the idea of beginning over."

"Yes, ma'am."

She didn't blame him for sounding a little confused. She hadn't answered his question. Before she could say she liked the wildness of the land, Eddie spoke.

"Boys, I want you to take supplies up to those bringing the cattle down."

"Yes, boss." They jogged away.

Grady yanked at Linette's hand. "Horses?" he whispered.

"We'll find some in the barn." Eddie led them toward the solid-looking structure.

They stepped inside. It took seconds for Linette's eyes to adjust to the dim interior. But the smells hit her immediately. Warm horseflesh, fresh hay, dust and new wood.

A horse neighed as if greeting them. "Grady, do you want to say hello to Banjo?"

Linette giggled. "You named a horse Banjo?"

"What's wrong with that?" Eddie's voice carried an injured tone.

"Absolutely nothing, I'm sure." She couldn't contain a snicker. "But how did you choose such a name?"

Eddie kept his expression serious, but his eyes twinkled. "When I first got him he was all strung out like a—"

"Banjo." She whooped at the idea.

The horse nickered.

Eddie leaned closer and whispered, "He knows we're talking about him."

Almost as if they were coconspirators, Linette thought, the idea dancing across the surface of her brain with unexpected joy.

"You better say hello."

Glad to be diverted from her foolishness, she moved toward the big black horse, with Grady clutching her skirts. "Hello, Banjo."

Grady relaxed slightly, interested in the horse.

Here was a chance to help Grady learn to trust Eddie. It would make life easier for everyone if he stopped shivering and withdrawing every time he saw the man. Or any man. "Grady, have a look at Mr. Gardiner's horse." She urged him forward.

He took one step, still hanging on to her coat.

The horse looked over the top of his pen and nickered.

"I touch him?" Grady whispered.

"You certainly can," Eddie answered. "Let me lift you up so you can pet his head." He grabbed the boy around the waist, but Grady screamed and kicked.

Eddie set him down abruptly and stepped back. Banjo snorted and spun away. Throughout the barn, horses whinnied and stomped.

Linette squatted and held Grady. "Hush. You're scaring all the horses."

Grady clung to her, burrowing his face against her neck. He stopped screaming but sobbed and shivered.

"I'm sorry," she whispered, not sure if she apologized more to Grady or Eddie. She held Grady until he calmed then straightened, allowing him to cling to her. Her heart poured out grief and concern at his heart-wrenching sobs.

"I think we better return to the cabin," she murmured.

They walked in silence toward the house. Grady's behavior troubled Eddie. Why should the boy be so frightened of him? Being rejected by his father didn't seem enough reason for such a reaction. Would Linette know if something else had happened to upset the boy?

They stepped into the cabin. Cassie looked at Grady. "What happened? Why is he crying?"

Grady straightened his face. "I not crying."

Eddie glanced at the cookhouse. "I don't know if this is a good time, but if I don't introduce you to Cookie, she'll nail my hide to the wall."

Linette's gaze darted toward the cookhouse and she shuddered. "She sounds like a curmudgeon."

Knowing Linette would be pleasantly surprised, Eddie only said, "You'll have to judge for yourself. Does everyone want to go over?"

"I'd love to have tea." Cassie grabbed her coat.

The four of them crossed the yard to the cookhouse.

Linette hung back as they approached the door, clinging to Grady as if the boy could protect her.

Eddie carefully kept his face expressionless as he opened the door. "Cookie, I brought company."

Cookie swept across the floor. "Why, this must be the young woman who came to—"

He broke in before Cookie said anything about marrying. "She's visiting for the winter. May I present Miss Linette Edwards and Mrs. Godfrey. Linette, this is Cookie—Miz Liza Mc—"

"Never mind the Miz stuff. Just call me Cookie." She wrapped Linette in a bear hug and banged on her back. "So good to see you, gal. You don't know how good it is. Welcome, welcome." Every word was accompanied by another smack that jarred Linette's whole body.

"Cookie, you might let her go before you break something."

"Well, I guess I plumb forgot myself." She let Linette escape.

"You'll recover in a few minutes," Eddie said. Cookie's greeting seemed like justice.

Linette gasped and sent him a hard look.

"Hey, don't blame me. She's like that with everyone. Cookie, how many times have I told you to have a little respect for breakable bones."

"Ah, pshaw." Cookie flicked a towel at his leg. It connected and stung. He knew there would be a welt. Cookie didn't even bother to give him a second look.

She turned and wrapped Cassie in a likewise-crunching hug.

Cassie gasped for breath when Cookie released her to turn to the boy clinging to Linette. "And who is this little man?"

"Grady Farris."

Cookie squatted to eye level with Grady. "And aren't you a handsome young fella. How old are you?"

Grady held up four fingers.

"Why, I'd say that's old enough to join us for tea, right, boss?"

Eddie waited, expecting Grady to disappear into the folds of Linette's coat, but he beamed at Cookie. His eyes glistened like sun off the snow. He looked sweet and innocent, not drawn and fearful. Seems he didn't object to the friendship of women. "I'll leave you ladies here while I get to work." He retreated.

Cookie made it to the door with a speed that seemed impossible with her big body. "Not before you have tea." She grabbed his arm and dragged him back to the center of the room.

He glanced at Linette, saw her amusement and jerked away to face Cookie as a bolt of something he could only think of as admiration flickered through his brain. "A little respect here." He struggled to contain his grin. Cookie didn't need to know he wasn't serious.

Cookie dropped his arm. "Sorry, boss." She neither looked nor sounded repentant. "Coffee?"

Eddie glanced longingly at the door but nodded. "Sounds good."

Cookie laughed heartily. "That's more like it."

So they sat at the long table. Linette made sure to position herself between Eddie and Grady.

Cookie poured their drinks then she put a platter of fresh cinnamon buns before them. "Eat hearty," she instructed.

Linette took a bite of the bun and sighed. "These are delicious. They practically melt in my mouth."

Cookie beamed. "Nice to have someone appreciate my cooking. The men—" she slid an accusing glance at Eddie "—wolf it down without comment."

"Isn't enjoyment the highest form of praise?" he asked. He consumed two rolls and two cups of coffee.

The door jarred open and Bertie strode in, his arms full of supplies from the storehouse.

Eddie made introductions again. Bertie reached out to shake hands with Grady but pulled back when Grady buried his face in Linette's sleeve. Bertie shifted direction and took Linette's hand as he asked about the trip.

Eddie rose. Cookie and Bertie could entertain the ladies. "Thank you, Cookie. Now I have a ranch to run." Eddie hurried for the door before Cookie could tackle him.

Cookie roared with laughter. Just before the door closed behind him, Cookie spoke to Bertie. "There'll be a wedding before the winter is out. Mark my words."

Eddie bolted as if he could outrun his churning thoughts.

Let Bertie and Cookie fall in love with Linette if they so desired. He didn't have a mind to do so. Sure, she was cheerful. But also stubborn and independent. Even worse, she got all prickly at the idea of acting like a proper lady.

No. He anticipated sharing life with a woman who welcomed the chance to be the lady of his big house, a woman who would bring to this wild country the sort of life that had taken centuries to establish in England. A woman who would do his family name honor.

* * *

The sound of the door slamming crashed through Linette's mind. Her face warmed. Eddie had not been pleased by Cookie's prediction. Not that it robbed her of hope. She trusted the Lord to help her. In the meantime, she would enjoy learning about life in the West.

Bertie sat across from them and Grady shrank to Linette's side. She placed a reassuring hand on his quivering shoulder. His reaction to Eddie's touch worried her. How would they spend a winter together in tiny quarters if Grady screamed at his touch and retreated at his presence? The poor man would feel unwelcome in his own house. That would not serve any of them well. Besides, it seemed unnatural and unhealthy for the boy to be so afraid of men.

She turned her attention back to the conversation around the table. Cassie spoke more freely and friendly with Cookie than Linette had heard her speak with anyone to this point. Turned out both of them had once lived in the same area of Ontario and even had some mutual acquaintances.

"So you and your man were planning to head west?"

"I didn't want to go, but that's what George wanted. He sold everything and quit a good job. Now we have nothing." She swallowed hard and corrected herself. "I have nothing. Not even a home." She ducked her head but not before Linette caught a glimpse of tears.

Cassie hadn't shared her husband's dreams. No wonder she was annoyed that men made the decisions. "You have a home here."

"For the winter. Then what?"

"Whatever the Lord has in store for both of us. And Grady."

Even if returning to England wasn't a dreadful prospect, she wanted to stay here. Foolish it might be, but she still saw Eddie as ideal, saw him through her earlier reactions while reading the letters he'd written to Margaret. His words of hope and faith in the new land, his description of the mountains, his references to his family and his duty as an obedient son had all served to give her a vision of a man who was strong and noble.

Her opinion of him hadn't changed in the slightest despite his resistance and continued denial of her plan. He simply needed time to get used to it and see how ideal she was as a rancher's wife.

Cookie chuckled. "Could be you'll both find what I've found with Bertie. I wouldn't trade that man for ten thousand acres of the best rangeland in this here country." She leaned closer to her husband. "He thinks the world of me, too."

"That I do, my love." Bertie patted his wife's generous arm.

Linette wasn't interested in that kind of marriage. Love, she feared, would eliminate her right to make choices and follow the dictates of her heart.

Cookie pushed to her feet. "Most of the men are out, but I still need to make a meal for those hanging around. Excuse me while I tend to my duties. Feel free to stay and keep me company."

Grady's head had been nodding for several minutes.

"One little man is ready for a nap," Linette said.

"It doesn't take two of us to put him down. I think I'll stay and visit with Cookie."

Linette was glad if Cassie found something to make her happy and she prepared to leave. Cookie accompanied her to the door. "If you need anything, don't hesitate to say so."

Linette glanced past Cookie to the cinnamon buns under the tea towels. "I wouldn't mind learning to bake like you do."

"It's easy as falling off a log. I'll gladly show you." Cookie laughed and made to slap Linette on the shoulder. She thought better of it and dropped her hand.

Chapter Seven

Eddie needed fresh air and hard work. He saddled Banjo. Remembering Linette's amusement at the name of his horse, he chuckled. Guess it *was* funny if you stopped to think about it. Linette had certainly considered it a joke.

Enough of thinking of her. He shifted his thoughts toward little Grady and the way he'd reacted when Eddie touched him. "I can't believe that boy screamed. I'm not such a bad guy, am I, old friend?" He'd seen how Grady shrank back from Ward and every other man on the place, so had to believe it wasn't personal. "I wonder what happened to make him so afraid of men." He remembered that Grady's mother crossed the ocean to meet her husband. How long since the man had left? "I suppose it could be that the boy hasn't spent much time around men." But the screaming when Eddie touched him seemed extreme. "They've upset my quiet little life," he muttered to Banjo as he led him from the barn. "I'm not happy about it, either." He swung into the saddle and headed down the trail to join his men.

Ward and Blue were already gone, but they led pack-horses. Eddie would soon overtake them.

The more he thought about Grady, the more he wondered if it wasn't more than not seeing many men. He scrubbed at the back of his neck. Had some man done something cruel to Grady? Or perhaps Grady had witnessed a man hurting his mother. He tried to think what Linette had said about the pair. She'd met them on the boat. Had they been in cabins or steerage?

He decided he would ask more questions though he wasn't sure how it would change anything. He'd seen frightened animals. Sometimes you could simply walk into their world and strong-arm them into capitulation. Other times, you had to give them space and let them figure out you were safe to be around. He kind of figured he would have to give Grady space. He chuckled, causing Banjo to perk his ears in curiosity. "You wouldn't understand, but it's going to be a little hard to give the boy room when the place is only three hundred square feet."

Banjo tossed his head as if comprehending every word his master said.

Eddie laughed. He saw the boys ahead and flicked the reins to hurry Banjo toward them.

Ward waited for Eddie to fall in at his side. "Hey, boss. Miss Edwards is a right pretty gal."

"Guess so." He thought her coloring a little uncertain. And she was on the small size. He'd thought Cookie would crush her in her enthusiasm. Again, he thought it a form of justice at the hands of another for a woman who had forced her way into his peaceful life and turned it topsy-turvy.

"Boss, I don't want to speak out of place…"

"Go ahead. Speak your mind."

"Well, Cookie said she came out to get married but you're not interested. That so?"

He knew his life was open to examination by everyone on the ranch. He was being asked if he had an interest in Linette. He had none other than to see she got back safely to her father as soon as spring arrived. Back to an arranged marriage with a man that brought a twist of disgust and fear to Linette's mouth.

He squeezed his fists about the reins. Even if Linette was too small, dressed poorly and had ideas of helping misfortunates, she didn't deserve that.

He turned to Ward. "I expect my intended will change her mind and join me in the spring."

"Then I guess any of us can court Miss Linette." Ward grinned widely.

"Suit yourself." Things might be looking up. If Ward had an interest in Linette then it would make her presence in his life less intrusive. He smiled as he rode on ahead, though his smile didn't go any deeper than his face. Why should he feel it necessary to take care of Linette? She sure wouldn't welcome such a sentiment.

He saw the cows ambling along, being moseyed toward the winter pasture. The crew moved them at a slow pace, letting them find the easiest path, giving them time to graze, but still keeping them headed in the right direction.

He checked the horizon. No threatening clouds. They might not get any more snow for a few days, but he knew better than to count on it. Last year he'd lost several hundred head in the heavy snow. His father had no idea what the country was like. He saw only the numbers and losses. His reprimand, given in a letter, had been strongly worded.

Eddie didn't intend to repeat his mistake.

He spoke to each of the men, assured them more supplies were coming with Ward and Blue. Satisfied that the men had the herd under control, he headed back to the ranch.

Darkness engulfed him by the time he reined in at the barn. He led Banjo inside, unsaddled him, brushed him thoroughly, filled a manger with hay and left the barn. Many times he had returned home after dark, to an empty, cold cabin. Now a light beckoned from the window, drawing him irrevocably to its welcome. He paused outside the door, but when he heard Linette's laugh, eagerly he reached for the handle. He stopped, turned and looked at the big house. Linette laughed again and he forgot the unfinished manor on the hill and stepped into the light.

Linette stood in the middle of the room, a blindfold on her eyes as she tried to catch Grady, who giggled and jumped away. "You're too quick for me, Grady."

Grady saw Eddie and fear wreathed his face. He ran to Linette and clung to her skirts.

Linette slowly removed her blindfold. "You're back."

It seemed unnecessary to respond, but he nodded as he pulled off his heavy coat. He took his time hanging it on a hook. His silly, unexplainable eagerness at seeing the cabin lit up and stepping into its warmth had been snatched away by Grady's fear.

Linette edged Grady to Cassie's side and slipped over to Eddie. "I'm sorry he's so frightened. I wish it weren't so."

"But it is." Eddie knew he sounded weary and he

was. He wanted to relax before the warmth of the stove and enjoy the evening. But Grady's fear palpitated through the room.

"Have you eaten?"

He shook his head.

"We waited for you."

The smell of venison stew enabled him to push aside the problem of Grady's fear. "It smells good."

At Linette's signal they gathered around the table and Eddie said the blessing.

"It's good," he said after he had tasted the food.

"Thanks to Cookie, who has been kind enough to teach me. Cassie has discovered she and Cookie are from the same town."

Cassie smiled. "I know her sister."

Eddie had never seen the woman smile. It took ten years off her face. Seemed she might find the winter pleasant enough because of Cookie's company. He shifted his gaze to Grady who pressed as close to Linette as he could. Now, if only the boy would shed his fearfulness.

Cassie helped Linette do the dishes without any prodding then took Grady to bed as she'd done the previous nights.

He pulled his chair closer to the stove and propped his feet on the wood box. "How do you know Margaret?"

"Margaret and I met at a tea given by Viola Williamson."

"You say that name with a curl of your lip. Is she a distasteful woman?"

She flashed him a grin. "She's a very nice woman.

A distant relative. And sister to Lyle Williamson, the man my father wants me to marry."

"Ah. I see."

"Viola gives the best teas. In the summer she puts up linen shelters and serves cold lemonade and sweet cold tea. She invites young ladies and their mothers. There is music and plays and games. Margaret and I got matched up for charades. Then we were seated together at tea."

"What did you like about her?"

Linette ducked her head as if embarrassed. "She told me about you and let me read your letters."

He'd often regretted his inability to put down words of affection, but now he was grateful he hadn't. Knowing Linette had read his letters left him feeling exposed. Why had Margaret shared them? It didn't seem as if she put proper value on their relationship. Or perhaps her parents regretted their agreement to let her move so far away. Had they influenced Margaret's decision?

But surely, once they knew of the big house and his plans to live a genteel life such as Margaret was accustomed to, they would realize it wasn't a mistake to let her go. "Did you write Margaret and tell her about the house?"

Her gaze caught his in silent challenge before she gave a tight smile. "It's done and waiting to be posted." She nodded to the letter on the shelf beside his own.

Had she written as he wished?

She sighed as she read his unasked question. "If it's a fine house she seeks, I told her she'd find it here."

Somehow she managed to make it sound as if it would be a poor excuse for marriage. Perhaps. But didn't most women put a great deal of stock in what a man could provide? Seemed Linette didn't. He decided to change the subject. "How did you meet Grady's mother?"

She tipped her head and looked troubled. "I wandered about the ship, exploring everything and meeting as many people as I could. It was the first time I'd had a chance to converse with such a cross section of people. Dorothy Farris was on the lower decks. She appealed to me to help her."

"Because she was ill?"

Linette lowered her head. "It was more than that."

"Someone was bothering her?"

Linette nodded. "Her only companion was Grady and he wasn't much protection."

"Do you think Grady knew what was going on? Perhaps felt threatened by it?"

Linette still looked at her lap. "Once I found him outside a cabin crying for his mother. When I asked, he said she was inside. The door was locked and a man ordered me away when I knocked."

Eddie's jaw protested as he chomped down on his molars. It was as he suspected, though he couldn't guess how much Grady had faced. Threats? Physical abuse? More? He didn't want to imagine anything done to the boy, but something had made Grady fearful beyond reason. "It might explain why he is afraid of men."

"I suppose so. The poor child."

The air shimmered with embarrassment at the subject they discussed. Her cheeks flared like a summer rose of palest pink.

He stood to stir the fire and put on more wood.

"I thought I saw bruises on his face a couple of

times, as if he'd been struck, and I know his mother didn't do it."

Eddie groaned. He suspected there were bruises Linette hadn't seen and, even worse, damage to little Grady's soul.

"I don't know how to help him," she whispered.

Eddie didn't know, either. "About all I can think of is to encourage him to see men as his friends."

"I guess the more time he spends around you the better then."

He snorted. "Considering his reaction, that might prove a challenge."

"It's a shame he is so frightened of you."

"Yes, but what are we to do about it?"

Her gaze bored into him. He couldn't imagine what he'd said to bring that burning look to her eyes. Then she banked the fire. "Give him time, I suppose."

"I will bid you good-night." She scurried away and a few minutes later crawled into bed with Cassie, Grady between them. He moaned a little at the disturbance. What had the poor child seen or experienced? The subject of what Dorothy Farris had done—or rather, endured—was not a topic proper ladies took part in. But Eddie needed to understand Grady's fear.

Eddie had asked what they could do about it. He'd made them partners. It meant her plans were succeeding.

"What were you two talking about?" Cassie whispered.

"How I met Margaret. And what awful things Grady might have seen on the boat."

"What things do you mean?"

Linette edged closer and whispered as softly as she could. "His mother was afraid of one of the other passengers. I think he was being inappropriate."

"You think he was—" Cassie didn't finish. One didn't even mention the shameful things that went on in secret. "Where was Grady?"

"Once I found him locked out of a cabin, but I can't say about any other time. Like I told Eddie, I saw bruises on Grady more than once."

Cassie let out a short sigh. "Poor little mite. Sometimes life is so unfair."

Linette couldn't argue with her.

She whispered good-night to Cassie and turned over, but she didn't sleep right away. Miserable thoughts of Grady's past tangled with joyous thoughts of success in proving her worth to Eddie. But the latter held little importance alongside Grady's needs.

Next morning, she rose with a plan in mind. Over breakfast, she put it into action. "Would you object to Grady and me wandering around the ranch?" she asked Eddie. She hoped her eyes told him she had an ulterior motive for her request—to help Grady grow comfortable around the men.

His steady look searched beyond the surface.

Finally he nodded and she believed he understood her silent message. "I've no objection. I'll be out in the yards today."

He headed for the door. Not until it closed behind him did Grady jump down from the chair to play.

"Cookie has invited me to visit anytime I like," Cassie said. "So while you venture around the place, I'll go over there."

"I'll go with you and discuss what I can make for

dinner before I take Grady for a walk." Cassie looked relieved to think Linette might not bother her as much about meal preparation anymore.

It took only a few minutes to tidy the little house and then Cassie, Linette and Grady crossed to the cookhouse. Linette spent a pleasant hour planning meals. Cookie invited her back in the afternoon to help bake cakes.

The sun was warm overhead, the snow melting and a breeze drifting down from the mountains when Linette took Grady outside.

"You can run and run here," she said to Grady.

Squealing, Grady raced down the trail toward the barn. Eddie lounged against the fence watching. Grady, unaware of Eddie's presence, turned at the corner of the corrals and raced back. Several horses nickered at his laughter.

Linette caught him and turned him about. "Let's say hello to the horses."

They edged toward the fence. She lifted Grady to the top rail so he could touch the horses that came for attention. He laughed as they snorted a greeting.

Suddenly he noticed Eddie in the pen and drew back.

Eddie pretended not to notice the boy as he scooped up droppings with a pitchfork.

"It's okay," Linette soothed. "Do you think the horses would be ready to play if they were afraid of Mr. Gardiner?"

"He not hurt horses?"

"No. And he won't hurt little boys, either."

Grady wasn't convinced and wanted down. He took Linette's hand and pulled her away from the corrals.

Eddie eased closer. "Take him along the road toward the other buildings across the creek. You'll come to the wintering pens and pigsty. Some of the men are working down there. I've instructed them to ignore the boy until he's ready to make friends."

"Thank you." How thoughtful and kind he was. He would be an excellent partner in assisting her to help others. She wanted to say so, but Grady tugged at her, wanting to escape.

Once Grady felt he was far enough away to be safe, he slowed his pace to examine every detail—the rocks beside the trail, the leaf that blew across the path, the raven flying overhead with a raucous call that made him laugh.

The wooden bridge was solidly built over a frozen stream sheltered by bare-limbed trees. On the span they paused to admire the view. A pig squealed and Grady looked up at Linette, his mouth a surprised *O*.

She chuckled. "Do you want to see some piggies?"

His blue eyes bright with excitement, he nodded and raced across the bridge. He noticed a man near the pigsty and ground to a halt. Slowly he backed toward Linette.

She knelt beside him. "Grady, not all men are frightening. Most are very nice people who would like to be your friend. Mr. Gardiner especially wants to be your friend. You need to give him a chance."

Grady shuddered and clung to her side.

She recognized the person by the pigs as Ward Walker. "You remember that man from yesterday. He works for Mr. Gardiner. Mr. Gardiner would never let a bad man live here, so you can be friends with him, too."

Ward touched the brim of his hat. "Ma'am." But he said nothing more and turned to fiddle with a gate.

Linette stood up. "Can we get close to the pigs?"

"Right up to the fence," Ward said as he continued his work, though Linette wondered if he actually did anything productive. Warmth wrapped about her heart as she realized Eddie had coached them all to be present for Grady but give him the space he needed. Again, she admired Eddie's kindness. Just think of the things they could do together, helping those in distress. It filled her heart with such joy she wanted to laugh out loud.

Grady kept his eyes on Ward until he got close enough to see the pigs nosing around in the feed trough, snorting and pushing. Fascinated, he watched and forgot about Ward even when the man walked past him, heading toward the larger pens where a number of cows milled about.

She let Grady watch the pigs for a long time. Then she interrupted him. "We have to go back so I can make dinner."

"I stay?"

"Do you want to stay with Mr. Walker?" Ward moseyed along the path.

Grady jerked back as he noticed the man. "I go with you."

Linette smiled an apology at Ward as they walked away. "One day, young man, you will realize these men can be your friends."

"Not make me?"

She stopped to face the child. "Of course not. You can't force someone to be friends. It comes when you realize they are good people who care about you."

"Not hurt me?"

Had there been others besides the man on the ship? "Grady, who hurt you?"

He looked past her, his gaze seeking the distance. She guessed he was seeing something in his past. When she called his name, he blinked. "Grady hungry."

"Then let's go make dinner." It had been a little glimpse into what had happened to the boy. She could hardly wait to tell Eddie about their walk and Grady's little confession. They could work together to help Grady learn to trust men. Another step toward showing Eddie how they could be a team.

Remembering his reaction to a similar statement in the big house, she decided she wouldn't speak of it in those terms.

Chapter Eight

After lunch, Eddie climbed the hill to the house and stepped into the quiet interior. With some hard work, the place would be ready for occupancy by spring. A fine house for a fine lady. He grabbed a length of oak trim, measured it and cut it. Tension he hadn't been aware of eased away. There was satisfaction and peace in the work.

A few hours later, his growling stomach and the growing darkness forced him to stop. He set his tools to one side. He'd return next morning and spend the day working.

As he made his way down the hill, the light from the cabin beckoned. Beyond the doors lay something he wasn't used to—warmth, welcome, a hot meal…

Inside, the smell of cinnamon and ginger greeted him. As did Linette's smile.

He paused, caught between the unfamiliar welcome and a resistance filled with the voice of his father and his promise to Margaret. Turning to hang his coat and hat on the hook behind the door, he pushed his thoughts back into proper order. "Food smells good."

"Once again Cookie has been kind enough to offer me some instruction. Under her supervision I made ginger cookies."

"Ah. That explains the cinnamon smell as I stepped in the door."

"Cookie said they were your favorite." Her voice strummed a bass chord in his heart.

Their gazes collided, caught for a moment, just long enough for him to feel a flash of something unfamiliar before her gaze darted away.

Linette passed around potatoes, carrots, fried pork chops and canned applesauce. Later, when the plates were cleaned, she served tea with cookies still warm from the oven.

He pushed back from the table. "Excellent meal."

Linette grinned. "Thank you, sir. I told you, I'm a fast learner."

He recalled what had accompanied her statement of being a fast learner—a promise he'd beg her to stay before the winter was over.

His pleasure in the meal faded. The interior of the cabin seemed less welcoming.

Cassie took Grady to the bedroom shortly after the meal. Linette didn't linger more than a few minutes before following them.

He finally relaxed. Life in the cabin could be pleasant enough if she would be content simply to pass the time while waiting for traveling weather.

Before he fell asleep he came up with a plan to divert Linette's single-mindedness.

The next morning was Sunday. Linette wondered if Eddie did anything to honor the day.

"We have a simple worship service in the cook-house," Eddie explained. "Nothing fancy, but it's the best we can do."

Linette liked the idea just fine. "It sounds perfect. I tried to guess how you managed to make Sundays special with no church out here. I read one story about a missionary who held services wherever he went. Didn't matter if it was in a tent, a sod shack or even in the open air. Wouldn't that be special, worshipping God in His own cathedral?" She went to the window to glimpse the mountain peaks to the west. "No church built by man could rival the majesty of God's creation." She turned to Eddie, saw him watching her with surprise, and—dare she hope—a hint of appreciation. "Wouldn't you agree, Eddie?"

"I think," Eddie said slowly and softly, "He gave us the great outdoors to enjoy and to make us realize how small we are and how mighty He is. Then we would acknowledge our dependence on Him. We'd see how great is His grace that He considers us with such favor. Perhaps that is the kind of worship He desires."

Linette stared, darted a look at Cassie and saw from the expression on her face that Eddie's eloquence had surprised her as much as it had Linette. She couldn't find a response as her thoughts lifted Heavenward, carried on the wings of his words. "I like the way you put it."

Eddie shifted from foot to foot and shrugged. "Let's get over to the cookhouse."

Linette held his gaze a moment longer, feeling again, as she had several times in the past few days, a sense of connection. He would no doubt deny it, but they shared the same awe at God's creation visible around them in the form of mountains, streams and even storms. They shared the same need to establish new roots in a new world.

He broke eye contact first to look out the window. "The men are already filing in."

It took her a moment to pull herself back to the here and now. How could she so easily forget that Eddie didn't want to use the new world to do new things? She followed the direction of his gaze in time to see a man disappear into the cookhouse. "Come on, Grady." She held her hand out to the child, but he backed away, retreating under the table. So long as she remained next to Eddie, the boy would not come to her. Sighing her frustration, she moved across the room and called Grady again.

Darting frightened glances in Eddie's direction, he scrambled to her side and clutched her hand with both of his.

"Grady, Mr. Gardiner is not going to hurt you."

He whimpered.

Eddie grabbed his Stetson and jammed it on his head. "Not to worry. It takes time to put aside fears." He stepped out the door and held it for the others. Grady shivered against Linette as they slipped past Eddie.

Eddie fell in at her other side, casually keeping two feet away so as to not further frighten Grady. They crossed the yard and entered the warmth of the cookhouse. The benches had been placed on one side of the table; Bertie faced them from the other side, a Bible tucked under his arm. Cookie sat on a chair at his side.

She rose as they entered. "Grady, boy. Come sit with me."

Grady saw all the men and pressed closer to Linette's side. She pushed forward to an empty place on the back bench, carefully putting herself between Grady and the others. Cassie settled on the end of the bench on Grady's other side.

Linette looked about. Eddie had not followed her. Instead, he sat on the far corner of the bench in front.

Someone sat beside Linette. "Morning, ma'am."

She turned. Ward Walker, all slicked up and polished for the day. "Good morning." Her gaze slipped toward Eddie.

He nodded and smiled, not a bit disturbed by this arrangement. Rather, he seemed pleased.

Her head buzzed with a thousand protests all as troublesome as a swarm of insects. She wasn't prepared to be so easily dismissed. She signaled her warning with her eyes but he turned away as Cookie cleared her throat.

"Shall we begin?"

Linette gave her attention to the pair at the front.

Bertie opened the service with a prayer. Cookie, with more enthusiasm than skill, led them in singing three familiar hymns then Bertie read a passage about the prodigal son. He closed the Bible. "I once wandered far from God eating of the husks of life. It took hitting bottom for me to turn around and look for God. He was there waiting all the time. Folks, He always is. No matter what we need, He can supply." He spoke several more minutes, then closed with a prayer.

The cowboys shifted, as if uncertain what they should do next with two visiting ladies in their presence. Cookie rose to the occasion. "I'll make tea for you all. Stay and visit. Make the ladies feel welcome."

Cassie hurried to help Cookie, but was shooed away. "Go visit. Enjoy yourself."

Roper edged forward and asked Cassie how she enjoyed the country.

Linette didn't catch her answer as Ward asked at her side, "Miss Edwards, are you liking the country?"

"Like I said before, I love it." She sought Eddie, found him standing across the room, grinning.

More protests buzzed loudly in her brain.

"Not too wild for you?"

Good manners forbade her from walking away from Ward and telling Eddie exactly what she thought of his enjoyment of her situation. "Not at all.'"

"I have some land north of here. Intend to have my own place just as soon as I can get me a few head of cows. It ain't much. Not fancy like this. But it's mine."

Linette nodded, sensing the man's enthusiasm. "It sounds great. I wish you every success. When will you take up residence?"

"Not for a while. Ain't had no cause to make the move. Maybe that will change now." Did he sound hopeful? Had Eddie said something to encourage the man?

She glared at Eddie with a burning look.

He flicked a glance her way and then turned his back to her.

Oh! The man was impossible beyond description. Did he think she would simply substitute another man for him? It wasn't possible. She recalled Eddie had said something very similar about her substituting for Margaret.

"Come on," Ward said. "Let's get tea and cookies."

Later, after they'd returned to the cabin and eaten a

simple lunch, Linette tried to think how best to inform Eddie that she wouldn't be diverted from her purpose and that she had no intention of wasting her time with a cowboy, though no doubt Ward was a very nice man. Just not a man her father would accept as her husband.

But before she found a chance, a knock came on the door.

"Company." Eddie didn't sound a bit surprised. He opened the door. "Come on in, boys."

Ward and Roper stepped inside.

Eddie's smile practically broke his face in half. "Thought you ladies could stand some visitors for a change. So I'll leave you to visit while I take care of some business." He grabbed his coat and ducked out, leaving four awkward adults behind.

Linette's thoughts raged. How dare he assume she would welcome this any more than would Cassie, who set aside her knitting with such vehemence Linette wouldn't have been surprised to hear something rip. Thankfully, Grady had fallen asleep in the bedroom so didn't have to endure this…this invasion.

"Ladies, if this is awkward…" Ward twisted his hat.

Linette pushed aside her anger. It wasn't their fault. "Of course not. Come on in. We'd love to hear about your ranch—" she indicated Ward "—and about your plan in life," she said, indicating Roper.

They edged toward the table and each pulled out a chair and sat down. Cassie, her face revealing anything but welcome, shifted her chair to face them.

Linette filled the kettle. How did one entertain a pair of cowboys on a Sunday afternoon? From what she'd read, they played cards or chewed the fat, which meant they sat around spinning yarns. Well, she had no problem learning more about the country.

"What brings the two of you to northwest Canada?" she asked the men.

They talked easily about the cattle drives they'd been on and the country they'd seen.

"Working for Eddie is good," Ward said. "He's a fair boss and the both of us have year-round work."

Roper nodded. "What about you ladies? Where have you come from and why here?"

Linette turned to tend to the tea. How much did the pair know? Did they know she'd come with plans to marry Eddie to escape her father's arrangement? But she had no intention of confessing so. "I want a life where women are allowed to follow their hearts."

Both men looked at her, confusion in their eyes.

Ward spoke slowly. "Where does your heart want to go?"

Where, indeed? So many things filled her thoughts. Escape, for sure. Freedom to tend to those who were hurting and in need. Those were the motivations she gave to Cassie and Eddie. But hidden deep inside lay a secret reason. She saw in Eddie something she'd admired from the first letter Margaret read. She had no words for the feeling. She only knew it was there.

She realized the others waited for her answer and she gave a little chuckle. "I'm not sure how to answer other than to say I grew tired of the restrictions society places on women in England and hoped to find new opportunities here."

A moment of silence greeted her response then Roper turned to Cassie. "Mrs. Godfrey, what brought you to the West?"

Cassie considered the man for a moment then sighed. "A boat, a train and a stagecoach."

Linette laughed along with the others. She knew Cassie meant to be dismissive but had instead been funny. Something warm flickered through the other woman's eyes at their amusement.

They visited until Grady called from the bedroom. "'Net?"

Linette excused herself and went to the boy. "Come out and visit."

He shook his head and clung to her hand. "I scared."

She sat on the bed and pulled him onto her lap. "Grady, I don't know what's happened to you to make you so fearful, but you are safe now. I won't let anything bad happen to you. Eddie won't let anything bad happen to you. Cassie won't let anything bad happen to you. Nor will Cookie, or Bertie or any of the cowboys on the ranch." She said it with total confidence, knowing her words were backed up by Eddie's character. "You can trust me on this."

Grady snuggled close.

"Do you think I'll take good care of you?"

He nodded.

She asked the same question with Cassie's name.

Again a nod.

Then with Eddie's.

Grady shivered. "He big."

"Yes, he's strong. That means he can take care of you really well."

Grady shook his head. "He big. He strong."

Linette closed her eyes. Had a man used his strength, his power, to hurt Grady or perhaps his mother? How could she explain strength as a good thing? "Grady, if you needed something big and heavy carried, would you ask me or Eddie to help?"

He didn't answer.

She wrapped him closer. "You'd ask Eddie because he could do it and I couldn't. Sometimes we need strong people to help us."

He considered her words then sat up. "I not move anything big."

She laughed. "You know that's not what I mean, you little scamp." She rose to her feet with the boy. "Now, come along and say hello."

He jerked his hand free. "I stay here. Okay?" His eyes pleaded.

"Fine." She couldn't force him to forget his fears. *Please, God, heal his little heart.* She returned to the other room. "Sorry."

Cassie gave her a worried look. "Where's Grady?"

"He prefers to stay in the bedroom."

Roper stood. "We'll be on our way."

Ward scrambled to his feet as well.

Roper paused at the door. "The boss said the boy was afraid of men. Sorry to hear that. But we won't be doing anything to feed that fear. Thank you for a pleasant afternoon." He donned his hat and stepped outside.

Ward grabbed his Stetson and smiled at the ladies. "'Twas a very pleasant afternoon. Thank you." He shifted his attention to Linette. "Perhaps you'd like to see my ranch someday." He twisted his hat round and round in his hands. "Think you might see lots of opportunities there."

"Perhaps." She closed the door behind him and leaned on it.

Cassie grinned at her. "I expect he'd marry you at the drop of a hat."

"Perhaps." Her predicament couldn't be so easily solved, and if Eddie thought otherwise, he would soon learn differently.

The next morning she wakened and listened. Eddie moved about in the other room. He lifted the lid on the stove and added wood. He moved to the table. Was he reading? Perhaps writing another letter? Would he beg Margaret to join him? A great ache filled Linette until she was forced to clamp her teeth together to keep from moaning.

She'd dreamed she'd be valued as a pioneer wife, able to share the work of building a new life in the West.

Lord, help my plan to succeed. Help Eddie see me as a woman to share this life as a partner, a helpmate.

She hurried to make breakfast. As soon as Eddie finished, he announced, "I'll be working on the house most of the day."

Linette allowed herself only a small smile. This was exactly what she'd hoped for.

"I go see piggies?" Grady asked.

She wanted to rush ahead with her own plans but couldn't ignore the child's wishes. "As soon as we clean up."

Cassie scurried about helping, more eager than Linette had seen her before. "I told Cookie I would help her this morning," she explained. "I so enjoy talking about where we used to live." She paused, a faraway expression on her face.

Linette studied her. Seems Cassie preferred living in the past to facing the present, whereas Linette felt just the opposite. There was nothing in her past she wanted to return to except to keep in touch with her family. Especially her brother. When they were younger she'd enjoyed following him around and imitating some of his activities. She'd ridden a horse astride, raced a wagon down the road, done a number of adventuresome things with him until their father and mother discovered the nurse wasn't supervising closely enough to suit them.

A new nurse, given the task of seeing Linette turned into a lady, put an end to her fun.

She shook away the memories and regrets.

She'd expected marriage to Eddie to change all that, give her back what she'd lost. She stiffened her spine. She wasn't about to give up hope.

Linette took Grady for a walk while Cassie hurried over to visit Cookie.

Grady skipped ahead murmuring to himself. She caught up to him, hoping she might learn something from listening to him, but she couldn't make out his words. He ground to a halt. She stopped and glanced about to see why he'd grown so quiet.

Her attention on the child, she hadn't noticed Eddie leaning against the fence, his arms crossed, one foot resting on the tip of his cowboy boot. He appeared relaxed, yet she felt his alertness as clearly as if it had found wings and flew before her face.

The sun flashed in his eyes. His steady watchfulness never faltered. Hadn't he said he was going to the big house? Had he changed his mind? What did he want? And why did her heart pound against her ribs at the sight of him?

His gaze lowered to Grady and he slowly stepped away from the fence and bent to pick up a rope. He moved to the middle of the pen and began to circle the rope over his head in a wide loop. With great ease and grace, he danced the loop down to the ground and up again. Then he lowered it over his body, hopped out of the circle and swung it over his head.

Grady, as fascinated as Linette, moved closer to watch, mesmerized by the twirl of rope.

Eddie continued the show for several minutes. Then casually, he let the rope fall to the ground, gathered it into neat coils and hung it over his shoulder. He turned, touched the brim of his hat. "See ya." He headed for the barn.

Neither Grady nor Linette moved.

Slowly she drew in a breath. She suspected he'd put on the show for Grady but allowed herself to hope a part of him was trying to impress her, too. The thought filled her with hope that he had begun to view her differently.

"What did you think of that, Grady?"

He stepped away from the fence. "Can I see piggies now?"

She laughed as she took his hand and headed toward the bridge. "You aren't about to give in easily, are you?"

No more than she was.

Eddie stood in the house and stared at the piece of wood in his hands. Why had he put on that little show with his rope earlier? For Grady, of course. He wanted the boy to be curious about him, maybe get up enough courage to talk to him. But he kept wondering what Linette thought of his roping skills.

Not that her opinion mattered one little bit.

He turned back to the task at hand—measuring and

cutting the wood trim. The finishing details took time but he was determined to do them right. Margaret deserved the best. The house was much smaller than either of them was accustomed to in England, but it was still a beautiful house. Margaret could entertain important people and fine ladies.

Never mind that fine ladies and gentlemen were few and far between in the territory.

An errant thought blasted through his mind. The kind of people Linette favored as occupants of the house were everywhere, even here. Widows like Cassie. Orphaned or abandoned children like Grady. Even some of his cowboys. Quiet, good men with a background of hurt.

"Hello. Can I come in?"

He jerked toward the sound. Was he imagining Linette called?

The main door closed with a gentle thud. "Hello?" Her voice sounded closer.

What was she doing here? He had struggled for the past hour to erase her presence from the house and picture Margaret there instead. Now she would undo all his hard work. "In here," he called. He intended to finish the family dining room first. As Linette said, the view over the ranch, the coziness of the quarters, made it one of the nicest rooms in the house.

She stepped into sight and rubbed her hands together. "I thought you might be able to use another pair of hands."

"I have half a dozen men I can call for assistance if I want help."

She ignored his dismissive tone. "It seems they are busy elsewhere."

He considered her. Would she leave if he asked or simply disregard him if it didn't suit her? No wonder her father felt he had to marry her off to someone who would control her. Best he keep that opinion to himself. "You know anything about carpentry?"

She tipped her head and looked thoughtful, though he didn't miss the teasing twinkle in her eyes. "I know the difference between a nail and a hammer. Does that count?"

He intended to be disapproving, discouraging, insisting he didn't need her hanging about getting in the way and distracting him. Instead, he laughed. "That's valuable information, I'm sure. Certain to be a great help."

She recognized the teasing in his words and chuckled. "You can never tell."

He held her gaze, feeling her smile, and something more. A challenge. Never one to pass up a challenge, he nodded. "Let's see how useful you can be. I was about to nail this trim into place." He indicated the window frame he was finishing. "Hold the end in place."

She clamored to the window, but instead of attending to the task, she stared out the window and sighed. "I could never get tired of this view."

He joined her to enjoy the sight. Slim and Roper jogged past the buildings.

"How was your visit yesterday?" He'd sent Ward and Roper in the hopes of giving Linette other prey to stalk.

"It was very pleasant."

He waited, hoping for some indication as to how she felt, but she gave him nothing. "Boys are headed for town. Carrying the letters to Margaret." Margaret would soon know the truth about the house he'd built for her.

Linette didn't speak. He felt her silence as solidly as the hardwood in his grasp. What did she think as she watched the men walk away? Was she accepting that her stay here was temporary?

"Let's get to work." She grabbed the end of the window trim and eased it into place. She eyeballed the other end. "You got a level?"

He blinked. For someone who barely knew a hammer from a nail, it was an informed question. "Let me check it." He did and she adjusted the end with ease.

"How do you know about levels and hammers? It hardly seems…"

"Ladylike? My parents couldn't agree more. You going to tack this in place or leave me holding it for the rest of the day?"

Feeling a little as if he'd been tardy about his work, he reached around her to nail it. In order to get the end he had to press close to her. Close enough to feel warmth from her body, breathe in the smell of cinnamon and more. A scent completely unlike those he'd grown used to. If he'd had a free hand he would have smacked himself. Of course she didn't smell like cows or cowboys. More like flowers and home.

He chomped down on his teeth and drove in the necessary nails. He obviously needed a long hard ride or a good dose of salts to cure his foolishness. "You can let it go now." He placed each nail carefully and stepped back to study his work. It looked satisfactory.

Now to keep his mind focused on the task. It was easy. All he had to do was turn to the right and grab the next piece of wood. Instead, he turned right and met Linette's gaze. He should thank her. But his tongue refused to move.

She grinned, her eyes dancing with amusement. "I learned a tiny bit about carpentry when I helped one of the servants build a shed." Her humor fled, replaced with a mixture of regret and determination.

He'd seen that look before. Knew it signaled a decision on her part to dig in her heels and fight for what she wanted.

"When my father learned what I was up to, the poor man lost his job. I've always regretted that."

Slowly, she turned full circle to study the room then returned to face him. "Did you do all this work yourself?"

"I had the boys help."

"How did you learn?"

"I worked on the estate."

Her eyes darkened. "Aren't rich boys supposed to play the wastrel?"

He shrugged. "Some, I suppose. Others are encouraged to be useful."

"Unlike daughters who are expected to be only ornamental."

"I never thought of it that way."

"You have sisters. Are they allowed to be useful? Or even to have a choice about what they want?"

"I've never considered it." He'd been too busy trying to prove he could do all that was expected of him.

"No, of course you didn't." She sighed deeply, as if chasing away dark thoughts. "Tell me about your sisters."

Glad to be free of the direction she'd headed with talk of how women were treated, he smiled. "Jayne is almost twenty." He and Jayne had been good friends. Mostly, if he had to venture a guess, because they were the two oldest and Jayne was sensible and intelligent. He paused to consider the younger ones. Seems they were in the nursery or under the watchful eye of a governess, so he didn't feel he knew them as well as he knew Jayne. "It's hard to think of them getting older. I haven't seen them in such a long time. Bess must be seventeen now and Anne, fourteen."

"But who are they? What do they like?"

He chuckled. "I seem to remember them clustering about each other giggling."

She wrinkled her nose. "You make them sound like silly ninnies. I'm sure they're not."

He'd never given it much study, but now that he did, he realized his father tended to dismiss them. Yet he and Jayne had shared some insightful conversations before he left. "Jayne and I were closest growing up. She liked studying languages. She's promised to a young man. They haven't set a date yet. I think Jayne would like it to be soon, but Oliver seems to have other ideas."

Linette nodded. "And Bess?"

"She has a beau, too, but Father forbids her to see him."

"Why?"

"He's the son of the groom."

"And that says it all. Not good enough for a Gardiner."

"She wouldn't be happy living the life he could offer and he lacks the education to be worked into the family business."

"So she has no choice in the matter?" Her voice dripped disapproval.

"I think my parents know what is best for her." Intending to forestall the impending argument, he continued, "Anne is our baby. She's been spoiled, I expect. She has only to smile prettily and everyone gives her what she wants. If that fails, a little pout will work." Remembering the girls, he chuckled.

Linette laughed, too.

Talking about his sisters had filled him with missing them.

"Maybe they'll visit someday, though I know Jayne will never leave her beloved Oliver."

"Never is a long time." She looked pensive as if missing her family, too.

That was good, he assured himself. Maybe she'd be ready and willing to return after a few months away. Exactly what he wanted. So why did he consider patting her shoulder and saying it got easier with time? He turned, picked up a piece of wood and cut it to fit.

She held the piece in place without needing instructions. And she talked.

"Austin is my only brother. He's a year older than me. We were best of friends until Father took him into the business. Then we hardly saw each other. And when we did, Austin felt duty bound to agree with Father's opinions."

Eddie heard the sour note in her tone. "Did he agree with your father's plans for you?" Seemed to him if the situation was as intolerable as Linette believed, her brother should have intervened.

When the board was in place, Linette stepped back. She tugged at her earlobe. "I think Austin felt sorry for me, but like he said, neither of us had much choice about what we would do with our lives." She sighed heavily. "I think Austin would have preferred to farm rather than work in an office, but Father wouldn't hear of it." She shrugged. "Guess it proves men aren't always able to make free choices, either."

He nodded. "We all have duties and obligations." He returned his attention to the project at hand and cut the next piece of trim.

Linette sprang forward to help. "Mort—that's the man who let me help construct the outbuilding for storing grain—he said it needed to be solid and tight to keep the grain dry. He said a man's character is revealed by the quality of his work. 'Course, he didn't say the same about a woman's work, but I expect it's true." She held a piece of wood in place. When it was secured, she stepped back. "I'd say Mort was right. For instance, I can tell much about you by what I see here."

He paused to study her, filled with curiosity. "Is that a fact?" Not that her approval or assessment mattered. Still, he couldn't keep from asking, "What do you see?"

She went to the windows. "Remember you said the world needed art and artists to see the beauty of the world? I think the fact you set the house here so these windows provide a view of the mountains reveals that you have an artist's soul." She practically choked back the word. "I mean eye."

He tucked a smile behind his heart. It felt rather nice to think he had an artist's soul—or eye—but he wasn't about to let his thoughts wander down a trail he didn't want to take. "I laid it out this way so I could see the ranch operations."

"If that's all that mattered, why not over there, behind the cookhouse?" She pointed to the hill she meant then turned and caught his gaze, holding it in a demanding, challenging look.

He wouldn't admit he'd looked at several building sites and chosen this one for the precise reason she'd given—the marvelous view of the mountains. Any more than he'd confess—even to himself—how it pleased him to have her recognize his motive.

She turned to study the room. "I know you'll say you only followed plans drawn up in London when you built this place, but..." She went to a corner hidden behind a door and examined the baseboards. "Did you place these?"

He admitted he had.

"Perfect fit. I see you are careful even on things no one might see or notice. That tells me you are honorable and have integrity."

He tried to laugh off her comments. "Or that I'm certain my father would notice any mistakes and point them out."

She again drilled him with her demanding gaze. "Can you say that's your reason?"

The word *yes* came automatically to his mind, then he reconsidered and discovered a truth he'd been unaware of. "Only partially. I would do the best job I could regardless of who saw it. After all, God sees and expects us to do our best."

She grinned. "I knew it." Suddenly she sobered. "Did you know it, too?" Not waiting for an answer, she pointed to the patch of sun pooling at the foot of the windows. "It's almost lunchtime. I'll have it ready in a few minutes." She looked about at what they'd accomplished. "Not bad. Not bad at all." Then she scurried away.

He watched out the window as she trotted down the hill. She paused at the doorway of the cabin to glance in his direction. She must have seen him still there, for she lifted her hand in a quick wave. He didn't turn away until the cabin door closed behind her.

Then he slapped his forehead. She'd done it again. Intruded on his plans, his world.

How long before he heard back from Margaret?

Perhaps he'd get Ward to help with the carpentry, then if Linette insisted on coming up the hill, she could get to know Ward better.

Chapter Nine

Linette hummed as she and Cassie cleaned up after lunch.

"You're mighty pleased with yourself," Cassie said, sounding curious as much as anything.

"I spent the morning helping Eddie in the big house. I think he is beginning to accept me."

Cassie let out an impatient sigh. "Accept you or just your help?"

"Either way, it's a start. He'll soon see I'm suited for ranch living. If you stay with Grady for his nap, I'll help him this afternoon, too."

Cassie picked up her knitting. The afghan was steadily growing large.

"You never did tell me who you are knitting that for."

"For myself. I have no one else, if you care to recall."

"I'm sorry. Perhaps you'll find someone out here. Roper seemed rather interested. I think he's half in love with you already."

"I'll marry again if I can." She jabbed her needle

through a stitch. "A woman needs protection of a man. But it won't be for love. No value in that."

Linette didn't answer, but she couldn't argue. Love had no place in the lives of those she knew. Certainly her mother and father seemed to tolerate rather than love each other. Mother ventured no farther than her sewing room and her lady friends. Father's time and attention were devoted to enlarging his holdings and amassing more money. Her aunt was the only woman she knew who spoke freely of loving her husband and, as far as Linette could see, it made her aunt far too pliable and ready to jump at every little suggestion her uncle made. Linette had no desire for such a life.

"I'll stay with Grady if you still have a mind to traipse up the hill, but it seems to me he's a man who knows what he wants."

"And it isn't me? Is that what you're saying?"

Cassie lowered her knitting and met Linette's gaze. "The man was quite clear on the matter."

Linette pulled on her coat before she faced Cassie again. "I have until spring to change his mind and I intend to make the most of my time. I'll be back later."

"No rush. I can manage Grady. Maybe we'll go over and see Cookie."

Linette took her time climbing the hill. She'd seen the flash of surprise darkening Eddie's eyes when she'd said he had integrity. He'd surely looked at her with more interest than he'd previously revealed. She'd shown herself capable of working at his side. Surely he was learning her value…an asset to help him build a new life here. She would not think of the letters even now starting their journey to Margaret. She could imagine what Eddie had said, likely they were words of love urging her to join him.

But if Margaret changed her mind... Her heart dipped toward her toes. She had until spring. She prayed it would be long enough.

"Boys, turn the tailenders into the pen then head for the cookhouse." Only the weak and young cattle were brought to the ranch. The rest were in nearby pastures where he could keep an eye on them. "Cookie is sure to have some hot coffee and fresh bread." Eddie's gaze went unbidden to the little log cabin across from the cookhouse as Slim and Roper urged the animals toward their winter home. He'd left only three days ago, before the weather had taken a turn for the worse, but it seemed months since he'd last stepped into the comforting warmth of the little house and he looked forward to it with unusual eagerness. "I think we've all earned a warm bed and hot meal."

"Yeah, boss. And now you can stop worrying about your cows." No doubt Slim spoke for all the cowboys.

"Now we can watch them and feed them," he corrected. "I'm not prepared to let them fend for themselves if the snow keeps coming." It had started snowing soon after they left and continued intermittently while they were gone. He'd worried about the occupants of the little cabin but assured himself they'd be safe and sound. Still, he couldn't wait to see for himself. "I'm grateful we got them down before it got any nastier."

The men rode after the cows and Eddie reined toward the barn, glancing at the cabin again.

A movement on the hill beyond caught his attention. A handful of Indians slid past, only the sound of muted horses' hooves and the whisper of a travois broke the silence. No doubt they were headed to join other Indians in their wintering grounds to the south. He hoped they'd have sufficient supplies.

He watched until they slipped out of sight. Seeing the Indians had given him an idea on how to teach Grady to trust him.

He continued toward the barn where he took his time taking care of Banjo, brushing him thoroughly, feeding him a scoop of oats, cleaning his saddle.

The cold bit into his lungs as he stepped out into the bright sun. Sparkling crystals filled the air. He turned toward the cabin. Something dark disappeared around the corner of the cabin. He crept toward the spot and edged along the wall until he could peek around the corner. Linette. His breath whooshed out. Not an intruder or wolf.

But what was she doing? It looked as if she planned to bury something in the snowbank.

"Linette?"

She dropped whatever it was she held and spun around, her eyes wide. "You didn't take long enough."

"You think I should stay out in the cold?"

She darted a glance to the brown blob at her feet.

"What is that?" he asked.

"Nothing."

"Don't look like nothin' to me." He squinted at it. "Looks like—"

She stepped forward and tried to hide the lump. "It's nothing."

He crossed his arms and leaned back on his heels. "Uh-huh." He waited.

She shifted back and forth. Couldn't meet his gaze. "Oh, very well. You might as well know the truth." She stepped aside and stared at the lump. "It's supposed to be bread, but it won't rise." Her voice quivered. "It's the second time this has happened." She dropped to her knees and scooped a hollow in the snow. "You weren't supposed to see it." She dug the hole deeper and shoved the lump into it.

"Bread, huh?" He purposely kept his voice flat though amusement trickled through him.

"Cookie said it was simple." She pushed snow over the hole and pounded it. Hard. Every slap made Eddie blink. "Simple for her. Not for me."

Did her voice catch?

She planted her hands on the packed snow and leaned forward. What was she doing? Praying? He couldn't think how praying would salvage the dough. Her shoulders twitched. She sniffed.

"Linette?" He took one hesitant step forward. "Are you crying?"

"No." But the word ended on a sob.

He fell to his knees at her side. "It's only flour and water." Or whatever went into the mysteries of making bread. "Nothing to be upset about."

Her sobs ended. She faced him, stubborn determination hardening the bones in her face. A tear clung to her lashes. "You don't understand."

He patted her shoulder. "It's only bread," he soothed.

"My father was right." Her words choked with pain and defeat. "I'm only good for sitting and painting."

Her father had certainly bruised her heart. The agony in her voice drove arrows through his heart. He wanted to reach inside and yank them free, end the pain. Both his and hers. "I like your paintings."

A tear made a silvery trail down her cheek.

He'd said the wrong thing. But what was the right thing? "Linette, you can learn to bake bread."

She looked beyond him.

"Look how far you've come. And I don't mean simply crossing the ocean and most of Canada, though that's admirable in itself. I mean from a young society woman to a pioneer." She flicked a glance at him. Did he imagine she showed interest? "You can build a fire in the stove. You have learned how to make corn bread and how to fry bacon. Remember your first reaction to a slab of pork?" He chuckled, earning him a surprised look. "You've come a long way." He meant much more than her culinary abilities. He quieted, took a deep breath and released the words he deemed safe, though they were but a sliver of all he felt. "I admire your spunk and courage. I admire your spirit." She'd make a good pioneer wife.

Too bad that wasn't what he wanted or needed.

She grew still then she wiped tears from her face. Determination darkened her eyes. "I refuse to give up."

He sat back on his heels to study her.

A riot of emotions raced across her face. Her determination seemed to weaken, grow fragile, and then she scrambled to her feet. "I did succeed in making cookies. Care to try some with tea?"

He bolted to his feet and followed her to the cabin, grateful the moment ended before he'd tossed all his good intentions to the wind and decided a pioneer wife would suit him just fine.

Grady glanced up as Eddie entered. His eyes widened and he stiffened but then sank back to playing with his growing collection of rocks and bits of wood plus a handful of carved animals several of the men had crafted for the boy.

At least he hadn't withdrawn under the table and didn't cling to Linette's skirts. A notebook lay open on the table. Linette closed it and set it aside as she put out tea and cookies.

A little later, he noticed her notebook on the shelf. He'd seen enough to guess she wasn't writing. "Were you drawing something?"

She grew still and seemed to consider her answer. "I'm afraid I feel the need to capture life in my sketchbook."

He wondered why she seemed so apologetic. He certainly didn't object to the activity, but perhaps she wondered if he might. "What did you capture today?"

She picked up the book and opened it to reveal a simple pencil drawing of the interior of the cabin. It should have been crude, even barren, but the few lines portrayed warmth and charm.

"You make it look appealing."

Her eyes lit with humor. "Isn't it?"

He chuckled, beguiled by her smile. "Not many would see it as so."

"I guess it's all in the eyes…and heart…of the beholder."

He considered her statement, uncertain how to respond. Did she see everything this way? He answered his question. She did. Except the man her father meant for her to marry. "Perhaps you see things through an artist's eyes." He realized he'd used the same words she used to describe his choice of where to build the house and wondered if she'd notice.

Her smile deepened, her eyes darkened and he guessed she did notice. For a moment, he allowed himself to share a tenuous feeling of connection.

Behind him Cassie sighed and stopped his useless thoughts from wandering further. "Linette sees through rose-tinted glasses. She's always saying everything will turn out fine."

Linette chuckled. "Those aren't my words. They're God's. He says, 'All things work together for good to those who love God.'"

Suddenly Eddie was filled with curiosity as to how she viewed everything. "Did you do drawings of your trip?"

"Certainly."

"Would you mind showing them to me?"

"So long as you don't mock my immature efforts."

"I'd never mock." He sat at the table, across the corner from her, and she opened the first page. "This is our ship." He saw steaming smokestacks and a captain with a steaming cigar.

He laughed. "I think you're mocking the man."

"Only a little." She bent her head over the sketchbook and turned the pages.

There were drawings of the ship's dining room, caricatures of many of the passengers that made him chuckle. A young woman who might have been pretty except for her thinness and the strain in her eyes.

"Who is that?"

Linette sucked in a sigh. "I'd forgotten this. Grady, come here."

The boy played near Cassie—about as far away

from Eddie as he could get in the small room. He got to his feet, shot a fearful look at Eddie and remained motionless.

Eddie prepared to move away but Linette shook her head.

"Give him a chance." She spoke to Grady again. "Come and see the picture I drew of your mother."

Grady sidled up to Linette's far side. When he saw the picture a sob choked from him. "Mama." He touched the picture gently. "Mama's gone?"

"Yes, honey." Linette pulled him to her side and pressed a kiss to his blond head. "Mama's gone but you're safe with us."

"I have her picture?"

"Tell you what. I'll make a copy for your very own and keep this one safe. Okay?"

He nodded, touched the picture again and moved away.

Eddie felt the boy's pain like a spear to his heart and wished Grady would allow him to hug him. Instead, he sat motionless as Grady again settled on the floor with his playthings and carefully kept his back to them.

Cassie, bless her heart, patted his head and squeezed his shoulder.

Linette turned a page in her book and Eddie brought his attention back to the sketches. He looked at her pictures of the train, the stagecoach, then the mountains. He stared at the different ways she portrayed them—distant and pale, close and majestic, sometimes harsh, sometimes gentle.

"I never stopped to think the mountains have so many moods and yet, as I look at your drawing, I see they do."

"I can't wait to see them in their spring finery."

He couldn't, either.

And then there were two side-by-side sketches of the big house. One seemed to breathe warmth and welcome; the other looked cold and imperious. He stared at the pictures. "Why the difference?"

"A house has moods, too." Linette closed the book. "That's all." She took the pencils and sketch pad to the bedroom. She'd stay hidden there except there wasn't any point in hiding. She could only hope Eddie hadn't seen what the pictures of the big house meant. Bad enough he'd discovered her trying to hide the evidence of failed bread making. She smiled. It had provoked him into saying he admired her. *Thank You, God.* He might not have been so approving if he'd understood the drawings of the house. The formal one revealed the house as a manor house ruled by an aristocratic woman. The other showed the house as a home and sanctuary—a place of welcome to all.

It would not benefit her plan for him to guess she saw the second with her at the window. Thankfully she hadn't drawn herself there nor drawn Margaret in the window of the first.

She pressed her palms to her chest. He was learning to appreciate her. Surely that was a step toward her goal. Buoyed by the thought, she returned to the main room, paused to study each of her paintings as if she'd never seen them before, then moved to the window. Unable to look at the big house without being reminded of her foolish drawings, she moved to the pantry shelf and needlessly tidied the contents. Then she shifted to the bookcase.

"You're welcome to any of the books there," Eddie said. "In fact, anything there."

"Thank you." She'd been curious about the items on the shelves but out of respect for his privacy, she'd only glanced at them. Now she pulled out a box that she'd wondered about. "Do you mind?"

"Not at all." Both her words and his smile were inviting and she tried hard and without success to ignore the sudden racing of her heart.

She lifted the lid to reveal a beautiful hand-carved chess set.

"Do you play?" he asked.

"I love the game."

"Any objections to playing right now?"

"Not unless you have objections to losing."

He laughed. "I think you'd better give me a chance to see if you can beat me."

"Prepare to be challenged."

They set up the game and she soon learned they were pretty evenly skilled. She won the first game but only, she guessed, because he underestimated her. He didn't expect her to be his equal. A lesson he would do well to apply to more than a chess game.

He won the next match.

Grady shoved aside his playthings. "I'm hungry."

Linette bolted to her feet. "Is it that late already?" She served a simple meal of creamed peas and boiled eggs on toast.

"My nurse used to make this every Sunday," he told her. "It was my favorite meal."

"Mine, too." Linette's smile came from a warm spot deep within. She couldn't break free of his look as they silently shared enjoyment of a favorite childhood meal.

"Comfort food," he said with a chuckle that landed in her heart with a happy sound.

She laughed, feeling for certain they'd made progress during the past few hours.

Then Grady's hand slipped as he tried to cut his toast and she turned to help him.

They laughed often as they ate the simple meal and finished with bread and jam. Even Grady laughed when Linette and Eddie reached for the jar of jam at the same time and sent it skidding to the edge of the table. Only Eddie's quick reflexes prevented it from falling to the floor.

Later that evening, Linette couldn't force herself to head for bed as soon as Cassie and Grady left. She wondered if Eddie felt the same way, as he appeared to be prepared to sit by the fire and visit. She counted it as further evidence of progress in gaining his acceptance.

"I saw some Indians pass earlier today," he said. "Moving to their winter camp. I wonder why they aren't with the others."

"Others?" She kept every emotion out of her voice, but the stories she'd heard about Indians tensed her muscles.

"The larger bunch went by a few weeks ago. Usually they travel together."

He didn't seem concerned with their presence. Nor had she been alarmed at the few she'd encountered in her travels. "There was an Indian lad in Edendale. Would he be part of this group?"

"Probably."

"He was sick, probably with hunger."

"The boy? Was he alone?"

"The storekeeper said he'd been hired by a freighter

who no longer had need of him." She doubted she managed to keep the anger out of her voice. "The boy looked like he hadn't been allowed a decent meal in a long time. I asked why he hadn't been given food."

Eddie dropped his chair to all fours and stared at her. "You said this to the storekeeper?"

Linette snorted. "No, I saw the freighter and confronted him. Asked him if he starved his mules and expected them to serve him well."

Eddie's eyes widened. "Took kindly to that, did he?"

She chuckled. "I expect if I was a man he would have used his fists to give his opinion. As it was, he settled for directing a stream of brown spit to one side and telling me in very colorful language to mind my own business."

Eddie sighed deeply and shook his head. "Some might have not been so generous. Out here a man considers his business to be his own."

"I guess you know by now that I don't turn my back on someone in need. In my mind, people are equal. Doesn't matter their station in life or their race." She silently challenged him with her words. "Would you turn your back on someone in need?"

A grin began at the edges of his mouth and drew his lips wider. "I allowed you and Cassie and the boy to stay, didn't I?" His eyes reflected his amusement, but something more. Something that allowed her to think he didn't regret his decision, didn't see it as a hardship.

Her heart tipped sideways and poured out a bolt of hot hope. "Why would the Indian boy trust himself to the man? Why would he give up his freedom?"

Eddie studied her a moment before he answered. "He won't likely trust so easily again, will he?"

"I expect not. It's a hard lesson to learn."

"'Spect so. What happened to the lad?"

"I got him a hot meal and arranged a ride on top of the stagecoach so he could join his family."

Eddie held her gaze for a moment more. "Can't say I'm surprised." He pushed to his feet, signaling an end to the evening. Then he seemed to think of something and sat again and leaned back, tipping his chair to the back legs. "Who taught you to play chess?"

"My brother, Austin, and I learned under his tutor."

"You've mentioned your brother several times. You must miss him."

"I miss him dreadfully. We used to spend a lot of time together until—" She didn't want to ruin the day by mentioning how her freedom had been curtailed.

He grinned. "Until your father learned that you weren't acting like a proper lady."

She relaxed. So long as he saw the humor in the situation and didn't judge her as unsuitable because of her activities. "Yes, and then he joined Father in the business. Pushing numbers across a page is how he described it. Father saw to it that Austin had little time for frivolous activities unless they were with a proper young woman."

"Has he found one?"

"Sorry?" She wasn't sure what he meant.

"A proper young woman."

She laughed merrily. "If you saw what Father considers suitable young women—" She shuddered. "Poor Austin. I wish he could come to Canada and live an adventure."

"What's to stop him?"

It was a strange question from a man who lived to

fulfill family obligations. Might it provide an opportunity for her to point out how stifling obligations were? "I suppose he feels duty bound to do as Father dictates."

Eddie nodded.

She'd planted the thought that a person might wish to be free of obligations. It was enough for now.

"I'm heading out in the morning to hunt some game."

"I will bid you good-night. Thank you for playing chess with me."

"It is I who should thank you for giving me an opportunity to play with a worthy opponent." His smile seemed like a blessing and she ducked into the bedroom with hope and joy warming her insides.

He'd soon realize how much they had in common and see that duty wasn't reason enough to marry Margaret.

But what did she offer? A marriage of convenience? Though what was wrong with that? Convenient sounded very close to comfortable...or even wanted.

Eddie was gone when Linette rose the next morning. After breakfast, Cassie took Grady with her to visit Cookie, leaving her by herself in the cabin.

A little later, a scratching sound came at the door. Linette listened. It came again. She tensed and rose slowly. For the first time she was apprehensive that she was alone. Very alone. Though she hoped a scream would bring people from every direction. With that assurance, her nerves steadied. She set aside the shawl she was crocheting as a Christmas gift for Cassie and went to the door and cracked it open. "Why, hello." It was the boy she'd helped in Edendale. And beside him a woman who looked about ready to faint.

"Remember me? Little Bear." The boy patted his chest to indicate it was his name. "My mother, Bright Moon," he murmured with silent appeal.

Linette helped the woman inside and to the nearest chair, where she unwrapped the bundle in her arms to reveal a baby. A very new baby.

Little Bear stepped to her side. "Baby brother."

"Where is your father? The rest of your people?"

The boy struggled with English but managed to explain his mother had been too weak to keep up with the others and his father had gone looking for food.

"You did right to bring her here." Within minutes she had hot sweet tea for the woman. She spread syrup on several biscuits and handed a plateful to both the woman and her son. They ate slowly, savoring each bite. The woman nodded toward the furs in the corner that Eddie slept on.

Linette understood her silent appeal and spread the furs. The woman lay down, cradled the baby to her breasts, which likely had little to offer by way of nourishment. Both baby and mother soon fell asleep. The boy sat cross-legged at their side, his gaze never leaving them.

Linette filled a pot with meat and vegetables. She didn't know how long the little trio planned to stay, but when they left they would go with full stomachs and a jar of stew.

The woman slept until the baby's weak mewling woke her. She nursed the baby, her eyes dark with worry and fear.

Linette offered food. "You need to eat."

The boy translated.

The mother nodded and squeezed Linette's hand in gratitude. The boy accepted food as well but stood at the window as if he felt the need to keep watch. As they ate, Linette filled a jar.

She glanced up at the sound of several horses riding hard. The boy jerked from the window and murmured something to his mother. They scurried to the door.

"Wait," Linette called. "Take this."

The boy grabbed the jar and bent his head in thanks. They slipped silently away. Apart from the unfolded furs on the floor and the used dishes on the table, she could almost believe they hadn't been there.

Outside, the men were making a racket.

She went to the step to see what the cause was. Three ranch hands she recognized had a fourth man tied—an Indian. Ward held a rifle at the man's back.

She grabbed her coat and headed to the fray. "What's going on here?"

"We caught this Injun trying to steal one of Eddie's cows," the young man, Cal, said.

The suspected thief was most likely the father of the two boys and husband of the woman she'd just helped.

"There's only one way to deal with a rustler," Slim said, his expression indicating he would not give an inch on frontier justice.

Cookie, Bertie and Cassie stepped from the cookhouse, Grady behind them. Several more men came from the barn.

"Where's Eddie?" Bertie asked.

Ward answered. "Out hunting wild game. Even he doesn't butcher a young cow."

Linette trotted closer, confronting the knot of men.

"This is his decision to make. Why not tie the man in the barn and wait for him?"

Ward and Slim exchanged looks.

"Look," she tried again, "I know it's none of my business, but maybe Eddie would like to handle this himself."

Again they silently consulted each other. Ward shrugged. "If you think it best." He sounded less than convinced, but he directed the men to lead their prisoner away.

Linette watched until they were out of sight then hurried to the cabin. Grady had retreated inside and pulled a chair to the window to watch. His eyes were wide with fright. "That a bad man?"

"Maybe he and his family are hungry."

Cassie followed on her heels. "The men weren't happy about your interference. Cookie said they have to act swiftly and justly in order to prevent losing so many head they might as well pack up and go home."

Linette wanted to protest that many a man turned to stealing if he was starving, but she kept her thoughts to herself. There was only one person she had to convince.

She watched out the window for Eddie's return, hoping to speak to him before the men, but he approached the ranch from the other side. Even before he dismounted, his men crowded around him.

She could not leave the man to be hanged or shot. Not when he had a wife and children to feed. She grabbed her coat and hurried toward the barn.

Eddie stepped out before she got there. He saw her and strode in her direction. He grabbed her elbow, turned her aside. "We need to talk."

"I had to stop them from carrying out their plans."

He grunted—a sound full of distress.

"What would you do if your wife and children were starving and a thousand cows grazed close by?"

He led her to the far side of the cabin…the same place they had first confronted each other.

Her heart thudded deep in the pit of her stomach. Despite a few times that offered hope, it was plain things had not changed a great deal in the recent weeks. She had a choice. Give in to the opinion of Eddie and his men, which would no doubt earn her favor in his eyes, or risk disfavor and defend the Indian.

She didn't even hesitate over her choice. "Remember that Indian boy I told you about in Edendale?"

He nodded.

"He showed up on the doorstep this afternoon with his mother who had a newborn baby at her empty breasts. They're all starving to death. I fed them and gave them a jar of stew. How long do you think that will last? How long before the baby dies…before they all die?"

"A thieving man of any race has to be stopped."

"Rather than force the man to steal, give him enough meat for the winter. Isn't that a better way to stop him?"

Eddie looked at her as if she'd lost her mind.

She pressed the matter. "Does not God say He wants us to show mercy? Hasn't He shown us undeserved mercy?"

Eddie looked past her and sighed deeply. "This is what your father had to deal with?"

She drew up tall. "I told you from the first I will not turn my back on those in need. I've said my piece. I'll let you decide what is fair and right." She turned and walked away, her head high, her heart beating hard.

Lord, give him a heart to show mercy. Spare these poor people.

If Eddie didn't help, the family would starve to death. And she'd have to reconsider her desire to marry him, which left her facing the fact that her father would find her, drag her home and insist she marry according to his wishes.

She shuddered and prayed Eddie would live up to her opinion that he was a noble man who wouldn't turn his back on another in need. She included herself in that statement.

Chapter Ten

$\sim$

What was right and fair?

Eddie stared after her. The woman certainly had definite ideas about the matter. Shouldn't she stay inside the house and let the men decide such things?

He turned toward the big house. She'd never sit quietly indoors and ignore the challenges of creating a new world. She seemed to think her ways would make the new world better. His insides twisted mercilessly. New world. New ways. Those in the old country favored the old ways. And why not? They had worked for centuries. Why not here?

He released a blast of air from his tight lungs. Her interference left him facing a dilemma—show frontier justice or show mercy. Which was right? His heart said one thing, his brain another. He kicked at a lump of snow then crossed to the barn where the cowhands waited. Young Cal swung a rope before the Indian, taunting him with the loop he meant to throw over the rafter above their heads.

Ward and Slim didn't look quite so eager for a hanging and poor Roper looked ready to bring up his lunch.

"Boys, you know that big old steer mixed in with the breeding stock?" All winter they'd joshed about how good the critter had it just because he refused to leave the yard.

"Yeah, boss." Slim sounded relieved, as if he understood what Eddie had in mind. The others merely looked curious.

"I couldn't find any deer and we're getting real short of meat. I think fresh beef would be great. What do you all think?"

The whole works cheered. "Nothing like well-fed beef," Slim said.

"Yes, sir." Eddie looked about. "Cal, Ward, Slim— butcher that steer. Cut off the back quarter, wrap it in canvas and throw it in the back of the wagon."

"Boss?" Cal didn't want to believe what he'd just heard.

"I think we have plenty enough for sharing. Anyone disagree?" His words were soft, but not one of the boys missed his silent challenge.

"Nope." The three tromped off.

"Let the man go," he said to Roper.

The Indian shook his wrists once then faced Eddie.

Eddie wasn't sure how much of the conversation the man understood. "I'll give you the hindquarter. You don't need to steal from me. If you're in need come and ask for help."

The man nodded slowly as if struggling to comprehend. "Boy right. He say not all white men bad. I go now. Not wait. Family need me."

Eddie nodded. "I'll bring the meat later." He had seen enough signs to guess the Indians camped in a grove of trees a few miles away.

He hummed as he headed for the cabin. Linette would be pleased with his decision.

He stepped into the warm room. Linette glanced up from a tiny garment she was folding and his heart stalled. Baby clothes. How he wanted babies to fill his house...his heart. Babies of his flesh and blood. He drew in air that caught several times on the way in. Did she have a secret she hadn't revealed? A hidden pregnancy?

"I saw the man ride away." Her face beamed with gratitude. "You let him go."

"I told the boys to butcher an animal. I'll take some of it to him."

"I knew you would."

From the other side of the room Cassie snorted. "Bertie says they're a thieving bunch."

Neither Linette nor Eddie even looked at the woman.

"What do you have there?"

"I brought this with me, intending to use it as a pattern if I ever needed it. Well, I think I need it." She held up the tiny sweater. "I want to give it to the baby."

She meant to give it away. Thank goodness. His heart resumed a normal pace. "Do you want me to take it when I deliver the meat?"

Her expression grew thoughtful. Shifted to determination. He knew her answer before it came.

"I want to deliver it in person. Make sure Bright Moon is okay."

"It's not a fit journey for a young woman." He knew the fact wouldn't influence her.

"I thought by now you would realize I will not be controlled by such things. When are you going?"

He hesitated. "What if I forbid you to come along?"

Her look held steady. "Why would you do that?"

"It could be dangerous."

She shook her head, unconvinced, unyielding. "I crossed the whole country getting here. Is it any more dangerous than that was?"

"I'm wasting time while daylight passes." He turned to leave.

She bolted to her feet. "I'm ready."

Could he hope to trot away and escape her? He snorted. She'd likely trot right after him.

"I'd like to give the mother something, too. But I have nothing except..." She paused. "My coat."

He shook his head in disbelief. "I expect they have lots of furs to wrap themselves in." He would forbid her giving away her coat, but he didn't think she would take kindly to orders from him. "What they need is food. Why don't you take a sack and fill it from the supply shed."

She clapped her hands in delight. "I'll do that."

He remembered a woolen blanket in a box of belongings and said he'd get it as well.

"Thank you for being so generous. You are a good man." She took a sack from the shelf, grabbed her coat and headed for the door where he still stood.

She saw him as good? Or was she simply pleased to get her own way? What did it matter either way? Except it did. "I'll go with you and get the blanket." He stole a glance at her. Her face fairly glowed. She liked helping these people. She didn't seem to care about race or station of life, rich or poor, respected or outcast. The knowledge seeped through the cracks in his heart brought about by the many comments of disapproval over his lifetime, the frequent whispered and hurtful words about his birth, and softened their sharp edges.

Together they marched to the storage shed and selected a container of loose tea, dried apples and raisins. He lifted the lid on the box and pulled out the blanket.

The wagon rumbled past on the way to the cabin. "The beef is ready to go." He took the sack of food to the wagon then they headed up the hill.

It was easy enough to follow the trail the Indians had left. The cold had deepened throughout the day and it was growing late.

"We should perhaps wait until morning," he suggested.

"I'm okay. Besides, I fear that baby will perish if his mother doesn't get adequate nourishment."

Eddie didn't mind pushing on. He was used to the cold but Linette wasn't. She might suffer for it. She'd been pampered and protected all her life. He pulled the buffalo robe tighter about her knees and edged a little closer on the wagon bench to protect her from the chilly air.

She made no protest at his actions.

They smelled the smoke from the Indian camp before they saw the tepee.

Linette gasped. "They'll freeze."

"They've survived centuries doing things their way."

She relaxed. "Of course, you're right."

The Indian man lifted the flap and stepped out to greet them. "Red Fox." He tapped his chest to indicate it was his name.

His son ducked out after him. "Little Bear."

Eddie gave his name and Linette's then accepted an invitation to step into their abode. He'd been inside native tents before, but Linette had not and she glanced about with interest then hurried to the woman resting on the furs.

"How are you feeling?"

Little Bear translated for her. "She say much better. Stew good."

"I brought the baby a gift and Eddie brought some food."

Eddie put the sack on the floor.

Red Fox crossed his arms and stood up proud.

Linette saw that he was about to refuse their offering and spoke again to the woman. "White women give gifts to each other when there is a new baby. This is my gift to you." She indicated the sack.

Little Bear explained what she'd said and the woman nodded.

Linette handed her the baby sweater. "I hope it will help keep him warm."

The woman took the sweater and chuckled softly. She spoke to Little Bear. A quick smile crossed his face before he translated for Linette.

"Mother say thank you and baby now have to live to prove worthy of the gift."

Linette turned to Eddie, a radiant smile on her lips, then spoke to the mother again. "I will pray for him to grow into a strong, noble man."

When her son explained what Linette had said, the woman nodded vigorously, her eyes expressing her appreciation so clearly that no words were necessary.

"Snow come," Red Fox said.

Eddie didn't ask how the quiet man knew, but understood they must hurry. "Let's get the meat unloaded." He and Red Fox slipped outside to do so.

A few minutes later Eddie and Linette were back in the wagon. Red Fox stood at Linette's side. He touched her arm as he spoke to Eddie in words Eddie did not understand.

Red Fox stopped, searched for English words and shook his head. "She good woman. You keep her. Now go. Snow come."

Eddie needed no more urging. The cold had deepened enough to hurt his bones. "Stay close to preserve your body heat," he urged her when they settled on the wagon bench.

Five minutes after they left, snow began to fall in big lazy flakes.

"He knew." Linette sounded pleased that Red Fox had been correct.

"They seem to feel the weather."

She lifted her face to the heavens. "It reminds me of the first day I was here. It snowed then, too."

"Except for the fact we are two months further into winter and it's about twenty degrees colder." He didn't point out that darkness was falling and the wind had picked up. They could be in for a snowstorm. He'd hunkered down against many storms but never with a woman to guard and protect.

"You're worried about us getting home safely."

"I admit I am." Eddie knew they would need divine intervention to make it back, and he didn't mind asking for it. Without closing his eyes or relaxing his grasp on the reins, he prayed aloud, "God, protect us and guide us home."

The snow fell heavier, making it hard to see the tracks they had left only a short time ago. He leaned forward, peering into the swirling snow. A shadow caught his eye. It moved like quicksilver. It wasn't the shadow of a tree. It was a wolf. And likely only one of several.

He didn't say anything. Didn't want to alarm Linette.

"What was that?" She'd noticed.

Not that he was surprised. But he didn't answer.

"There it is again. It's some kind of animal."

He held the reins tightly as the horse grew nervous. He leaned back for the rifle he had behind the seat.

"It's wolves, isn't it? I read about them." Her hard tone informed him she knew enough not to think this was a lark.

He couldn't put his hand on the rifle. Didn't dare loosen his grip on the reins. "My gun is behind you. Can you reach it?"

She shifted away, letting a blast of cold air separate them. "I've got it." She handed it to him but left space between them for him to maneuver.

"I need you to hold the horse. Think you can do that?"

"I can do whatever I put my mind to."

For once he didn't mind her stubborn determination. He showed her how to hold the reins. "Don't let up no matter what."

He cradled the rifle against his shoulder and watched for the slinky shape of a wolf.

A shadow erupted from the darkness. It left the ground, grew larger. The horse whinnied and jerked away.

"Hold him."

"I have him."

The wolf disappeared in the darkness before Eddie could get a shot off. They'd been the animal's intended target. Sweat pooled in Eddie's armpits. He didn't dare miss next time. He had no intention of becoming wolf food. Nor of letting Linette be torn by vicious fangs.

He squinted into the shadows of the trees. Was that a moving shape among the snow-shrouded branches? He cocked his gun and fired. A yelp! Had he shot one of them?

Something thudded in the wagon. He turned in time to see a wolf coming at them from the back.

Linette glanced over her shoulder and gasped.

Eddie didn't have time to reload. Instinct took over and using his rifle as a club, he clouted the animal as hard as he could. The wolf yipped and stumbled back. For a second he faced Eddie, challenging, then he jumped over the side and disappeared.

"Are you okay?" Linette demanded, her voice quivering.

"Yes. Are you?"

"Yes." But the wail in her voice told him just how frightened she'd been.

He reloaded and glanced about. After a few minutes he decided he had succeeded in scaring off their attackers. "I think they're gone." He put the rifle across his knees, ready to use, and took the reins. He had to pry her fingers loose. He gripped the reins with one hand and pulled her close to his side with the other. "You did good."

She clung to him, her fingers knuckling into the lapels of his coat. The grasp seemed to go further, deeper, right into his heart to wrap around it and squeeze from it admiration and something sweeter that he didn't want to identify at the moment.

"We'll soon be home."

She didn't speak.

"You held the horses. You didn't panic." Not once had she screamed. "You make a good pioneer woman."

She gave a thin laugh. "I've been trying to tell you that."

"So you have." His words rumbled in his chest, easing back the tension that had held him for the last few minutes.

She relaxed her grip, but continued to press to his side. "You're a good rancher. You scared off the wolves. You handled the situation with Red Fox well, showing wisdom and compassion. You're a born leader."

Each word drifted through his mind like a warm summer wind, full of the perfume of affirmation, full of sunshine and blessing. He tightened his arm across her shoulders.

For this moment he would allow himself to bask in her approval. For the rest of the trip he would enjoy sharing the challenges of frontier life with her.

Linette groped from one heartbeat to the next, one breath to the next. Her fear would not subside.

Eddie seemed to think she'd shown courage. But as she'd held the reins, stories she'd read filled her mind—men hurt by wolves, scarred for life. Or worse—torn to pieces. She knew how the animals hunted in packs, diverting attention to one or two animals so the others could surprise their prey. If the horse had bolted and they'd been thrown from the wagon they would have been easy victims. She would not be responsible for such a predicament. She'd held the reins so firmly they'd bitten into her palms.

Now she clung to Eddie's side trying to calm herself.

Together they'd evaded the attack. He'd finally seen her as suitable for pioneer life. Her heart should dance with joy, but she felt vulnerable, shaken. As much by the way she found strength and comfort pressed next to his heart as from the threat of being torn to shreds by the wolves.

She sucked in air, pushed her turmoil away and carefully examined her emotions, skipping the terror part, which was understandable and explainable.

He'd said the words she'd longed for. But they didn't satisfy the way she'd expected them to. She wanted his offer to marry her. But she wanted more. No. She shook the thought away. All she wanted or needed was a marriage that would allow her to live in this new country and establish new rules for how a woman could conduct herself.

She pushed upright, pulled the furs around her. "Until we get safely home I'll be keeping a close watch for them to reappear."

"Indeed. So shall I."

She squinted into the deepening darkness, concentrating every thought on the shadows around them.

The wagon clattered down the hill. The barn door opened and four of the men stood with lamplight behind them. Ward reached for the horse. "Beginning to worry about you, boss. Didn't know if we should go looking or not."

"Thanks, boys. It's nice to know I can count on you. We ran into wolves on the way home."

Several talked at once. "How many?" "They attack?" "Where?"

"I'll tell you about it in the morning. I need to get

Linette to the house. Ward, send two more men to help watch the herd."

He jumped down from the wagon. When he reached for Linette she couldn't make her limbs move. He lifted her down and carried her to the cabin as Ward took the wagon away to the barn.

Cassie threw open the door. "Is she hurt?"

"I'm fine. I can stand." But her protests sounded weak even to herself.

"She's cold." Eddie carried her to the stove, grabbed a fur from his bedroll and wrapped her tight. "Cassie, is there tea?"

Cassie brought a cup, but it was Eddie who held it to her lips and urged her to drink.

The warm liquid eased down her throat. She hadn't realized how cold she'd grown. Terror had driven away such ordinary concerns. "I'm fine." She reached for the cup with stiff fingers.

He pressed his fingers over hers, holding the cup steady as she took another swallow.

Their eyes caught over the rim and his gentle smile threatened to take the fragile strength from her hands.

"You did well," he said. "Real well."

Before she could reply, Grady crowded close to her side.

Cassie hung over Eddie's shoulder. "What happened?"

Eddie told the story, making it sound even more adventuresome and Linette more heroic than she had been. His gaze flashed back and forth between Cassie and Linette. Each time, she felt something wrench inside her—a strange twist of both hesitancy and eagerness.

She shifted her attention to Grady, whose eyes had grown wide as Eddie retold the events.

"Eddie save you?" He looked at Eddie with new-found awe.

Eddie laughed. "No more than she saved me."

His approval warmed her as much as the tea and the fire and she let the fur slip from her shoulders. "Thank God we made it home safely."

"Amen." Eddie's voice deepened and against her better judgment she glanced at him. The depth of emotion in his eyes stunned her, left her struggling to find equilibrium.

It was only because they had shared a frightening experience. Only that he'd finally admitted she would make a good ranch wife. Only that they were both grateful to be safe and sound.

Later, in bed, Linette could not fall asleep. Each time she almost did, she'd jerk awake with a wolf lunging at her throat.

She heard Eddie moving about in the other room and wondered if he was having the same difficulty.

His arms about her would calm her fears. Would it be appropriate to put on her heavy robe and go to him?

Appropriate or not, she would not do so. She'd proven her courage to him. Now she had to prove it to herself.

She would not seek or desire anything from Eddie but a marriage offer. She would not allow her heart to overrule her head. Nor would she let her emotions turn her into a weak, needy woman.

The next day Eddie and his men hunted wolves. They found one dead where he and Linette had encountered the animals and tracked half a dozen others. The trail headed toward the wintering herd.

Eddie urged his horse to a trot. "If they've attacked the herd—"

There was no need to say more. The men with him kept pace. They met Ward and the others before they reached the herd. Two wolves hung from Ward's saddle.

"What happened?" Eddie asked.

"A pack of them came at us last night. Good thing we were prepared and able to stop them. Got these two. The others slunk away."

"What direction?"

Ward pointed.

"I'll track them. Blue, you come with me. Ward, head back to the ranch." He gave Ward the wolf carcass he'd picked up earlier. "The rest of you keep a sharp eye out for more attacks."

Blue was the steadiest man, the most accurate shot of those who worked for him, and together they followed the tracks for the better part of two hours.

"Boss, looks like they've left the area."

"For now." There wasn't any point in going farther. "Let's head on home." The shadows had lengthened and covered the feet of the trees. He would be glad to get out of the saddle and have a hot drink. And some food.

They retraced their steps. By the time they reached the barn, darkness had settled in.

Ward knelt outside the barn, working by lantern light. He'd already skinned two of the hides and nailed them to the wall. He worked on the third carcass.

He looked up as Eddie and Blue approached. "Everything okay?"

"The rest of them have hightailed it to the mountains."

"Glad to hear it."

Eddie grunted agreement and led his horse inside. As soon as he took care of the animal he headed for the cabin and flung the door open to warmth and gentle lamplight.

Linette sprang forward. "I was getting worried. Here, let me help you." She assisted him as he unwrapped his woolen scarf and removed his heavy coat.

"I'm fine." Though it felt nice to have someone fuss over him.

Cassie sat by the stove knitting and Grady played at her side.

"You must be cold," Linette said. "Sit by the stove. Have you eaten? I saved soup for you."

Home sweet home. He sat by the warm stove and took the bowl of soup she offered.

She sat at the table watching.

"The wolves seem to have moved on," he said in answer to her silent question. "I killed one last night and Ward killed two later. He's at the barn skinning them."

"So everyone and everything is safe?"

He nodded.

"Thank God."

"Amen to that." He finished the soup and handed the bowl to her as he failed to stifle a yawn.

"I expect you're tired."

"It's been a long day."

"Well, we'll say good-night." The three of them departed to the bedroom and a few minutes later he threw himself on his bedroll and put out the lamp.

Despite his concern about wolves stalking his herd,

he felt warm and content. He had almost fallen asleep with a smile on his lips when he recalled what he'd said to himself earlier. Home sweet home.

The thought was very close to what Linette had promised. And that he would be begging her to stay before winter ended. He clamped a lid on such errant ideas.

The big house would be every bit as welcoming. Margaret would take equally good care of him. Or would she assign the task to a servant? He didn't have the energy to think of an answer.

Linette lay on the bed praying her gratitude for Eddie's safe return. Throughout the day, Cookie and Bertie had told tale after tale of disastrous encounters between men and wolves to the point Linette thought she'd run into the cold and bury her head in the snow to block the words.

After they left the cookhouse and returned to the cabin, the minutes ticked by with the reluctance of a boy headed for a whipping.

She spent much of her time staring out the window hoping, praying for a sign of Eddie's safe return.

Cassie watched her. "Aren't you the one always saying God will take care of things? So why are you worried?"

"You heard Cookie and Bertie. He could be hurt. Or killed."

"And then what would you do? Isn't that what's bothering you?"

Linette had jerked around to face Cassie. "Of course. What else would it be?" But deep inside, she wondered if her concern went beyond the marriage she hoped for, planned for.

How absurd. She simply wasn't thinking straight because of the tension. That's all it was. All it could be.

And now he was back safely. Likely sleeping while she lay in the dark reliving each waiting moment.

She made herself think of something else. The shawl she worked on. Her attempts at bread making. What had she done wrong? Were the wolves as big as she imagined?

One way to find out. She'd ask Eddie if she could see the dead animals.

She waited until after breakfast. "I'd like to see the wolves."

Eddie set his cup down with a crash. "They've left for good, I hope. Besides, didn't you see enough of them the other night? One practically leaped at your throat."

She clutched her throat and cast a look at Grady. Thankfully he seemed occupied playing beyond the stove and didn't appear to have heard the comment. "I meant the dead ones."

"Oh." He gulped the last of his coffee. "They've been skinned out."

"I'd still like to see."

"Then come along. I'll take you to the barn."

She scurried into her coat and followed him out the door. Before they reached the barn, she saw Ward admiring the pelts stretched out on the wall.

Her steps slowed. She'd never seen death this close.

Ward stepped to one side as they reached the pen. "These are prime pelts." He brushed the fur beside him. "See for yourself."

She moved closer, pulled off her mitten and stroked the fur. The wolves had beautiful heads. Like a majestic dog. "It's a shame they had to be killed."

An explosive noise came from Eddie and she jerked about to face him. He scowled at her. "Don't be feeling sorry for them. That one—" he indicated the pelt farthest to the right "—tried to kill us." His anger filled the air like a blast of hot air. "I suppose you'd prefer I rescued them. Turned them into pets."

"I meant nothing of the sort. I only admired their beauty." She kept her tone neutral though she wanted badly to answer him in kind.

He scrubbed his chin. "I just can't stop thinking of how close we came—" He shook his head and shifted his attention to something beyond the barn, though she guessed he saw nothing.

"Eddie, we're safe. Everyone is safe. You said so yourself." She pressed her hand to his arm in an attempt to comfort him.

He shrugged, forcing her arm to drop. "Yes. Everyone is safe." He ducked into the barn.

Linette didn't follow. He needed time alone.

Ward cleared his throat. "I know what you mean about killing such noble animals, but sometimes it's necessary."

"I understand." All kinds of things were unpleasant but necessary.

Ward leaned against the wall and tipped his hat back. "Too bad it's snowed again. I'd hoped to take you to see my ranch."

Eddie stepped from the barn. "You could put runners on the wagon and take it in the snow."

Linette shot him a look fit to curl the leather on his boots.

"Boss, you wouldn't mind?"

"Not at all. I think Linette would enjoy it. Wouldn't you?"

"Perhaps another time." She spoke to Ward, keeping her voice as gentle as possible when inside she burned like a raging forest fire. How dare Eddie encourage Ward? "Cookie promised to give me another lesson in baking bread." She turned to Eddie and made no attempt to disguise how she felt. "I am determined to learn that skill." Just as she was determined to convince Eddie she would make a good pioneer wife. For him. Not Ward.

His expression remained stony, as if to inform her nothing she said or did would change his mind.

"Good day to you both." She strode toward the cabin as if hurrying could put out the fire within. But it only fanned it hotter. What was wrong with the man? How could he be so blind? So stubborn? Yes, he'd said she'd make a good pioneer wife, but not for him. For anyone but him. It burned clear to the depths of her marrow to think he continued to reject her.

Chapter Eleven

"Boss, I get the feeling she's still got her hopes pinned on you. She barely sees me." Ward, like Eddie, stared after Linette's departing figure.

Eddie grunted. He'd made a mistake in telling her she'd make a good pioneer wife. He'd given her hope, when he only meant to compliment her. Although, if he was honest, in the heat of the moment, his heart pounding with fear, he'd been glad enough to hold her. No reason she should read more into that than two brave, frightened souls helping each other.

"Take care of—" He didn't finish. Let Ward figure out for himself what to do. He crossed the bridge and went to the wintering pens. With a practiced glance he checked on the animals till he felt satisfied they were in excellent condition. Come spring he'd begin his new breeding program. In the coming years he expected to see the results in healthy, hardy cattle that brought top dollar. Leaning his arms on the top rail of the fence, he relaxed as he watched the cattle eating the hay he'd insisted the men put up during the hot summer months.

His sense of balance returned and he ambled over to the barn, where Slim worked alone on the harnesses.

"Where's Ward?"

"Gone to check on his ranch. Said to tell you he'd be gone for a few days. Hoped it was okay."

"Fine by me." He joined Slim at the workbench. Eddie relaxed further. Ward would not be sending Linette adoring eyes. Until he returned. In the meantime…

Slim wasn't much for talking just to hear his voice, so they worked in companionable silence for the most part.

Far too soon it was time to return to the cabin for dinner. If his stomach wasn't so demanding he would forgo the meal rather than face Linette.

Slim left the barn, paused to look over his shoulder. "Boss, time to eat."

Eddie nodded and strode for the door. He'd faced floods, snowstorms, angry drunks and attacking wolves. No way would he hesitate to walk into his own cabin because he'd offended Linette. Yet his steps lagged as he headed across the yard. He paused with his hand on the doorknob and listened. All quiet. He sucked in air and opened the door.

The aroma of roast beef greeted him. Along with a smile from Linette. He tried to believe the smile reached her eyes. But she turned away quickly. "It's right ready. Grady and Cassie, come to the table."

He shucked off his coat and sat with the others. "A very nice meal," he offered.

"Thank you. Like I promised, I'm a fast learner."

He nodded. If he wasn't mistaken, her voice carried a note of warning. Which he chose to ignore. He'd made himself clear from the beginning and if she refused to listen, well, that was her problem.

He finished his meal and prepared to leave the cabin.

"I'd like to walk with you," she said as she put on her coat.

"You aren't asking, are you?"

"How astute of you to notice."

He looked at Cassie, who poured hot water into the dishpan.

She shrugged.

No sympathy from her.

Linette stepped outside. He closed the door gently behind her. "Where would you like to go?"

She tipped her head toward the big house. "That way is fine."

They passed the cookhouse. She said nothing. They reached the bottom of the hill. She said nothing. They climbed the snow-covered path. Still nothing.

The roast beef sat heavily in his stomach. Whatever she meant to say, he wished she'd get it done with.

They reached the front doors of the house and she stopped, turned slowly and faced him, her eyes burning like hot embers.

"Do not think you can toss me off on some poor unsuspecting cowboy. My father would have no regard for such a marriage. He would send his henchmen to drag me home."

"What about the convent?" He knew before he spoke the words how she'd react.

Her look practically scalded him. "I came West to start a life free of artificial restrictions. I mean to get it."

He leaned closer, not giving her fury any quarter.

"Miss Edwards, I told you from the beginning I mean to marry Margaret. So how, pray tell me, do you intend to live this life?"

"I will find a way." She spat the words out like bitter seeds. Then the fight left her. She shifted as if to hide the fact from him and looked at the far mountains.

"Linette." He touched her arm. "You'll make someone a fine wife. A fine pioneer wife."

She blinked, brought her gaze back to him. "Someone like Ward, you mean?"

He began to nod then changed his mind. It was exactly what he meant. But he couldn't say it. He didn't want to upset her further. But something more than concern about her reaction stopped him. He would not give it a name.

"I'm sorry," he murmured. Though for the life of him he couldn't say what he was sorry for. He swung his attention to the house. "Did you want to come in?"

"I don't think so, thanks. I plan to spend the afternoon with Cookie." She sauntered down the hill and into the cookhouse without so much as a backward look.

He jerked about. It wasn't as if it mattered what she thought. Only he hoped— What? What could he hope for? He toured the house, reminding himself of all the plans he and his father had discussed. Tried to forget the eagerness Linette showed for certain rooms. How she meant to use the extra rooms to help those in need. He came to a halt in the room that would be the family parlor. The room where Linette had exclaimed over the view and helped him put up trim. Where she'd pointed

out the good job he'd done and likened it to him being
an honorable man.

He tossed aside the piece of wood that he held, having no idea when he'd picked it up or why. She saw him
as an honorable man but he'd acted like a scoundrel
trying to force her into Ward's sphere.

All because she had succeeded in making him confess she was a pioneer woman. And in the confessing,
he'd allowed himself to see her working side by side
with him, building a new life in a new world.

In effect, he'd punished her for his own wayward
thoughts.

He meant to make up for it. But how?

Linette liked pretty things. She liked color. All part
of her artistic nature. If he thought the store in Edendale would have artist's paints, he'd ride into town and
purchase some for Linette. But so far as he could recall,
the shelves had only necessary supplies.

Surely among his books to be shipped there'd be
one or more that she'd enjoy. But they wouldn't be arriving until spring.

Except he had a box he'd never opened because he
didn't have room or need for anything more in the little cabin. A box his mother had packed to help him set
up housekeeping.

Eddie jogged down the hill, past the cookhouse, kept
his gaze from the cabin and went to the storage shed.
The crate stood in the far corner. He pried the lid up
and began to pull out items. Some pretty dishes and
an assortment of table linens. No doubt Linette would
enjoy the whole lot, but there was hardly room for them
in the tiny kitchen. He dug farther. Miniature portraits

of his parents. He set those aside. They belonged in the big house, not in the log cabin. He lifted a fine woolen blanket and wondered if the ladies had need of it. When he saw what lay beneath it he laughed. Mother's dancing lady. A porcelain figurine of a woman in a swirling pink gown holding a china rose to her nose.

Eddie held the figurine in his hands. It was one of his mother's most prized possessions. She'd had it since before she married Randolph Gardiner. Why had she sent it with Eddie?

Memories of his mother and other family members filled him with loneliness. Sighing, he turned the dancing lady over. He studied the bottom as if hoping for clues as to why his mother had sent it.

Nothing but the name of the manufacturer.

He sat back on his heels. She'd never said where she got it. He'd always assumed it was a gift from someone. But if from her parents or a friend, wouldn't she have said so?

That left one possibility he'd never considered.

His real father had given her this. He almost dropped the figurine. Who was the man? Eddie would never know because his mother refused to discuss it. She must have endured so much shame and ostracism until Randolph Gardiner married her. His position in society forbade anyone from treating her, or Eddie, poorly.

He owed his father a great deal. There was one way to repay the kindness—fulfill his father's expectations.

Deciding the figurine belonged in the big house next to the likenesses of his mother and father, he set it aside and dug deeper.

A china teapot. Plain brown but so much superior

to the tin pot they'd been using. He returned everything else, nailed the lid down again and headed for
the cabin.

Since her return to the cabin Linette had renewed
her plan to make herself invaluable to Eddie. She'd already tried everything she could think of—learning to
make meals, helping at the house. She'd even helped
fight off wolves. How much more could she do? Learn
to make bread, but she knew it would not influence his
thoughts any more than the cookies and biscuits and
roast beef had.

The door opened and Linette glanced up. Her heart
caught on its next beat.

Eddie! Had he changed his mind?

"I brought you something." He held out a china teapot.

"A Brown Betty teapot!" Cassie sprang to her feet
and set the kettle to boil. "Finally. Some decent tea."

Wild hope rushed through Linette. Surely this
meant something more than tea without the tinny taste.
"Thank you, Eddie. Where did you find it?"

"There's a crate of things out in the shed. Thought
I'd poke through it and see if there was anything we
could use."

We? He'd been thinking of them. Her hope settled
in to stay.

He put the pot on the table and leaned back on his
heels, grinning as if all was right with his world.

She smiled back, feeling as if her world returned
to balance.

Their look went on and on until Cassie grabbed the

teapot from under Linette's elbow. "I am going to enjoy a cup of tea." She paused and gave Linette and Eddie a serious look. "If no one has any objections."

Linette jerked away to stare at the stove. "I'm going to try making bread again. This time I'm going to succeed."

"I'm sure you shall." He sounded so confident she stole another look at him.

His smile faltered. "I was afraid I was rude earlier today, so I—" He pointed toward the teapot and shrugged.

"You brought a gift."

He nodded, then with a wry smile shook his head. "My way of apologizing."

"Apology accepted." Surely her voice didn't quiver, but she feared it did.

"Tea is ready. Who cares for some?" Cassie asked, handing them each a cupful.

The three of them pulled chairs around the stove as Grady played with his growing assortment of toys. No one seemed impatient about supper. Linette certainly wasn't. This bit of kindness and concern filled her heart with hope.

And something more that she wasn't prepared to look at too closely for fear she would be alarmed at what she saw. A growing fondness for the man.

Eddie finished his tea and strode the three steps to the window, peered out then turned. "Linette, would you like to go for a walk?"

She'd been staring at the mixing bowl she'd used for the failed bread dough, wondering what she'd done wrong. She'd asked Cookie to explain the procedure again and still could not understand where she'd veered from the woman's instructions. She gladly pushed the task aside and grabbed her coat to join Eddie.

They walked past the barn, past the wintering pens as he explained the advantages of the cows he'd chosen, the way he fed them and a bunch of things that had never before mattered to Linette but now seemed the most important information on the face of the earth. They climbed the rough trail beyond the pens. He took her hand to guide her over the rocky path. They came to a grove of dark pines where they stood with the sun on their cheeks.

Still hand in hand, they watched a raven rise from the trees, squawking at the intrusion.

"Every time I came up here during the summer, if I sat real quiet, I could watch a deer and twin fawns," he told her. "They tiptoed from the trees to nibble at the grass."

"Maybe I'll get a chance to see them in the spring."

He faced her, an inscrutable expression on his face. Was he imagining her at his side throughout the changing seasons? The thought strengthened her resolve. She would, with God's help, prove her value to Eddie's plans. She intended to tell him so, but before she could say anything, he spoke.

"I need to help the boys repair a fence the bulls broke down, but I thought you might enjoy seeing this place." He dropped her hand and led the way back down the hill then strode off, leaving her at the cabin staring after him.

Why had the walk ended so abruptly? It was as if he regretted taking her there. Or perhaps he regretted taking her hand to assist her? Or…dare she hope he was beginning to see how suited they were to one another and the thought frightened him?

She clung to the notion as she returned to the cabin. Perhaps all her efforts were bearing fruit. A smile curved her mouth. By spring he'd be rejoicing over her presence rather than fighting it.

"I'm going to work on the house," Eddie announced the next day as he pushed from the breakfast table. "I could use a hand measuring the baseboards."

Her heart took off like a horse freed from a pen. Her eyes jerked toward him. He had asked her to accompany him. Surely that meant he had changed his mind about her. She calmed her racing heart. "I could help."

"You might want to bring your sketchbook."

She couldn't force her eyes away. Her father had scoffed at her art as useless. But Eddie seemed to appreciate her drawings. Even his comments made her realize he understood the emotions she tried to capture. Try as she might, she couldn't stop pleasure from blossoming in her heart at his approval.

"The sun is shining. The mountains glisten with fresh snow," he said. "Might make a good picture."

He wanted her to capture the sight? She certainly itched to see the view and draw it. But even more, she anticipated discovering what this change in him meant.

Cassie reached for her coat and handed Grady his. "I'll take the boy with me to see Cookie."

The interruption enabled Linette to break from Eddie's gaze. She sucked in air as if she'd forgotten to breathe. "I'll get my things." She rushed to the bedroom where she kept her supplies, but at the trunk she hesitated. She wanted to prove to Eddie how capable she was. He'd seen her failure at baking bread. Did he also need to see how she wasted her time drawing pictures? Though her skill wasn't entirely wasted. She'd copied the sketch of Dorothy Farris for Grady and been pleased at the boy's pleasure.

But she'd done that in her spare time while Eddie was away. Now she needed to prove she had some practical value on the ranch and she returned to the other room without the sketchbook.

Cassie and Grady had left.

"Couldn't find it?" Eddie asked.

"What?" As if she didn't know what he meant.

"The book you draw in."

She shrugged. "It's only something I do when there's no work to be done."

He pinned her with his dark gaze. "Are you refusing to draw a picture because I requested it?"

She shook her head. "That's not why."

"Then would you mind drawing a picture of the mountains for me?"

To refuse would be churlish. She returned to the bedroom and scooped up the sketchbook and her pencils then followed Eddie up the hill. She went immediately to the window while he built a fire in the round-bellied stove in the room that would serve as the family dining room and parlor. "Oh." The word escaped her. "Beautiful. I can see why you want to capture the sight. But there is no way I could do it justice in black and white." How she itched to pull out her canvases and oils. But she wondered if crowding the cabin would give Eddie the impression she didn't put proper value on the comfort of others.

"My mind can fill in the details." He joined her at the window.

She simply stared at the view as they waited for the fire to drive the cold from the room. Oh, how she loved this room. She wanted to be a part of this house, a part of this ranch, a part of this land. She wanted to be part—

She silently commanded her thoughts to stop. She did not want to be part of this man's affections. She would not give up control of her heart. Not even to belong here. She would, instead, prove her value as a woman who contributed. "I'm ready to get to work."

His gaze went to the sketchbook on the window ledge.

Her gaze went to the stack of wood next to the wall. "I'll give you a hand with those first."

He looked about to argue then nodded. "If you wish."

For two hours she helped him measure, cut and nail the boards in place. While she worked she had no trouble keeping her thoughts in place except when her glance went to the window and she watched the changing face of the magnificent Rockies.

He cut another board, but rather than nail it, he straightened. "I'll be back in a moment."

She stared after him as he disappeared into the kitchen area.

A few minutes later he returned with a wingback chair and put it before the windows.

She gaped at the chair. It was green. Exactly as it had been in her imaginings.

"I'm done until you do what you promised." His words jerked her back to his request.

"I don't recall making any promises." Not out loud to him.

"A drawing of the mountains." He indicated she should sit.

She hesitated but only out of caution. Her insides burned to capture the sight. Giving in to her yearning, she dropped to the chair, pulled her sketch pad to her lap and started to work.

Peripherally she heard Eddie leave the room and return with a second chair matching hers. He parked it close to hers, facing the window, and sat quietly at her side as she worked. But her attention and imagination were on the scene before her. The lines flowed from her mind to the paper. The ruggedness of the mountains, the contrast between the snow and dark green pines, the neatness of the red farm buildings.

After a while her neck ached and she straightened and looked around. "How long have I been drawing?"

Eddie grinned. "More than an hour, I expect."

She groaned. "I didn't mean to waste your time or mine."

"Let's see the finished product." He reached for the sketch pad.

"It's only rough."

He studied it. "This is not a waste of time. May I have it?"

"Of course."

He carefully tore the page from the pad. "I'd like

to frame it and hang it in this room." He tried to close the pad. The pages stuck. He turned them one by one. And stopped to stare.

She stifled a groan. She hadn't meant for him to ever see the drawing of him confidently riding his horse.

"This is me. I look like...a cowboy."

She laughed as much from relief as amusement. He hadn't seen anything extraordinary in her depiction of him. But even at the time she'd struggled to see him as only a means to an end—a way to gain escape from her father's plans. Not as a strong, handsome, trustworthy, noble man. She jammed a log in the flood of his admirable qualities rushing to her mind. "Don't you think of yourself as a cowboy? A good cowboy, from what the men say about you."

"I ride because my tasks require it. Sure, I enjoy it, but that's not uppermost in my mind." He glanced about the room. "Just as I enjoy working on this house, but I don't do it for that reason."

She thought she understood his reason—build a house that would win Margaret's favor. The pleasure she'd enjoyed as she sketched fluttered like a dead moth. Did she stand a chance against such devotion? How could she possibly hope to get him to change his mind?

He went on as if talking to himself. "It's a job entrusted to me by my father and I am determined to prove I can handle the responsibility. Prove, I suppose, I am equal to the task. That my father was right in assigning it to me."

"You feel the need to prove yourself to your father? Yet he must trust you a great deal to send you over here with the responsibility of finding land, purchasing a huge herd of cows and building a house that would make anyone proud."

"It's more of a test than a sign of trust."

She thought it was an odd answer. "What sort of test would that be?"

He made a deep-throated sound. "To see if I'm fit to be a Gardiner."

She shifted so she could study his expression. His smile was mocking, as if he'd said more than he meant to or perhaps regretted sounding so hurt. But the look in his eyes spoke volumes. She knew—just knew—his words revealed a lifetime of doubt and striving. She held his gaze as the knowledge slid sideways into her heart and burned a raw path. "Why do you need to prove such a thing?" Her words scalded her throat.

"Because I am not a Gardiner."

"But your name—it *is* Eddie Gardiner. Yes?"

His smile tipped to one side. His eyes darkened. "I was born before my mother married my father. My real father was not in the picture. My mother has never revealed one detail of how I came to be. She said that part of her life ended when she married Randolph Gardiner and it was up to me to make sure he never regretted taking me as his son." He seemed to do his best to smile widely, but she read in the set of his lips a world of wondering if he'd truly been accepted.

She curled her fingers into her palms to stop herself from reaching for him. Her circumstances were vastly different. She was her father's biological daughter. Never once had she doubted her value in his world. As a commodity. A business advantage. A bargaining chip. She knew she wasn't valued for who she was or what she wanted. This trip to Canada had been her first victory.

Her nails dug into the heels of her hands. Never would she give up the freedom she'd won. Never would she give up the independence she'd struggled so hard to win. But Eddie's unspoken pain beat relentlessly at her thoughts. He ached from not feeling totally accepted. She understood he would not acknowledge it. Never admit anything more than a commitment to live up to Mr. Gardiner's expectations. "I expect he is pleased with how well you've done." She glanced around the room to silently emphasize his success.

He shrugged. His gesture seemed to indicate more defeat than indifference. He glanced about the room and then turned to look out the window. "Father does not understand how different things are out here. How I must make decisions based on the circumstances of the moment. Anything I do that differs from his plans is under suspicion."

She turned the idea over in her mind, finding that it scratched at her insides. "How much has he planned for you?"

His laugh was short. "Every detail he could think of, because he doesn't believe I can handle decisions on my own."

"Does that include the woman you will marry?"

He refused to meet her look, instead stared steadily out the window.

"Ah. You don't think I'd pass inspection?" Somehow that didn't surprise her. Her father could be abrasive and had offended any number of people in his quest to claw his way to the top. Though she wasn't sure what he hoped was at the top or even where the top was.

Eddie sighed heavily.

She guessed he felt a need to earn the favor he never felt he qualified for. She glanced about the room she had grown to love. "Did he design the house?"

"Certainly. Though I made a few changes to better suit the setting."

"Like what?"

His grin was genuine. His eyes lit from within as if he spoke from a secret, joy-filled spot.

Her insides mellowed knowing she'd distracted him from worrying about his father's expectations.

"This room. According to the plans, it should face the other direction, but that would have been a mistake, don't you think?"

"Indeed. As I'm sure he would agree if he ever saw this view."

Eddie sobered. "I hope so." He studied the sketches before him as if they held some dark secret. "I have been entrusted with a job. I intend to do my best. I aim to honor my father for giving me his name and a family. I pray it will honor and please God as well."

She waited, but he didn't look up from his contemplation of the drawings. His commitment to his family and God was noble and honorable. "I think your father would be proud of all you've done."

He stared at her drawing of him on horseback. Then with a deep sigh he set the sketches aside and jumped to his feet. "Enough of this. It's time for lunch."

When he reached for her hand, she didn't refuse. Whatever his father required of him, the older man was far away, restricted to reports by mail. She said so to him and he laughed.

"Maybe so, but I can't help feeling he's watching over my shoulder."

Chapter Twelve

Why had he revealed his insecurities to Linette?

She had been understanding and sympathetic, though.

But what did it matter what she thought? He would succeed. The house would soon be done. Margaret would come. Linette would accept defeat and leave. He shoved aside the questions as to where she would go and what would become of her.

Only one more thing he aimed to accomplish. Since he'd seen the Indians and their travois, he had been secretly working on a project that he hoped would convince Grady that men weren't to be feared. At least, not all men. He eyed the boy as he ate his meal beside Linette. "How long does he nap?"

"About an hour." Linette sounded puzzled by his question.

"Good. That's just about right." He spoke directly to Grady. "I'll have a surprise for you when you wake up."

"'Prise?" the boy spoke before he realized it was Eddie he addressed, and then he ducked his face into Linette's shoulder.

It was enough to give Eddie hope. It would only take some fun together for Grady to forget his fear of men.

"I ready for sleep." Grady scrambled down and disappeared into the bedroom.

The three adults exchanged looks and laughed. Linette followed the boy and a moment later came out chuckling. "His eyes are shut tight. Don't suppose you can tell me what you have in mind?" Linette's eyes filled with teasing lights.

"Nope. You'll have to wait just like Grady."

She laughed. "But I can't spend my afternoon napping like Grady, so it's harder for me to wait. Couldn't you give me a little hint?"

He leaned back on his heels and scratched his head, pretending to be in deep thought over her question. "I don't know if it would be fair. After all, I planned it especially for Grady. Of course, you'll have to come with him or he won't come." Would she latch onto the little nugget he'd dropped for her?

"Ah. So we have to leave the house? Will we be outside?"

"Best dress warmly." A grin tugged at his mouth as she narrowed her eyes and studied him.

"A ride? No, a walk? You've got something special to show us?"

Linette looked intrigued and tapped a fingertip to her chin.

That rhythmic movement drew his gaze to her chin. Its firmness signaled a determination that he already had firsthand knowledge of. She pressed her bottom lip into a thin line that made her look so serious he had to chuckle. "All I'll say is it isn't a cow." And if he hoped to have the surprise ready by the time Grady woke up, he would have to leave the house and head for the barn. Yet his limbs refused to move and his gaze wouldn't veer from watching her fingertip.

She lowered her hand and shook her head. "I simply can't imagine what it might be."

He dredged up enough effort to turn and grab his coat. "I'll be back in about an hour. You'll have to wait until then."

"Maybe I'll go for a walk and see what you're doing."

She followed him across the cabin at his heels. Although he couldn't see her he felt her presence as clearly as sunshine on bare skin. He swallowed hard, promising himself he would not turn and meet her face-to-face. He knew if he did he would be close enough to see the way her eyes flickered from pale to dark brown as her emotions fluctuated. He hadn't yet learned to interpret those subtle shifts, but knew they signaled deep feelings—like anger, and maybe the opposite. Maybe if he turned, confronted her, they would darken with something else. He couldn't even explain what he hoped to see.

Best not to turn. Then he wouldn't have to witness anything or try to decipher what it meant. Or why it mattered so much. He should be thinking of Marga-ret anyway. She would have received their letters by now. Would she be eagerly packing and making plans? He grabbed the door. "Be a good girl and wait here."

Only after he'd pulled the door closed behind him did he realize he'd relegated her to the same status as Grady—a child. He hesitated. Should he go back and apologize?

A burst of laughter came from the other side of the door.

Linette wasn't offended by his remark.

A stampede of emotions raced through him. Pleasure at her amusement. Satisfaction that he had her interest. And something unfamiliar that crept to the fore. A feeling unlike any he'd experienced before.

Connection?

He shook his head. That didn't make a lick of sense. He wasn't a bit interested in Linette. Didn't feel anything toward her but... He struggled to find a word.

Responsibility. That was it. He was stuck watching out for her—for Cassie and Grady too—until he could send them back.

Maybe he'd track down Grady's father and make him take responsibility for his son, though the idea of Grady being with someone who didn't value him didn't sit well.

And Cassie? Well, he'd seen the way Roper looked at her. She could do worse than marry a cowboy.

As for Linette, he would send her back to her father. A bitter taste filled his mouth as he thought of her married to an old man.

He went to the barn and set to work finishing his surprise. An hour later he returned to the cabin.

Linette must have been watching because she stepped out when he was still fifty feet away, Grady clutching one hand. Both were dressed warmly.

Eddie struggled to keep amusement out of his voice. "I see you're ready."

"Ready and waiting for your surprise," Linette called.

"'Prise?" Grady whispered.

Eddie stepped aside to reveal a toboggan. It was admittedly crude. Likely Linette was used to much better. "I did the best I could with what I had."

She clapped her hands and squealed. "You know what this is, Grady?"

The boy shook his head.

"A toboggan. It's for riding down the snow-covered hills. It's great fun. As much fun as racing horses."

"Another of your adventures with your brother?"

Her gaze brushed Eddie's and pink colored her cheeks. He didn't think it was from the cold. "My father was very displeased when he found out."

"And yet you sound totally unrepentant."

"I am. Like I said, I have no use for pretentious rules of conduct." Her chin went up. Her eyes flashed in challenge.

He heard distant warning bells. Echoes of his father's words. *A Gardiner always lives up to expectations. They are pillars of society.*

He ignored the distant call. He only meant to have a little fun and help Grady learn that men wouldn't hurt him. No one could object to that.

"Let's try it out." He headed for the hill. The snow on the north slope would make decent sledding. Linette fell in at his side. Grady carefully kept her between him and Eddie. But he came along eagerly enough.

They trudged to the top of the hill and stood on the crest looking down their intended path.

"I'll do a run first. Test it out. Then I'll take Grady down." And before Grady could protest, Eddie positioned himself on the toboggan, gave himself a little push and raced down the hill. He hit a bump, righted himself quickly and zipped to the bottom, coasting a hundred feet before he jumped off.

He waved at the pair watching from the top of the hill. Linette and Grady returned the wave and cheered. Now for the long trek back to the top. He leaned forward into the hillside and climbed. At the top, he paused to catch his breath. Again, Grady carefully kept Linette between himself and Eddie.

He plopped the toboggan down and waved a hand at Grady. "Your turn." Eddie sat on the back of the toboggan and patted the space in front of him. "You sit here and I'll keep you from falling off."

Grady whimpered and shrank back.

Linette squatted before him. "It's a lot of fun, Grady."

He shook his head, his eyes wide with what Eddie knew was fear.

"Eddie isn't going to hurt you. You know that."

Her complete confidence in him brought a grin to his mouth and a warm feeling to unfamiliar places in his heart.

But Grady wouldn't take another step closer. He looked down the hill where Eddie had ridden the toboggan, slid a glance toward Eddie and sighed deeply. Suddenly he brightened and grabbed Linette's hand. "You go, too."

Linette straightened and considered the spot in front of Eddie. "I don't think there's room."

How had she gone from touting how safe it was for Grady, to being as reluctant as the boy? Eddie wouldn't hurt either one of them.

He edged back and patted the wood before him. "Lots of room."

Grady tugged on Linette's hand.

She didn't move.

Eddie repeated her words. "'He isn't going to hurt you. You know that.'"

Her gaze darted past him, restlessly seeking a place to light, then she swallowed hard and met his eyes. Hers were wide with unnamed emotions. He knew his were challenging. He wondered if her mouth was as dry as his.

Grady waited for Linette to move.

Eddie wanted to take the pair for a ride. For Grady's sake.

Only, it wasn't the thought of Grady sharing the toboggan with him that made him feel nervous with both anticipation and dread. He knew he would later regret this action, but at the same time figured it was worth whatever price he must pay.

She took a step toward him, her gaze never faltering from his.

He dared not blink for fear the pair would dart away like a couple of shy deer.

She reached his side, shifted her gaze. Pink stained her cheeks as she studied the small space they would have to share. "Come on, Grady." She eased down to the wooden seat and fussed about getting Grady settled.

"Ready?" She fit easily, as he expected she would, her head right at his chin, a familiar scent of flowers teasing his nose. He gave a shove. "We're off." Only, they didn't move.

"We seem to be stuck here." Linette giggled. With the added weight, it took both of them pushing off the snow to get them moving.

"Hang on. Here we go," Eddie said.

The toboggan picked up speed. Grady squealed once then was silent. Eddie wished he could see the boy's face to know if he was excited or scared.

They tilted to the right. The toboggan was harder to control with the others on it and he leaned hard to the left to keep them upright. They shot over a bump and flew off the ground. He couldn't see past Linette's head and had to balance them by feel. They landed on the edge of the toboggan. He threw his weight the other way, but it wasn't enough. They hit the ground, and snow blasted into their faces. They rolled in the snow, a tangle of arms and legs. When they stopped, Linette lay sprawled over his chest. He stared into her snow-dusted face just inches from his, her eyes wide…

"You okay?" he murmured, brushing snow from her face.

"I'm fine." She scooted away. "Grady?"

Eddie sat up and looked around for the boy. He lay spread eagle a few feet away. "Is he hurt?"

They scrambled to their feet and struggled through the snow to him. The boy's eyes were closed, and he shook all over.

"Grady?" Linette dropped to her knees at his side. "Are you hurt?"

Grady's eyes opened. He looked at Linette then darted a glance at Eddie.

Linette examined him with her hands.

But Grady pushed them away. "Fun," he wheezed.

"He's laughing." Eddie stared at the boy. "He's not hurt. He's enjoying this."

Linette sank to her heels. Eddie squatted beside her and they both studied Grady, who giggled.

Linette flopped to the ground and laughed as well.

Eddie shook his head. "You two are crazy."

"Crazy is fun." Linette managed to strangle the words out between giggles.

Amusement tickled his insides and gained momentum. A burst of laughter exploded, releasing something in his heart that had been tight most of his life.

He tried to stop. He almost succeeded, but then he looked at Linette and her giggle triggered an answering laugh from him. Finally he admitted defeat and flopped down in the snow next to her and let the laughter wash through him.

After a few minutes all three of them grew silent but no one moved.

Eddie couldn't say what the others were feeling, but he was relaxed and mellow. Then he grew aware of heat building in his arm, springing from where his elbow brushed against Linette's shoulder. She'd been the cause of him laughing so hard. She had a way of seeing the fun, the possibilities, the positive in every situation. He'd learned to appreciate that.

In his peripheral vision he caught a glimpse of the big house. Margaret's house. He scrambled to his feet and stared at it. He hadn't yet had a reply to his letter to Margaret. But he had no doubt she would agree to come once she heard of the fine place he'd built. He brought his emotions under control. "Grady, do you want to go down again?"

The boy hesitated, sought Linette's opinion.

"I think I'll stay at the bottom of the hill and watch," she said.

Her voice sounded strained. Was it from laughing so hard? Or had she noticed his sudden withdrawal? He wanted to explain, but what could he say? He'd enjoyed the laugh. What's more, he enjoyed her company. But nothing had changed. He still intended that she should leave come spring and he still expected Margaret to join him and become his wife. Surely she understood that. Sometimes a man had to make difficult choices.

Now, if he could only persuade *himself* nothing had changed. In hindsight, he realized things had begun to shift days ago when she had fought off the wolves. Or perhaps earlier when—

It didn't matter when or where or how.

It only mattered that he recognized it and must put a stop to it.

He looked directly at the boy, avoided searching Linette's face, afraid he'd see more than he cared to.

Or perhaps she would see more than he cared her to.

"Grady, if you want to ride down again, you'll have to climb the hill."

Grady hesitated, darted a glance back and forth between the two adults and then plowed up the hill with Eddie at his heels. There was a moment when Eddie wondered if Grady would change his mind about sharing the toboggan for the ride down. But he climbed on in front of Eddie, all the while careful to avoid looking at him.

They rode down the hill without upset and zipped past Linette where she stood waiting for them.

Grady tumbled off the toboggan as they slowed to a stop and ran to Linette, squealing delight. "It's fun. You come again?"

"I think I'll stay here." She bent and hugged Grady. "I'm glad you're having fun." She smiled at Eddie. "The toboggan was a good idea."

He couldn't help noticing her smile didn't reach her eyes. Any more than he could miss the coolness in her voice. "Glad it's working out."

Only, he didn't feel as pleased about Grady's progress as he should.

Linette watched Grady return up the hill with Eddie. The boy was losing his fear of Eddie thanks to Eddie's efforts.

He'd be able to face life with a lot more confidence. Enjoy the fun parts of ranch life rather than clinging to the womenfolk indoors.

The smile curving her mouth at acknowledging these things did not reach her heart.

She'd known from the start she shouldn't get on the toboggan with Eddie. It was far too intimate. His arms about her, the feel of his breath on the side of her face, the tangle of arms as they rolled in the snow…

She swallowed hard against the tightness in her throat.

Freed by the moment, unexpected feelings had surfaced, only for a flash, but long enough for her to picture herself in the big house, filling it with dreams and life and—she gulped—love. Her unguarded eyes had surely revealed the overflow of her heart.

Eddie had read her growing regard for him. He'd jerked away as if stung. He did not return her feelings. Resisted the possibility.

Her insides twisted and she shifted her attention from the pair at the top of the hill. Feelings didn't enter into her plan. She only wanted him to see her as a partner. Capable. Suitable. She expected no less and wanted no more.

There was plenty enough time for the good Lord to change things, make Eddie see that she would make a better wife than Margaret any old day.

She didn't need any silly wishes for more. Such feelings left her vulnerable, uncertain of herself.

She shivered as Grady and Eddie sped past her on their downward journey. They tumbled from the toboggan, laughing together.

Eddie pulled the toboggan to her side.

She kept her gaze on the hilltop. But the sight of the track they'd recently sped down mocked her. Made it impossible to forget that moment in the snow when his eyes flew open and he looked deep into her gaze. His look had slipped past her reservations, past her control, past her pain, straight to a tender, aching spot in her heart that cried silently for his touch.

With the same stubborn determination she'd claimed as she crossed the rugged, unsettled continent, she pushed aside the foolish thought.

The pair climbed the hill. The toboggan raced past her again. Grady's giggles tickled her ears. Eddie had taken the boy from fearful to joyful. He would no longer need Linette to shield him from Eddie. The boy could accompany Eddie to the barn alone.

"I'm going indoors." She started for the cabin.

Grady scrambled after her. "I go with you."

She reached for his hand. Maybe he wasn't quite ready to move on without her. Shouldn't she regret the fact? But she didn't.

Eddie fell in step at her side. "It's a beginning."

A beginning for Grady, but was it the beginning of the end for her? Would she wind up trudging away from the ranch as dejectedly as she left the hill?

Right then and there she vowed she must protect her heart from wayward emotions and keep her eyes on the goal of getting Eddie to agree to a marriage based on rational decisions. She was surely the best woman for the job of being his wife in this appealing frontier.

Feelings did not enter into the situation.

When they reached the cabin, Eddie stayed outside.

"I'll take the toboggan to the barn," he said.

Linette hadn't spoken as they crossed the yard, but she couldn't let him leave without acknowledging her gratitude for what he'd done for Grady. She faced him, her emotions hidden behind solid walls of determination. "Thank you for doing this."

"My pleasure."

She wouldn't read more into the words than a polite response.

"Grady, thank Eddie for the toboggan ride."

The boy hesitated.

Linette nudged Grady to reply.

"Thank you." His words were barely audible.

She realized the boy and man were much alike—hurt by fathers, uncertain about trusting. Perhaps she also shared the similarity. She silently prayed for God's healing for all of them.

Two days later, Eddie bit into a slice of fresh bread. "I could get used to this." She'd learned to make bread that gladdened a man's heart.

Linette grinned. "I could get used to success."

He concentrated on the meal before him. Success. What did that mean to her? Becoming his wife as she had said from their first meeting.

There had been no letters from home yet. Likely a

number waited at Edendale. He and the men had been too busy to ride to town. Plus, the snow continued to build up. But when the letters did arrive, he was certain there'd be a reply from Margaret. She would come. He knew it. After all, he'd built the house to please her. Little did she know he'd taken note of the preferences she'd stated and incorporated many of them into the plans he and his father drew up. Margaret belonged here.

She would sit in the wingback chair near the window as she did needlework or cradled a child. She would serenely tell the cook what to prepare for dinner.

Would she struggle to learn how to cook bacon? Or to learn to bake bread?

Would she exclaim over the view? Want to capture it on canvas? Sketch it?

He shook his head. He would not picture Linette in the room. She simply did not fit. He would not tell her so, but his father never mentioned the Edwards name without getting a sour look on his face, as if he'd bitten into a fresh lemon.

He finished his meal and pushed from the table. But before he could leave the cabin, a call came from outside.

"Hello, the house."

"Company," Cassie announced from the window. "A cowboy."

Eddie reached the door before the man could knock and threw it open. "Clyde, howdy." He shook hands with the cowhand from the OK Ranch. "Everything all right?"

"Dandy as can be. I'm not here looking for help but

to invite you all to a Christmas party next week at the ranch." He glanced beyond Eddie to the womenfolk.

"Come in." Eddie introduced everyone as soon as Clyde shed his heavy winter wear.

"The boss figures this is a chance to get together."

Eddie nodded. "Good idea." He'd plan a similar event when the house was finished.

Clyde had coffee and they shared more conversation. As soon as he departed, Cassie and Linette peppered Eddie with a string of questions about the upcoming party. He couldn't blame them for being excited. They'd not been off the ranch for weeks.

They were ready to go. Linette tried not to wriggle and squeal with anticipation like Grady, but the idea of a party at the neighboring ranch thrilled her. The cowboys sat astride their horses, but Eddie had hitched horses to a wagon to carry the women and Grady. Cookie, Bertie and Cassie crowded together on the back bench. Grady and Linette sat beside Eddie on the front. The air shimmered with excited talk.

This was a chance for her to be with Eddie at a social, fun occasion. She intended to make the most of the opportunity.

Things between them had shifted though she couldn't say if was for the better. On one hand, he seemed to enjoy the evenings they spent together, sometimes with Cassie there, more often with her gone to bed with Grady. They often played chess. Just as often they simply sat and chatted. They liked to talk about the same places they'd visited in England.

"Seems odd we never bumped into each other,"

she'd once said and immediately wished she could suck the words back into her mouth when he grew serious.

"Not so odd, I suppose."

She heard what he didn't say—that his father would never knowingly, willingly cross paths with her father. Knowing she didn't fit into the well-planned life laid out for Eddie seemed an impossible barrier. It was up to her to prove otherwise. Make him see she could be accepted on her own merits. Tonight the social gathering and party atmosphere would hopefully provide a chance for him to see her in a different environment and to appreciate her.

She joined the conversation of the others in the wagon as they made the journey to the OK Ranch, but her mind hummed with possibilities. She'd primed Cassie to mention how well Linette had adjusted. Linette would tell the others how much she liked the country and not one word of it would be false. She fit here and Eddie needed to see it. To admit it.

They arrived at the ranch house—a long, low building alight with candles in every window and along the veranda.

Grady sucked in air and held it. He squirmed forward, reached out as if to touch the glow.

In the low light, Linette's and Eddie's gazes met and held. One thing they shared openly was a desire to make life good for Grady and they smiled at the boy's excitement. The look in Eddie's eyes, the glow in her heart shifted from Grady and Christmas to something beyond reason—a silent hunger she had no wish to acknowledge, much less name.

She tore her gaze away and turned to the open door where a man waited to welcome them.

Roper dismounted from his horse and hurried over to help Cassie down from the wagon. Linette watched the pair out of the corner of her eye. Roper had shown his interest at every opportunity, rushing to greet Cassie when they went to the cookhouse for coffee, escorting her across the yard, asking her to walk with him. He'd visited at the cabin several times both with and without Ward. Cassie was always polite but uninterested. She said she would never belong to another man.

"What happened to your plans to marry so you can have a man's protection?" Linette had asked her.

"I changed my mind. I see now I can make it on my own and I intend to."

Linette had understood and shared the sentiment. But if she didn't belong to Eddie and the ranch, her father would insist she belong to Lyle Williamson. It was a fate worse than imprisonment. At least on the ranch she could do something of value.

"Linette?"

Shaken from her thoughts, she realized Eddie waited to help her down. She sucked in raw air and rested her fingers in his palm. The cold air nipped at her cheeks. Her hands had cooled considerably on the trip, yet heat seared up her arm from his touch. Only nervousness, she informed her confused brain. If they married, touches would be common. She understood that. It did not need to set her heart to fluttering like a handkerchief held out in a brisk wind. Having so informed herself, she concentrated on the magic of the candlelight from the house and withdrew her hand as soon as she stood solidly on her feet.

Eddie waved to indicate they should all proceed to the house.

Linette followed the others, glad of the chance to shift her nervous reaction to excitement, though she was still acutely aware of Eddie beside her.

He led her forward. "This is Sam Stone, owner of the OK Ranch."

Mr. Stone welcomed them into the house. "Merry Christmas."

"Oh," Grady said, his one word full of wonder.

Linette's thoughts echoed his amazement. A huge tree stood in the far corner, adorned with red bows and white candles. Red bows swung from every doorway, every bookshelf. In the midst of the long room a U-shaped table stood draped in white, with a mixture of china dishes. The aroma of roast turkey and cinnamon filled the room. "It's beautiful."

"The credit goes to Miss Amanda Oake, my foreman's sister." He waved the pair forward to be introduced.

Linette immediately liked Amanda. Her eyes were clear and caring, her lips full and merry.

"Thank you. I love Christmas and have planned this for weeks."

Amanda and a shy-looking woman with very dark eyes and black hair were the only women, apart from those from Eden Valley Ranch. Amanda introduced the other woman as Mary, her kitchen helper. Linette guessed her to be Indian or Métis.

They circled the room, meeting and greeting the others, then settled at the table. Eddie held a chair for Linette and she sat at his side. Roper made sure he did likewise for Cassie as she grabbed a place beside Linette. Grady was escorted to the kitchen to join Mary's little brother.

"You could do worse than Roper," Linette whispered to Cassie as she half turned away from Roper.

"You think marriage is an escape, but you don't realize it's only a form of control." Cassie's low whisper was harsh with disapproval.

Linette leaned closer. "Not if you don't give your heart."

Cassie studied Linette a moment, her expression disbelieving. Her gaze shifted past Linette to Eddie and back and her mouth twitched. "No doubt you believe you can achieve that."

"Certainly." She flicked her napkin to her lap. All she had to do was ignore the way her skin itched at his nearness, pretend she didn't jolt when he accidently brushed her elbow, convince herself all she wanted was an escape as Cassie said. "I will not be chained by emotions."

Cassie snorted.

Sam Stone rose to ask the blessing, making impossible any further conversation on the matter.

With Mary's help Amanda served mounds of creamy mashed potatoes, pitchers of succulent gravy, platters of tender turkey and a wide variety of vegetables.

Conversation buzzed around the table. For the most part, the men talked about the weather, the cows and the country until the food had all been placed on the table, then Amanda clapped her hands to get their attention. "Let's talk about Christmas. I want everyone to tell us a favorite memory of the season. I'll begin. I was a teacher at a girls' school and I enjoyed seeing the girls dress in their finest and be on their best behavior. I do believe if they'd acted more like that every day I would not have been so ready to give up my position." She laughed merrily and the others joined in.

She turned to the cowboy next to her.

He spoke in a soft voice, as if his memories were sweet. "I remember plum pudding and roast goose."

One by one, others shared memories. Then it was Roper's turn. "I grew up in an orphanage, so we didn't do anything very special, but every year some kind benefactor gave us each an orange for Christmas. Nothing has ever tasted better."

Linette nudged Cassie. "There. Don't you feel sorry for him?" she whispered. "He needs a family. You need a family."

Cassie gave her a dismissive glance before she turned to tell about the last Christmas before her husband died. "We lived in a little rental house. George had a job in a mill. I knit him a sweater that fit him perfectly. We didn't have much, but we were content."

The table was silent a moment at the knowledge of what she'd had and lost.

Then it was Linette's turn. She had to scramble to find a good memory. She'd allowed the later years to eat up those earlier pleasant times. "I remember the year my father took me out to see the stars on Christmas Eve. It was marvelous." Her voice caught and she nodded that she'd finished.

Eddie found her hand beneath the table and squeezed.

No doubt he thought she was homesick, but she was thinking how she'd felt special that night when her father took her in his arms and lifted her toward the sky.

Eddie began to speak and she slipped her hand away.

"I believe my favorite memory would have to be

the year all four of my grandparents were with us. My eldest sister was a baby and the house rang with happiness." His voice ended suddenly.

Linette ducked her head lest anyone see the pain in her eyes as she wondered if Eddie thought the joy in the home was over a child belonging to both his parents—a joy that would never be extended to him. For a heartbeat she ached to reach out and squeeze his hand in sympathy and understanding, but she must guard her reactions to him. Seemed both her body and her heart had wills of their own.

She clasped her fingers into a tight knot and didn't move.

They devoured mounds of food then Mary brought in plum pudding and mince pie to cheers of appreciation.

"It's so nice to enjoy food I didn't prepare," Cookie said for the sixth time. "Besides, my food can't hold a flicker to this. You are an excellent cook, Amanda."

"Hear. Hear." Sam lifted his glass in a toast.

The whole crowd voiced their approval.

Amanda nodded serenely. "I had lots of help."

One by one the ladies finished and pushed their plates away. The men accepted seconds and some thirds of dessert.

Amanda shoved her chair back to signal the meal was over. "Let's move to one side while the table is removed." She signaled to the OK men who whisked the table away and arranged the chairs in a circle around the room.

Linette saw the expression of anticipation on Amanda's face and wondered what she had in store.

Amanda waited until everyone found a place to sit.

"One of my favorite memories is when we played parlor games. So please help me in re-creating my fun time."

A murmur of protest came from many of the cowboys.

Linette kept her eyes lowered, not wanting to hurt Amanda's feelings, but she didn't want to play games. In her experience they often provided a chance to mock someone, usually her because she had dreams that, in her parents' opinion, exceeded possibilities.

Only a marriage based on mutual benefit would allow her to achieve even a fraction of the things she dreamed of. Yet, she feared she could easily forget she wanted nothing more than a business deal.

Amanda good naturedly ignored the protests and divided the group to play charades. The cowboys were good sports and let her forge ahead.

To Linette's relief the acting was humorous and any mocking was directed toward one's self. She could handle this. It was her turn. She unfolded the scrap of paper and silently read the words: "What Child Is This?" Too bad Grady was still in the kitchen. She could have used him as a prop. She stood and faced the others, cradled her arms and swayed as if rocking a baby.

"Baby?" Eddie guessed.

She nodded, smiling encouragement at him.

His gaze locked on hers. She couldn't pull away. If they married, would there be babies? Sweet little boys with dark eyes and dark hair. Precious girls with intelligence and spirit. If she had daughters she could encourage self-sufficiency and independence just as she was sure Eddie would encourage the same in sons.

Sons and daughters. Her tongue stuck to the roof of her mouth. She tried unsuccessfully to swallow.

"Baby?" Cassie prompted. "Baby Jesus?"

Linette jerked her attention to the other woman and shook her head. She made a motion as if playing the piano.

"Lullaby?" Eddie said.

Again their gazes collided. It took all her reserves of strength to jerk away. She made a questioning gesture and expression. Cassie guessed the name of the song and Linette gratefully returned to her seat, her ears burning with something more than embarrassment. She could not—would not—allow herself to think of being held, kissed, cherished by Eddie. His heart belonged elsewhere. She understood that. She didn't mind. She didn't want his heart. Only his name and a rightful place in his home.

Margaret would hate it here. She'd made as much clear to Linette. That freed Linette to pursue a marriage without love.

Exactly what she wanted.

The rest of the evening passed in a blur. She watched the proceedings without taking part any more than she must to keep anyone from commenting.

Then finally Eddie announced it was time to leave, signaling a sudden rush of goodbyes.

Linette had been quiet much of the evening. Eddie watched her out of the corner of his eye as they headed home. Had someone said something to hurt her? Had the holiday memories made her homesick?

Homesick was good. It could well provide the impetus for her to abandon this marriage idea and return home. But it felt so wrong. He wanted to hold her and comfort her.

They arrived back at the ranch and he asked Roper to take the wagon for him. "Cassie, would you take Grady? I'd like to show Linette something."

Cassie took the boy and ducked into the cabin.

"I should—"

He'd anticipated Linette's argument. "It's a lovely night. So clear."

She turned to study the sky. "It's beautiful."

"You should see it at the top of the hill." It was too dark for him to guess at her reaction. "Let me show you."

She nodded and he turned toward the path. She stumbled and he caught her elbow. He tucked her hand through his arm and felt her stiffen. There was a constraint between them he couldn't explain, any more than he could explain why he cared. Except he did. So much he wanted to stop right here in the dark and figure it out.

Instead, he led her across the bridge, past the pens and up the hill.

She dropped his arm as they reached the top and tilted her head upward. "It's beautiful. I feel like I could reach out and pluck handfuls of stars from the sky."

"Me, too." And if he could, he would fashion them into a necklace and hang them around her neck. It hit him like a blow to the head.

He had begun to care for her.

He took a step backward. When had this happened? When she'd made bread? Or when she had failed at her attempt? When she'd sketched a picture of the ranch for him? Or when he'd noticed the paintings she'd hung on the walls and realized she was the artist? It had happened slowly but surely from the first day when she'd stepped from the stagecoach with the expectation of becoming his wife.

She *would* make a great ranch wife. At the acknowledgment his heart plopped to the bottom of his boots. Except for one thing—he'd asked Margaret to reconsider. And until he heard from her, he wasn't free to speak of his feelings to Linette.

She sighed and faced him. "Thank you for bringing me here."

"I thought you might enjoy it. Thought it might remind you of happy times at home." He wanted to cheer her up. "You seemed a little unhappy at the party. Is something wrong?"

"Not at all. I suppose it was a little overwhelming. But didn't Amanda do a great job?"

"Indeed." He waited, knowing there was more to her quietness all evening, hoping she would tell him. "Linette." He touched her shoulder. "If there is anything wrong, I hope you would feel free to tell me. Would you?"

She kept her head downturned. "Of course."

Her answer came too quickly. He touched her chin and lifted her face to the starlight. Stepped closer so he could read her expression. Her mouth trembled. She seemed so sad his heart gave a vicious kick to his rib cage and he caught her with both arms and drew her closer. He studied her for a fleeting second then caught her trembling lips with his and steadied them with a kiss.

She gasped and pulled away.

He was as shocked by his actions as she. He backed up and scrubbed at his chin. "I'm sorry. I didn't mean that to happen. I just wanted to make you feel better."

She turned to stare down at the ranch where lights flickered in the cabin, the cookhouse and the bunkhouse. "It's me who should apologize. If we're to be married I expect we would kiss." She made it sound like bitter medicine.

"Seeing as that's not in my plans, my apology is even more heartfelt." He regretted that fact a thousand times more than the kiss, but as a man of honor he must stand by his word and his offer of marriage to Margaret. A Gardiner was, above all, honorable. "I'll see you to the cabin."

She managed her way down the hill without accepting his help. He left her at the door. "I have to make sure the horses are okay." The others would have seen to it, but he couldn't enter the cabin right now. Her presence was too close.

Chapter Thirteen

Linette prayed for sleep to block out her foolishness.

She'd seen his kiss coming. Had enough time to duck away. But she'd let him kiss her. It was true, if they married they would kiss. She'd wanted to know how it felt. Told herself she could keep her heart under lock and key.

But her good intentions had proven useless.

She pressed her fingertips to her lips. How could such a simple touch ignite such depth of longing? She pushed aside the feelings and questions. She only wanted to marry Eddie to escape her father's plans. At the same time she'd keep her heart intact so she could follow its dictates.

Lord, help me. Give me a secure heart. Keep me anchored in Your love. I need no more. I am safe in Your hands. Keep me strong.

A thought came to her mind. Why was she fretting so? Eddie made it clear he hadn't changed his mind. Oh, what a tangled mess she was in. Wanting to marry Eddie. Not wanting to love him. It seemed so simple at the start, but with each passing day she was discovering how complicated it was.

How could she ensure her emotional safety?

The next morning, Eddie was gone when she got up. He returned a little later for breakfast. Linette's gaze was drawn to him under cover of her lashes. He seemed unchanged by the kiss.

"The party last night made me realize I'm unprepared for Christmas," he said. "It looks like the weather will hold, so I'm going to Edendale to get some things. Anything you ladies need?"

Linette glanced at Cassie. Neither of them had any money. She'd given the last of her funds to the Indian lad on her way to the ranch. But she had supplies in her trunk. "We're fine."

When he left a few minutes later she watched him ride from the yard. Would he return with letters from home? One from Margaret saying the news of the big house convinced her to change her mind?

Even if such a letter came she still had until spring. God could work many a miracle in that time. Even in the heart of a man.

"I'm going over to see Cookie," Cassie said.

"Go ahead. I have a few things to do here."

"You want to come, Grady?" Cassie asked the boy.

"See Cookie?"

"Certainly."

The pair left. Linette hurried to her trunk and pulled out the shawl she had begun crocheting for Cassie. She lacked the skill Cassie had at knitting, so had tried this instead.

She glanced at the other gifts she planned to complete in time for Christmas. Time was drawing short, so she worked on them till suppertime.

That evening Eddie came home after dark.

His hands were full of mysterious parcels when he entered the cabin. Linette waited to see if he offered mail.

"No mail has come through for several weeks. The roads are blocked by snow," he said in response to her silent question.

Relief flooded through her. A reprieve again. "Can we get a Christmas tree?"

He glanced about. "It would take up most of the room here."

"Maybe we could set up one at the cookhouse."

"I like that idea. Let's take Grady tomorrow and find a tree."

They set out right after breakfast, riding in the wagon. Linette could have refused to accompany him, but it would rob Grady of the experience. She had only one goal in mind—make Christmas enjoyable, thus proving in one more direction her capability and suitability as a pioneer wife. No, she mentally corrected, she had two goals. She also wanted to prove to herself that she could enjoy an outing with the man she hoped to marry without her emotions running awry. It should be easy with little Grady sitting on the wagon seat between them.

"First time," Eddie said.

She jerked about to face him, startled and confused by his words. "First time?"

Smiling, he tipped his head to indicate Grady perched between them and she understood his meaning. It was the first time Grady had sat beside Eddie without showing some nervousness. Instead, he leaned forward, anxious to find the perfect Christmas tree.

Linette grinned widely at Eddie, as pleased by Grady's progress as he and equally pleased to silently share the pleasure of the moment with Eddie. It made her feel as if they shared something special.

She sucked in air and turned to face forward as they headed past the barn and outbuildings up a trail toward the trees. She'd have to work much harder at keeping her emotions tucked away. But she was determined to do it. Linette Edwards could do anything she set her mind to.

"We get a tree here?" Grady pointed toward the first spruce they saw.

"We'll go a little farther," Eddie said. "If you think you can wait."

Grady edged back marginally. "Not too long?"

Linette laughed, her gaze drawn relentlessly toward Eddie. He laughed, too, and her pleasure deepened.

All because of the boy, she insisted, and turned her attention back to Grady. "Do you remember having a Christmas tree before?"

He nodded vigorously and turned his bright blue eyes toward her. "Mama take me to see Gramma and Gramps. They gots the biggest tree ever."

Eddie groaned. "The biggest tree ever?"

Grady nodded some more.

"How are we going to best that?"

Grady studied him a moment. Linette couldn't see the boy's expression but read tenderness and humor in Eddie's.

"It not have to be the biggest tree," Grady allowed.

"That's a relief." Eddie made a show of wiping worry from his brow.

His teasing brought a chuckle from Linette and their gazes collided with such force her lungs forgot to work.

She might have remained trapped if the wagon hadn't bounced. Perhaps it was best not to look directly at him until she figured out how to tame her wayward emotions. So she forced herself to keep her attention on the passing scenery. Not difficult except for the way his voice called to her as he talked about all the places up this trail he'd visited.

"A waterfall. Rushing rivers. And you should see the cows grazing in green valleys. It's a beautiful country."

"It certainly is." Almost beautiful enough to hold her attention.

"This looks like a good place." Eddie pulled the wagon to a halt and jumped down. Grady allowed Eddie to lift him to the ground. Linette would have gotten down by herself, but there was no graceful way to do it, so she took his hand and accepted his assistance.

Grady looked about. "Big trees." His words were spoken with awe.

"Bigger than the tree you had before?" Eddie asked.

Grady started to nod then stopped. "Maybe."

Eddie chuckled. "We won't cut down one that's too big to get into the cookhouse. Cookie might not like it if we push her out in the cold."

Grady giggled. "She whack you."

Linette laughed out loud. Eddie laughed, too, and their gazes caught and held. She couldn't help it. Nor did she regret it. The man had a nice laugh and when he smiled, his whole face appeared wreathed in sweetness. Oh, my. She was not doing well at teaching her emotions submission. Thankfully, Grady demanded Eddie's attention and the pair headed for the woods in search of the perfect tree.

"You coming?" Eddie called.

"The snow looks awfully deep. I think I'll wait here."

"Okay." He turned back to Grady. "You follow in my footsteps so you don't disappear in a snowbank."

"Okay." And with complete trust and confidence he tromped after Eddie, who broke a trail the boy could follow.

Follow in my footsteps.

The words of a father to a son. *Oh, Lord, give this dear boy his father.* She'd left her address with Grady's father and instructions to contact her when he changed his mind. Perhaps the next mail delivery would include word from him.

In the meantime, Grady was learning to trust men and had a good example to follow in Eddie.

They went only a few feet and stopped. Slowly they circled a tree, looking it over with great concentration. Then they had a serious talk. Linette couldn't hear what they said, but there was a lot of head nodding. Then Eddie signaled for Grady to stand back, and with solid blows, he used his ax on the tree. It swayed and swished down. It took the combined efforts of a man and a little boy to drag it to the wagon. Linette allowed them to do it by themselves. She enjoyed watching them together too much to offer help.

The tree safely in the wagon, Eddie lifted Grady back to the seat then turned to Linette.

"Didn't expect you to let the men do all the work."

She could tell from his tone that he teased. "I was doing my share."

He drew back to stare at her. "How?"

She cocked her head to one side as if it should be obvious. "I was enjoying the entertainment."

He hooted and slapped his thigh. "So this was all for your amusement?"

"Absolutely. Didn't you know it?"

The way he looked at her felt like the sun warming her skin. "I do now. Happy to be of service." He touched the brim of his hat then held out his hand to help her onto the wagon seat. He whistled as he went to his place and took the reins. Every few minutes on the trip back he chuckled for no apparent reason and looked at her with laughter in his eyes.

Linette felt vastly pleased with herself that she'd made him laugh.

All too soon they arrived back at the ranch and he pulled up to the cookhouse.

Slim and Blue hustled toward them and helped carry the tree inside. It was soon standing in the corner of the dining room.

Cookie sighed. "It's just like home."

From the expression on the faces of the cowboys gathering in the room, Linette guessed they all agreed.

This was her chance to prove her abilities. "Who has decorations?"

Cookie nodded. "I have a few things."

Linette looked around at the others. "Everyone bring something and we'll decorate the tree right after lunch."

"What can I bring?" Grady whispered.

"We'll find something."

"Ma'am," Slim said. "What do you have in mind?"

She guessed they didn't have any fine ornaments, but she'd noticed how they often slipped a bright feather into their hatbands and she'd seen the colorful saddle blankets many of them used. She pointed it out to them. "Anything like that." It would take time to create things, so they agreed to meet and decorate the tree midafternoon.

Three hours later they again gathered in the cookhouse.

Grady wanted to be first. Linette had helped him color Christmas shapes on pages from her sketch pad then cut them out and put yarn hangers on them.

The cowboys had been very creative. Ward had a collection of feathers he tied to the tree. Slim had managed to tie bright threads from a blanket into bows. There were bits of ribbon and other assorted things. Cookie had six bright red Christmas balls. Linette added the ribbons she'd crocheted. Cassie had fashioned bits of colored paper into beads and hung them in clusters.

Only one person remained to contribute—Eddie— and everyone turned to him. He had something hidden beneath a wrap and now revealed it. "An angel for the top. I found it in the crate Mother sent."

Linette began to think that container held everything a person might want.

"Grady, you can help me put the angel on top." Eddie lifted the boy, and the two of them perched the angel on the uppermost branch.

They all stood back and admired the tree.

"We should celebrate with tea and cake," Cookie said.

No one argued.

Later that evening, after Grady and Cassie had retired to the bedroom, Linette and Eddie sat by the stove. She thought of suggesting they play chess, but neither of them seemed inclined to stir.

"You've made us all look forward to Christmas this year." He seemed to approve of her efforts. "Thank you."

"Being out in the West doesn't mean we shouldn't enjoy the season."

"I guess it takes a woman to plan it though." He shifted to consider her. "Not everyone would think to include the cowboys, too."

She nodded and caught a thrill of victory to her heart. "I'm not like everyone else."

"So I'm learning." He grinned. "Though you made it pretty obvious from the start." His eyes twinkled. "Every time I see you in the big overcoat I am reminded. As if I need reminding. I don't think you'll ever give me a chance to forget."

She tried to think how to respond. How to make him see that women didn't have to live in the constricting molds from the old country.

Eddie lay on his bedroll. Today was Christmas—a day full of promise and possibility. He stared up at the still-dark ceiling and let his thoughts fill with pleasant prospects.

Grady rushed from the bedroom. "Get up. There's presents."

When Eddie didn't move, Grady yelled, "Get up. Get up."

Eddie grabbed the boy and tickled him. Grady was

so excited about Christmas and gifts he didn't protest but squealed with laughter.

Linette stepped into the room, saw Eddie wrestling with the boy and laughed. She met Eddie's gaze and her smile crept into the bottom of his heart.

What was this strange feeling? Admiration? Certainly. Friendship? He hoped so and hoped it was mutual, though she seemed skittish around him as if she was afraid. Which made not one lick of sense. He'd never seen Linette afraid. Not even when they were attacked by wolves. His smile deepened as he thought how brave she'd been. If only he hadn't written Margaret and again offered her marriage. But he had and he would honor his word as he must.

Grady squirmed free and bolted to Linette's side. "Let's eat. Hurry."

Again Eddie's gaze caught Linette's. They smiled at Grady's excitement. The air crackled with something more. She must have felt it, too, because she jerked toward the stove. Did it frighten her? Or entice?

Cassie joined the others at the breakfast table. Grady's excitement spread to all of them and they rushed through the meal, took only a few minutes to clean up then hurry across to the cookhouse.

All the cowboys gathered in the big room, dressed in their finest. Eddie wished he could take a picture of them staring at the decorated tree. A pile of gifts rested beneath the green boughs.

Cookie handed them each a cup of spicy tea mixture as they headed for the tree. All eyes turned to him. He was in charge.

He looked around the group. They were family now. And they accepted him. To them he was Eddie Gardiner, not the adopted, illegitimate son. He sucked in air to smooth the roughness in his throat. "I hope you don't see me as simply your boss, because we're family. Some of us have relatives in distant parts of the world. Most of them have no idea what our lives are like now. But we understand the demands of this new world. We know the necessity of working together, helping each other through the difficult spots. To each of you, Merry Christmas." He held his cup up in a toast and the others joined him. There was a clink of china against china and a chorus of "Merry Christmas."

"Now, who gets the first present?"

Grady's face almost disappeared in his big eyes.

"Grady?"

The boy nodded.

"Let's see what we can find." Eddie reached under the tree and pulled out the gift he'd made—a small wooden horse and a wagon for it to pull.

Grady tore the paper from the gift and yelled his approval.

Everyone laughed.

Eddie passed around gifts. Cassie and Linette had managed to make scarves for all the men. Cookie had made each a selection of candy. Grady got more carved animals from the men and a beautifully illustrated picture book made by Linette. The men had made each of the women a writing tray to hold their paper and correspondence.

Eddie pulled an unwrapped present from behind the tree and gave it to Linette.

"An easel," she said on an exhaled breath.

He couldn't tell if she was surprised or pleased. "I thought you might like to do some painting."

Her gaze burrowed deep into his. Was she remembering the afternoon she'd sketched a picture for him? Was she wondering if he considered her talent a silly pastime unsuitable for a pioneer woman? "This country is so pretty. I've often wished I could take a picture, but a painting is even better."

"Thank you." Her eyes darkened before she handed him a package.

He folded back the brown paper to reveal two pictures of the house on the hill drawn at different times of the day.

"Ward made the frames," she told him.

"Thank you. I'll hang them in the new house."

The air between them was heavy. With longing and dreams? No. He jerked away. She had only one purpose in mind—marry to avoid her father's despicable plans for her. And he had his offer to Margaret to honor. All they shared was the moment.

Winter set in for real after Christmas. Snow came in blankets then disappeared in a warm Chinook. The temperature fluctuated. On warmer days Eddie continued work on the house, grateful for Linette's company and help. There was something isolating about being alone in the house. On colder days he made sure the cows were taken care of, fed the horses then stayed indoors, often playing with Grady as the women sewed and cooked. The place was warm and cozy and despite the crowded conditions no one complained.

But he liked evenings best. Cassie normally retired to the bedroom with Grady leaving Linette and Eddie to themselves.

Sometimes Linette painted, but after a few minutes would step back. "The light is too poor."

He didn't say much. He enjoyed watching her but knew it would make her uncomfortable if he said so. She viewed her painting as useless and would seldom paint in the daytime, saying there was work to do.

But whatever they did, they talked. He learned more about her home life. How her parents insisted on forcing her into a mold of their shaping.

"I wanted to join a mission and help the homeless and ill." Her half laugh, half snort held self-mockery. "You can imagine my parents' reaction to that. They threatened to put me under lock and key."

"It still surprises me they allowed you to come here." He couldn't imagine the place without her now. Her presence made winter enjoyable.

She lowered her gaze. The air seemed heavy and he wondered if another snow was about to descend, but the sky was clear. The heaviness came from her. "There's only one way I can escape my father's plans."

She expected him to be her means of escape. For her sake, he wished he could be. But he couldn't. Besides, what man wanted to be only a way to avoid an unpleasant fate? He changed the subject to ask about her brother. They both found talking about their siblings a pleasant topic.

They often discussed their faith and would spend time together searching out scriptures in his Bible. He came to look forward to those times, finding himself both challenged and encouraged by the depth of her faith in God's love and the extent of her knowledge of God's word. "My nurse taught me well. From her I learned to find answers to life's problems in God's word. No matter what, I know God's love is sufficient."

He realized he did not have the same rock-solid assurance she claimed. But over the winter months with Linette he found his faith growing like a spring garden warmed by the sun and watered by a gentle rain.

He told her much, too. About the things he'd faced as he'd started a ranch in the virgin land of northwest Canada. "I had to decide the best place for the buildings. I had to select the grazing land. Then there were Indians, wild animals and wolves to deal with. And no guidebook to show the way."

"God guided you."

"Seems He must have."

She tipped her head and studied him.

He wanted to escape her probing gaze but wouldn't allow himself to be a coward. Whatever she saw, whatever she measured, he was man enough to accept it.

"Your father would be proud. And rightly so. You have succeeded beyond what most have. Your ranch is solid. The animals are doing well. The men look up to you, trust you."

Her approval was honest, open. It watered his soul. "I hope my father sees it the same way."

One afternoon, he glanced up at the approach of a horse. One of the men from OK Ranch rode into the yard. "Got your mail." He handed him a bundle.

Eddie thanked him. He'd been pretending the roads were too muddy for a trip to town, but now the inevitable had come. Spring was here. He could no longer delay sending Linette back. It had been the plan from the beginning.

He flipped through the letters. He didn't see one from Margaret and sighed in relief. It only meant postponement.

He'd been playing a game of make-believe in order

to see Linette in the cabin, to look forward to spending time with her, to picture her as the woman in the big house. But he wasn't a child controlled by pretend. It was time to stop playing and return to serious business.

He strode toward the cabin to deliver the three letters for Linette, all from the same return address but in different handwriting. No doubt each member of her family had written with news.

"Mail," he called as he stepped into the cabin.

She spun to face him, her mouth drooping as if reality had caught her by surprise as well.

If only they could stop time. Enjoy a few more days…weeks…months. But how long would be long enough? He was only avoiding fate.

He handed her the letters addressed to her and sat down to read the rest. There was a letter from an acquaintance wanting to come West and wondering if he might visit Eddie until he found a place of his own.

Jayne had written a letter full of wedding plans. She expected Eddie to return for the event though she still didn't give a date. He folded the pages and returned them to the envelope. Then he could find no more excuse for avoiding the letter from his father.

He slit it open and read words that made him feel as if he'd failed again. Instructions on caring for the cows. As if Eddie hadn't done so successfully for two years. Directions for every aspect of the house. Eddie had managed quite well without his father's supervision, though his father would no doubt wonder how it was possible. *I understand you are living like so many of the Northwest we hear about, ignoring legal and moral obligations and being consumed by the flesh.*

Furthermore, I hear you are still living in a cabin fit for a trapper but not a Gardiner. He effectively made it clear the Gardiners held up a standard Eddie never quite achieved. *Mr. Edwards has expressed his shock that his daughter should be treated in such a fashion. He is threatening to take legal action against the Gardiners. He says he expects certain benefits in compensation even if you marry his daughter. I warn you, nothing good will come of this. Get rid of that woman immediately. Wash your hands of her.*

He turned the page over. Nothing had been said of Margaret. Did she intend to come? Was he expected to return to London to marry her?

He bolted to his feet. "I'll be back later." He strode up the hill so quickly his heart pounded by the time he reached the house.

Linette barely heard Eddie leave as she read her father's letter. It was full of threats. *I expect documentation about your marriage by return mail or I shall take severe action toward the Gardiners. I have it in my power to destroy them utterly and completely.*

Little did he know that Linette would be returning without proof of marriage. Returning to her father's plans. She could only hope Lyle Williamson would find more suitable prey before she reached home.

She'd failed. Yes, she'd gained Eddie's respect for her as a suitable ranch wife. But not his offer of marriage. Now it seemed the best thing she could do was return home and deflect her father's intention of destroying Eddie's good name.

She'd prayed all winter for things to change.

They hadn't.

She must accept God had another plan for her. Perhaps like Esther of the Bible, she had something noble to achieve by accepting her father's will. *Oh, Lord, I submit to Your will but please, please may it be something other than marrying a man I despise.*

She glanced out the window as a horse rode by. It was Eddie headed toward the mountains. How long before he escorted her to town and saw her on the stagecoach back toward London?

The sun shone brightly and she headed outside. She ached to store up a well of memories of this place and this time. She wandered through the yards, paused to breathe in the sweet scent of the budding trees, then climbed the hill where she and Eddie had once tobogganed with Grady. She drank in the sight of the majestic mountains.

There was only one thing she would beg for and that was that Grady be allowed to stay with Cookie and Bertie. They would provide him with a loving home. She would take him with her except she knew her father would turn him out on the street as soon as she stepped into the house. Lyle Williamson would offer no more or she might view the marriage differently.

Cassie would likely be content to continue as Linette's maid at least until they were back in the old country.

For some time she sat there praying and planning. Then she returned to the cabin and prepared a meal.

Cassie and Grady returned from the cookhouse. But Eddie did not come in. "We'll go ahead and have supper without him," she said after a considerable time.

Had he decided not to join them? Or had he encountered difficulty in the hills? The men would surely know if they needed to go after him.

She tried to comfort herself with that knowledge, but as darkness fell and he still didn't return she pressed to the window, praying for a glimpse of him. She couldn't say how long she stayed there, only that her legs hurt from standing, her eyes ached from staring into the dark. Rain spattered the window and she shivered. *Lord, bring him home safely. Please.*

A noise outside the door drew her from the window. Eddie burst in, tossed his dripping Stetson to the hook and shed his wet coat. A puddle circled his feet.

She grabbed a towel and rushed to help him. "You're soaked."

"I'm fine." He took the towel and wiped his face.

"I'll make tea. I saved supper for you."

"I'm hungry."

She warmed the food, boiled water for tea and served him.

He thanked her and ate and drank in silence. Finished, he pushed his plate away. "Thank you. Now, if you don't mind, I'm tired."

Her cheeks stung at the way he dismissed her. She'd hoped he'd say where he'd been, but at least he hadn't told her to pack up for her return home. She gladly accepted the reprieve and ducked into the bedroom.

Eddie longed for her to stay. But he knew it was best if she left.

Unable to stop thinking about the letter from his father, he had left right after breakfast. He rode from the yard. The grass was greening in the lower pastures but the higher elevations would still be snow-covered. He didn't need to check them to know it.

He had to think. Sort out this confusion twisting his brain into a knot.

His direction took him away from the ranch. He'd ridden a few miles then reined in and studied the landscape. Wild. Open. Great for cattle if a man learned to work with the land instead of against it. He'd learned quickly he couldn't do things the same way they'd been done in the old country.

He turned his horse about and stared at the mountains.

Majestic. Bold. Unmovable. Unshaken by storms, by snow, by heat or cold.

I will lift up mine eyes unto the hills, from whence cometh my help. My help cometh from the Lord, which made heaven and earth.

Easily that passage came to mind. He and Linette had discussed it during the winter.

"God led me," she'd said, referring to her trip west. "I called to Him and He answered me and delivered me from all my fears."

Did she still believe God had delivered her now that spring was here and he had the onerous task of informing her she would have to leave?

He'd dropped from the horse, took the reins and walked. Over and over he'd informed himself it was time to tell her.

It had started to rain. But he'd stayed out rather than have to return and confront her.

He didn't want to tell her to leave. He didn't want to send her away.

But he'd asked Margaret to marry him.

The fact that she hadn't replied made him wonder how successful he'd been at convincing her. Perhaps he could write and retract his offer before she decided to come.

He stared at the mountains. Something about them made it impossible to avoid the truth.

It wasn't only because of his offer to Margaret that he hesitated. His father didn't like Mr. Edwards. His father had instructed Eddie to send Linette home. Actually he probably didn't care where Eddie sent her so long as it got her out of the Gardiner sphere.

Eddie had been trying all his life to live up to the expectations of that name. Would he ever succeed?

"Your father would be proud." "You've done a good job." "You're a good leader." Words he longed to hear, but they hadn't come from his father.

They'd come from Linette.

Linette who faced challenges fearlessly. Who played a sharp game of chess. Who painted and drew pictures that stirred his emotions.

Linette who showed kindness to all regardless of race and station in life.

He didn't need to prove anything to her. She accepted him as he was, not because he was the son of Randolph Gardiner. Her approval was honest, open, free.

Why would he send her away and lose all that?

Morning came and he still couldn't think clearly. He hurried from the cabin and saddled his horse. He meant to ride hard and far, but instead headed for the big house, approaching from the hillside so no one would note him. He strode into the house and went immediately to the windows overlooking the ranch.

He belonged here, was part of the developing country.

All his life he had worked for what he had here.

He knew who he was. Not a Gardiner by birth, but that no longer mattered. He was Eddie Gardiner, the man who built Eden Valley Ranch. The man who ran it successfully.

More than that, he was a man loved by God. Accepted by the One who created the mountains and plains. It was time he was honest to the depth of his soul. Here, in the wilds of northwest Canada, he had found acceptance such as he'd never before known.

One time he'd kissed Linette. One time only. But that one fleeting touch had been the most honest moment of his life.

He loved her. He wanted to share his life with her. He wanted to fill this house with a family they'd have together.

With every honest breath, his heart beat harder, more insistently.

He had one thing to do before he could ask her.

He must write Margaret and withdraw his offer then write his father and inform him he intended to follow his heart.

If that meant he had to give up running the ranch... well, so be it. With Linette at his side, he would start somewhere else.

His mind made up, he returned to his horse, rode to the barn, took care of his mount then hurried to the cabin and gathered up pen, ink and paper. The cabin was empty. He climbed the hill to the house and sat down to write two letters.

Before he began, he bowed his head and asked the Lord to guide him then he let honest words flow to the paper.

Finished, he sealed the letters and marched back down the hill. He found Slim and sent him to town with the missives.

Now to pick the right time to tell Linette of his decision.

It took determination to wait until after supper. "Linette, come for a walk."

She stopped, her hands clutching the pot she dried, sucked in air and tucked in her chin. "Of course." She put the pot on the shelf, removed her apron and hung it carefully on a nail by the washstand then reached for her heavy coat.

"It's warm out. Your shawl will be enough."

She rehung the coat and took her knitted shawl instead.

He held the door for her and fell in step beside her. He lifted an arm, wanting to pull her to his side, but she hurried ahead.

They passed the barn, crossed the bridge and went beyond the pens, up the hill to a spot they'd visited before. He knew she would welcome his offer. Hadn't she come for the very purpose of marriage to him?

He caught her hand and pulled her to a halt beneath the aspens heavy with the scent of spring buds. The sun was nearing the horizon. He turned her to watch the sunset—flares and ribbons of mauve and pink, purple and orange filling the western sky. And then the sun dipped out of sight, leaving the sky orange in its wake.

"It's so beautiful," she whispered.

He rested his hands on her shoulders and watched a moment longer. Then he slowly turned her to face him.

Her smile slid sideways and vanished.

He touched her cheek. "Don't look so afraid."

She lifted her chin and faced him. "I'm not afraid."

"I'm not about to tell you I'm going to send you home."

Her chin dropped hard. "You're not?"

"Linette, I want to marry you."

She blinked. "Really?"

He had so much to say but the words stopped halfway up his throat. "Not just because you've proved you would make a good ranch wife. I want you to stay. I want you to be part of my life."

The uncertain, surprised look in her face made him realize he was doing a poor job of saying what his heart felt.

"Linette." He took her upper arms in his hands and bent closer. "I love you. I want to share my life, my dreams, my heart with you."

She splayed trembling fingers over her chest. She looked so vulnerable. So uncertain.

Had he surprised her so much with his confession of love? "I know you look at marriage only as an escape. You weren't expecting an offer of love. Maybe you don't even welcome it. But it doesn't matter. I love you. And if you can't love me back, it's okay. I'll still love you." He hoped somewhere inside her lay a tender feeling toward him. He prayed there was a tiny seed of sweet regard that, with nourishment, would someday grow into love. He intended to provide the nourishment.

Giving her time to refuse, rejoicing when she didn't, he caught her mouth with his own, letting his kiss say all the things he felt, hoping, trusting she heard his silent promises. He lifted his head, smiled at the confusion in her eyes. "You will marry me?"

She nodded. "I told you you'd change your mind."

Chapter Fourteen

Linette's breath stuck halfway up her throat.

He'd offered marriage. Exactly what she wanted. But he'd offered more than she bargained for. His heart.

She couldn't decide what to think except it frightened her. She hadn't expected love. Didn't know if she was prepared for it. Love meant so much more than a marriage of convenience. It meant relinquishing her dreams in deference to his plans.

But in return, she'd get his devotion. The thought reached into her heart and squeezed it, flooding her veins with a combination of anticipation and caution.

"What about Margaret?"

"Let's sit."

They sat on the crest of the hill as the light faded from the sky.

"I wrote Margaret and my father, informing them of my choice." Eddie's laugh carried a note of regret and he took her hand between his. "Father suggested you might not be suitable to become a Gardiner."

"I guessed as much."

"Sorry. Remember my father isn't sure *I* am suitable to be a Gardiner."

Her defense on her own behalf died. "I can't imagine always feeling the need to prove yourself. Besides, he is so wrong. He needs to visit and see for himself how well you've done."

"He'd only see what he wanted to see." His expression brightened. "But I came to a conclusion this afternoon. I know who I am. God made me and He's in charge."

"Amen. He holds you in His hand and directs your steps."

"Like a good shepherd."

She laughed. How often had they discussed the Twenty-third Psalm over the winter months, considering the differences between raising sheep and cattle?

But what would Eddie do if his father forbade their marriage?

"How soon can we be married?" he asked.

She hesitated but a second. "As soon as possible, I suppose."

They talked about how their marriage would change things.

"What about Grady?"

"He'll live with us in the big house."

His ready answer gave her the strength to dismiss her fears.

They didn't return to the house until late. At the door, she stopped. Did they kiss again? What were his expectations?

As if he'd read her mind, he gently turned her into his arms, allowing mere inches to separate them. "I'm willing to do things your way. Whatever you're comfortable with is fine with me. I pray at some time you'll grow to love me, but if you don't, we can still have a great marriage. I promise."

She sighed her relief and rested her head against his shoulder. He wanted her to say she loved him but she could not squeeze the words from her fearful heart.

"I'm sorry." Love frightened her, but how could she explain it to him when she didn't understand it herself?

"I'm not complaining." He cupped his hand to the back of her head and held her gently. He pressed his cheek to her hair and she was almost certain he kissed the top of her head.

"I will be a good wife," she murmured against his jacket front, breathing in his warm scent. "I'll work hard."

"Linette, you don't need to prove anything to me. I love you just the way you are."

He held her a moment longer then led her down the hill and shooed her away to bed.

In the dark, she whispered to Cassie, "He said he'll marry me."

Cassie bolted upright, making Grady murmur a complaint. She settled back down. "I don't believe it."

"It's true."

"Will we all get to stay, then?"

She found Cassie's hand on top of the covers and squeezed it. "What would I do without you and Grady? Of course you get to stay."

"I'm happy for you. It's what you wanted."

"Thank you." She shifted to her side and stared into the darkness. It was why she'd come West—to marry a man who would allow her to escape her father's plans. She hadn't counted on him falling in love with her.

You don't need to prove anything to me. I love you just the way you are.

Love? What was that? Didn't it turn her into a pawn, the way she'd been as her father's daughter?

Eddie was not like her father.

But she couldn't push away the fear of giving herself wholly and completely to another. Unless she retained control of her heart, she feared she would lose who she was to him.

The next morning, she accompanied Eddie to the cookhouse where he called for attention. "Linette has agreed to become my wife."

Nice of him to put it that way when they all knew she'd come with the specific intention of marrying him. But it pleased her that he made it sound as if it had been his idea.

"Didn't I tell you so?" Cookie exclaimed as she engulfed Linette in one of her massive hugs.

Eddie managed to keep his arm about her shoulders and protect her from some of Cookie's enthusiasm, then she turned to pat Eddie's back in congratulations.

Linette felt the thuds clear to her fingertips and feared Eddie would suffer internal injuries.

One by one the cowhands who were present filed by shaking Eddie's hand and taking hers in a polite gesture. All of them said they were glad she was going to stay and help Eddie run the ranch. Even Ward offered his congratulations.

"Guessed you weren't interested in my little ranch."

At first she giggled at their comments then she began to squirm. "Eddie has done quite well without my help so far. I expect he could continue to manage without me."

Eddie squeezed her to his side. "They know a woman's touch makes all the difference. Especially a woman as wise and generous as you."

She waited until they were alone to question him. "What did you mean about me being wise and generous?"

He laughed hard. When he noticed she didn't join in his merriment, he sobered. "You really don't know?"

She shook her head, not caring her fears and uncertainties likely showed in her face.

He took her hands and pulled her close. She tipped her head to search his eyes as he spoke.

"Linette, you show kindness to all, you try to help people no matter what their race or color or social standing. You speak your mind but in a way that causes people to respect you. You stopped my men from hanging an Indian who didn't deserve such a fate. And brave? I never expected to see a woman stand up to the wolves the way you did." He pressed a kiss to her nose. "I understand you think you have to prove you are something more than a beautiful woman who can be used as part of a business deal." His voice deepened as if the words pained him and her heart did a slow tilt toward him.

"But my dear sweet Linette. You don't need to prove anything to anyone. You are beautiful." He kissed her on each cheek. "But you are so much more. And I cherish each and every bit of you—your personality, your faith and your..." He paused, eased back a few inches and touched her chest over her heart. "Who you are inside."

She swallowed hard several times, struggled with a

sense of breathlessness as his words washed over her, cleansing away self-doubt and fear, leaving her whole.

She loved this man for the gift he'd given her.

But when she tried to say the words, they stuck in her throat.

If he noticed her struggle he didn't say anything, just pulled her close again and held her gently. "I need to go." He caught her chin with his fingertip and lifted her face to kiss her sweetly and quickly. "I'll be back later and we can talk more."

But it was easy in the following days to talk about other things. She sensed his patient waiting but the knot in her throat would not let go. In fact, it seemed to extend to her heart and bind her feelings behind prison bars.

One day she glanced up to see a line of Indians riding by and realized winter had begun to relinquish its hold on the land.

Eddie came from the pens and stood at her side.

"They're moving out to hunt for food. Unfortunately there is little left for them. Buffalo hunters have killed most of the huge herds. And now the people are confined to specific areas. It's a tough life."

"I hope they'll be safe. I wonder how Bright Moon, Red Fox and their boys are."

They watched the long line snake by. A man turned aside and headed down the hill toward them, a woman at his side. "It's them," Linette squealed, running to meet the family.

Bright Moon showed them the baby, wearing the sweater Linette had given him.

"His name Little Shirt." A chuckle accompanied

Red Fox's announcement. "White woman give little shirt."

Linette grinned, happy at their choice of name. The baby had put on weight. In fact, they all looked considerably better than last time she'd seen them.

"Mother has gift," Little Bear said.

Bright Moon handed her a pair of baby moccasins, ornately decorated with beads.

Linette choked up. "Thank you," she managed to say past the tears clogging her throat.

"You are great white woman," Red Fox said, holding his hand out as if in benediction.

From the hill came a cheer. The whole tribe faced them.

Linette waved then thanked Red Fox and hugged Bright Moon and the boys. The family returned to the others and the Indians continued their journey. Linette watched until they were out of sight.

"The great white woman. I like that." Eddie had his arm about her shoulders and pulled her close to rest his forehead against hers. "You are appreciated by men of both races. How does it feel?"

She considered his question. "It feels fine."

He gave her a little shake. "And yet you still doubt. Linette, my love. When will you believe you are accepted and more...honored and loved?"

She shrugged. "I don't know."

He kissed her forehead. "I pray for the day but until then know this, I love you just as you are."

"Sounds like a wedding vow."

"It is. I am yours for as long as I live. You have my heart, my love, my everything."

"Eddie…" Her voice broke. "I don't deserve so much."

He gave her another little shake. "But you do."

She nodded as tears gathered in the back of her throat.

How she wanted to believe him. Say to him the words he wanted to hear. Was it stubborn pride that prevented it?

Lord, help me. I came for a marriage of convenience. That's all I wanted. Now it seems I must choose if I want more. But something in my heart is stuck. Broken, even. Show me how to fix it. Please.

She was tired of the constant warfare between what she wanted to give Eddie and what she wanted to keep for herself.

Her heart.

Later that day Eddie went to Linette. "Let's inspect the house." He wanted her to see it as hers. He wanted to feel her joy in making plans. "It's yours now. You can choose how to use the rooms, how to decorate them."

They climbed the hill to the house and she went immediately to the window overlooking the ranch as he knew she would. "I want this to be our main room so we can enjoy this view every day."

He chuckled. "Why doesn't that surprise me?"

She would have stayed there, content to ignore the rest of the house, but he took her hand and drew her away. She inspected the kitchen as if seeing it for the first time. "I can see myself working here."

"I expect it will be a pleasant change after the

cramped quarters of the cabin and the tiny stove, which you've managed to cook very nice meals on."

"I enjoyed it." She faced him. "Are you sure about this?"

He looked at the wooden worktable. "Is something wrong with it?"

"What if I never say the words you want?"

She'd read his longing so clearly. He ached for her to say she loved him. Wondered what held her back. Not that he had any reason for complaint. She was gentle, loving and kind to him. Just as she was to everyone.

He pulled her to his chest, pressed her head to the hollow of his shoulder where he'd discovered it fit very nicely. He rested his cheek against her hair. "Linette, I love you enough for the both of us. Yes, I pray you will someday learn to love me, but so long as you can accept my love I'm okay with this arrangement."

She wrapped her arms about his waist and held him tight. "You are a good man."

It had to be enough for now. But someday, God willing, there would be more.

A few days later, Linette turned as Eddie strode into the cabin. Her lungs tightened with—

She couldn't say what. Or perhaps she didn't want to admit it.

"I'm going to help the men move the herd up to new pasture." Eddie pulled Linette into his arms and searched her face with hope. But she couldn't give him the words he wanted. Yes, he'd said he would wait. No demands. Yet she felt his longing as clearly as she felt the air fill her lungs. "Take good care," she said, and boldly lifted her face and kissed him.

He hugged her tight then hurried away.

She watched him go then climbed the hill to the house.

The house was almost finished, but Eddie said he would complete the work before they were married. They hadn't yet set a date. She knew he wanted to hear back from Margaret, officially freeing him from his offer. But she wondered if he also waited for a reply from his father. What if his father forbade the marriage? He would never choose her over his father's approval.

She went immediately to the row of rooms upstairs. They were in a separate wing from the family rooms. Meant for the Gardiner family. But she saw them as suitable for an entirely different purpose. A place of healing and rest for the hurting and weary. She had already moved cots into two of the rooms and now she mentally furnished them and imagined them occupied.

Racing horses' hooves caught her attention. She hurried to a window in time to see Slim race to the barn and throw himself from the saddle even before the horse stopped. The horse was lathered in a way Eddie would frown on. Slim raced to the barn and pushed the big doors open.

Something was wrong.

She dashed from the house and jogged down the hill in time to see Slim rattle from the barn in the wagon.

"Wait," she called.

He saw her and shouted, "…hurt." But he didn't slow down.

Had he said Eddie was hurt? She was certain he had and she sank to her knees to watch the wagon bounce along the trail. She didn't move until it disappeared from sight.

And then she returned to the big house to the windows that allowed her a view of the ranch. From where she stood, she could see the wagon before it reached the barn. Before it could be seen from the cabin or any of the buildings below her.

Lord, keep him safe.

Her knees failed and she sank to the chair, never taking her eyes from the window.

How badly was he injured? Her heart beat double time.

What if he was worse than injured? The blood congealed in her veins.

She couldn't imagine life without him. She'd give up every dream, every desire, if it meant she could share the rest of her life with him.

The truth hit her with such force she groaned.

She loved him. But she'd never told him.

Why had she waited so long? Perhaps she would never get the chance now.

She'd held back her words because of her father. Fearing Eddie would somehow turn into a man like him. See her as currency to be used in a business deal. But Eddie was not her father. Never would be. Eddie loved her. And she knew her heart was safe in his care.

Oh, why had she been so stubborn? So prideful?

Why had she feared so much to love a man? A verse her nurse had taught her came to mind. *There is no fear in love; but perfect love casteth out fear...he that feareth is not made perfect in love.*

God's love was perfect and complete. It enabled her to love a man, to say the words to him.

Tears washed her soul.

She'd wasted so much time. Maybe lost her chance.

Lord, forgive me. Please give me a chance to tell him how much I love him.

She remained at the window until she saw a twist of dust far to the north then dashed from the house and down the hill to await the wagon.

She prayed it wasn't Eddie, but if it wasn't him it would be one of the other men or some unfortunate stranger. She couldn't guess how badly the poor injured party was, only that the injury was severe enough to send a man back for the wagon.

The wagon drew closer, surrounded by a guard of men. It took her only one quick glance to see Eddie wasn't among those on horseback and with a cry straight from her fractured heart, she raced forward.

Ward dropped from his horse and caught her in his arms. "He looks worse than he is."

"Let me go." She struggled in his arms, straining toward the wagon.

"Best let us clean him up first."

"I must see him." She broke from his grasp and made it to the back of the wagon before anyone could stop her.

"Eddie." His name wailed past her teeth.

He lay motionless on the wooden wagon bed. Blood covered his face. She scrambled up beside him, kneeling at his head but not touching him. Afraid to, lest she hurt him further. "What happened?"

"His horse stumbled in a hole and threw him into a rock. Knocked him out cold."

Ward touched her back. "We need to get him inside."

She thought of the bedroll where he always slept and

quickly made a decision. "Take him to the big house. He'll be more comfortable there." The bed she'd pictured as respite for a wounded stranger was about to hold the one she loved.

The wagon jerked forward and Linette pressed her palms to the floor to keep her balance. "Eddie, wake up," she whispered.

But he showed no response.

Blood wept from his hairline and she lifted her fingers but drew back without touching his skin. Would she make things worse? She didn't know and wished she'd defied her father and entered a hospital to train as a nurse.

"Let us carry him in."

She hadn't noticed they'd pulled up to the house and she shifted aside so four men could tenderly lift Eddie from the wagon and carry him up the stairs. She rushed ahead, grabbed a handful of blankets from one of the storage crates and tossed them to the bed.

Through it all Eddie made not one sound. Didn't even flinch.

Linette pressed her lips together to keep from crying out. She sucked in air and pushed resolve into her trembling body. "I need water. A basin. Towels."

Someone put a chair next to the bed and she sank into it, never taking her attention from Eddie's face. *Please, Lord, let him open his eyes.*

Ward set a small table beside her, along with a basin of water. Eddie still did not stir.

She wet a cloth and tenderly, gingerly, patted at the blood. "I can't tell where it's coming from." Her voice shook like a wind-battered leaf. She rinsed the rag out and finished cleaning his face. He was so pale. So still. Only the rise and fall of his chest assured her he was alive.

Fresh blood flowed down his cheek and pooled in his ear. She sponged it off and pushed his matted hair aside to search for the wound. It gaped a few inches above his ear, blood flowing steadily. She tried to push the edges together but there was too much swelling. She rinsed the cloth again then pressed it to the wound. The blood flow stopped.

She ran her gaze over the rest of his body. "Is anything broken?"

"Don't seem to be," one of the men replied.

"He's been out a long time," Ward said, his voice tight with worry.

Worry Linette shared. Eddie was too quiet. Deathly still. "I don't know what we can do but wait. I'll watch him until he wakens."

Roper stepped back. "Come on, boys. The boss will expect the work done when he wakes up."

One by one they slipped away until only Ward remained. "You'll be okay on your own?"

She nodded. "I'll give a holler if I need anything."

He nodded. "We'll check on you in a bit."

Then she was alone with Eddie and she let the tears flow unchecked. "Don't you die on me, Eddie Gardiner. I never got a chance to tell you I love you."

She checked the wound. It still oozed and she applied pressure again. *Please, God. Please, God.* She couldn't form any more of a prayer but knew God heard the cry of her heart.

Cassie stepped into the room, a covered plate in her hands. "Any change?"

"He hasn't moved. Not once."

"You need to eat." She handed Linette the plate.

Linette stared at it. "What's this?"

"Supper."

"It can't be." She glanced toward the window. The sun almost touched the mountaintops. "How long have I been here?" She'd been vaguely aware of one or another of the cowboys slipping in and leaving again. Cookie had come once, tsked and left again.

"At least six hours."

She turned toward Cassie. "Six hours and he's still unconscious." Her voice caught. "That's not a good sign."

Cassie shook her head. "Everyone is praying."

Linette nodded, but strength seeped from her body. She set the plate on the table lest she drop it.

"I'll be back after Grady is asleep." Her friend patted Linette's shoulder then slipped away.

Linette fell on her knees at the side of the bed, clutching Eddie's limp hand in hers, willing him to waken. "Eddie, I love you. Don't leave me. I'm so sorry I didn't tell you sooner. Don't leave me. Please, God, don't take him from me."

She wasn't aware darkness had fallen until Ward entered and set a lamp on the table. She didn't recall returning to the chair, but she sat close to the bed still holding his hand.

"I'll sit with him while you rest," Ward offered. "Cassie made up the bed across the hall."

"I can't leave."

"You'll be close. I'll call if anything changes."

Still, she didn't move.

"You need to keep up your strength."

A cry filled her mouth and she clamped her fist to

her lips to stop it from escaping. Did he mean Eddie could remain like this for a long time? Or did he mean Linette might be faced with a funeral and the sorrow accompanying it?

She bolted from the room, threw herself on the bed and sobbed into the pillow.

She must have dozed off, because she was startled by a sound from the other room and dashed across the hall. "Eddie?"

It was Slim. "Sorry, Linette, there's been no change."

"I'll be back in a moment to sit with him." She did a quick toilet and rushed back to the house. Dawn spread fingers of pink across the sky as she threw back the door.

Upstairs, the men had gathered.

"He's not going to die." She stared hard at each in turn, not shifting until each had lowered his eyes. "Is there a doctor in the area?"

Slim shook his head. "Don't know. Never heard of one. Closest is Fort Benton."

She turned to Ward. Eddie had often said he was the best rider. "Ward, ride to town and ask around. I don't care how far you have to go. Bring back a doctor if there's one anywhere at all."

"It's several days to Fort Benton. Do you want me to go that far?"

"Go a reasonable distance. But hurry."

He was already out of the room.

She turned back to the others. "Now, go about your business and stop hanging around as if it's a death watch. I'll stay with him."

They hesitated until she shooed them away.

Finally, alone again, she sat at Eddie's side. Someone had brought fresh water and she gently washed his face and hands, as much to have something to do as anything. As she worked, she talked softly. "Eddie, I know God's in control, but it's hard to trust Him when you're lying here so still. Please wake up. I know you can't hear me, but I will say it anyway. I love you. Wake up and hear me. I love you."

The men came, one by one, and left again. She knew they were concerned about their boss.

Cassie brought tea and toast. Cookie lumbered up the stairs and wheezed a few minutes before she sighed sadly and left again.

Linette wanted to order all of them to stop acting as if Eddie was dying. He couldn't die. *Please, God.*

From outside she heard a horse gallop into the yard. She sprang to the window. Ward had returned, but he was alone. She searched the back trail for a slower horse, a buggy or wagon, but saw nothing. She turned as Ward clattered into the room.

"Ain't no doctor within a hundred miles."

She sucked in dry air that made her cough. "Then we'll wait and pray."

"Brought the mail." He set a bundle of letters on the table.

She glanced at them. Saw the return addresses. Randolph Gardiner in bold letters. Eddie's father had written. Would he threaten dire consequences to Eddie if he proceeded with his plan to marry Linette?

She recognized the handwriting on another letter as Margaret's.

She jerked away. Nothing mattered but seeing Eddie wake.

The day slipped away without him moving. Again, Slim insisted she lie down in the other room. And again, she fell asleep crying and praying.

She bolted awake. The room was dark. Silent. Her heart raced. Eddie had called. She'd heard his voice as if he stood at her bedside. She raced across the hall to Eddie's room where a lamp on the table gave the place a golden glow. Roper sat on a chair at the bedside. She dropped to the floor at Eddie's side. "Eddie?" But he didn't move. Didn't show any sign of response.

Her heart still beat a hard tattoo against her ribs. What had wakened her? "Eddie." She spoke his name louder. "Eddie, wake up."

Nothing. She sank back on her heels. No sign of a response.

Roper guided her to the chair. "It will soon be morning."

She shook her head. "It's dark as coal out there."

"It's always darkest before dawn."

His words slid through her like life-giving rain to a drought-stricken desert. He hadn't likely meant them as anything more than an observation, but they gave her hope. She would not give up even though there'd been no change.

Vaguely she realized the light in the room increased, that Roper turned the lamp off and slipped away.

But her every breath, every thought, every energy focused on Eddie, willing him to live. Over and over, she murmured his name. Sometimes gently, other times demanding as if she could order him to wake up.

"Eddie, I love you." She would say the words again and again in the hope he would waken and hear them.

Her head fell forward. She jerked upright. She must stay awake. If he only regained consciousness for a second, she would not miss it. She would not miss her chance to tell him she loved him.

Chapter Fifteen

Cassie brought Linette food. She ate it because Cassie wouldn't leave until she did. As soon as Cassie left she knelt by the bed, clutching Eddie's hand and praying.

She squeezed his hand tight.

His fingers curled against hers.

Had he moved or had she imagined it?

She jerked back to look at him. His eyes were open. They were clouded with confusion and perhaps pain. He struggled to keep his eyelids open, but he was awake. She cupped his face in her hands. "Eddie. I love you."

"I love you, too." He closed his eyes.

"Eddie?"

But he didn't respond.

She dashed away tears she hadn't known she shed. Was it a sign he was returning or—she groaned from deep in her soul—was it goodbye? She clung to the belief he would recover. But at least he'd heard her words of love.

He opened his eyes again before dinnertime and smiled at her before he drifted off again. Her heart overflowed with gratitude, which grew and multiplied as he wakened several more times throughout the evening.

She didn't want to leave him when darkness fell, but Slim insisted. She lay on the bed unable to sleep despite fatigue that numbed her bones. *Thank You, God. Thank You.* She couldn't stop saying the words.

The next day he wakened for longer periods and was able to take a bit of nourishing broth provided by Cookie.

The following day he tried to sit up, groaned and grabbed his head.

She eased him back to his pillow. "Lie still. Give your head a chance to heal."

"Right." He breathed hard then grabbed her hand. "I dreamed I was in a dark tunnel and you called me. I followed your voice back." He fell asleep without releasing her hand.

She gladly sat at his side, their hands together on his chest. A bit later he stirred again.

"I dreamed you said…" He didn't finish.

She realized how desperately he needed to hear her words, how he feared to believe he'd heard them. "It wasn't a dream. I should have told you before, but I was stuck in my fear and pride." She cupped her palms over his cheeks and leaned closer, drinking in the hunger in his eyes, the strength of his features. "Eddie Gardiner, I love you." She pressed a gentle kiss to his lips, fearing she would hurt him. He smiled beneath her kiss and pulled her to his chest.

Slowly in the following days, he gained strength and stayed awake for longer periods. But the letters on the table haunted her."You have letters. Margaret and your father wrote."

He groaned. "Read them to me."

"I don't know if I should."

"I don't intend to have secrets from you. Read Margaret's first."

She nodded. Her fingers trembled as she opened the letter and unfolded the one page.

Did Linette not make it clear that I am not interested in leaving the comforts of London? I thought you would have married her by now. She is by far more suited to that life than I. I wish you both the best.

Linette smiled at Eddie. "I tried to tell you as much."

"So you did, but I had to make sure Margaret hadn't changed her mind." He sounded weary.

She considered delaying the news in the next letter until he was stronger.

"Read Father's letter. I won't rest easy until I know what he's said."

She couldn't refuse after that and she quickly opened the envelope and read the words aloud.

Eddie.

No "Dear Eddie." Not a good beginning.

I forbid you to marry that woman.

Your duty is to obey me.

And a bold signature. *Randolph Gardiner.*

The trembling had spread to her stomach and she wished she hadn't eaten.

"Linette, would you get pen and paper?"

With leaden feet she did as he asked and held the items to him.

"Would you mind writing as I dictate? I fear I am not up to doing it myself."

"Of course." She could think of nothing she wanted less to do.

"Dear Father, I received your letter today. All my life I have done my best to honor you, not only because I wanted to be a good son but because God has instructed us to honor our parents. However, I fear I must disobey you in this matter."

Linette ducked her head over the paper. Could he mean he would choose her over his father?

Eddie continued and she wrote again.

"It is my honor and privilege to have met Linette Edwards and I can assure you she is more than worthy of marrying any man...even a Gardiner. I intend to make her my wife as soon as preparations can be made. New paragraph, if you please. I realize you might want to make other arrangements for the ranch, but I invite you to examine the records, ask others in the area about the operation and you will discover that I have done an excellent job. If you find my work satisfactory I am willing to stay on but not as a foreman or supervisor. I will stay on in one condition—you make me a full partner. Awaiting your pleasure in this matter."

"Eddie, you can't mean it. Where will you go? What will you do?"

"Don't you mean where will *we* go?"

"Of course."

"We'll manage fine. We could start a small place like Ward has. Now hold the paper for me to sign."

She did so then sealed the letter in an envelope.

"Get one of the boys to take it to town today."

She found Slim and gave him the letter then returned to Eddie's side.

She perched on the edge of the bed. "Are you sure about this?"

"All this—" he waved his arm to indicate the house, the ranch "—means nothing without you to share it with."

A smile threatened to split her face. "Is it any wonder I love you?"

He caught her hand and pulled her close to kiss her. "I will never grow tired of hearing those words. Now, when can we get married?"

She laughed. "Don't you want to wait until you can stand?"

A month later

Everyone from OK Ranch had come. At Eddie's request a minister had come from Fort Calgary for the occasion.

Linette wondered aloud if Eddie was ready. It had taken him ten days from the accident before he could stand without dizziness and another ten days before he could ride a horse. But he insisted he was back to normal. They'd had so many sweet times as he recovered.

She told him how she'd wakened, as if shaken by an unseen hand, in the middle of the night, and knelt at his bedside calling to him. He insisted it was her voice calling his name that enabled him to fight his way from the darkness of unconsciousness.

They talked about what they would do if Eddie's father asked them to leave the ranch. She'd tried to share Eddie's optimism but couldn't deny a bit of sadness. She had come to love the place, the residents and the house. But the fact that he would give it all up for her filled her heart with sweetness.

Eddie had invited others from around the area to the wedding.

Linette laughed in surprise as the stagecoach she'd arrived on rattled into the yard and men jumped off the top and climbed from the coach. "You seem to have the regard of everyone in the area." She hugged Eddie's arm.

She and Eddie stood on the bridge, facing the visiting minister and the gathered crowd. The trees were dressed in spring finery and the water rushing under the bridge filled the air with gurgling music. Cassie and Roper stood at their sides. Roper barraged Cassie with longing glances. Linette smiled. Roper had a tough journey ahead of him, but if she could change Eddie's mind, if Eddie could teach her to love, then Roper could win Cassie's heart.

The minister spoke and drew her attention to the dear man at her side. They exchanged vows and sealed them with a kiss full of promise and trust.

Cookie insisted she would provide a meal to rival the Christmas feast at the other ranch and she did them proud.

During the meal, the stagecoach driver sidled up to Eddie and Linette. "All winter I wondered if Eddie here would come to his senses and see what a prize you are. Glad to see he came round."

Eddie pulled her close and pressed his cheek to her hair. "Not half as glad as I am."

She wrapped her arms about Eddie's waist. "Nor half as glad as I."

The driver sauntered away, his eyes on the cinnamon buns Cookie put out.

Grady considered Linette with a worried look. She pulled him to her side. "What is it, little man?"

"I stay with you?" He addressed Linette, but darted a quick glance toward Eddie.

She'd assured him over and over that he had a home with them, but he needed to hear it again.

Eddie drew the boy closer. "You will stay with us."

Grady nodded. "You be my new papa?"

Eddie hugged the boy. His eyes glistened as he met Linette's gaze over Grady's head. "I would be honored to."

"I love you," Grady said.

"I love you back," Eddie replied and opened his arms to pull Linette into a three-cornered hug. "I love you both."

"Me, too," she whispered. "Me, too."

Grady edged free to grin at the assembled people.

Linette turned her face up to Eddie. "I suppose this is a good time to admit I was more than a little in love with you even before I came."

His eyes flickered amusement and heart-stopping love. "You don't say? How is that possible?"

"From the letters you wrote to Margaret I kept thinking, there's a man worth loving."

He cupped her chin. "It took your faith in me for me to see I deserved more than my father's name."

They still hadn't heard from Eddie's father, but she refused to let the concern about what he'd said mar her day.

"Our future is in God's loving hands," Eddie said.

It didn't surprise Linette that he'd read her thoughts. "I am so happy."

"Me, too." He kissed her, a sweet, promising kiss.

Whatever the future held, she could gladly, eagerly face with Eddie's love and God's care to guide her.

Epilogue

Linette wandered through the house checking each room. She straightened the covers on each bed, adjusted the curtains at a window and paused to admire the china in the dining-room cupboard—a gift from the owners at OK Ranch. She had grown to love the house, but nowhere as much as this room with the windows overlooking the ranch, and her footsteps returned there as if drawn by a cord to her heart.

Below, Roper rode into the yard and waved a bundle at Eddie. Eddie took it, glanced at it then turned his gaze toward the house, unerringly finding Linette in the window. He waved a long white envelope.

Linette clutched her arms about her. It was the long-awaited, dreaded letter. She looked over her shoulder and mentally began saying goodbye to the room and mentally began packing their belongings.

Eddie found her sitting in the wingback chair before the window. He knelt in front of her and wrapped his arms around her. "Whatever this says, nothing changes so far as I'm concerned. I have all I want right here in my arms."

"Open the letter," she begged.

"Not before you tell me it doesn't matter what it says."

She stared into his eyes, deep into his heart and saw the promise of his faithful love—a love she had grown to cherish more with each passing day. "I only care because I know the ranch is important to you."

"Nothing matters but you and me together."

"If you're happy, I'm happy." Her heart overflowing with joy, she leaned forward and kissed him. "Now open the letter."

He sat at her knees and carefully broke the seal on the envelope to withdraw a sheaf of official-looking papers.

Her heart kicked against her ribs. "He's removing you from the ranch."

Eddie read the documents. "I don't think so." Suddenly he laughed. "He's made me half owner. I will be in complete control of what he calls 'Northwest Canada operations.' He will retain control of major monetary investments over five thousand dollars." Eddie whooped. "He's basically given me the ranch." He bolted to his feet and pulled Linette up to face him. "The Lord has done great things for us."

"Above and beyond what we thought possible."

They hugged each other and kissed then Eddie turned to the rest of the mail. "There's a letter to you."

She took it. "From Father." Inside she found a note and explanation that the funds of her dowry had been placed in Eddie's name at Fort Macleod.

Eddie barely glanced at the letter. "It's your money to do with as you want. I have no need of it and don't want you to ever think I had an eye to gaining this by marrying you." He kissed her to prove he was teasing.

"I know exactly what I want to do with it."

Eddie chuckled. "Let me guess. First, you want to finish furnishing the rooms in the guest wing then make them available for people in need and you want to use the money to help them."

She giggled. "What are you, sir? A mind reader?"

His eyes flashed humor. "Wouldn't take much of a mind reader when you talk about it every chance you get. Well, Mrs. Gardiner, you have my complete approval to do whatever you want."

She wrapped her arms about his neck. "Is it any wonder I love you so much?"

He sobered. "Your love will always be a wonder to me."

She nodded, equally sober. "And yours to me." They searched each other's gaze for a moment, found the assurance they knew they would and kissed—a kiss full of promise and hope and joy and so many more things.

* * * * *

THE COWBOY'S
UNEXPECTED FAMILY

Owe no man any thing, but to love one another.
—*Romans* 13:8

To families. To my children and their children. May you build sweet memories, establish worthwhile traditions and grow in love and care for each other. I wish this for all families.

Chapter One

Eden Valley, Alberta
Summer 1882

Cassie Godfrey's dream was about to come true. She could see it there before her eyes. She could smell it, and practically taste it. Twenty-five years old and she was finally about to become self-sufficient.

"I'm not sure this is a good idea." The cowboy sitting next to her sounded worried but she dismissed his concern. She'd heard all the arguments she cared to hear.

"I'll be fine." She jumped from the wagon seat and headed to the back where her things waited to be moved to her new home. Only one small problem remained. Or perhaps it was a large problem.

She had no house.

Roper Jones climbed down slowly, reluctantly. "Where you planning to sleep?"

"Eddie lent me a tent." She'd spent the winter at Eden Valley Ranch where Eddie Gardiner was boss and had recently married Linette. When Linette had discovered Cassie living in the Montreal train station after the death of her husband, she had gathered Cassie under her wing and taken her to Eden Valley Ranch with her. After Linette and Eddie married, they'd insisted Cassie was more than welcome to remain and share their big house but it was time for Cassie to move on. For months, ever since she'd reached the Eden Valley Ranch, her dream had been growing. There was a time she thought a secure future meant depending on a man, but she'd grown to see she didn't need a man to take care of her. She could take care of herself. It had become her dream and that dream was about to be realized.

"You're mighty determined." Roper's chuckle sounded a tiny bit regretful. He hoisted the tent and a couple of bags from the wagon and headed for the little patch of land Cassie had persuaded Mr. Macpherson to sell her. He'd been reluctant about selling to a woman but she pointed out she was the head of her household—although she refrained from mentioning it was a household of one—and a widow, which entitled her to file on a homestead.

"Guess if the government would allow me to own one hundred and sixty acres for a homestead, I can buy a small lot." Her words had persuaded him, and no one else had raised an objection.

Roper set her things on the ground and leaned back on his heels. "Cassie, this doesn't seem like a good idea to me. Why not come back to the ranch?" His grin did nothing to erase the disapproval in his eyes.

She planted her feet on her own piece of land and sighed. "I realize you're only wanting to help but believe me this is exactly where I want to be and what I want to do." She turned full circle, mentally measuring the boundaries of her lot. It lay behind Macpherson's store, close enough that she could supply the bread for his store, once she had a stove, as part payment for the lumber for her house. Yet it was far enough to be out of sight of the freight wagons, stagecoaches and riders passing the store.

Roper followed her visual inspection until they'd both gone full circle and ended looking at each other. He was a pleasant enough man with a ready smile tipped a little crookedly at the moment. Stocky built, solid even. A good head of brown hair mostly hidden under his cowboy hat. A square face. His hazel eyes were always full of kindness and hope, though she'd gone out of her way to make it clear he need not pin any hope on her.

"Why must you insist on this foolishness?" He swung about to indicate the vast open prairies, the rolling foothills, the bold Rocky Mountains. "Ain't nothing but nothing out here. A few cows. A few cowboys. A store. A settler or two."

Her gaze took in the wide land and for a moment rested on the mountaintops that seemed to poke the blue sky. As always they made her feel stronger, and she brought her mind back to Roper's concern. "And Mr. Macpherson," she added, "just a holler away."

"Who's to protect you from wild animals? Either the four-legged or two-legged kind?"

"Indeed. And who has protected me in the past? Sure wasn't my dead husband." She'd been so afraid sleeping in the railway station. "Nor my dead father. Certainly not my still-living grandfather." She made a grating sound of disbelief.

"Must be the good Lord 'cause it sure ain't your good sense."

"Think what you will." She turned away to examine the stack of belongings. "Thanks for bringing me to town and unloading my stuff."

"You're telling me to leave?"

"Don't recall saying so but shouldn't you get back to the ranch?"

"You're bound and determined to do this?"

She faced him squarely. She would reveal no flicker of doubt. "I'm bound and determined."

"Nothing I say will convince you to reconsider?"

"Figure you about said it all and still I'm here."

But he didn't move and she avoided looking at him. He'd already made his opinion clear as spring water. As had Linette and Eddie.

"It goes against my better judgment to leave you here alone."

"This is something I have to do." She didn't bother explaining her reasons, afraid they would look foolish to anyone else. But she was through feeling indebted to someone for her care.

He pressed his hand to hers. "Cassie, at least let me help you set up some kind of camp."

The weight of his hand, the warmth of his palm, the way he curled his fingers around hers made her realize how much she would miss him. But when he reached for the tent, she grabbed his arm to stop him. "I'll be fine. Don't worry about me." Even though she had pointedly ignored him all winter it was comforting in some strange, unexplainable way to know he was there, on the periphery of her world.

But she would not depend on anyone. She'd long

ago learned the cost of doing so. She had to make her own security. She fussed with the ropes around the rolled-up canvas tent. "I plan to manage on my own."

He edged past her, shuffled toward the wagon, never taking his eyes from her.

She did her best to keep her attention on the pile of belongings at her feet but couldn't keep from glancing his way when the wagon creaked as he stepped up.

He sighed loud enough to make the horse prick up its ears. "Look, it ain't like I'm asking to be your partner or anything like that." He grinned as if to inform her he considered the idea plumb foolish. "Just want to make sure you're going to be okay."

"I'm going to be just fine." She lifted her hand in farewell.

With a shake of his head, he drove away.

She watched until the trail of dust hid the wagon. Only then did she turn and face her predicament. She had land of her own. A nice level bit of ground with trees surrounding it and the river a few steps away.

She had plans to support herself, and a tent to provide temporary shelter. She had a pile of lumber that would become her home.

There was only one small hitch.

She had no notion of how to transform that pile of lumber into a house.

First things first. She would erect the tent and prepare camp.

Three hours later, she had managed to sort out the ropes and stakes for the tent and put it up. Sure it sagged like a weary old man but it was up. She'd unrolled her bedding along one side and slipped her derringer under her pillow. Whatever Roper thought of her she wasn't foolish enough to be unprepared.

Macpherson had provided a saw, hammer and nails with the lumber. She carried them to the pile of lumber and stared helplessly. She had no idea how to begin.

God, I know there must be a way to do this. Surely you can help me.

But she heard no voice from the clouds, nor did she feel a sudden burst of inspiration. As usual she'd have to figure it out on her own.

Roper muttered to himself as he headed toward the ranch. Stupid woman. If he didn't know better he would think she was crazy in the head. But he'd watched her all winter, seeing the pain and defiance behind her brown eyes and wanting to erase it.

From the beginning Cassie had been as prickly as a cactus. Over the winter she'd mellowed. Her black hair had gone from dull and stringy to glistening and full. Morose, even sour, at the start, she'd started to laugh more often.

He shook his head and grunted. But she'd changed in other ways, too. She'd grown downright stubborn and independent.

He adjusted his hat to suit him better and swatted away an ornery fly that wouldn't leave him alone.

Growing up in an orphanage he'd learned if he helped people, made them laugh, life was more pleasant for everyone. He'd become adept at smoothing out problems in order to maintain peace.

He ached that Cassie refused to let him help in any way.

"Shoot. Best thing I can do is forget all about her."

Something else he'd grown good at—letting people go. He'd learned the hard way not to expect permanence. Still he'd be giving Eddie every excuse known to man to ride to town until he was certain she was well settled. In fact, he'd leave the job and stay in town if he could think of any reasonable excuse. After all, he had no particular ties to the ranch. To any place for that matter.

But he could think of no reason to hang about town other than to make sure Cassie was safe and happy. Seems she was only too happy to see him gone so maybe he'd accomplished one of his goals.

A dark shape on the trail ahead caught his eye and he blinked. He pulled the horse to a halt and stared. Rubbed his eyes and stared some more.

He'd seen mirages of trees and water but he'd never seen a mirage of kids. He squinted hard. Three kids. Four, if that squirming armload was another.

He called to them as he edged the wagon forward.

The huddle of young 'uns left the trail and ran toward the trees a distance away.

"Now hold up there."

The kids picked up speed.

Roper quickly secured the reins and jumped to the ground, breaking into an awkward trot. His bowed legs weren't made for running but he didn't let that slow him much.

One of the kids hollered, "Hurry."

Another started to cry.

He couldn't bear to hear a kid crying and he slowed. But just for a moment. Kids didn't belong out in the middle of nowhere all alone. It wasn't a bit safe. He forced his legs to pump harder and closed the distance.

The biggest one turned and faced him, a scowl on her pretty little face. "Leave us alone!"

He skidded to a halt and took their measure. The girl looked about twelve, maybe a little older. She held a trembling younger girl maybe two years old. Roper couldn't see anything of the little one but the fine golden hair and impossibly tiny shoulders. Then there was a boy a year or two younger than the older girl. And between them, face full of fear and defiance, a young lad of maybe six or seven. The look on each face held a familiar expression...one he had seen time and again in the orphanage that had been his only home. It spelled fear. And trouble.

He held up his hands knowing the bunch wasn't ready to see the folly of their attitude. "I mean you no harm but I can't help wondering what four young 'uns are doing out here halfway between nowhere and nothin'."

The eldest two exchanged glances, and a silent message passed between them. The boy answered. "None of yer business."

Roper backed off a step but rocked on the balls of his feet, ready to grab them if they tried to escape. "Long way from here to someplace." They'd been headed away from Edendale so he guessed that wasn't their destination of choice. "You might get a little hungry and thirsty."

The girl glared at him. "We don't need no help."

He sighed. Where had he heard that before? And he didn't like it any better from the lips of a young gal with nothing more than the company of three younger kids and a gut full of determination than he had hearing it from Cassie. "How about you let me give you a ride at least?"

Again that silent communication. The young lad signaled to the older girl and they lowered their heads to hold a confab.

He waited, letting them think they were in control but he had no intention of turning around and leaving them there.

They straightened, and the oldest answered, "We'll accept a ride. For a little ways."

"Best we introduce ourselves," Roper said, and gave his name. "I work on a ranch over in the hills there."

Three pairs of eyes followed the direction he indicated and he could see their interest. He turned to the kids. "Now tell me who you are."

The big girl nodded. "I'm Daisy. This is Neil." She indicated the older boy, then nudged the younger one. "Billy, and Pansy."

"Suppose you got a last name."

"Locke."

"Well, howdy." He held out a hand but they shrank back. He waited, wanting them to know he meant them nothing but kindness. Finally Neil grabbed his hand and gave a good-size squeeze. The boy had grit for sure. Guess they all did to be out here alone.

He led them to the wagon. They insisted on sitting together in the back. He climbed to the seat but didn't move.

"Mister?" Daisy sounded scared.

He shifted to face them. "It might help if I had some idea where you want to go."

Again a silent discussion then Daisy nodded. "We're looking for our pa. He set out to get himself some land close to the mountains. Maybe you heard of him. Thaddeus Locke."

He'd heard of the man. One of the only settlers in the area. Last time he'd been mentioned in Roper's hearing was last fall. "Where's your mother?"

"She died. Before she did, she made us promise to find our pa." Daisy's voice quivered but she held her head high.

"Well, let's find him, then. Mr. Macpherson will know where his farm is." Macpherson knew everything about everyone within a hundred miles. 'Course that didn't mean more than a couple hundred people, not counting Indians. Roper turned the wagon about.

"You don't know where our papa lives?" Neil asked.

"Can't say as I do." The kids murmured behind him and he glanced over his shoulder. Little Pansy rested her head against Daisy's shoulder, big blue eyes regarding him solemnly, unblinkingly. The kid had been aptly named with eyes as wide as the flower. "We'll soon be at Macpherson's store." The collection of low buildings clung to the trail ahead, trees of various kinds clustered behind the buildings. His gaze sought the little area behind the store. As they drew closer he saw Cassie had almost managed to get the tent standing, but it swayed like a broken-down old mare. He chuckled. Wouldn't take more than a cupful of rain to bring it down and soak everything inside, including her if it happened while she slept. The canvas flapped in the wind. Fact was she might not have to wait for rain to topple the tent. A breeze made by bird wings would do the trick.

"Whoa." He jumped down and went to the back of the wagon.

Already Neil was on his feet with Pansy and he

helped Daisy to the ground as Billy scampered down to join them. All four regarded him with wary eyes.

He pushed his hat farther back on his head and returned their study. "Your ma would be proud of you." Where had that come from? The words must have been dropped to his tongue by the good Lord because the three older kids beamed, and Pansy gave him a shy smile that turned around in his heart and nestled there. "Now let's find your pa."

They trooped into the store. Macpherson leaned across the counter talking with another man. Roper recognized the North-West Mounted Police officer, Kipp Allen. "Howdy, Constable. Didn't see your horse outside."

The man nodded a greeting. Even though he lounged against the counter, he had a way of holding himself that let you know he saw clear through you. "He threw a shoe. He's down at the smithy." His eyes shifted to the young 'uns and he straightened, his gaze watchful.

Roper paid him no mind. "Macpherson, these here are the Locke kids looking for their pa, Thaddeus Locke. I'll give them transport if you tell me where I can find him."

Macpherson blinked. Just once but enough for Roper to wonder what secret the man had. "Best you be asking the constable."

Roper shifted to meet Allen's study. "I'm asking."

The Mountie's eyes softened and he faced the children. "I'm sorry to inform you that your pa passed away last winter. I buried him on his property."

Neil and Daisy drew in a gasp.

Orphans. Just like him. Roger remembered well the loneliness, the discouragement of it. How many times had he held his breath and watched a man and woman come to the orphanage for a child? Waiting. Wanting. Hoping. Never chosen. The matron tried to comfort him. "People want to know your background." But he had no background. No name. Only what someone had given him after he was discovered as a squalling infant on the doorstep. "You'd do well to forget about a home and family," she'd said.

He tried to heed her advice and turned his attention to helping others. Making them laugh. Teaching them how to smile for strangers so they would be chosen. Helping others find a home helped him find his joy and satisfaction.

But as he grew older and left the orphanage he forgot the matron's sound advice. Until it was too late. He learned the hard way that his background mattered more than who he was. After that experience he knew he would never belong in a forever family.

Small whimpers brought Roper's attention back to the children. Billy's eyes were wide as dishpans. Pansy stuck her fingers in her mouth and burrowed against Neil's shoulder.

"What…how'd he die?" Neil squeaked out.

The Mountie closed the distance between himself and the children. Roper automatically stepped away, out of respect for the sorrow visibly carved on their faces.

"Son." The man clasped Neil's shoulder. "I regret to have to tell you that he froze to death. Near as I can figure he went out in a storm to check on his animals and got turned around trying to get back to his cabin." He let the news sink in. "I have admiration for a man who is willing to face hard things rather than shirk his responsibilities. You kids can be proud of him."

Although the kids seemed to welcome the praise, Roper couldn't help wondering if staying safe for his family wouldn't have been more responsible than worrying about a couple or three animals.

The Mountie straightened. "We'll see you get back to your mother."

"Mama's dead." Billy blurted out the announcement, then sobbed into Daisy's dress.

"I see. What other family do you have?"

Daisy's mouth worked silently for a moment. Life had dished out a lot of bad news for them. No doubt she reeled inside, making it difficult to recall things.

"Mama had a brother but we haven't heard from him since I was Billy's size."

"Do you know where he was at the time?" The Mountie pulled out a little notepad, ready to jot down the information.

"We were living in Toronto then. It was before Papa decided we would do better to move West. He always wore a suit. I think I remember Mama saying he was a lawyer. Maybe. I can't be certain."

"Do you remember his name?"

"Jack. And Mama's name before she married was Munro."

"Can you spell it?"

Neil answered. "I can. I saw it in the Bible." He spelled it.

The Mountie wrote it down, closed his notepad and stuffed it into his breast pocket. "Fine. We'll locate him for you. In the meantime, we'll have to find a place for you to live." He turned to Roper. "I expect Mrs. Gardiner would take them in."

"Normally, yes." His boss's wife shared her home with anyone who needed it. "But she's been awfully sick. The boss has been plenty worried about her. I 'spect he'd say no to the idea."

"Then I'll have to take them back to the fort."

"And then what?"

"No one will likely take four but we'll split them up between willing families. Or..." He didn't finish the thought.

But Roper knew.

Send them to an orphanage.

Daisy stepped back, Neil at her side. They pressed Billy behind them and Pansy between them both holding her tight.

"We aren't going," Daisy said.

"We're sticking together," Neil added.

And then Roper heard himself say, "I'll look after them."

The kids relaxed so quickly he was surprised Pansy didn't drop to the floor.

Billy poked his head out between his older brother and sister. "You will?"

"Now wait a minute." The Mountie held up his hands. "You live in a bunkhouse when you're not out on the range. You expect to bunk these children with you or carry them on horseback across the mountains?"

"Well, no." Put that way it sounded pretty dumb. But something about their predicament forced him to speak and act on their behalf. "But I'll think of something." Eddie wouldn't object to giving him some time off. If he did, there were other ranches that could use another cowhand. His smile tightened. Eddie was a good boss. Roper liked working for him. But he wouldn't let these kids be sent someplace they weren't wanted. No siree.

The sound of a pounding hammer came from behind the store. The corners of his mouth lifted. "I know a young woman who will help me care for them." If he could make her see what a good arrangement this was for all concerned. It was perfect. God sent. He could help Cassie get set up. In return, she could help care for the kids until the uncle came. Then he'd be at ease about moving on and letting her run her business.

The assurance in his voice caused the Mountie to study him carefully. Then he shook his head. "'Fraid I can't simply take your word for it." He turned to the kids. "I'll find a wagon and be right back for you." He headed for the door.

The kids pressed tight to each other, fear vibrating from them.

Roper leaped forward, catching the Mountie before he could open the door. "Constable, there's no need for that. Give me a chance to make arrangements." He bored his eyes into the Mountie's but the man had more experience staring down people and Roper thought he'd blink before the Mountie finally relented.

"Tell you what. I've got to check on my horse and finish my business here. That'd give you enough time to arrange things?"

What he meant was that was how much time he'd allow Roper and his silly idea. "It's all I need."

"I'll be back shortly." The Mountie pushed past him, and strode down the street.

Roper wanted to holler at him to take his time but knew the Mountie would do as he chose. Instead, he turned to contemplate the kids and his predicament. All he needed was a convincing argument. But if Cassie got all independent and resisted the idea, what would he do? He needed help from the good Lord and he uttered a silent prayer. "Come on, kids. I think I know just the place for you." As he shepherded them out the door, he prayed some more. If ever he needed God's help—and he had many times in his life—it was now.

Chapter Two

Cassie had heard a wagon stop at the store but she paid it no mind. Her thoughts were on other things.

She pulled out a length of wood and dragged it to the site she'd chosen for the house and laid it alongside the other three she'd put there. She still had no idea how to proceed. Did she build the floor and put the walls on top? Did she make the walls and build the floor inside? How did she put in the windows?

She sat down on the stack of lumber and stared at the four pieces of wood. If she had the money she'd hire someone to do this. Someone who knew what they were doing. Someone who would expect nothing in return but his wages. But she was out of funds. Roper's offer to help flashed across her mind but she dismissed the idea. She did not want to be owing a man for any reason. She bolted to her feet. She'd ask Macpherson what to do, and she'd do it. By herself.

Her mind set, her back stiff, she turned and staggered to a stop as a wagon drew up before her property.

Roper jumped down, leaving a boy on the seat. She thought she glimpsed two or three more kids in the wagon but she must be dreaming. Why would Roper have kids with him? She supposed the boy could be headed out to work at the ranch, though he looked too young to have to earn his way in life. But if Roper took him to the ranch Eddie and Linette would see he was properly treated. He could be a companion for Grady, the four-year-old boy Linette had rescued on her ocean voyage from England.

Roper crossed the grassy property and stopped two feet from her. "See you're about ready to move into your house." His grin mocked her.

"Check back in a week or so and your grin won't be so wide."

He glanced at the lumber on the ground. "Guess you know what you're doing."

What he meant was, *You're lost in the fog.* "I was about to ask advice from Macpherson. Who are those kids?" Three pairs of eyes peered at her over the edge of the wagon and the boy on the seat watched with unusual interest.

Roper removed his hat, scratched his head until his hair looked like a windblown haystack then shoved the hat back on, adjusting it several ways until he was satisfied.

She'd never seen the man at a loss for words. "Roper, what are you up to? You haven't kidnapped them, have you?"

"Nothing like that." He stared at the wagon and the kids, who stared right back.

"Well, what is it like?" She alternated between watching Roper and watching the kids as wariness continued to creep across her neck like a spider.

He faced her so quickly she stepped back, as much

from his bleak expression as from being startled. "The kids' mother is dead. They came West hoping to join up with their pa but they just heard he's dead, too."

Cassie's heart dipped low, leaving her slightly dizzy. She remembered what it was like to hear your pa had died, recalled what it felt like to suddenly be homeless.

"I said I would keep them until their uncle sends for them. Or comes for them."

"Roper, how will you look after four children?"

"I will."

She didn't bother pointing out the obvious arguments. "Why are you here?"

He gave her a look rife with possibilities and she didn't like any of them. "I know how to build a house. I could put this up for you in short order."

"We've had this discussion."

He snatched the hat from his head. "Hear me out. What I have in mind is a business proposition." He paused, waiting for her response.

"I'm listening." The word *business* appealed to her. She had every intention of becoming a successful businesswoman.

"I plan to take care of the kids until the Mountie finds their uncle. But I can't do it alone. If you helped I would pay you by building your house." He grinned, as pleased with himself as could be. "I'll stay here, in a tent, as long as it takes me to build it."

She stared at him, turned to study the kids who listened intently. She wanted to help. Not for Roper's sake but because her heart tugged at her. She knew how uncertain the children would be feeling right now. She hoped their uncle would welcome them, unlike her grandfather who had never welcomed Cassie and her mother. He'd made it clear every day how much it cost him, though the way he'd worked Ma she knew he'd gotten a bargain in the arrangement. Cassie didn't want the children to feel as lost as she had felt, but if she went along with Roper's suggestion would he end up thinking he had the right to control her life? She would never give up her dream of being self-sufficient.

The youngest boy sank back in the wagon. "She don't want to help us," he muttered.

The words were slightly different than the ones that had echoed in her head from the time she was nine until she'd run off to marry George, but the ache was the same. The need to be accepted, to feel secure.

Before she could reason past the emotion, she turned to Roper. "It's a deal." She held out her hand, and they shook. He held her hand a moment longer than the shake required, his eyes warm and thankful. She clamped her lips together and tried to deny the feeling that the two of them had stepped across an invisible line and entered strange new territory.

He released her hand and turned to the children. "Come on, kids. You're staying here."

They scrambled from the wagon and edged their way over to face Cassie. She felt their uncertainty like a heat wave.

She wanted to ease that fear. "You'll be safe here as long as you need."

The oldest girl teared up. "Thank you. Thank you."

The oldest boy's expression remained guarded. Cassie knew he wouldn't easily accept words; he'd have to see for himself they were more than empty promises.

Roper introduced them all and at Cassie's request

they gave their ages: Daisy, thirteen; Neil, twelve; Billy, six; and Pansy, two.

Cassie quickly assessed them. They seemed weary and afraid but not defeated, especially Daisy who appeared competent in her role as mother, her watchful brown eyes never leaving her siblings.

Neil, too, seemed strong though not yet grown past childhood. His brown hair was in need of a cut, she noted as he stared at Cassie with the same deep brown eyes as Daisy.

The two younger children were both fair-haired, like their older sister, and blue-eyed and clung to their older siblings.

They all shuffled their feet and grew exceedingly quiet as the Mountie crossed from Macpherson's store.

"You kids ready to go?"

Cassie shot Roper a look full of hot accusation. He had neglected to say anything about the NWMP having a claim to these children. What else had he not told her?

"Constable, they'll be staying here with us." Roper included Cassie in his announcement.

The Mountie looked about slowly, taking in the pile of lumber, the tiny sagging tent and likely a whole lot more. His gaze stopped at Cassie. "Are you in agreement with sheltering these children temporarily?"

She nodded, too nervous to speak as he studied her. His look seemed to see a whole lot more than the tight smile she gave him.

His gaze again went to the tent.

Roper stepped forward. "I guarantee they'll be as safe and dry as any kids setting out with their folks in a wagon."

He might as well have said things would be a little rough.

The Mountie didn't answer for several minutes then shook his head. "This is most unusual. Two unmarried people caring for a family. However, I've had reports about a group of Indians stirring up trouble and I need to check on them before I head back to the fort. Should be gone a few days. I'll leave the children in your care until then. When I get back, I'll make my decision." He donned his Stetson to indicate the interview was over and headed back to the store.

Tension filled the air after he left. Cassie searched for something to ease the moment, but as she glanced about, the enormity of the situation hit her.

"Where is everyone going to sleep?" She waved her hand toward her tent that grew more bowed with each puff of wind. Obviously that wouldn't be sufficient.

The kids considered the tent. As if the thought of so many inside was too much for it to contemplate, the tent collapsed with a heavy sigh.

Billy giggled. "It got tired and laid down."

For some reason his words tickled his brother and older sister and they pressed their hands to their mouths, trying to contain errant giggles. They failed miserably and stopped trying.

Pansy's eyes widened and she gurgled at their amusement—a sweet pleasing sound that brought a smile to Cassie's mouth.

Their reaction was likely the result of all the emotion of the past few hours, Cassie reasoned. She glanced toward Roper. As he met her gaze, he started to chuckle.

"I don't see what's so funny about the prospect of sleeping out in the open." But there was something infectious about the laughter around her and she could no longer keep a straight face.

They laughed until she was weak in the knees and had wiped tears from her face several times.

As if guided by some silent signal they all grew quiet at once.

"I'll put up a temporary shelter," Roper said. He headed toward the pile of lumber.

Neil sprang after him. "I can help."

"'Preciate that. Let's find something to build half walls with."

"Half walls?" Cassie asked.

"Temporary but solid. I'll get some canvas from Macpherson to cover the top. It will be warm and dry until we get the house done."

Neil grabbed the end of a board that Roper indicated.

Cassie trotted over and reached for a second board.

Roper caught her shoulder and stopped her. "I can handle this."

Did he think he could simply take over? "We need to discuss our arrangement." She edged away from the children so they wouldn't hear the conversation. "I want to be clear this is only while the children are here."

"Cassie, that's all I expect." Something about the way his eyes darkened made her think of retracting her words. But only for a quick second.

"I don't need or want help for my sake."

He lifted his gaze to the sky as if seeking divine help then grinned at her.

She gave his amusement no mind. "I'd pay you if I could."

"You take care of the kids." He tipped his head toward the quartet. Neil had joined the others and they regarded her warily. "I want nothing more."

"Good. So long as you understand completely."

"You've made yourself more than clear. Now about the children…"

"Of course." She had no idea how she could manage until they had some sort of shelter and a stove, but she'd keep her part of the bargain and care for them. She squared her shoulders as she joined them. "When was the last time you ate?"

"We're not hungry," Daisy said but the way Billy's eyes widened with hope and little Pansy stopped sucking her fingers, Cassie knew Daisy did not speak for the others. "I'll make tea." She headed for the tent to retrieve her stack of dishes. She lifted the canvas and crawled inside, fighting the billows of rough material. A moment later, she backed out with her hands full.

Billy giggled.

"Shh," Daisy warned.

He sobered but the way his lips trembled tickled the inside of Cassie's stomach.

"I feel like a bug crawling out from a hole." She grinned and ran her hands over her hair.

"Pretty big bug." Billy's smile flickered and sputtered to an end as Daisy poked him in the back.

"He doesn't mean anything bad. He just hasn't learned to think before he speaks." Daisy's stare dared him to say anything more.

"Have, too."

Cassie chuckled. Obviously the boy didn't seem inclined to listen to Daisy's warnings, silent or otherwise. To distract him, she said, "Billy, why don't you gather up some firewood?" There was plenty of it lying about. Neil had gone back to helping Roper so she asked Daisy, "Could you help with these things?" She indicated the kettle and the box of supplies.

Daisy jiggled Pansy farther up on her hip and grabbed the kettle.

It was on the tip of Cassie's tongue to suggest that Daisy put her sister down but she wondered if either of them were ready to be separated and decided to leave it be.

It didn't take long to get a fire going and hang the kettle over it. Roper paused from his work to drag logs close.

"Benches," he explained, and she thanked him.

She took the biscuits and jam out of her provisions and when the tea was ready she called Roper and Neil. The other children hovered beside the fire, Pansy still riding Daisy's hip.

Roper hung the hammer over the board walls he had started and squatted to begin a mock fistfight with Neil. "You hungry, boy, or do you want to stay here working?"

"I'm hungry." Neil batted Roper's harmless fists away and tried to jab Roper's stomach.

Roper bounced away on the balls of his feet, still throwing mock punches.

As Neil laughed, the other three watched, their expressions relaxed, the guardedness gone from their posture.

Cassie studied them. Strange how the kids seemed to feel comfortable with Roper. Maybe because he was always laughing and teasing. Didn't he know there were times to be serious? Times to think about the future?

The pair reached the campfire.

"I haven't a cup for everyone until I unpack some boxes." She indicated the crates nearby. In one of them were dishes purchased from Macpherson that she planned to use when she served meals to people passing through in need of a feed and willing to pay for it.

"We'll share," Daisy said and offered a drink to Pansy from her cup. "Neil and Billy can share, too." Her look ordered them to agree without fuss and they nodded.

Cassie dipped her head to hide her smile. Daisy had taken on the role of mother. She didn't have much choice but Cassie wondered how long it would be before the others, especially Neil, decided otherwise. Still smiling she lifted her head and encountered Roper's gaze. He darted a glance at the kids and winked at her.

Winked! Like she was a common trollop he found on the street. Her cheeks burned. Her heart caught fire. How dare he?

He left his perch by Neil and plopped to the log beside Cassie. "My apologies. I didn't mean to offend you. I meant only to signal that I understood the way you'd read the children." He kept his voice low as the kids shared their drinks. "Neil and Daisy are both strong. So far they work together for the good of all. I hope it continues until their uncle arrives."

Cassie stumbled over her thoughts. She'd misread his action and now she was embarrassed and uncertain how to undo it. Best to simply face it honestly and move on. "Apology accepted and please accept my own regrets for being so quick to jump to offense."

He nodded but the air between them remained heavy with awkwardness.

"Those biscuits for eating?" Billy asked, eyeing the plate of biscuits and jam.

"Billy." Daisy grabbed his arm. "Mind your manners."

Neil watched Cassie with a look of uncertainty that made her forget any lingering embarrassment. How well she understood that look. Even more, she knew the fluttering in the pit of one's stomach that accompanied it. She wanted more than anything to put a stop to the kids feeling that way—and equally as much to lose the memory of that sensation.

"Billy, you're right. I've forgotten my manners as the hostess. Thank you for reminding me." She grabbed the plate and handed it around. "Take two," she insisted. She stopped in front of Neil. "We don't know each other and you might not be here long enough that we ever do but while you are here, you are safe. I expect each of you to be cooperative and polite but I'm not about to change my mind when you slip up. I won't kick you to the curb." She chuckled softly and glanced toward Macpherson's store. "Guess it might be a little hard seeing as there isn't even a street let alone a curb." She returned her gaze to Neil. "What I'm trying to say is you can trust me."

Neil held her gaze for a heartbeat then took two biscuits. "Thank you."

She didn't expect to win his approval overnight but it was a start. She held the plate and the remaining biscuits out to Roper.

He shook his head. "Give them to the kids. I'll go out early tomorrow and rustle up some more food."

Seems she would be depending on him far more than she cared to. Her whole goal had been to be free of obligation and debt. She ached to say it again but not while the children were listening.

The kids finished their food, handed Cassie their cups and quietly thanked her. They sat on their crude log benches, fingers twitching, their gazes darting about and long sighs escaping their lips.

Their restlessness made her skin tingle. "Go ahead and play while we have some more tea." She refilled Roper's cup and they watched as the kids hurried away to the other side of the walls Roper had constructed. As soon as they were out of sight, tension grabbed Cassie's muscles. This was a far cry from what she'd planned. Her agreement to work with him felt like a walk back into the very thing she meant to escape. "How long do you think it will take to contact the uncle?"

"I wouldn't venture a guess. Why? You already wishing I was gone?"

"You make me sound rude and ungrateful. I'm not. I just have plans. Goals. Don't you?"

He stared off in the distance for a moment, his expression uncharacteristically serious. Then he flashed her a teasing grin. "Now that you mention it, I guess I don't. Apart from making sure the kids are safe."

"I find that hard to believe. Don't you want to get your own ranch?"

He shrugged, his smile never faltering. "Don't mind being free to go where I want, work for the man I wish to work for."

She wanted him to admit to more than that. "Wouldn't you like to have a family of your own?"

The corners of his eyes flattened. The only sign that he wasn't still amused. "I never think of family."

She puffed out a sigh. "Family can be a pain."

He shrugged again. "Wouldn't know. Never had any except for the other kids in the orphanage." He laughed. "An odd sort of family, I guess. No roots. Changing with the seasons."

She didn't answer. Her grandfather had made the word *family* uncomfortable for her but that was different than what Roper meant. She didn't know how to respond to his description of family. With no response coming to her mind, she shifted back to her concern. "Roper, about our arrangement. I—"

He chuckled. "I know what you're going to say but this isn't about you or me. It's about the kids."

"So long as you remember that."

"I aim to. I got rules you know. Like never stay where you're not wanted. Don't put down roots you'll likely have ripped out."

She guessed there was a story behind his last statement. Likely something he'd learned by bitter experience but she didn't bother to ask. "I plan to put down roots right here." She jabbed her finger toward the ground.

"That's the difference between you and me." The grin remained on his lips but she noticed it didn't reach his eyes.

She studied him. "I'm guessing taking care of other people's business is another of your rules."

He laughed out loud at that. "Seems I got more rules than I realized."

Whispers and giggles came from behind the wooden walls. "Do you think they'll be okay?"

"You did good in telling them they'll be safe here." His grin seemed to be both approving and teasing.

How did he do that? Never quite serious. Always positive. Certainly different than how her grandfather had been. Thinking of the older man, she shifted her concern to the children. "They will be safe as much as it lies within me to make it so." And they'd never be made to feel like they were burdens. Not if she had anything to do with it.

"Good to know." He eased to his feet. "Watch this." He tiptoed to the half walls, glancing back at her with a wide grin. He held his finger to his mouth to signal her to silence then he edged around the corner and jumped into the children's view, yelling wildly.

Pansy screamed, Daisy gasped loudly enough for Cassie to hear her, and then started to laugh. Neil let out a yell. At the same time Billy hollered and ran diagonally across the lot.

Next thing she knew, Roper was tearing after Billy. "I'm going to catch you."

Billy looked over his shoulder, saw Roper bearing down on him and ran so fast his short legs could have churned butter. Not far behind Roper, Neil joined the pursuit.

Cassie jumped to her feet. What were they doing? Had Billy done something to annoy Roper? Was Neil trying to protect his brother? Aiming to protect the kids, she picked up her skirts and ran toward them.

Roper caught Billy and lifted him into the air. "Gotcha." He plopped the boy on the ground, knelt over him and tickled him.

Cassie slowed to a halt. It was only play!

Neil reached them, and threw himself on Roper's

back. Roper flipped to his stomach, Neil still clinging to him.

"You got me. Oh. Ow. Let me go."

Both boys piled on him, tickling and play fighting. At least she hoped it was play and by all the laughing she guessed it was. She knew little about play. Seemed her whole life had been work and if not work, then soberness and trying to please. Fun did not fit into either category. Somehow she thought it was that way for all children. Apparently Roper didn't agree.

Daisy joined her, Pansy again riding her hip. "Don't worry. The boys won't hurt him."

"I was worried about the boys."

They looked at each other and laughed. Pansy gave a shy smile from the shelter of Daisy's neck.

Cassie gave the little gal some study, taking in her wondrously big blue eyes that, in a few years, would bring grown men to her beck and call, and her fine blond hair that could use a combing. Suddenly she realized all the children were travel soiled. They would need baths and food and clean clothes and—

The enormity of the task she had taken on hit her like a falling pine. How could she possibly manage?

She sucked in air to relieve her anxiousness. It was a business arrangement that would result in having her house built, she told herself. It would help her achieve her dream. It was temporary and two of the kids were big enough to lend a hand. She could do this. She pushed her shoulders back as if stepping into a harness, and like a horse leaning into a load, she turned toward the fire.

Daisy followed on her heels. "I intend to do my share around here."

"Fine. Let's get the dishes done then heat water for baths."

"I guess we are pretty dirty. Mama would scold us for sure." Her voice quivered.

Cassie faced her. "I expect she would be proud that you've managed so well."

Daisy nodded. "Roper said Ma and Pa would be proud of us."

"Indeed."

She washed the few dishes, handing them to Daisy to dry. Pansy sat at Daisy's side, content to watch. As soon as they'd washed and dried the last cup, Cassie dragged out the big tub.

Roper saw her intent and he and Neil hauled more water from the nearby river.

As the water heated, Roper finished the walls and somehow built a frame for the roof on which to drape the canvas he purchased from Macpherson. With Neil's help he brought over the stove Cassie had ordered and set it up in the new shelter.

Cassie eyed it with joy. She'd be able to start baking bread for Macpherson and paying off her loan a lot sooner than she'd anticipated.

With the kids helping, Roper soon had Cassie's bed roll in one corner of the shelter, furs and blankets arranged for the children next to her bed. The stove and a crude table he'd put together made an area where she could work and feed the kids.

They dragged the tub under the canvas and filled it with water.

"I'll bathe Pansy," Daisy insisted.

Cassie didn't protest. She hadn't ever bathed a baby. Nor a two-year-old. Her heart clenched as she recalled her hope for babies. Twice she'd thought she'd welcome an infant into her arms but twice it wasn't to be. They had never drawn breath after their births.

She turned away, unable to catch her breath, and slipped outside before anyone noticed.

Roper found her there. "What's wrong?"

"Nothing." She stared toward the sun dipping behind the mountains and breathed slowly, evenly.

He gently touched her shoulder. "Are you regretting your decision?"

"It was an act of God."

His fingers tightened on her shoulder. "Are you talking about the children?"

She closed her eyes and pushed back a groan. Of course, he meant the children in the tent. "No, I don't regret my decision. It will benefit me to get my house up as soon as possible."

"You didn't mean the kids, did you?"

His quiet question, the gentleness in his voice tugged at her soul, made her want to wail out her pain. But she'd learned to hide her hurt, bury her feelings. She didn't know any other way of dealing with life. "I better go check on them."

He blocked her retreat. "I think they can manage quite well without us. Let's go for a walk."

"I'm really too tired."

"I want to show you where I'll set up my camp in case you need me for anything."

She stiffened her spine. "I think I can manage."

He chuckled. "I'm sure you can but this is a business deal, remember? The kids are my responsibility."

Somehow he had taken her elbow and herded her toward the river and a grove of trees.

"I'll take the tent that collapsed on you and pitch it here." He pointed. "If you need me, you have only to holler."

"I won't be hollering."

"I expect not. But I feel better knowing anyone could and I'll hear them."

He meant the kids could call for him. "Why would they need you when I'll be right there in the same tent or whatever you want to call it?"

"No reason. Just as there's no reason to get all prickly about it."

"Prickly?" She swallowed hard. "If I am it's because you make me sound like I can't manage on my own."

He held up his hands in a sign of protest. "It never crossed my mind."

"Well, then. So long as we understand each other." She headed back to her site.

He chuckled softly, and followed her. "Oh, I get it."

She ignored the note of triumph in his voice. How could he possibly comprehend? He had no idea of the events that had shaped her life and made her want nothing half as much as she wanted to be independent. Self-sufficient. "I don't need anyone," she muttered.

"Sounds mighty lonely to me."

"You can be lonely with people around." Thankfully they had reached camp and he didn't get a chance to respond.

The sound of giggling stopped them, and they listened.

"That's about the happiest sound in the world." Roper seemed pleased, content even.

"How can they be happy? Their parents are dead. They're orphans." Their lives were full of uncertainty.

"A person can be as happy as they make up their mind to be."

She'd heard the words before. "Linette said the same thing when we first arrived at the ranch." She didn't believe it was that simple any more now than she had then. People made demands of a person that made happiness impossible. It was why she intended to survive on her own.

"I figure you might as well choose to be happy as miserable."

She heard the shrug in his voice. "Sometimes it isn't up to you."

"I suppose you're right in the sense that our lives are in God's hands and ultimately we have to trust Him. But knowing that makes it easy to enjoy life, don't you think?"

Grateful for the dusk that hid her expression, Cassie murmured a sound that could be taken as agreement if he chose to interpret it as such. But inside, protests exploded. Didn't God let man have a choice? Because of free will, not all men lived by God's rules. Not all people were kind. Not all of life could be enjoyed.

She realized Roper was waiting for her answer. "Sometimes you have to work to get what you want from life. I trust God to help me achieve my goals." Saying it out loud solidified it in her mind. God had given her the opportunity to own a plot of land and now, by caring for the children, she would get her house built much faster, and no doubt better, than she could have done it. God had given her what she needed. She would apply all her skill and strength to making it work. "Now if you'll excuse me, I need to take care of my share of the responsibility."

"And I need to get my camp set up while I can still see." Still, he hesitated as if he wanted something more.

She searched her mind but could think of nothing more she needed to do. "Good night, then."

"Good night. Call out if you need anything." He turned and strolled away.

She watched until he dipped down toward the creek, out of sight. Yet she felt how close he was, how ready to come to her rescue.

He would soon learn she could manage on her own.

Chapter Three

Roper tethered the horse nearby then pitched the tent. When he finished, it had a nice taut roof line. He gathered up firewood and built a fire.

He stretched out on the bank, stared at the flickering flames and listened to the murmur of voices from up the hill. Everyone was secure and happy. He'd managed to deal with two issues at the same time. He could help Cassie put up her house and keep the kids safe and together.

More than that, he'd played with the boys and seen them relax. Now to do the same for the girls. Daisy took her responsibilities so seriously it might take her a while to let go. But Pansy could well prove the greatest challenge of them all. She was so young. So shy. He smiled up at the star-laden sky as he recalled how she ducked her face into Daisy's shoulder when she made eye contact. She was comfortable enough to laugh only when Neil or Daisy held her.

But Roper wanted to see her comfortable enough to let Cassie and himself hold her and play with her.

All he had to do was gain her confidence.

He also meant to get Cassie to stop trying so hard. What was she aiming to prove, anyway? Everyone knew she could do whatever she set her mind to. She was like a stubborn badger in that way.

He'd once watched a furry little badger digging a hole, dirt flying faster than a man could shovel. The badger encountered a rock in his path and simply dug around it.

Cassie was almost as belligerent as a badger, too.

Why didn't she accept life and enjoy it? Made no sense to fight it all the time.

He smiled as he thought how to deal with the quintet up the hill. In the morning he'd spend some time playing with them so they'd forget their troubles.

His breath eased out in a long contented sigh. He'd struck a great bargain in getting Cassie to agree to help him with the children in exchange for him putting up her house. He chuckled into the dark. What had she planned to do with that pile of lumber without his help? He could picture her fashioning a structure as shaky as the tent she'd put up.

Why was she so prickly about accepting help? He could build a good solid-frame house in a matter of days.

Mentally he planned the construction. He might have to drag it out longer than necessary in order to care for the young 'uns until their uncle made arrangements. But Cassie would know if he purposely dilly-dallied. He'd need a solid explanation she'd accept.

He sat up briskly and drew his knees to his chest. "Of course. That's the answer." She'd need a cellar to store her supplies in. It would take him a few days to dig one. Satisfied with his plan, he lay back again.

The sounds from up the hill subsided. Everyone was tucked in for the night. He kicked sand over the fire and went into the shelter of his tent. But he didn't immediately fall asleep as he normally would. Instead, he thanked God for the opportunity to take care of both Cassie and the youngsters.

Next morning Roper was up with the dawn and bagged four partridges. He dressed them and roasted them over his fire. By the time he heard Pansy's shrill voice, the birds were ready for breakfast and he marched up the hill.

Neil and Billy were outside, bleary-eyed in the morning sun.

"Morning, boys. I brought some breakfast in case anyone's hungry."

Both pairs of eyes immediately lost all sleepiness.

"I'm hungry," Billy said.

"Never mind him. He's always hungry." But Neil's gaze didn't waver from studying the roasted birds.

Daisy led Pansy from the tiny abode. As soon as the little one saw Roper, she lifted her hands to her sister and insisted on being carried.

What would it take to get the littlest one to warm up to him? At that moment, Cassie stepped out, head down as she fingered her hair into submission in a ragged bun. Her distraction allowed him plenty of time to study her. Her black hair glistened like sun off water. She had a leanness to her that once made him think her frail. She'd soon disabused him of that notion. She was about as frail as a sapling clinging tenaciously to the side of a mountain in the midst of winter storms and summer heat. His heart sunk to the bottom of his chest. He'd had little success getting her to warm up to him.

Cassie grew still and sniffed, catching the scent of his offering. She lifted her gaze—full of interest until she saw him. Then the interest faded to resistance.

Must she always be so prickly?

"Brought breakfast," he murmured before she could say anything.

She opened her mouth, glanced around at the expectant children and closed it again as if she needed to reconsider her reaction. "I expect the children are hungry. I've got a few more biscuits, as well." She ducked back inside and reemerged with a pan to put the birds in and tin plates for everyone. "I dug out the dishes from my supplies." She passed around plates for each.

"Guess I'll need to build us a table and benches." He slipped the birds from the spit as he talked and wiped his knife on his pant leg before he set to carving them.

The children watched in total fascination. Even little Pansy, although she kept her face pressed to Daisy's shoulder, watched his knife slice off portions, drool wetting her sister's dress. Seems it had been a few days since this bunch had had a good feed. He put a piece on each plate and Cassie added a biscuit. The youngsters perched on logs but no one took a bite.

Roper sent Cassie a questioning look. She shrugged. Then her mouth pursed as if she realized something. "I expect you're all waiting for someone to say grace."

Four heads nodded.

"Ma said we should never forget to thank the good Lord for His mercies," Daisy said.

"I sure am thankful for breakfast," Billy said. "It smells awfully good." He swallowed hard.

Roper blinked as every pair of eyes turned to him. "Me?"

"You're the man," Neil pointed out. "Ma said it was a man's job to lead the family. I said grace when Pa was away." His chest swelled with pride then sank again. "But I'm just a kid."

The expectation of these youngsters made Roper want to stand tall. Yes, he was a man. One who seldom thought to say grace when he was out on the trail and this wasn't much different. Not that he couldn't. But at the cook shack, Cookie or her husband, Bertie, said grace. It had been a long time since he'd spoken a prayer aloud. In fact—

"I could do it if you want I should," Neil offered in an uncertain voice.

"No, I'll do it."

The children reached for each other's hands. Billy reached for his hand on one side. That left Roper with one hand to extend toward Cassie. He hesitated. Would she refuse this gesture?

Daisy gave them both a look that was half scolding and half confused.

He reached for Cassie's hand and she slipped hers into his as she darted a look at him from under black eyelashes. One eyebrow quirked as if daring him to read more into this than he should.

A grin threatened to split his face.

She sighed, and nodded toward the cooling food.

Still smiling, he bowed his head. Suddenly his mind went blank. What did Bertie or Cookie say? He should be able to remember. Cookie, especially, bellowed the words loud enough to brand them on his brain. "Dear God. Thanks for the food. Thanks for health and strength." Cookie normally said more. Sometimes a whole lot more but he must have paid more attention to the aroma of the food waiting his attention than the words because they had disappeared. "Amen."

The children attacked their food.

He didn't realize he held Cassie's hand in a deadly grip until she jerked his arm to get his attention. With an unrepentant grin, he freed her. He held her gaze for several seconds before she huffed and turned to her food. He got a kick out of teasing her.

A few minutes later the children finished and stared at the slower adults.

He felt their unasked question. "What?"

Neil and Daisy exchanged a silent look that spoke volumes.

"Spit it out." He swallowed the last bit of biscuit and put his plate on the ground before him. "You might as well say what's on your mind. After all, we're going to be together for a time." He figured it would a few days for the Mountie to take care of his business. He hoped he could then persuade the man to leave the children with them while he contacted the uncle. Daisy nodded. "Ma made us promise we'd make sure the little ones are raised right and that we continue some of our practices that both Ma and Pa held as important."

He guessed Daisy was going someplace with this information but he had no idea where and turned his questioning gaze to Cassie, wondering if she got the drift, but she merely shrugged.

"What practice did you have in mind, Daisy?"

Daisy glanced at Neil who nodded encouragement.

She took a deep breath. "Ma, and Pa before he left, always read to us from the Bible after breakfast. And they prayed for us to have a good day and be safe. You could be like Pa."

Roper stared. He guessed he looked as surprised as he felt. Being raised in an orphanage, he had no knowledge of this kind of thing. Of course, he knew families had traditions but he thought that meant trimming the Christmas tree or going to Grandma and Grandpa's house for Sunday dinner.

He swallowed hard and clamped his lips together. The idea of playing pa to these youngsters…

It sounded mighty appealing but he had no idea how it was done.

He managed to find his voice. "I got no Bible."

Daisy turned to Cassie. "Do you?"

She nodded. "I'll get it." She hustled to the shelter, and disappeared from sight. They all stared after her.

Roper had to wonder if the children felt as awkward as he. But likely not. This was familiar to them.

Cassie returned and handed him a Bible bound in brown leather. He trailed his fingers over the soft cover.

"It was my husband's."

He lifted his head to meet her gaze. He knew she'd been married before. Their first introduction referred to her as a widow. Yet holding this solid proof of a lost love did something unsettling to his insides. "You sure you don't mind us using it?"

She shrugged. "It doesn't do much good tucked in the bottom of a bag, now does it? Besides, the children have made a request. Shouldn't you try and fulfill it?"

He opened to the first page. *Presented to George James Godfrey on the occasion of his sixteenth birthday by his loving parents.*

Swallowing a lump of guilt, feeling as if he had inadvertently ventured into private territory, he quickly turned the page. *This certifies that Cassie Ann Mudd-bottom and George James Godfrey were united in Holy Matrimony.* He sputtered back a snort of laughter. *Muddbottom.* Some of his mirth leaked out. He felt Cassie's considering look and flipped the page. *Births and deaths.* He should not read this. It was too personal. But his eyes did not obey his brain. *Baby boy Godfrey. Baby girl Godfrey.* She'd had two children? Where were they? The answer lay in the record before him. They were born and died the same day. *Oh, Cassie. I had no idea.* If they'd been alone he would have spoken his sympathy. Maybe even risked her ire by pulling her into his arms and patting her back.

Instead, he sucked in a gulp of air and continued turning pages till he got to the pertinent stuff. He cleared his throat and read, "'In the beginning God...'" He read to the end of the chapter then slowly closed the book.

The children sighed as if content. The feeling lasted about thirty seconds before he realized they waited for him to pray for their safety throughout the day. Just as their pa had.

He sat up taller and squared his shoulders. He wasn't their pa, but he could do this. "Let's pray." They all bowed their heads. Even Cassie. His throat tightened as he glanced at them. Maybe this was how fathers felt, though he wasn't sure how to describe the feeling. Protectiveness, or responsibility or... He swallowed back a lump at the word that sprang to his mind. Joy. Joy at such a privilege. It was his first real taste of being part of a family and he rather liked it. Even as a portion of his brain reminded him of one of his rules. *Don't put down roots. You'll only have them ripped out.* It wasn't a lesson he cared to repeat.

He ducked his head before anyone wondered what took him so long. "Dear God in heaven, who made the earth and everything in it, please watch over us today. Keep us safe. Help us be happy. Amen."

Daisy got to her feet, shifted Pansy farther up her hip and gathered up the dishes with her free hand. "I'll wash them."

Neil headed for the water bucket. "I'll fetch more water."

Billy glanced about. "What should I do?"

"Get more firewood," both older children said at once and the entire family set to work.

Roper fingered the Bible on his lap. He wanted to say something to Cassie about her losses. But he didn't want to upset her. Seemed being reminded of two dead babies and a deceased husband just might do that. But he enjoyed sitting by her side and didn't want her to leave. "Do all families do that?"

She jerked and seemed to gather herself up from some distant spot. "Do what?"

"Read the Bible and pray each morning. Is that what all families do?"

She turned then and considered him with such brown-eyed intensity he had to force himself not to squirm.

"I'm guessing they didn't do so in the orphanage?"

"Nope. We stood for grace. Ate quietly and without complaint even when the food was thin gruel, then gathered our dishes and carried them to a big tub before we marched to our classrooms."

"No Bible instruction?"

He chuckled at the idea of wasting time on such an activity. "On Sunday we were given religious instruction. When I was about ten there was a sweet old man who came in and told Bible stories and made it seem like fun. A lot of us became believers when he was there. But he only came a couple of years. The rest of the time we had stiff preachers who intoned a sermon for us." He realized his voice imitated their mind-numbing monotone and he grunted. "Haven't thought about it in a long time. I remember the sessions were so boring some of the little ones would fall asleep. If they were caught they'd be punished. I made sure they didn't get caught."

Her eyes sparked with curiosity and a warmth that sent satisfaction into his soul. He liked having her regard him with eyes like that.

"What did you do?"

"To keep them from getting caught? If we were allowed to sit where we wanted, I sat with the little ones and played finger games that didn't attract any attention but kept the little ones watching." He illustrated by having the fingers of one hand do a jig on the back of the other. "It was nothing special but they had to keep alert to see when I'd do something."

"And if you couldn't sit with them?"

"Then it was harder. But one of the things I did was send a tap down the line. Everyone would pass it on to the little ones."

"Seems you felt responsible for the younger children."

He considered the observation. "It wasn't really responsibility. Not like Daisy. It was more like I wanted everyone to be happy."

Her grin tipped the flesh at the corner of her eyes upward. "I think you haven't changed a great deal."

He tried to think how he felt about her evaluation. He decided it was true and he didn't mind that she'd noticed something he did without thinking about it. "Back to my original question." He tipped his head to indicate the circle where the children had sat. "Is it normal? You have a family. Is that what you did?"

Her eyes darkened. The smile fled from her face. What had he said to bring such distress to her face? Whatever it was, it had been unintentional.

But how could he undo it when he was at a loss to explain it?

The ground beneath Cassie's feet seemed to tip as a thousand memories crowded her mind. "My father died when I was nine so I don't recall much about being a whole family." Except she suddenly did. "I remember sitting on my father's knee as he read aloud. We were in a rocking chair. A lamp glowed nearby so it must have been evening. Mother was in the kitchen so it was just me and…" She stopped the words that had come from nowhere. Just her and those comforting, secure arms. "Just me and my father." The memory ached through her. She concentrated on breathing slowly and deeply. She forced strength into her voice. "Seems I recall my father reading to me at night. He heard my prayers before Mother tucked me in and kissed me good night."

"Didn't you keep doing the same things after he was gone? I guess I would…both to honor him and preserve the memory."

"Things changed after he died." Her grandfather didn't allow such extravagances. *The child is big*

*enough to put herself to bed. I'm not supporting you
to spend time coddling her.* She pushed to her feet. "I
better get to work." She went to join Daisy at the dishpan. "I'll dry," she said to the girl.

Roper strode away in the direction of Macpherson's
store. She wouldn't watch him go. Nor voice any curiosity about why. But hadn't he said he'd build her
house? Shouldn't he be doing so? He liked to make
everyone happy, did he? She sensed it was more than
that. Seems he had a need to make sure people were
well taken care of. Well, she silently huffed, she had
no need of his help. She'd learned to depend on no one.
She had all she needed right here on this little bit of
land. She glanced about at the piles of lumber, the neat
little shelter Roper had erected. Yes, she'd accept his
help in exchange for providing care for the children.
But she'd never make the mistake of expecting it nor
of counting on it.

Daisy persuaded Pansy to sit on a log at her side as
she dried the dishes. "I want to thank you for allowing us to stay here and I promise we'll do our best not
to be any trouble."

Children are nothing but trouble. The words rever-
berated through her head in her grandfather's harsh
voice. How could such a coldhearted man raise a son
who turned out to be a loving father? Why had the better of the two died? Seemed bitterly unfair in her mind.

She hated that these children should feel the same
condemning words hovering in the background and
vowed she would not do or say anything to make them
real. She dried her hands on the towel and turned to
Daisy. With her still-damp hands, she clasped the girl's
shoulders and turned her so they were face-to-face. "I

don't consider you the least bit of trouble. In fact, it would be mighty lonely if I were here by myself." Yet that was exactly what she intended once the children were gone. "Besides, isn't it to my benefit? I get help to build my house."

Daisy considered her steadily, then, satisfied with Cassie's assurance, nodded. "Still. I wouldn't want you to regret it."

"I promise I won't." As she returned to her task a flash drew her attention to the side. Roper stood with two spades over his shoulder, so new and shiny the sun reflected off them. He stared as if he'd overheard the conversation. She favored him with a challenging glare, silently informing him not to read anything into her confession of loneliness. It was meant to reassure the children, not give him an argument to pursue.

"What's with the shovels?" Far as she could figure he needed to wield hammer and saw, not shovels.

He moved closer so she saw the green glints in his eyes. "Got to thinking. Didn't you say you plan to bake bread for the store?"

She nodded even though he knew the answer.

"And feed travelers?"

She didn't bother to nod again.

"Seems you might be needing a cellar. You know. To keep things cool in the summer and stop your canned goods from freezing in the winter. So me and Neil are gonna dig you one."

No way could she hide her surprise and she knew he read it on her face by the way he grinned in satisfaction. He held her gaze for several seconds.

She tried to tell herself she didn't notice the way his eyes flashed pleasure at coming up with an idea that seemed to please her. Tried to convince herself he was only doing what he always did—making sure people were happy. But try as she might she couldn't deny a little start of something both sweet and reluctant. It was sweet to have someone appear to care about what might please her. But she dare not let herself think past that. A woman in her situation could do no better than maintain her independence.

Still grinning, Roper called Neil and handed him a shovel. Together they marched to where she'd marked the boundaries of her house and began to dig.

An hour later they'd made little progress.

She began to suspect digging a cellar hole would consume an inordinate length of time.

Had that been his reason for suggesting it? Not concern for her at all but only an excuse to hang around and do for her what she preferred to do for herself?

He'd always balked at her independence.

She glanced about at the children. Daisy brushed Pansy's hair and talked softly to her. Neil worked alongside Roper trying his best to dig at the same pace as Roper, which was impossible yet Roper told the boy how well he was doing. Billy carried the dirt to the designated area. How could she tell Roper she suspected him of delay tactics?

She didn't need or want him trying to take care of her.

Chapter Four

As Roper and Neil dug, Cassie turned her attention to other things. First, she had to prepare meals for the children and Roper. With the stove set up in the little shelter, she could bake, using this time to her advantage to start paying off her debt at Macpherson's. She mixed up a hearty stew of meat and vegetables and as it simmered, she cut lard into flour for biscuits. By noon, she had several dozen baked and cooling.

"This place is steaming hot."

She turned at Roper's voice behind her and brushed a strand of hair from her burning face. "I'm baking."

"Both yourself and biscuits, I presume."

She grinned at his teasing.

"You need a breeze going through here." He ducked outside and made a racket on the wall. Then the canvas rolled up and blessed cool air blew through the shack. Roper peered through the opening. "I can roll it down at night."

"Oh, that feels good." She fanned herself. "I didn't realize how hot it was."

He came in again and eyed the biscuits covering the table. "You've been busy."

"Dinner is ready." She reached for the pot then realized she had no place to put it.

Roper grabbed a towel and took the pot. "Come see what I made."

She wrapped a selection of biscuits in a towel and followed him outside. "A picnic table. Perfect. Now we can eat outdoors in comfort."

He set the stew in the middle of the table. "I thought you could use it for feeding travelers, too."

"Thank you, but—" Oh, dear. How were they going to manage working together if he constantly took care of her when she was determined to take care of herself?

Though, on her own, it would take a little longer to build a house and get herself organized. Macpherson understood she'd take time to get established.

"Just part of the business deal." His dismissive tone warned her not to make a fuss about it.

She stifled a sigh. She might as well take advantage of all this arrangement offered. So she tucked away her resistance as Daisy passed around the plates and cups.

Cassie waited for the children to sit, then chose a place that wouldn't put her near Roper. She didn't want to be forced to hold his hand again during prayer. But as soon as she was seated, Neil and Billy slid down on the bench opposite her and made room for Roper to edge in and sit directly across from her, an unrepentant grin on his face. He'd correctly read her attempt to avoid him.

She barely restrained herself from wrinkling her nose at him but let him guess at the silent message in her eyes. *Don't think I've changed my mind about want-ing to keep this businesslike.*

He winked, and when he saw her draw her eyebrows together in affront, he sighed. "Cassie, don't be look-ing for offense when none is meant."

She forced a smile to her lips but figured it looked as wooden as it felt.

Roper wagged his head in mock frustration. "Cassie, Cassie, what am I going to do with you?"

She tipped her chin. "You could try saying the bless-ing so we could eat before the ants find us."

The children giggled.

Roper chuckled. "Very well." He eagerly reached for her hand, giving her a look that said he enjoyed her discomfort. Then he bowed his head and uttered a few words. "Amen."

When she jerked her hand free, his eyes practically glittered with triumph. Oh, bother. By overreacting to an innocent, meaningless touch of hands, she'd given him reason to think it meant more than it did when she only wanted to remind him this was a business deal.

They ate in companionable silence except for Pansy who fretted.

Daisy hushed her. "She needs a nap."

"Finish your meal, then put her down," Roper said.

"And the dishes?"

Goodness, the child had an overblown sense of re-sponsibility. Cassie patted her hand. "I can manage a few dishes."

Daisy nodded gratefully, scooped up her little sister and disappeared inside the shack. For a few minutes Daisy's gentle murmurs blended with Pansy's fussing, and then all was silent.

Roper helped Cassie clean up the table. "Daisy reminds me of you," he said.

"How's that?" She filled a basin with hot water, and began to wash the dishes. She scrubbed the plates and Roper dried them.

"She feels she has to do everything herself."

"Independence is good, especially when she has no one else." Seems that should have been self-evident even to a man like Roper, determined to help everyone he met.

"But is that true?"

"Her father and mother are dead. Who knows what her uncle will decide about their future? Seems the best thing they can do is learn how to manage on their own, expect nothing from anyone else."

"What about people who want to help?"

She couldn't tell if it was hurt or warning that made his voice so low and decided it was safest to assume the latter. "I suppose she has reason to wonder what other people want in return."

"I don't want anything but to help. What do you want?"

Maybe she'd been talking more about herself than the children. "I expect nothing from them. I hope they understand that."

"Your words are contradictory."

"Maybe so. But it seems best to count on no one but yourself." She had to change the direction of this conversation before she said more than she meant to… things she hadn't even reasoned out yet. "How long do you think it will take to dig the cellar?"

He shrugged, his gaze lingering on her as he understood her attempt to avoid explaining herself. "Depends on how hard the ground is. And I don't want to overwork young Neil. He's determined to match me shovelful for shovelful. Besides, I don't want him to think the only thing I want from him is work. In fact, I've decided to take a break for some play." He paused. "If you have no objection."

"Of course I don't." Did he think all she cared about was work? "The children should certainly be allowed a little fun."

Maybe he was right. She seemed to know little about how to play.

"You'll join us, won't you?" Had he read her mind and determined to teach her?

"I have biscuits to deliver to Macpherson's."

"You might wake Pansy if you go into the shack."

Cassie scrambled to find an excuse to avoid joining Roper and the children. Before she could, Roper waved to the boys.

"Who wants to play a game?"

Neil and Billy perked up and raced toward him. Daisy slipped from the shack and hesitated.

"You, too." Roper waved to her. "Everyone's going to play." He shot Cassie a challenging look. "Play refreshes the soul."

Cassie swallowed hard.

"Come on. We'll go down by the river so we don't wake Pansy."

The boys ran after him, while Daisy followed more slowly, cautiously, as if uncertain she should let herself play.

It was Daisy's hesitation that convinced Cassie to join the parade. Daisy was still young enough to enjoy a game or two. She shouldn't let her responsibilities take away that pleasure. So Cassie linked arms with Daisy. "Let's see what he's up to." She could feel the girl relax beneath her touch.

Roper glanced over his shoulder and grinned.

Cassie knew he'd heard her and, furthermore, she guessed he might have some inkling as to her motive. Though she felt a strong urge to wrinkle her nose at him, she hoped the toss of her head convinced him of her lack of concern for his opinion.

Roper waited until they all reached the bank of the river. "Who knows how to play Sneak Up on Granny?"

No one said they did.

"I'll be granny. You line up there." He drew a line in the sand. "I'll stand here." He went about twenty feet away. "When I turn my back, you try and sneak up on me. When I shout 'stop,' don't move because when I turn around and see you moving, you go back to the start."

"What's the point of the game?" Cassie refrained from saying it sounded silly because she recognized the voice in the back of her head as that of her grandfather. *Waste of precious time.* For that reason alone she would play the game and waste as much time as she pleased.

"If you can sneak up on me and touch my shoulder without me catching you moving, you get to play granny."

Cassie snorted. "Great. I've always had a hankering to play granny." She drew her lips in, hunkered over like an old woman and smacked her gums loudly.

The three children giggled and Cassie knew a sense of satisfaction. Was this how Roper felt when he made others happy? She shot him a look, wondering if her surprise showed.

Their gazes caught and held, and the look of triumph in his eyes seared away something she couldn't identify. Didn't want to acknowledge. All she would admit was it felt good and right to make the children laugh. It seemed fitting to see them enjoy life.

She would not listen to the strident voice of her grandfather telling her to stop wasting time.

The children toed up to the line he'd scratched in the ground. She did the same as Roper took his place ahead of them.

"One, two, three." He counted, turning his back.

Neil raced forward. Billy took a giant leap. Daisy tiptoed.

Cassie took one cautious step, and then another.

"Stop."

Neil skidded but not in time. Billy was in midair and landed with a thud.

Roper chuckled. "Boys. Back to the start."

Daisy and Cassie grinned at each other. He hadn't caught them.

"One, two, three." He turned away again.

Billy and Neil tried to make up for lost time but Cassie edged forward, knowing she must be ready to stop quickly.

"Stop."

Again the two boys were sent back to the start amid groans.

Roper gave Cassie and Daisy a long stare as if daring them to waver. Neither of them did.

They continued. Cassie was within two feet but Roper called stop so often she daren't move. She tensed. One step was all it would take. As soon as he began to turn away, she leaped forward and reached out to clap his shoulder. At the same time he hollered stop and turned to face her, and they collided.

She staggered, off balance and about to fall, until he caught her, his hands warm on her arms as he steadied her.

She looked deep into his hazel eyes, saw his concern over bumping her. Her heart beat a frantic tattoo against her breastbone. Longing rose up within her, a hunger to be valued and appreciated. To be cared for.

No, she told herself. Such feelings were a weakness she would never allow herself. She'd learned far too well how they made her vulnerable. She shook free from his grasp. "Guess I'm granny now." Surely he wouldn't notice the trembling in her voice.

"Guess so." His voice grated as if his throat had grown tight.

They returned to play although she had little interest. She wasn't a bit sorry when Pansy's cry brought an instant end to their game as Daisy rushed back to get the little one.

The rest trooped after her.

"I'm going to take biscuits over to Macpherson's and see if he can sell them." Cassie headed for the little shack as if she had a sudden deadline.

"Come on, boys. Let's get that cellar dug." Roper sounded as cheerful as ever.

Why had she wasted so much time? It was Roper's fault. Something about him enticed her to forget her responsibilities and goals.

All winter she'd avoided him as much as possible without being rude. Or maybe sometimes, especially at first, she hadn't cared if she happened to be rude. All she could remember of the first few weeks at the ranch was the pain of her losses and despair at how desperate her situation was.

When Linette had found her sleeping in the train station in Montreal she'd cajoled, enticed and begged Cassie to accompany her West on her trek to meet her future husband. Cassie had agreed because it had seemed better than her current situation. Anything would have been better. She didn't know she would end up in a tiny log cabin, barely big enough for one adult let alone three adults and a child. Even worse, Eddie was not expecting to marry Linette and said he had no intention of doing so. Not that Linette was deterred. She said she would prove to him she'd make an ideal pioneer wife.

Cassie smiled. The attraction between Linette and Eddie had been obvious from the first but it had taken the pair most of the winter to acknowledge what the rest of them saw.

She pressed her palm to her chest. She missed Linette. And Grady.

She missed Cookie, too. From the beginning, the big-hearted woman seemed oblivious to Cassie's sharpness and showed her nothing but kindness. Slowly, between Linette and Cookie and the gentle attention of the cowboys at the ranch, Cassie's wounds had healed. She'd gone from thinking she had no choice but to accept whatever kindness and protection a man would offer to knowing she could live life on her own terms.

It wasn't something she meant to give up. She had a life to live. Work to do. A business to establish.

She filled a large bowl with biscuits, covered it with

a clean tea towel and headed over to Macpherson's store. A couple of cowboys lounged against the counter as she stepped inside. Within minutes most of the biscuits had been purchased.

Macpherson snagged one of the biscuits for himself and tested it. "These are good. Reminds me of my daughter, Becca. She used to bake the best biscuits. Many a man stepped into the store solely to see if she had any baking on hand."

Cassie couldn't remember much of what she'd heard about Macpherson's daughter. "She moved away, didn't she?"

"Married herself a fine young man, Colt, and adopted two orphaned children. They have themselves a little ranch northwest of here. I expect them to visit this summer."

Cassie chuckled. "You're obviously proud of them."

"A fine bunch." He indicated the crumbs of biscuit on his fingers. "Bring me more of these as soon as you can. You set up to bake bread yet?"

"I'll start today."

Glowing with satisfaction she returned to her place. Oh, didn't that sound good! *Her place.* A business about to take off. A house soon to be constructed, thanks to Roper's help.

She ground to a halt at the corner of the shack and watched Roper digging her cellar. Her house. Her cellar. Her land. It seemed Roper was contributing far more to this arrangement than she. What would she owe him? Nervousness quivered in the pit of her stomach. She didn't like to owe anyone. She sucked in air to calm the fluttering, and reminded herself that it was a business agreement. So he could help the children.

Or was it an excuse so he could take care of her?

He glanced up, saw her watching and slowly straightened.

Her eyes must have given away her doubt and confusion for he climbed from the hole and strode toward her.

She shook her head to clear it, and ducked into the shack where she made a great deal of noise pulling out a bowl so she could set the yeast to rise.

"Cassie? Something wrong?" His voice came from the doorway.

"The biscuits sold like hotcakes. Macpherson was very pleased. Asked if I could start providing bread." No doubt she sounded falsely cheerful.

It took only three steps for him to close the distance between them. "That's good news. So why do you look so troubled?"

She could deny it, tell him he must be imagining things. But her doubts had a tenacious grip on her thoughts. She straightened and slowly faced him. "Why are you doing this?"

He looked around, not knowing what she meant and searching for a clue. "Doing what?"

She waved her hand around the little shack, then pointed to indicate the activity beyond the canvas walls. "Everything. Why are you digging a cellar? Offering to build my house? What do you expect in return?"

He stepped back and his eyebrows knotted. "Cassie Godfrey, you are one suspicious woman. I told you what I want—to help the children. I grew up in an orphanage. Never knew anything about family. I saw kids ripped from their siblings. Do you think I could stand back and let that happen to these youngsters when I could do something to prevent it?" His voice had grown harsh. "I'm more than willing to dig your cellar and build your house if it enables me to help them. I thought you understood that."

She sighed. "Family isn't the ideal dream you seem to think it is."

"And yet I doubt it's the curse you seem to consider it." He swung about and strode from the shack.

She stared after him. Was that what she thought?

Her earliest memories had been pleasant enough but then… She shook her head. She didn't know what she thought. Except that she intended to have a batch of bread ready to deliver tomorrow.

She set to work, pausing only to make supper and hurrying through the meal so she could return to her baking, though, if she admitted the truth to herself, she wasn't half as busy as she acted.

She simply did not want to face Roper any more than she must and feel guilty about his accusing looks. No. She'd keep busy running her business and she'd not allow anything to divert her from her purpose.

As soon as breakfast was over the next morning, Roper headed for the cellar hole, his insides burning with frustration. Prickly Cassie, always seeing ulterior motives. She'd avoided him last evening. He'd hoped for a change in her behavior at breakfast but she'd slid her glance over him as if he were invisible.

"I hope my bread turns out," she murmured as if nothing else mattered.

Before he reached the cellar, he veered off toward the river. In his present frame of mind he wasn't decent company for a young lad. He grabbed his rifle. They could always use fresh meat. On second thought…

He hitched the horse to the wagon.

Neil appeared at his side. "Whatcha doing?"

"Need to take the wagon back to the ranch and get my saddle horse." Eddie had told him to help Cassie if she'd let him so he wouldn't have been concerned when Roper didn't immediately return.

"You coming back?"

At the sound of fear and uncertainty in the boy's voice, Roper's anger fled. "I'm not about to ride out on you." He clamped his hand to Neil's shoulder. "I said I was going to build Cassie's house and I will. I said I would look after you until your uncle came and I will. Never doubt it. But I need a saddle horse to hunt meat for us."

Neil nodded.

Billy and the girls watched him from the trees. "I'll be back. Take care of yourselves and help Cassie." He spoke out of his own heart's desire. He wanted to take care of them all…but Cassie didn't want his help.

He closed his eyes and willed his inner turmoil to settle. He had nothing against a woman having a business if she had the hankering. But Cassie's desire went beyond what was necessary or expedient. She seemed set on proving something. He had no idea what.

"You gonna tell Cassie you're going?" Neil asked.

"I'll let you."

"You should tell her yourself," Daisy interjected, sounding quite certain.

The four watched him closely.

"Ma always said—" Neil started.

Here we go again. Them wanting him and Cassie

to act like their ma and pa. He didn't want to disappoint them but he had no idea how to be a pa any more than he had a hankering to put down roots. A no-name cowboy didn't expect to belong any place for long. As he'd said to Cassie, he liked being able to say when, where and with whom. "If it will make you happy." He knew his voice revealed his frustration as soon as Daisy clutched Pansy closer and Neil reached for Billy's hand. He was getting as prickly as Miss Cassie.

If such a little thing eased their minds, he could do it graciously. "You're right. I should tell her." He flashed them a grin as he tromped back up the hill to the shack where pots and pans clattered. Hat in hand, he paused in the doorway.

Cassie glanced up, saw him and pointedly returned to her work.

"I'm going to take the wagon back to the ranch and get a saddle horse."

Her hands stilled. He felt her indrawn breath.

"Do you want to come along? You and the youngsters?"

She didn't look directly at him but he caught a flash of eagerness. Then it disappeared, and she grunted. "Thought you were taking the wagon back."

"Uh-huh." Of course, he couldn't bring them back on a saddle horse. "Eddie might be willing to lend us a wagon."

"No need. I can't go. I've got work to do." She nodded at the bowl of dough and set of bread pans. "Check and see how Linette is, though, if you don't mind, and say hi to Grady for me."

"I can do that. You'll be okay until I get back?"

That brought her about so fast he chuckled.

"I think I can manage just fine, thank you."

"See you later, then." He was still chuckling as he returned to the wagon and bid the youngsters goodbye.

Later, he pulled the wagon onto the Eden Valley Ranch property and drove past the ranch house. From the dining room window overlooking the yard, he saw Linette watching and waved. At least she was feeling well enough to be up and about.

Eddie trotted from the barn. "Roper. Nice to see you back. Are you here to stay?"

"No. Sorry, boss, but you won't believe what I've been doing."

"Tell me about it. No, wait. You better come to the house and tell Linette at the same time."

Roper jumped from the wagon and fell in step with Eddie as they headed up the path to the house. "How's Linette?" When he left, Eddie was worried that she was so sick.

"She's fine."

"Good to see you grinning from ear to ear. Not all hangdog like you were when I left."

Eddie laughed. "She tells me she's in the family way. That's why she's ill."

Roper ground to a halt. He wasn't sure how a man should respond. "You seem happy." The idea of family filled him with a queasy feeling. It seemed an unnecessary risk.

"I feel like I'm walking on air."

"You don't mind that she's sick?"

"Linette assures me it's normal and temporary as her body adjusts to the new life growing in her."

Roper grinned. "Eddie Gardiner a papa! Now won't

that be something?" He couldn't wait to tell Cassie the news.

Eddie grinned wide enough to split his face. "It will certainly be something to behold." They reached the house and Eddie threw open the door.

Linette waited in the entrance, the picture of health.

"You're looking good," Roper said.

"I'm feeling fine. Better than fine." She sent Eddie a look full of love and adoration.

A hollow hunger hit Roper's gut and sucked at his soul. He pushed away the feeling. It was enough that Eddie and Linette were happy, he told himself. He was glad for them.

Linette led the way into the cozy room with big windows allowing a view of the ranch buildings. "Have you been with Cassie all this time?" she asked as they sat at the big table.

"I have and you wouldn't believe why. She sure didn't want me to stay and help but…"

Linette served tea and cookies as he told of finding the children and his agreement with Cassie.

"Boss, I'll be needing time off to help with the kids."

Eddie nodded. "Take as much time as you need. Your job will be waiting."

"I'm so grateful it's worked out that way. I've been praying God would somehow make it so Cassie would get help. She's so…"

Roper sighed. "Prickly."

Linette chuckled. "Actually I was thinking independent. She once told me she didn't feel she could trust anyone. Or was it only men she didn't trust? I can't remember but once she figured out how to start her own business she was set on proving she didn't need any help."

"She's still set on doing so."

Grady burst into the room. "Hi, Roper." He looked about. "Where's Cassie?"

"I left her in town. Remember, she said she was going to live there."

Grady climbed to Linette's lap and snuggled close.

Roper had often observed that Linette gave the child as much comfort as he sought. Grady was fortunate. He could have been placed in an orphanage. Roper had no complaints about his upbringing—he'd been fed and housed and taught to read and write. Even been taught about God. But he couldn't remember ever having a lap to welcome him. He couldn't even imagine how it would have felt.

"We'll visit her soon," Linette promised Grady.

After a few minutes the boy got down and found a collection of carved animals to play with.

Linette leaned closer. "Tell me more about the children and how Cassie is doing."

Roper told her everything he could think of. Even remembered to mention that Cassie was taking biscuits to the store and was busy baking bread for Macpherson to sell.

"Sounds like she's getting into business sooner than she thought possible, thanks to your help."

He shrugged a little. Too bad Cassie wasn't as appreciative as Linette.

Linette turned to consult Eddie. "She'll be needing some supplies. Potatoes, carrots. Some meat. Do you think Cookie would part with some of the jarred beef she did up?"

Eddie chuckled. "I think if I mention sending something for Cassie, Cookie will load a wagon to the limit." He turned to Roper. "Come along. Let's see what we can find."

They found plenty. Enough to see Cassie through much of the summer unless she started feeding huge crews. Roper took time to visit with Cookie and Bertie and the cowboys still around the place, then headed back to town with a full wagon and a saddle horse tied to the back.

Roper didn't mind in the least that he'd returned with the wagon he'd meant to leave at the ranch. His only regret was he hadn't insisted Cassie come with him. Next time he would.

He glanced back at all the supplies. It eased his mind to know she'd have plenty of provisions even when he couldn't bring in game. There was no way she could reject these gifts. Because he wasn't taking them back.

The wagon rattled as he drove toward home.

Home? Guess he was so used to calling any place he hung his hat home, so it naturally followed this was home for the time being. But the word had a more satisfying feel to it than a hat rack. Probably because he had youngsters to care for and a house to build.

Suddenly he realized it was the closest to home he'd ever known even if it was only temporary. Something pinched the back of his stomach. A sensation of intermingled regret, sorrow, hope and—

He'd long ago learned the futility of wishing upon stars or anything else, so he abandoned that way of thinking and turned his thoughts to estimating how long it would take to dig the cellar at the rate they were going.

Lost in his planning, he was surprised when he reached Cassie's bit of land.

No one raced out to greet him as he pulled to a halt, which provided a sharp reminder that this was not home. Then he heard Pansy's heart-wrenching cries. He bolted from the wagon and raced toward the sound.

Chapter Five

From the moment she'd watched Roper ride away, the wagon rumbling over the rutted trail, Cassie had been apprehensive. She was alone. Unless she counted the children, Macpherson, the smithy down the road and the riders who had come to town shortly after Roper left. No, she wasn't alone. Nor was she lonely.

And Roper had promised to return. The words came from a forbidden corner of her brain.

What difference did it make if he did or not? She could manage quite well by herself. But his words of promise embedded in her mind like warm sweets.

Even her busy hands did not keep her from wondering when Roper would be back. Only, she silently insisted, so she could hear news of Linette and the others at the ranch.

She marched outside for wood, and had her arms full when something tickled her skin. "What's on my arm?" she asked Daisy who hovered nearby.

Daisy squealed and backed away. "A—A—" She couldn't speak but her eyes spoke volumes. Mostly stark fear.

Her near panic was contagious, and Cassie dropped the load and backed away, watching as a snake writhed out from the wood Cassie had recently held close to her chest.

Cassie shuddered and swiped her hands over her chest and hair. "I hate snakes." She shuddered again and backed away from the woodpile. But she needed more wood. "Maybe Neil can get me some wood." She tipped her head toward the nearby trees. "I'm sure there's lots scattered about for the picking." But neither of them moved.

After Daisy called him, the boy stuck his head from the cellar hole that he continued to work on. "Can you get Cassie some firewood?"

He climbed from the hole. "There's a whole stack of it. Me and Roper made sure there was plenty on hand for several days."

Daisy and Cassie glanced at each other and shuddered. "There's a snake in there," Daisy said.

Neil shrugged. "Who cares about a little bitty snake? Come on, Billy. Let's get some wood for these sissies." He headed for the woodpile.

Cassie shivered. "It wasn't little. It was huge. And maybe poisonous."

Neil skidded to a halt. "How big?"

Daisy held out her arms to indicate a very large snake.

Neil edged away, reaching toward Billy and pushing him back, as well. "We'll get some from the trees." He kept his eyes on the woodpile until he was a good distance away.

Cassie could hardly contain her shudders as she returned to the shack, tiptoeing so she wouldn't wake

Pansy. She opened the oven door slowly, grateful it didn't squeak. The biscuits looked fine.

In a few minutes, the boys returned with their arms loaded, and Cassie had them put some wood in the stove.

"I'm not afraid of snakes, you know," she told them with mock confidence. Then she boldly marched to the stove and set the lid in place. "Thanks, boys, now I can get back to work."

Only it wasn't as simple as she hoped. Some of the wood must have been green for the stove smoked, the heat was uneven and she burned one side of a tray of biscuits.

The heat in the little shack grew oppressive but an hour later she had another tray of biscuits and bread baked a golden brown. She dusted her hands and looked about with satisfaction at all she'd accomplished.

Outside, sounds of the children playing came from the river. Knowing they didn't need her supervision she grabbed a spade and climbed into the cellar hole. Time to show she could manage on her own. With heartfelt determination, she set to work. The ground was hard and unyielding. After what seemed like hours, she'd made little progress. How did Roper manage to get the hole almost five feet deep in such a short time?

Roper. Who needed him? She jabbed the shovel into the ground sending a jarring shudder through her arms and into her shoulder joints. She hadn't asked him for his help. Didn't need him to dig a cellar for her. Gritting her teeth, she jumped on the top of the metal blade, bouncing until the blade edged into the rocklike ground. The wooden handle burned into her palms but she didn't relent until the dirt loosened.

Sweat beaded her forehead and soaked her chest. She ignored it. A woman must learn to manage on her own. Depending on a man made her vulnerable. Worse, it put her at his mercy. *You owe me. You have no choice. I say when and where.* Her heart threatened to burst with rage and sorrow. Her mother had jumped when Grandfather said jump. She'd given up every right even to her own opinion.

Cassie would never do the same. Never. She bent over the handle of the shovel, welcoming the pain in her blistered palms. Pain proved she was taking care of herself.

"Why don't you wait for Roper?"

At the child's voice she looked up to see Billy looking down into the hole. "I can do it myself." She tackled another bit of hard soil.

"You ain't getting much done."

"Thanks, Billy. Just the encouragement I need."

"Roper would do a hundred times faster 'n that."

"Probably he would." She grunted under a scoop of dirt. Seems each shovelful grew heavier. "But he isn't here and I am."

"He's coming back."

"Guess so. But this is my house. My cellar. My life. I can manage fine on my own."

Billy was quiet a moment. "I wouldn't like to be on my own." His voice was soft, tight with fear or perhaps sorrow.

Cassie paused, wiped her face on a corner of her skirt and grimaced at her blistered palms. "You've got your sisters and your brother so I guess you don't have to worry about it." Would siblings have made life easier for her? Likely not. They would have only given Grandfather more ammunition to use against her mother. But maybe if she had a brother or sister they could be partners—

She didn't need a partner.

Pansy started to cry and both Cassie and Billy turned toward the sound, listening as Daisy soothed the little one. Only Pansy wasn't being soothed and her wails intensified. After several shrieks, Cassie climbed from the hole and went over to Daisy who held her struggling, screaming little sister. "What's wrong?"

Daisy's eyes filled with distress. "I don't know. She just won't stop crying." Indeed, Pansy threw her head back and refused Daisy's attempts to comfort her.

"Is she hurt?" Cassie had to raise her voice to make herself heard.

"Don't think so. I was right there and all of a sudden she started to cry." Daisy bounced her sister but the way Pansy flailed about, Cassie feared she would fling herself from Daisy's arms.

"You better sit down before she falls."

Daisy struggled to hold the crying child as they moved to the table.

"Did you see anything?" Cassie asked Neil. "Maybe a snake?" She shuddered.

Neil shook his head.

Daisy's eyes widened and she quickly examined Pansy. "I don't see any bite marks."

"What's going on?" Roper's voice startled Cassie. She hadn't heard him approach. And her relief at seeing him overrode all her fierce arguments. Only, she excused herself, because she hoped he might have a solution to Pansy's distress.

"We can't get Pansy to stop crying."

Roper reached for the little girl but she pushed him away and screeched. "Is she hurt?" he asked.

"We don't know," Cassie said, her voice raised to be heard over the toddler's cries.

Tears welled in Daisy's eyes. "If only Ma or Pa were here. They'd know what to do."

Cassie studied the three young faces, all wreathed with concern for their little sister. Each set of lips quivered. Mention of their parents under the circumstances looked like it might release a flood of sorrow.

It was a loss they would have to live with the rest of their lives and nothing would change that. Best they figured out how to do it. She pushed to her feet. "Look, there's no point in wanting things you can't have. About all you can do is fix what you can. Make the here and now work."

"How are we supposed to do that when Pansy won't stop crying?" Daisy looked about ready to wail herself.

"I'll show you."

Roper kept trying to get Pansy's attention by clapping his hands and playing peek-a-boo. Cassie figured it did little but make the child scream louder.

Seemed obvious to Cassie this was one time trying to make people laugh wasn't going to work for him. She strode over to the shack where she scooped up a plateful of biscuits, a table knife and the can of syrup and returned to the table. "Sometimes the simplest solution is the most effective. Who likes syrup on their biscuits?"

The two boys plunked down on the bench across the table from her. Both eagerly said, "I do."

She prepared them each a biscuit. "How about you, Daisy? Would you like one?"

Daisy looked doubtful.

Cassie tilted her head toward Pansy.

Daisy understood what Cassie hoped to do and nodded. "Yes, please."

Cassie prepared another biscuit and handed it to Daisy who took it with one hand and bit into it.

"Umm. Good."

Pansy watched, her cries less intense.

"Roper?"

"Sure. A man can always stand a biscuit or two." He emphasized the last word and Cassie dutifully prepared two.

She did another, put it on a plate and set it on the table to one side of Daisy. "How about you?" she asked Pansy.

Pansy sobbed—a sad sound that tore at Cassie's heart. The little girl shuddered twice, then wriggled from Daisy's arms to sit beside her.

Cassie realized they all sat motionless, biscuits held before them as they watched and waited to see if Pansy would decide to eat or continue crying.

Pansy sucked back a sob, then took a bite of her biscuit.

A collective sigh escaped and they all turned back to the food. The quiet was blissful.

"Maybe she was sad," Daisy said.

"I think you're right." Cassie thought the whole lot of them had accepted being orphans without much fuss though once or twice she'd seen them huddled together and expected they shared their sorrow with each other.

The biscuit finished, Pansy's bottom lip quivered.

Cassie jumped to her feet. "Who'd like tea?"

Three children chorused, "Me."

So she made tea, poured canned milk into the children's weak tea and waited a couple of minutes to pour stronger tea for herself and Roper.

He watched her as if he wanted to say something. His patient intensity made her nervous. Was something wrong at the ranch?

"How is Linette?"

"Looking fit as a fiddle. Practically glows with health."

"Oh, good. I was a little worried when I left but she insisted I should proceed with my plans."

"She and Cookie sent you some things." He waved toward the wagon, which she hadn't noticed until now.

"I thought you were leaving it at the ranch."

He chuckled. "Needed it again. Come see."

The children had moved away to play quietly in a circle as if afraid to get too far from each other. Pansy no longer cried but occasionally shuddered.

Cassie watched them a moment, then she followed Roper to the wagon. She nearly gasped when she saw it full of supplies. "My goodness. I can't take all this. I have to—"

Roper's smile flattened. "Manage on your own? Do you have to, or do you insist on it?"

"I can't repay it."

"Who's asking you to? Cookie, Linette, Eddie and yes, me, we just want to help. We want you to succeed, to be happy."

She couldn't look at him. The words sounded nice. Comforting even. But where did helping end and owing begin? And what was she to do with all these supplies? There were jars of canned beef—Cookie's specialty— and potatoes, carrots, turnips, pickles, onions. With all this, she would be able to start offering excellent meals to paying guests. And, tucked away in the corner of the wagon, was a batch of Cookie's excellent cinnamon rolls. Her mouth watered at the prospect.

"Don't refuse help, Miss Prickly Cassie."

She finally met Roper's eyes. The teasing and kindness she saw there made her mouth feel parched. Made her eyes watery and her throat scratchy. "Can kindness really be given without strings attached?"

She hadn't meant to ask the question aloud but it was too late to stop the words from speeding from her mouth.

Roper chuckled. "I think you know the answer." He sobered and studied her. "Seems to me someone in your past has taught you otherwise, exacted a price of some sort when they gave a gift, but there are lots of people in this world who give out of love and concern. I think you know a few if you would just let yourself believe it."

His gaze went on and on, turning over rock-solid arguments in her mind, lapping at memories of her grandfather's miserly help.

She worried her lips, unable to divert her eyes from his intense gaze. She tried to tell herself she didn't see things she longed for in his eyes. From a deep well of doubt she brought forth a snort and returned her gaze to the contents of the wagon. "I'll find a way to pay for it."

Roper sighed long and hard. "I'll let you tell Linette yourself. She said she'll visit soon. Said it would do Grady good to play with other children."

Grady. She missed the little guy and would be glad to see him. Linette, too. She was the closest Cassie had ever had to a friend. The closest she'd ever allowed.

Cookie, too. Tears burned her eyes. She reached for the cinnamon buns. "The children are in for a real treat."

"I take it you're going to accept this gift?"

"Can't hardly send it back, can I?"

He chuckled. "Wouldn't make a speck of sense to even try."

"So we might as well unload it."

He grabbed a box of jarred beef. "Show me where."

They crammed most of the supplies into the shack crowding it even more. She desperately needed her house finished but her own efforts had done little to accomplish it. She stole a glance at her palms.

Roper noticed and caught her wrists. "What in the world have you done?"

She tried to snatch her hands away but his gentle hold was unrelenting. "Did some work."

"What sort of work?" His narrowed gaze filled with suspicion. "Tell me you weren't trying to dig out the cellar."

"Okay, I won't."

He made a noise rife with exasperation. "You need to take care of these hands. Come on, I have something in my saddle bags."

"I'm fine." Again she tried to extract herself but he led her from the shack and out to the table, completely ignoring her torrent of protests.

"Sit." He nudged her so she had no choice. "And stay there while I get the ointment."

Neil left the other children and hovered close by. "You should have left the digging for Roper."

Cassie sighed. Bad enough to have Roper nagging at her. Now a twelve-year-old boy had taken up the cause. "I was only trying to help." She wasn't helping

Roper. She was helping herself. It was her house, her responsibility not his.

Roper returned and knelt before her, turning her palms upward. He tsked and blew on them, cooling the heat in the blisters. But his attention did not calm her insides. He had flipped his hat to the table and she looked down at his brown hair, noting—not for the first time—the little wave that gave his hair a natural pompadour. She was a little tempted to flick her fingers through the wave and see if it flipped back into place automatically.

She swallowed hard and tried to ignore the proximity of the man. But she couldn't ignore the way he tenderly touched her hands, spreading a yellow ointment over the blistered area. "What is that?" Her voice sounded positively strangled but she couldn't help it. When had anyone been so attentive to her needs? Not in a very long time. Since she was a child younger than Neil, who rocked back and forth as he watched.

"It's something I use on my horse."

She jerked away.

He laughed up at her and captured her hands again, but his gaze remained locked on hers, edging past her hard-earned, hard-learned defenses and laying silent claim to a tender spot deep within that she had long denied—and intended to keep denying.

Correctly reading her silent defensiveness, he grinned. "Don't think my horse will mind sharing."

She huffed. "Maybe I do."

He bent back to his task. "What were you thinking? I'll finish digging the cellar. Cassie, when are you going to learn to leave the hard stuff to me? It's part of our agreement."

Again that demanding look.

Again she deflected it.

"Ma says some things are man stuff." Neil fairly burst with the need to speak his mind on the matter. "She used to say that when things were too hard for her to do. 'Man stuff for Pa to do when he got home.'"

Cassie shook her head. "I don't aim to be beholden to a man."

Roper had finished applying the ointment but still refused to release her hands. He pulled out a wad of white material and wrapped each hand.

How was she going to work with her hands bundled up in such a fashion? She'd leave the bandages on until morning then they'd come off so she could make bread.

Roper's gaze rested on her.

She didn't miss the fact that he burned with the need to say something almost as urgently as Neil. Then he ducked away to secure the end of the second bandage.

"Thank you." She tried to extricate herself from him, but he kept his fingers around her wrists. His hold was firm, yet his touch was so warm and gentle it clogged her throat with unfamiliar emotions. He perched beside her and watched her.

She studied some distant spot although she focused on nothing in particular except the need to maintain a protective distance from the emotions threatening to rage through her.

"Cassie, I don't know what happened to make you so prickly. I don't know why you feel you must stand alone when there are those who would stand with you. I expect it was something very hurtful. I'm sorry and I pray God will heal that hurt. But hear me carefully."

When she continued to stare at nothing, he released

her wrists to catch her chin and turn her to face him, waiting until she met his gaze. She immediately wished she'd continued to refuse as the kindness and concern in his face almost melted her resistance. The war inside her made her dizzy with fear and longing.

Seeing he had her full attention, he nodded. "Cassie Godfrey, we have a business arrangement. That means we each give something to this situation. You provide meals and shelter and care for the children. In return, I help with the children, dig your cellar and build your house. But hear me and hear me good. Even if we had no arrangement I would help you if you let me. I think you know that. No strings attached. No expectations except to do what Neil calls 'the man stuff.'"

She rocked her head back and forth. It sounded nice. But she couldn't trust such generosity. Best if she depended on no one but herself.

"Fine." He let her go, leaving her off balance.

She tried to clasp her hands together but the palms were too tender and she settled for folding her wrists at her waist.

"If that's the way it is at least we still have our business agreement." He headed for the cellar hole, grabbed a shovel and jumped down. In a few minutes, he pitched earth over his shoulder.

She felt his anger clear across the few feet and in the vigor of the dirt being tossed. But what else could she do? Accepting anything but business between them would give him the right to be angry at her anytime and for any reason. This way they would part when arrangements were made for the children. They would go their separate ways. It was for the best.

Scoops of dirt flew from the hole.

She did not look forward to living with Roper's anger even temporarily. She stared at her bandaged hands, remembering his gentle touch, and seemed unable to move.

Neil touched her shoulder. "You should be happy he can help you. My ma sure wished Pa was around to help her."

She nodded, her tongue suddenly wooden and unable to form a word even if she could have dragged it from her brain. She could not allow herself to be happy Roper was around for any reason—chalking up favor after favor.

Something he'd said slipped back her stalled brain. *I'll pray for you.*

Ah. No wonder she was feeling out of sorts. When was the last time she'd prayed? Several days ago if she wasn't mistaken. *God, I trusted You to provide this opportunity so I could be independent. Seems I've gotten a little confused about my intentions what with the children needing help and Roper striking an agreement.* Remembering how she'd originally thought his offer of a business arrangement was an answer to a prayer, she let her tension ease out. God had provided a way she could accept help without being in anyone's debt. She would accept it with gratitude and make the best of it. *I'll just be sure to uphold my end of the bargain.*

She pushed to her feet and set to work making supper. It was difficult with her sore hands but she managed and a little later announced the meal was ready. If Roper faced her with anger she would simply ignore it and do her duty.

Hadn't she learned that lesson over and over until it was branded indelibly on her brain?

Just as she'd learned to ignore the pain of those memories.

Chapter Six

Roper tossed the shovel aside at Cassie's call to supper. His muscles burned from exertion. A satisfying feeling. And it had effectively soothed his frustration with Cassie. He knew he was right when he guessed something, or more likely someone, had hurt her badly even though she neither admitted it nor denied it. He could only pray God would heal that hurt.

He paused in the bottom of the hole to stare up at the sky. Reading the Bible every morning with the youngsters reminded him of God's love and power. It was a good habit. If he ever had a family of his own, he'd do the same thing.

Whoa! Where had that come from? He didn't expect to ever have a real family. That would mean putting down roots…trusting someone would want him to hang around forever. That wasn't possible. Besides, he liked being free to do his own thing. Seemed he had to say it louder and more often of late.

He shifted his thoughts back to his morning prayer. *Watch over us. Keep us safe. Help us be happy.* A man could wish for no more.

Calmed by his prayer, he scrambled from the hole and jogged to the river where he ducked his head into the icy water and scrubbed off dirt and sweat.

Lacking a towel, he wiped water from his hair and shook his hands then trotted back to the table where everyone sat waiting. He grinned as he saw Cassie had carefully positioned herself across from the boys. As if he'd let that dissuade him. He sat at the end of the bench, next to Neil and nudged him over, chuckling at the scowl on Cassie's face. "Gal, I sure do like the welcoming way you have of looking at me." He hoped to bring a smile to her face or at least a flash of amusement to her eyes

He was pretty sure the flicker he saw signified uncertainty rather than amusement. Her mouth worked as if she wanted to say something but couldn't find the words. Then she turned away. "Glad to make you happy," she murmured.

He wanted to see her face better, look into her eyes and read her meaning, but she suddenly found the bench between herself and Pansy needed to be brushed off though he suspected there was nothing on it but imaginary dust.

Amusement continued to stretch his mouth. "You do make me happy," he murmured, not sure what he meant by it but knowing the words were true. He liked helping her. He liked sitting across the table from her, holding her hand as they prayed. He reached out to claim one hand now. Out of consideration for her tender palms, he wrapped his fingers around her wrist instead.

He also liked sharing the table with a woman and children. Doing what he could to ensure their safety and happiness. He knew it wouldn't last but he didn't figure to let that steal any joy from the present.

He bowed his head and thanked God for the food.

The "amen" said, the food passed, they all dug in.

"Good meal," he murmured, enjoying the tender beef, rich brown gravy, potatoes and carrots. "You're a good cook."

"Thank you. I'm hoping others will agree." She glanced about. "I think I could start offering meals to travelers. I'll let Macpherson know."

"I'll get some fresh meat in the morning." He saw her ready protest. "You might want to save the jarred meat for when you don't have fresh."

She nodded. Again the expression in her eyes revealed uncertainty. He wished he knew the source so he could fix it. He almost laughed aloud. Yup. She'd start running to him for help in fixing her problems all right.

Maybe in another life.

"There's a snake in the woodpile," Daisy announced.

"They were afraid of it," Neil said.

Daisy gave her brother an accusing look. "So were you." She turned to Roper. "Cassie had it in her arms." She shuddered.

"It must have been in the wood when I picked up an armload," Cassie explained.

Had she turned a little pale? Roper glanced around the table, seeing an unspoken message. Ahh, he understood. The children expected him to deal with the snake. He met Cassie's gaze. Would she insist she could handle this by herself or ask for help? She ducked away but he waited and slowly she returned her gaze to him. She swallowed hard enough he wondered if she would choke. Oh, but it felt good to think she needed him. He would make her ask. Make her acknowledge the need. Perhaps if she did it once...

Would she ever realize that his caring carried no obligations?

Except to appreciate him.

He mentally shook himself. Where had that come from? He wanted to help her for her sake not his. Maybe she needed a little prodding in asking for his assistance.

"A big snake, you say?" He made his voice sound worried. "Could have been a hognose." Not that he'd ever seen one. But he'd heard tell of them farther south. About the only poisonous snake he knew of around here was a rattler and if she'd held it in her arms—

He shuddered. It could have struck out, the bite filling her with poison. Every cowboy knew the symptoms. First, lips tingling, then a struggle to breathe then a person's muscles stopped working. Some people survived but their muscles were never strong afterward. If Cassie had been bitten, they would not be sitting around the table. He wouldn't be teasing her.

He rubbed at a spot beneath his breastbone that developed a sudden pain.

"Are you afraid of snakes?" Cassie asked him.

Neil laughed. "'Course he's not. He's a man."

"Nice to have your support." Roper squeezed the boy's shoulder. "I don't much care for the way they sneak around but I guess I'm not scared of them." He continued to wait, his eyes on Cassie.

"Would you—?" She puffed out her lips.

If only she would say the words, she'd learn that asking for a favor didn't require selling her soul.

"I'd like it if you could get rid of the snake." The words came out in a rush.

His grin stretched to its limit. "Of course I will." He rose and headed for the woodpile, two boys in his wake, chattering about how they'd take care of that nasty old snake. Roper chuckled. He guessed "they" meant him as the boys stopped a good ten feet from the pile.

He kicked the stack to alert any sneaky critters, then picked up one piece of wood at a time, carefully searching for snakes or other things.

"There it goes." Billy jumped up and down, pointing toward the woods.

Roper saw the little green snake slither away. "Only a garter snake. Harmless as a fly." He watched it disappear. "Don't expect it will come back."

Cassie and Daisy, with Pansy safely in her arms, watched from a wide distance.

Roper replaced the wood, dusted his hands and went to face Cassie. "I doubt it will return but from now on let me get the wood."

"You planning to make wood gathering your new job?"

He understood what she didn't say. She had no intention of depending on him for this simple job. Fine. "When you get wood, pick up each piece carefully. You give him a warning and he'll be glad to get out of your way."

Again, he read confusion and uncertainty in her eyes and was at a loss to explain it. He took her elbow, pleased when she made no attempt to pull away, and guided her toward the cellar hole where they could talk away from the youngsters. "Cassie, what are you worrying about?"

"I'm not."

"Something is troubling you. I've seen it in your eyes all during the meal and even now." When she would have turned away, he caught her chin and gently insisted she face him. "Have I done something?"

For several moments she studied him, searching his eyes. He was at a loss to know what she sought.

"You aren't angry?" The words were barely a whisper.

"Me? What would I be angry about?" He couldn't imagine.

"I insisted we stick to a business arrangement between us. You seemed upset. I thought—"

"You thought I'd hold a grudge? Even go so far as to inflict some sort of punishment in retaliation?"

He waited for her answer and it came in the form of a single nod. Despite his finger on her chin she refused to meet his gaze. He slouched down until he could see into her guarded eyes. "I'm not that sort of person. You should know that by now."

Her eyes widened. A flicker of something he could interpret as both surprise and acknowledgment crossed her face.

A sigh came from deep inside. "Cassie, maybe someday you'll explain why you are so prickly. And maybe, God willing, you'll see whatever your reasons, they don't apply to me."

This time he knew the look that flashed across her face was surprise and his heart swelled with victory at the thought she might be changing her view of him.

"Now that you're in a mellow mood I have some more news from the ranch." He paused. "Could be

Linette wants to tell you herself…" He considered the possibility.

Alarm made her features harsh. "You said she was okay."

"She is."

Cassie's breath whooshed out. "Then it could be that once you start an announcement, you ought to finish it." Her tone was as dry as a prairie wind. A chuckle rippled up his throat. This Cassie sure beat the prickly one of a few minutes ago.

She crossed her arms and gave him an I'm-waiting look.

He grinned. "What if Linette is disappointed not to be the one to tell you?"

She tapped a toe. "You're assuming you'd live to hear the words from her mouth."

He stared. "Live?" Then he realized she'd threatened him. In fun, of course. Delight as pure and sweet as fresh honey ran through his veins. "Why, Miss Cassie, I do believe you're intent on getting me to tell."

"I perceive that you are mighty sharp—especially for a man."

He hooted and slapped his leg as pleased as could be at her playfulness.

She quirked an eyebrow and continued to tap her toe but he knew he wasn't mistaken in observing that her eyes danced with amusement.

He forced his laughter back though it refused to leave his throat. He held his palms toward her in a gesture of defeat. "I'll tell. Just don't hurt me. Promise?"

She chuckled. "I promise. Now what's this news that you're making me wait for?"

He glanced about as if afraid someone would hear

and signaled her to lean closer. No need for such secrecy but he was enjoying this playfulness too much to bring it to an end.

He whispered in her ear. "Linette is going to have a baby." His breath disturbed strands of her hair and they blew against his face. He brushed them aside, smoothing them into place.

He'd never touched her hair before. It was so silky, he wanted to run his hands over it again but she drew back and stared at him.

"She is?" She laughed. "I knew it. I told her I thought so before we left. I'm so glad for them."

Her gaze grabbed his in a triumphant look and in it he saw her joy for her friend. Her smile flattened and he saw something else…something he guessed she was unaware of. A deep sadness. He remembered the writing in her Bible—the two babies who died the same day they were born.

He acted without thinking and caught her arms. "Cassie, I read about your babies. I'm sorry. It must make you sad to hear of Linette's baby."

She swallowed hard. She stared at his chest, then she blinked and jerked back. "That's water under the bridge. I never think about it. I've got the future to consider. Macpherson is expecting me to deliver biscuits and bread to his store." She spun away and returned to the shack so fast she left a dusty blur in her wake.

Cassie thundered toward the shack. She sank to her bed on the floor, pulled her knees to her chest and rested her forehead on them. Anger and pain intermingled in her throat like a bitter medicine.

She pulled in a deep breath and held it, forcing her emotions into order. But her anger refused to dissipate.

He had no right to talk of her babies. She did not want to think of that part of her life. The joy and anticipation of the little lives. The tiny flutters of their first kicks. Their growing movements and her growing belly. With the first one, George had shared every joy. But after their little son was stillborn, he refused to allow himself any joy over the second baby.

And he'd been right to fear it would happen again. The little one never drew a breath and they buried a little girl.

Cassie rubbed at her chest but it provided no comfort.

Roper had snooped. Read words that weren't his business.

She snatched the Bible from where it rested and opened it to the page of births and deaths. Her fingers trembling, her jaw clenched, she plucked at the page, drew it toward her until it grew taut at the binding. But before the paper began to tear, she dropped the page and smoothed it. She couldn't rip it out. This was all that was left of her babies. She bowed her head over her knees and breathed hard, fighting for calmness, peace…relief.

The backs of her hands grew damp and she swiped them on her skirt then scrubbed her eyes dry. Crying accomplished nothing. Work. That was the answer.

For a second she couldn't recall what it was she should do.

Then she saw the stack of biscuits and loaves of bread. She meant to deliver them hours ago but had been sidetracked by one thing, and then another.

What kind of way was that to run a business?

She pulled to her feet, her body strangely heavy, gathered up the biscuits and bread, and left the shack.

The children played nearby and Daisy watched her.

Cassie forced a smile to her lips and hoped it looked real. She did not allow herself a glance toward the house site but heard the thud of earth hitting the ground.

Sucking in a deep breath she squared her shoulders and headed for the store. Macpherson would be pleased with her work.

Work was the antidote to foolish emotions. She needed to keep that in mind and focus on what she could do.

A short time later, Cassie rushed back from the store. "Macpherson said he expects a stage before the day is out." It was already late in the day but a rider had seen the stage on its way. "Says he'll direct the travelers this way for a meal." She laughed, hardly able to contain her excitement. Her dream would soon be fulfilled.

Her words brought Neil and Roper from the cellar hole.

"Do you need any help getting ready?" Roper asked.

Cassie sobered. She didn't want him hanging about making her remember things put to rest. Besides, she meant to manage on her own. "I have things under control." Then she remembered her manners. "Thanks." Her grin returned as she hurried to the shack. She ripped the bandages off her hands and turned her palms to examine them. They'd be fine. She didn't have time to worry about a little discomfort.

Daisy insisted on helping and Cassie allowed it. The girl needed to know she pulled her weight.

An hour later a cake stood ready to ice. A meal was cooked and pushed to the side of the stove to stay warm. The rumble of a stagecoach brought her from the shack and she stared toward the store. She watched the passengers disembark—three men and a woman. As the driver tossed down packages, a cowboy reached out to lend a hand.

Roper joined Cassie. The children clustered around. The boys bounced on the balls of their feet. Pansy ran round and round in front of them. Daisy, ever vigilant, continually darted glances at her baby sister while observing as much of the activity around the stagecoach as she could.

Cassie wanted to join Pansy in making happy, flapping circles but instead, crossed her arms and waited. "Everything is ready." Her voice seemed high, as if she worried. Well, of course she did. Her future depended on providing meals that satisfied. Word of mouth would build her reputation.

Roper draped an arm across her shoulders. "You'll do fine."

She didn't need his encouragement. Of course she'd do fine. She'd done her best.

But her stubborn defiance couldn't block the echo of her grandfather's words. *Too slow. Sloppy. You forgot*—even when nothing had been forgotten. She pushed away the uncertainty the words brought. She was in charge now. She jumped for no one unless it pleased her to do so, but for a few seconds she let the weight of Roper's arm on her shoulders anchor her to her land.

A dusty man with a ragged beard and equally ragged hat headed in their direction. She recognized Petey, the driver. Behind him came the two men then the woman clinging to the arm of the third man. Cassie could tell by the curl of the woman's lips that she wasn't pleased by her circumstances. Behind her strode the cowboy.

Cassie stepped forward, leaving Roper's strengthening arm behind. "Welcome. The meal is ready. Seat yourself." She waved toward the table. She and Macpherson had discussed a price for the meal and she'd accepted his advice on setting a fee. She held a tin can toward the guests and they each dropped in their coins.

"Where can I wash?" the woman asked, her voice demanding.

Cassie hesitated to point to the basin perched on the butt end of a log, a bucket of water beside it. She'd put out a stack of clean towels. It was the best she had to offer and totally adequate. "The washbasin is over there."

The woman looked as if Cassie had offered swamp water in a slop bucket. Cassie knew that look, though it had normally come from above a mustache. She bristled.

"It's perfectly clean."

The woman sniffed. "I am not impressed with the wilderness."

"Come along, dear." The man, who must have been her long-suffering husband, urged her toward the basin. "You'll feel better after you've washed the dust from your face." He managed to edge her away.

"I'm covered with dust from head to toe. I need a full bath."

Cassie resisted suggesting she could have one in the river and turned back to the others. Instead, she caught Roper's gaze, full of laughter, and her spirits revived. How foolish to head out to the wilderness, then complain that it was wild. It was good to share her amusement with Roper. Then she snapped a mental door closed. She would not be involving Roper in the everyday aspects of her life.

The cowboy brought up the rear. He snatched off his battered hat to reveal a mane of blond hair that hadn't seen a pair of scissors for many months if Cassie had her guess.

"Lane Brownley, ma'am. Got me a little place just over there." He pointed in a vague northwest direction that could have been along the river, or toward the mountains or in the middle of nowhere. Not that Cassie cared for more specific directions. He dropped his coins in the can. That's what mattered.

"I'll gladly pay for a decent meal whenever I'm nearby, if you have no objections."

"That's what I'm here for."

His blue eyes matched the sky and shone as brightly as he grinned at her. "You and your husband got a good idea, setting up a stopping station here."

She blustered an embarrassed reply. "He's not my husband. He works for Eddie Gardiner at the Eden Valley Ranch."

"My apologies but I've seen him here several times over the past few days."

"It's the kids." She explained the orphaned children and how they had a business agreement to work together to care for them until their uncle could be reached.

Lane's eyes brightened. "Then you're planning to run this place on your own?"

She studied him without answering. Did he mean to take advantage of her situation?

Roper must have wondered the same thing. He stepped to her side and dropped his arm across her shoulder. "'Spect me or the boss or one of the boys will be stopping by mighty often."

Lane suddenly realized how his words had been interpreted and red crept up his neck. "Didn't mean it that way." He scuffled off to wash up.

Roper didn't step back but as soon as Lane bent to splash water over his face, Cassie ducked away and put a good six feet between them. From that distance she shot him a warning look. He needn't think he could make a habit of being protective.

He returned her hard look and after a moment she shifted her attention to the children.

Neil sat on a log with Pansy and Billy and watched the visitors.

Cassie waited until the guests were seated then took the potatoes to the table. Daisy brought the roast venison. They returned for the rest of the dishes only to meet Roper part way carrying gravy and carrots.

Cassie reached for the bowls but Roper shook his head. "I got them."

"But—" she sputtered.

Roper gave her a mocking grin. "Did you think I'd stand idly by and watch you and Daisy work? Nope." He took a step, then paused to face her. "Ain't gonna stand by and see some young upstart boy who thinks he's a cowboy come stomping in to make a nuisance of himself, either."

"He came to eat. He paid his money. I intend to serve him."

"And next time?"

"He pays his money, I feed him. Every time."

"Just make sure he isn't after anything but meat and potatoes."

Her nostrils flared. How dare he insinuate she would allow someone to take advantage of her? "You forget I can take care of myself." She kept her voice low so those at the table wouldn't hear but made no attempt to keep the defiance out of her words. Daisy had thankfully returned to the shack so didn't overhear this conversation. When would he realize she didn't need or want coddling? She grabbed the jug of gravy from him.

Roper put the carrots on the table, gave her a look full of judgment, then took the younger children and disappeared over the bank toward the river.

Cassie shrugged. Sooner or later he'd realize she didn't need him watching over her shoulder. She turned her attention back to her guests. "Help yourself and enjoy the meal."

The men dug in with gusto and if the way they hunkered over their plates indicated pleasure, then they enjoyed the meal.

The fine lady shivered as a fork scrapped against a tin plate. "I'd think a person charging for a meal would use real china."

Cassie smiled but didn't respond. China was fine in a restaurant but she wasn't running a restaurant.

The lady held up her hands. "I could do with a napkin."

Cassie fetched a small towel, which earned her an impatient sigh. Cassie glanced about trying to see the place as others would. The table was crude. The plates were tin. They ate outdoors. She'd been so pleased to get her business started that she hadn't thought of the deficiencies. "Once I get my place built I'll have things nicer."

"In the meantime—" The look on the woman's face said just how lacking the present conditions were.

Petey lifted his head, and wiped his mouth on his sleeve. "I remember you from last fall when I brought you out with Miss Edwards who was set on marrying Eddie. Glad they finally got hitched. You're doing okay, too, with this setup. I'll be back on a semi-regular basis and the bull trains will run until snow blocks the road. The drivers are always ready for a big feed. Once they hear about this place you'll find yourself busy as two beavers."

Cassie's tension released. "Thank you." It was hungry men who would make up the bulk of her business and they cared nothing for fancy tablecloths and napkins.

Lane leaned back with a sigh. "Best meal I've had since I left England three years ago."

"Wait. I have coffee, tea and cake." She bustled back to the shack and with Daisy's help served each customer.

The fancy lady spoke not a word of appreciation even though she ate every crumb of the piece of cake Cassie served her.

Cassie determinedly ignored the woman's constant sighs and furrowed brow. She'd grown adept at turning away such insignificant signs of displeasure. She glanced toward the river where she could hear the children playing and Roper's laugh.

A few minutes later everyone left. All except Lane. He sat with his elbows on the table watching her as she and Daisy scraped the dishes and stacked them to be washed. His attention screeched along her nerves as much as the sound of metal scraping metal.

Neil and Billy climbed up from the river, with Roper following on their heels, Pansy perched adoringly in his arms.

Cassie stared. They fit like hand and glove. Why wasn't Roper married with a baby of his own?

She choked back an unfamiliar emotion. Was it loneliness she felt? Impossible.

She shook her head to clear her confusion. It must remind her of her father and all she'd lost when he died.

Roper had been grinning down at Pansy but glanced up, saw Lane still at the table and instantly scowled. He shifted Pansy to one side and veered toward the table where he plunked down opposite Lane. "Where did you say you have this ranch?"

Lane barely pulled his gaze from Cassie and distractedly jerked his thumb over his shoulder. "That way."

"You got livestock? Farmland? Family?"

"Small herd of cows. Half a dozen horses. A pig and some chickens. Broke some land and planted oats for feed." He offered the answers in sharp bullets as if paying no attention to his words.

"Family?" Roper prodded.

"None this side of the ocean. I'm all alone."

Daisy giggled at the mournful note in the cowboy's voice and leaned close to murmur in Cassie's ear. "Think he's wanting to change that."

Cassie gave her full attention to the pan of hot soapy water as she scrubbed the dishes. She didn't know whether Daisy meant the cowboy was looking for a group of friends or if he had an eye on marriage. If the latter was his intention he'd soon learn Cassie had no such notion. But she certainly didn't object to taking a bit of his money in exchange for a home-cooked meal.

Roper reached across the table, grabbed the man's empty cup and put it among those to be washed. "Guess it's time to get back to work." But he sat at the table.

Daisy nudged Cassie but Cassie was already aware of the silent tug of war. In fact, Lane seemed the only one oblivious to Roper's broad hint to leave.

The stagecoach rattled away.

Lane finally swung his legs over the bench and pushed to his feet. "I best get on home and see to the chores." He paused at Cassie's side. "Appreciate the fine meal. You can count on me returning." He smiled.

She smiled back. To do otherwise would be rude. Besides, she didn't object to him buying a meal. "I'll be here serving meals."

His gaze lingered then he jammed his hat on his head and sauntered back to the store. In a few minutes he came into sight astride his horse, gave a quick salute, reined around and rode away.

Roper pushed to his feet. "Thought I might have to shovel him off the bench."

Neil laughed. "Maybe you should've given him a shovel and let him help dig the cellar."

"You're jealous, aren't you?" Daisy dried a plate as she talked.

"Me?" He rumbled his lips. "Not at all but I don't see the use of a man sitting around watching everyone work."

Cassie wanted to know who he'd watched apart from her and Daisy.

Roper put Pansy down. "Come on, Neil. Let's get some more water." He paused then, and faced Cassie. She saw the guardedness in his eyes. And something more. Something that made her uncertain.

Did he expect her to reassure him? About what? That she wasn't interested in Lane? How could she be? She'd only met him a couple hours ago. She'd known Roper since last fall and constantly pushed him away. He should know it would be the same with Lane. She wasn't interested in special attention from either of them. "I need to get these dishes washed so the children can prepare for bed."

He grabbed the buckets. His strides ate up the ground until he dropped out of sight.

A few minutes later he returned with water and Pansy edged toward him. He lifted her to his knees as naturally as if they'd always been friends.

Cassie knew his naturalness came from his life in an orphanage. "Do you keep in touch with any of the children you grew up with?"

His hands grew still. He stared at the table. Then slowly he lifted his head and faced her.

She tried to read his expression. Was it wary? Pained? "I'm sorry. It's none of my business." Normally she would have added that it didn't matter to her but she couldn't say the words.

Then he smiled. Goodness, the man had a way of smiling that made her forget every cross word, every harsh thought, every determination to keep her distance.

"It pleased me tremendously to see many of the little ones taken into homes. Some of the older ones were put out to work." His grin dipped crookedly. "Sometimes they were returned as unsatisfactory, which meant they didn't work hard enough or…" He trailed off and didn't finish. "Many times the kids weren't treated kindly and found a way to leave. Sometimes they came back to the orphanage. Others simply disappeared."

She held her breath waiting for him to continue, suspecting he wasn't talking just about others. She sensed the sadness, saw the tiny telltale signs of tension in the narrow wrinkles about his eyes.

"Roper, you believe so strongly in family. It surprises me you don't have your own."

Only the tightening of the skin around his eyes revealed he'd even heard her. Once her curiosity had been unleashed it couldn't be contained. "Why aren't you married with a little girl of your own?" Her gaze slid to the child on his knee.

"I'm a man with no past. No history."

"Why would that matter? Are you afraid of what your parents might have been?"

"Not me."

She saw him jerk a little as if he'd said more than he meant. "You think it matters to others?"

"I know it does."

"I take it that's why you have a rule about not putting down roots. They'll only be ripped out."

She sat beside him, rested her palm on his forearm, feeling tension beneath his shirtsleeve. This was a side of Roper she'd never seen. "What happened?" She sensed it had been painful.

He shifted a little, obviously uncomfortable with the subject. But he didn't pull away. He turned slowly as if reluctant to look into her eyes. She held his gaze, silently promising to hear him, to help him if she could.

He deserved it, trying as he always did to make everyone else happy. Who tried to make him happy?

"I worked for a man for several months when I was nineteen. The boss had a pretty little daughter a year younger. She treated me kindly. She told me her secrets of wanting adventure. Wanting to learn about the world. I believed—" he swallowed loudly "—that she cared for me. I saved my money. Had enough to buy us a train ticket to the east where I thought we'd buy passage on a ship to Europe. We'd see all the things she dreamed of. Just as soon as we were married."

He didn't go on.

She waited, increasing the pressure of her hand on his arm.

"When I told her of my plans she looked shocked. Said I'd mistaken her kindness for more than it was. She explained in a very clear way that I was not suitable. No one had any idea of my background. That simply wasn't acceptable."

"Roper, I am so sorry." She touched his cheek. "Background doesn't matter to everyone."

Something shimmered in his eyes for a moment, then he smiled and closed his thoughts to her. "I've believed for most of my life that God never closes a door without opening a window."

She stared at him. How could he believe so simply? So thoroughly? It wasn't because life had been easy for him.

"Like you." He shifted Pansy to one knee and jabbed a finger toward Cassie.

"Like me? I've never noticed open windows and doors especially in difficult situations." There'd been no escape from her grandfather until she'd met George.

There'd been nothing but closed doors when her babies died. All she could do was put one foot in front of the other until it became a habit.

Daisy came over and reached for Pansy. "This little girl is almost asleep."

Cassie glanced about. "It's getting late. The children need to get to bed." She welcomed the interruption and a way to avoid continuing this discussion.

Roper stood. "Just let me point out that this business venture of yours is an open door."

She nodded. "God's given me this opportunity. I intend to make the most of it. But I won't be owing to any man over this business. Nor will I be turning away any paying customers so long as they act decently."

"Like Lane?"

She lifted her chin as she stared at him. "His money is as good as anyone's."

Her newfound freedom would not be relinquished.

Chapter Seven

Roper lounged by his campfire knowing sleep would not come while his mind twisted round and round. Why was Cassie always ready to take a contrary view about everything he said?

He regretted only one thing. He wished he hadn't talked about her babies. The mention of them had hurt her badly. More and more he began to suspect Cassie's way of dealing with things that brought pain or made her uncomfortable was to pretend they didn't exist. Instead, she worked. Work was her way of forgetting.

But working for Lane Brownley? He'd seen the way Lane watched Cassie. The man had more than a good meal in mind. He couldn't blame Lane for seeing Cassie as a woman he'd like to take home as a wife.

But he had no right to poke his nose into Roper's temporary home. Roper bolted to his feet and kicked dirt on the fire. He was not the sort of person who believed in anything but temporary.

Suddenly, he laughed. He should warn Lane that Cassie was dead set on being independent.

* * *

The next morning, Roper's irritation lingered…a fact that churned his insides. All his life he'd been able to put aside the disturbing events of a day and greet the new dawn with joy and anticipation, but not today. And that only increased his frustration.

He tried to dismiss his feelings as hunger but a hearty breakfast didn't change anything.

As he jumped into the cellar hole, he called it worry. But no amount of searching his mind yielded anything that deserved his concern.

He tried to explain it as anything but what it was. Jealousy.

Roper jabbed his shovel into the ground and dug out a lump of dirt. He wasn't jealous of Lane. But something about Lane made his muscles twitch. The man was like a big overgrown pup.

Roper only wanted to protect Cassie from those sad, hungry eyes.

But she didn't welcome his protection. He grunted as he attacked another lump of dirt.

At least Pansy now welcomed his care. He recalled how she sat on his knee that morning while he read the Bible after breakfast and he breathed in the sweet, baby scent of her.

He'd tried time and again to win over the child but she would always turn away, bury her head against Daisy's shoulder or simply ignore Roper. But yesterday he'd succeeded in making friends. He'd hidden behind a tree and played peek-a-boo, letting her come closer and closer until she stood against the tree and giggled as he whispered, "Boo," just inches from her head.

He'd squatted to her level and let her study him

closely, let her feel her own way, see he meant no harm to her.

When she lifted her arms and said, "Up," he grinned clear through. After that she wouldn't let him put her down until they were back with Daisy and Cassie.

His pleasure at holding Pansy yesterday had dimmed when he saw the way Lane watched Cassie. He didn't have to have two eyes in his head to know the man wanted to spend all day mooning over her. And likely marry her and take her home before the week was out.

He threw spadeful after spadeful of dirt with unusual vigor. The muscles in his arms burned but not enough to make him forget Lane.

Neil leaned on the handle of his shovel. "How come you don't like Lane?"

Had he inadvertently mumbled his thoughts aloud? He stopped digging, wiped the sweat from his brow. "I got no feelings one way or the other about the man. Hardly know him from Adam."

"Yeah, but you don't like him. I can tell."

"Just don't want him hanging about wasting our time."

"Oh." Neil returned to digging but didn't even get his shovel into the dirt before he paused and looked about. "You think this hole is big enough yet?"

Roper stopped to consider. "You might be right. How did I miss that? We'll smooth it out and tomorrow start work on the floor for the house." Cassie'd be pleased at seeing some progress.

"I'm hungry," Neil said.

"I expect Cassie will call us soon. You run along while I finish here."

Neil scampered up the ladder and raced away, no doubt glad to be done digging.

He smoothed the bottom and tidied the sides. After he got the house up, he'd build shelves down here for Cassie to store her supplies.

A thought scratched at the back of his mind. When he finished here... When the youngsters' uncle collected them, he would have no excuse for staying. Not that he'd ever planned to. He recited one of his rules—*don't put down roots.* Another rule tagged along on the heels of the first. *Don't stay where you're not wanted.* How many times had he said that to half-grown orphans who were taken to a home to work? Work hard, he'd said. Aim to please. Be cheerful but if they are unkind, don't stay. He'd walked away from situations that made him feel small and useless.

Cassie would not want him to hang about helping. And he didn't have Lane's excuse that he lived nearby and appreciated home-cooked meals. Cookie made excellent meals and the ranch was not a shout and holler away.

He leaned on his shovel handle and contemplated his predicament. To think of leaving her alone hurt like a boil on his skin where it touched the saddle. Cassie was easy prey for young cowboys. And old mule skinners. Besides, who would gather her wood and make sure there were no snakes? How would she keep the water buckets full? It was a steep climb up from the river with two full buckets.

"Neil says you're done with the cellar." Cassie's voice over his head jerked him about so fast his neck cracked.

"Just tidying it up." He tipped his hat back as he

peered up at her standing near the edge. "Careful you don't fall."

Her look informed him his warning was unnecessary and unwelcome. Then she turned her attention to the cellar hole. "It looks roomy." She brought her gaze back to him.

Standing in a hole staring upward, the sky bright behind her, he couldn't see well enough to know for sure why she studied him so.

"I want to apologize for complaining when you said you wanted to dig a cellar for me—I mean, for the house."

Was it so hard for her to acknowledge he'd done it for her? Well, he wasn't about to let her get away with that.

He climbed the ladder.

She edged back, keeping a healthy distance between them.

He jabbed the spade into the ground and closed that distance until he stood two feet away, able to see the uncertainty in her eyes. "Cassie Godfrey, I dug a cellar because I knew it would make your life easier. I did it for you." He stared at her.

Her gaze shifted to a spot beyond his shoulder but he didn't relent. He wanted her to acknowledge he'd done it for her.

But her gaze darted to him and shied away again twice before she drew in a sharp breath and kept her eyes steady on his. "I know you did. Thank you." It was barely a whisper and no doubt made a large hole in her pride but it signified a small victory for him.

He reached out and brushed his knuckles along her jawline. "There. Did it hurt so much to admit it?"

Her eyes widened at his touch and she swallowed loudly but didn't pull away. In fact, if he let himself read a whole book into a glance he would say his touch made her aware of a hunger for everything she denied herself. He didn't know exactly what that was and didn't bother to figure it out as his rules rang loudly inside his head. But he didn't back away. Not yet. Not for another moment.

Her eyes shuttered. "You will never know how much it hurt," she murmured, hurrying back to the table.

Later that night he sat under the stars, listening to the night call of the birds, the rumble of the water and the occasional murmur of voices from up the hill. All he wanted was a chance to help Cassie learn that it was all right to accept help. That she didn't need to stand alone. There were friends all around. He knew Linette, Eddie, Cookie, Bertie and even Macpherson would willingly help Cassie at any time.

But that wasn't exactly what he pictured.

What he saw, if he allowed himself to be honest, was Roper Jones, orphaned, nameless, with nothing of substance to offer, helping Cassie as she welcomed guests and fed them.

A groan rumbled from his chest.

He didn't put down roots. He didn't stay where he wasn't wanted. He helped people find their happiness. Which wasn't the same as interfering with their business as Cassie had said.

He ducked his head. "Dear Jesus, You know who I am. I just wish I did. I have nothing to offer any woman except my help. Please enable me to do that, to protect her and the kids until their uncle comes." It was all he wanted or expected from this arrangement.

The next morning he opened Cassie's Bible for their customary reading. He slowly read the story of the rainbow. He'd heard it many times while in the orphanage, but somehow today, reading the words to Cassie and the children, his heart swelled with assurance of God's love and protection. He finished and was quiet a moment, letting sweet thoughts fill him. Then he reached for Cassie's hand on one side and Neil's on the other. This was his favorite time of the day—them all together and united under God's love. He prayed for their safety. "Amen."

He didn't immediately release either hand.

Neil pulled away first and was about to leave when Daisy told him to bring water and help with the dishes.

Neil grunted. "I'm going to help Roper."

But Roper was in no hurry to return to work. He studied Cassie's downturned head. Was something bothering her?

When the children left, she extricated her hand. "Do you think about God's promises?"

"Not as much as I should."

"Do you think they are meant equally for everyone?"

He thought of the deaths noted in her Bible and guessed she wondered if the promises were for her. He didn't know what to say. "God told Noah He would remember His covenant and gave us the rainbow to remind us. It assures me that God won't forget me."

Slowly her head came up and she searched his soul. He let her, wishing he had something more to give her than a faltering trust.

"Seems I mostly remember the times when I thought

He had forgotten me." Her voice faltered. "I saw no rainbow in my life then."

"What did you see?" How he ached to comfort her, hold her, bear her pain.

"Nothing. No one." She looked into the distance. "I learned to stand alone."

"God promises to never leave us or forsake us."

She jerked her gaze to him, doubt and defiance blazing from her eyes. "So where was He when I needed Him?"

"Did you look for Him?" Before she could answer, he spoke again. "Too often I've wandered about on my own, wondering where God had gone. It took way too long for me to realize God didn't move. I did." He'd learned the lesson at a young age. When—

When didn't matter. He no longer dreamed of the things he wanted when he was young. Home and family were out of his reach. He accepted that and looked for satisfaction in helping others.

She looked hard and long at him. But her resistance did not fade. "Maybe there are times when God expects us to stand alone."

It wasn't what he hoped she'd say. He saw her alone, afraid and hurting. "Oh, Cassie. You never have to be alone. I'll stand with you anytime you need it."

Her eyes narrowed. "No one can be always available."

He wanted her to reach out to him and accept his offer to be with her. But she was right. He couldn't always be there. "God is."

"I try to believe that but sometimes it's hard. Maybe even impossible."

"I'm no Bible scholar so I don't have any answers

for you." He paused as an assurance grew in his own soul. "Except to say I believe God is always with us. Even when we feel most alone."

"When do you feel most alone?"

The question stripped away a barrier he wasn't even aware of until now. "You remember the Christmas party at the OK Ranch?" The whole crew of Eden Valley Ranch had been invited to the neighboring ranch to enjoy a beautiful meal and play games.

She nodded.

"Remember how we went around the table saying our favorite Christmas memory? I always picture Christmas as family gathered around the tree. That's when I feel the loneliest." He glanced about the table, now empty apart from himself and Cassie.

Daisy washed dishes. Pansy played at her feet. The boys struggled up the hill, water sloshing from the buckets they carried. "This is the closest to family I've ever had. It's temporary, I know. No roots for me." Maybe if he said it often enough he would believe it as deeply as he needed to.

Cassie's warm hand on his arm brought his attention back to her. "I'm sorry." Her voice burrowed into his struggling thoughts.

Their gazes locked. Hers went on and on, past swirling waters of doubt and hurt, straight to a hungry, needy spot he hadn't been aware of until now. No. He'd known it existed but he'd long ago learned to ignore it. Now he felt as if dusty doors were creaking open and refreshing air and bright sunlight poured in. As her look of concern continued, he struggled in vain to push the door closed.

Then she jerked away and bolted to her feet.

"Thought you might be in a hurry to start building my house."

Her sudden movement enabled him to slam the door back in place. He took his time getting to his feet. "I'll get at it right away."

She was afraid of her emotions, he realized. She hadn't had as much time and practice at building solid doors, unlike the barriers he'd built long ago and reinforced as needed.

Cassie hurried to help with the dishes. Why had she lingered at the table and admitted to feeling alone at times?

Better to be alone than under someone's cruel thumb.

But Roper's words circled her brain. *God is with you. He will never leave you.*

But where was He when Grandfather made her life and Mother's life miserable? When her babies died? When George died, leaving her alone and penniless in Montreal?

He sent Linette. Made it possible to come to Edendale. Enabled her to start her own business.

Cassie straightened her spine. Yes, thank God, she had a fledgling business. It wasn't an opportunity she intended to waste. She put away the clean dishes and checked the bread. The loaves had risen so she put them in the oven to bake. She'd made biscuits after breakfast and taken them over to Macpherson. He'd thanked her and noted the amount in a ledger book.

"Heard a mule train is on its way. You'll have a meal ready for them?" he'd asked her.

"I will indeed." As she prepared a meal large enough

to feed the hungry mule drovers, she listened to the sound of sawing and hammering. If she'd known more about construction work she could have done this on her own. Of course, the children's need for a safe home changed her need to do it herself.

A harsh truth gripped her thoughts.

It had changed many things.

She stared at the pot on the stove. Her chest tightened enough to make breathing difficult. The circumstances were changing her. Changing how she did business.

A few days ago she'd arrived here with her goals clearly formed. She would build a house, work and create a business on her own. She would ask no one for anything.

She knew no other way to ensure she would be independent.

Why had she allowed that to change? Not because of the children. She could take care of them fine on her own.

All she needed from Roper were instructions on how to build a house.

The food for a big meal was as ready as it could be until she heard the men cracking their whips as they reached town. She went outside, toward the shell of the house Roper was constructing. She watched every move. How he measured and cut. How he drove in the long spikes, making it look easy. He measured again from corner to corner.

"Why do you do that?" she asked, following him back and forth as he had Neil hold the tape at one corner and stretched to the opposite one.

"To make sure it's square." He wound the tape measure up, apparently satisfied.

She needed to know how this ensured him it was square and what he would do if it wasn't but he trotted away for another board. She practically hung over his shoulder as he meticulously measured.

Slowly he straightened and faced her. "Did you want something in particular?"

She nodded. "I want to know what you're doing."

"Why?"

"I might need to know some time."

He shook his head and turned back to the board. "Muddbottom, if you ever need something built, you give me a holler, hear?"

She jerked back, almost tripping over a lump of dirt. A myriad of horrible feelings raged through her at the memories accompanying the sound of that name. "Don't ever call me that." She could barely squeeze the words through her tight throat.

He looked into the distance, exhaled noisily then slowly faced her. "Why not? Isn't it your name?"

She fought to push away the impact of that name. "It's a vile name belonging to my grandfather."

He set the pencil and tape measure on the board and edged closer. "Wouldn't it also be your father's name?"

"My father is dead and so is everything good associated with that name."

He was only inches away, his look endless and searching.

She scowled at him. "How do you know about it?"

He hesitated, then shrugged. "Read it in your Bible."

"You have no right to snoop." The births and deaths of her babies were also in the Bible. He'd seen them.

Seen fit to mention it when all she wanted to do was forget.

She stuffed her fist to her mouth to keep from crying out a protest and ran.

The only place she could hope to be alone was in the trees and she clamored through the underbrush unmindful of thorns tearing at her skirt.

"Cassie, wait."

There was nothing she wanted to hear from him. Nothing. He couldn't take back the words that brought painful memories from the deep pit where she'd buried them hoping they would never be resurrected.

She didn't stop running until she tripped over a root, and then she lay facedown in the leaves and needles, panting.

Her insides felt hollowed out, scraped cruelly by some sharp instrument. Her babies. Born two years apart. Perfectly formed. But neither of them had ever drawn a breath. They went from her warm sheltering womb to the cold lonely grave.

Oh, God, where were You then?

George hadn't blamed her in words but she was never in doubt that he silently thought she'd done something wrong.

But no more so than did she.

Oh, God, am I not to be allowed anything? Must I stand alone?

She knew the answer. *Yes.* Whatever she wanted or needed in life she must provide it herself.

No point in trusting God or a man to do for her what she could do for herself.

She scrambled to her feet, brushed the debris from her clothes, swiped at her face and smoothed her hair.

No doubt she looked a wreck but that was immaterial. She had a business to run and hiding in the trees, feeling sorry for herself would not lead to success.

She tramped back through the trees.

"Cassie?"

She practically bolted out of her shoes and stared at Roper half hidden in the shadows, sitting on a tree stump waiting.

"Are you okay?"

"I'm fine," she lied. She didn't know if she would ever be okay.

"I didn't mean to upset you."

"I'm fine." She didn't want to talk about her babies. Didn't want to ever mention them. The only way to deal with the pain was to push it so deep it would never surface.

And she'd done so successfully. Except for times like this when someone encroached into forbidden territory.

"I know you're not fine and I blame myself."

"Forget it."

"I don't think I can. I don't think you can. I seem to have an unfortunate knack for mentioning things that bring you pain."

She gave him a good hard stare, daring him to poke his nose any further into her business.

"I guess you don't much care for your grandfather."

She snorted. He had no idea. Suddenly she realized they weren't talking about the babies but about her grandfather. Her breath wheezed from tense lungs.

"I'm sorry about your losses." He spoke cautiously.

He did well to be guarded. She closed her eyes as a wave of pain clutched her insides.

"Never mind." She couldn't bear to say anything more.

"If you ever want to have a good cry I have two shoulders you're welcome to use." He grinned somewhat crookedly.

"I've done all the crying I intend. Now if I'm not mistaken, there is a house to build and food to serve." She stomped on. Let him follow or sit like a bump on a log. Made no difference to her.

But she tipped her head a little and relaxed marginally as she heard him clumping after her. Unbidden a picture came to her imagination of her resting her head in the hollow of his shoulder and crying out her pain and sorrow and confusion as he rubbed her back and made soothing noises.

She shook her head. She needed no comforting. All she wanted…needed was to get on with her plans.

Chapter Eight

$\mathbf{A}$ short time later, Cassie welcomed the sound of the mule train. One thing Grandfather had been right about. Work didn't allow time for self-pity.

The children stood beside her as the drovers pulled up to the store yelling and cursing at their animals.

Daisy covered Pansy's ears and gave her brothers a warning look. "If I ever hear you say those words I'll wash your mouth out with soap. Mama would want me to."

"You listen to your sister," Roper said. "A man doesn't need to talk like that to accomplish his work."

Cassie felt him behind her but didn't turn. She couldn't look at him, couldn't even think about him without being reminded of painful things. Instead, she counted the men. "Six?"

"I'm guessing they'll eat more like a dozen."

"I'm prepared for it."

As the men unloaded supplies for Macpherson she rushed to get the meal ready to serve.

Daisy followed, shepherding her brothers ahead of

her. "There's no need to stand around listening to that sort of talk."

Roper, as usual, hovered. "I'll give you a hand."

Cassie closed her eyes. Must they go through this again? She noticed Neil straining toward the activity at the store and it gave her an idea. "Why don't you take the younger children some place until the men have eaten?"

"Oh, yes, please," Daisy said, and handed Pansy to him. The little girl went eagerly, and Roper grinned.

"Glad to. Come on, boys. Let's go exploring."

Roper broke into a rough trot, bouncing Pansy until she giggled. The boys pushed at each other as they followed him down the hill.

He welcomed a chance to get away from Cassie's angry looks. He hadn't meant to upset her. But everything he did, every word he spoke brought forth her ire rather than her approval.

Playing with the kids would be a welcome relief from the sting of his failure.

"Where are we going?" Neil asked, falling in step on one side of him.

Billy trotted at his other side. Roper shortened his strides so the boy didn't have to work so hard to keep up.

"I bet there's treasure around here," Billy said. "Didn't Pa say he might find gold? Roper, where can we find gold?"

Roper chuckled at the boy's intensity. "What would you do if you found some?"

Billy picked up a handful of rocks. "I'd buy us a home."

The words fell into the air like hailstones, forceful, bruising.

Roper pulled Billy close. "I promise you will have a home." He had to believe going to a relative was the best thing for them.

Neil moved closer. "Daisy said you're an orphan like us."

"That's right." The boys considered him, as if checking to see if being an orphan had branded him.

He chuckled and playfully knuckled Neil on the arm. "It isn't the worst thing in the world, you know."

"What's worse?" Billy asked, his voice so mournful Roper's smile disappeared instantly.

"I can think of a few things. Being in a home where people are cruel. Not having anything to eat or a safe place to sleep." Losing two babies. He shook his head. He had to stop wanting to salve Cassie's pain. She didn't welcome it in the least.

Billy's breath released in a long sigh. "We sure 'nough have lots to eat. Cassie's a good cook. Don't you think so?"

"I surely do. I expect she's good at whatever she does."

Neil laughed. "Except putting up a tent."

Roper laughed, too. "Or building a house."

"Or digging a cellar." Neil laughed so hard he had to sit on the log beside Roper.

Billy didn't even smile. "You guys are mean laughing at her."

Roper sobered. "Ah, Billy. We aren't being mean. Just having fun."

Neil jumped to his feet and faced them. "We

wouldn't be mean to Cassie. We like her, don't we, Roper?"

Roper could honestly say he did. More than was wise, considering her reaction to him.

"Why don't you tell her?" Billy asked.

The boys waited for his answer. Pansy played with his collar.

"I don't think it would be a good idea."

Neil plopped down on the log again. "I guess if you say being an orphan is okay, I'll believe you."

"You'll be fine. All of you." A person couldn't change the facts but he could enjoy the good things of life. "Let's go look for treasure."

The pair dashed off, pausing to examine shiny rocks then running on.

A little later Roper lifted his head and tipped his ear toward Edendale. "Listen, I think I hear the wagons leaving. We better go back and help Cassie and Daisy. They'll need water and wood." It took concentrated effort to keep from jogging back to the camp.

Home.

Cassie.

Don't put down roots. Don't expect you can have family. Never stay where you're not wanted. She clearly didn't want him. But he could not drive the traitorous word *home* from his mind. The best he could do was ignore it.

He crested the hill, and drew to a halt. She stood at the end of the table, smiling widely. His lungs drew in air with a whoosh and he realized he'd been worried about her alone with rough men. Her and Daisy. To see the pleasure in her expression eased his concerns.

She glanced up. When her smile didn't falter, his

worry disappeared. She'd forgiven him for his earlier comments. Or forgotten about them, at least.

"You look pleased."

She nodded. "I am. The men each paid double what I asked." She shook the can. "I can hardly believe how well things are going. Every penny earned is a penny more I can pay Macpherson toward what I owe him."

"That's good."

"I don't like owing anyone."

"I kind of figured that out." He was glad to see her good humor returned. Too bad it couldn't be because of something he'd done. Perhaps he should start a list of things that upset her, topics he must avoid. Talk of her babies, which he could sympathize with. Use of her name, Muddbottom. That had something to do with her grandfather. Offers to help. He stopped because he couldn't avoid that. He'd never stop trying to help her.

He'd simply have to find more subtle ways of doing it.

He grabbed up two empty buckets and trotted to the river. When he returned he filled the kettle and the basins and the pots she used for washing up dishes. He made certain there was plenty of wood, then returned to the construction of the house, measuring, sawing and hammering at a steady pace, Neil assisting him.

Hoofbeats signaled the approach of riders. He straightened to consider the visitors.

"Who are they?" Neil asked.

Roper tossed aside the hammer and headed for the trio. "Cowboys from Eden Valley Ranch."

Slim, a thin man who lived up to his name. Roper had found him to be quiet and helpful. Ward, solidly built with a ready smile and a quick sense of humor.

He often tread where angels feared. And red-haired Blue—shy but thoughtful.

The trio swung down from their mounts.

Cassie put aside the paring knife and the potato she'd been peeling and hurried forward. "Welcome."

Ward pushed back his hat and looked about. "So this is what the pair of you are up to. Kids, a house… looks like a real home shaping up here."

Roper watched Cassie's shoulders stiffen and tried to signal Ward to stop his comments but Ward's attention had shifted to the children. "Hey, kids, these people treating you all right?"

Daisy and Neil had formed a flank with Pansy in Daisy's arms and Billy firmly between them. Daisy studied Ward then nodded. "They're good to us."

Neil added, "We help."

Slim held a package toward Cassie. "Cookie insisted we bring you cinnamon buns."

Roper chuckled as the children lost all wariness.

Cassie laughed, too. "Thank Cookie and tell her we truly appreciate them."

"I'll do that," Slim said. "But I'm to tell you she wants to know when you plan to visit."

"I'd love to." Cassie glanced about, her expression going from relaxed to stubborn. "Tell her I'm pretty busy now."

As Ward talked to the children and Slim talked to Cassie, Blue followed Roper to the construction site.

"This will be Cassie's home and give her a place to serve meals indoors in poor weather," Roper explained.

"She's really intent on this, isn't she?"

"Yes, I am," Cassie said as she hurried toward them. "Macpherson says I'll do well."

"Looks like you could use a hand." Blue waved to the others. "Come on, boys, let's help Roper with this floor."

Cassie sputtered a protest but no one but Roper seemed to hear.

The cowboys clattered to where Roper had several beams measured and cut. In a few minutes they had them in place and the spikes driven to secure them.

Roper saw Cassie's expression darken, and knew she resented their help. But she couldn't make herself heard above the hammering. She turned and stomped away. Out here people helped people. He vowed to speak to her about it before she offended someone.

A little later the three cowboys left.

This was his chance. "Cassie, you can't refuse every offer of neighborly help without offending someone."

"I don't want to be owing."

He'd expected her reply but still it clawed at his thoughts. He pushed to his feet. "Cassie, when will you learn not everyone demands repayment for kindness?" He strode away not wanting to hear her answer, sure it would be the same as always.

It had been a long and challenging day and Cassie couldn't wait for the forgetfulness of sleep.

Her emotions had been up and down all day. Up when the drovers paid her so well, up when the cowboys brought greetings from the ranch. Down when Roper scolded her for trying to turn away help from the cowboys.

A suspicion burst into her thoughts. Maybe he resented his part of their agreement, resented the amount of work he had to do. It wasn't as if she did anything in return. Their agreement had been for her to look after the children but she would do that, anyway, so it really didn't count. She must tell him he wasn't obligated to stay.

She could manage on her own. She wouldn't be lonely.

Especially for someone who had the bad taste to remind her of her babies.

Cassie tried to push the memories from her mind, tried to fall asleep so she could forget but every time she closed her eyes she saw her babies. Each wore a white dress as they were laid out in a satin-lined box. She stared into the dark, tried to focus on the sound of a fly buzzing against the canvas. The noise echoed in her head, annoying her.

It was too hot to sleep.

She pushed from her mat, pulled her dress over her head and stepped outside to the murmur of night noises. She filled her lungs until they ached. Still the unsettled feeling of loss and loneliness would not depart.

"Cassie?"

She jerked toward the sound. "Roper?"

He climbed up the riverbank and came to her side. "Yes. Can't you sleep?"

"Too hot." He didn't need to know the real reason even though he was to blame. But at the moment, she lacked the energy to confront him.

"I have something to show you."

"What?"

"Come and see." He signaled for her to follow him back down the bank.

She hesitated. But anything was better than staring into the darkness of her past.

He fell in at her side, took her hand. "It's hard to see."

She started to pull away and stumbled. Only his grasp kept her from falling so she let him guide her down the bank toward the river.

"Over here. Sit down." His blanket had been spread against the sloping bank.

She sat. He lowered himself beside her, crowding close as they shared the blanket. He lounged back as if in a chair. "Look up."

She did, seeing a beautiful clear night with the sky full of bright stars. Her breath eased out of her strangled lungs.

Cool air came from the river. She sank back to enjoy the sky. The blanket smelled faintly of horse reminding her of the life Roper normally lived. "Don't you miss being out on the range, riding and roping?"

"Can ride my horse any time I want. Mostly I'm content being here. Building your house. Helping care for the youngsters."

He truly sounded as if nothing else mattered. She tried to convince herself it didn't make her feel a tiny bit special. Now was the time to inform him he didn't need to stay.

But before she could say anything a star flashed across the sky and flared into a sudden death. "Oh. A falling star."

"Yup. Seen six already. I guess it's a meteorite shower."

"Another." She pointed and adjusted herself more comfortably on the narrow blanket which meant she edged closer to Roper, felt the warmth of his arm against hers.

Then the sky was still. She waited, afraid to take her eyes from the sparkling canvas lest she miss a falling star.

One crossed the sky and before she could comment another. "Two," she murmured. "They come and go so quickly. They die almost as soon as they're born." The meaning of the words flared through her heart, searing a white-hot trail. Her throat tightened and a scalding tear escaped each eye. She wiped them away. She did not intend to cry over deaths that came too soon and sudden.

But a torrent threatened.

Another star blazed across the sky and burned out. It happened so fast. Ended so quickly.

A sob ached from her throat. The tears scorched down her cheeks. She stiffened, determined to hide this embarrassing display of weakness.

Roper shifted to study her.

She prayed he couldn't see her tears or her twisted face in the darkness.

"Cassie, are you okay?"

She couldn't answer except for a muffled sound that even to her ears seemed more sob than denial.

He edged his arm under her neck and pulled her to his side. "I told you my shoulders are available anytime."

Heaven help her but she couldn't deny herself this bit of comfort, and she buried her face in the fabric of his shirt and let the tears flow. Once started she could not stop them. They tore from some secret place deep inside, a well of hidden, denied, bottomless sorrow. She clutched his shirtfront and hung on for dear life.

He made murmuring noises as he cradled her gently. It didn't matter that his sounds and words made no sense. They conveyed such a feeling of compassion and care that it made her cry harder.

Eventually, she cried herself dry. Too weak and spent to move, she remained in his arms as he stroked her hair. Gratefully he didn't seem to have a need to talk. She couldn't have said an intelligible word at the moment.

"Look." He pointed toward the sky. "Oh, you missed it."

But another flared across the sky. "That was a big one," she said.

"Good thing they burn up before they hit the earth."

She considered the idea. "Do you think there is a reason for bad things?"

He was quiet a moment. "I don't think God sends bad things. Wouldn't that make Him evil? But I think He can turn them into something good. Maybe He does so with such skill that we sometimes think He arranged the bad things."

She nodded. His words made more sense than the empty things well-meaning friends had said when her babies died. *This is God's will. They are far better where they are now...back with God.* "I don't see how God can make something good out of my babies' deaths."

His arm tightened across her shoulder. "Maybe the good is only found in God, not in our own hearts."

She tried to think what he meant but could not. "I don't understand."

He shifted to look into her eyes. He was close enough she could feel his breath on her cheek, but it was too dark to see his expression. "I think what I am trying to say is if I look inside, just at me, I see the hurt, the pain, the missing pieces. But if I look at God, maybe even let Him move into that area of my heart, I see wholeness, healing and love. Does that make sense?" He sat back. "I'm not much good with words."

She touched his cheek, liking the feel of his rough whiskers. "Your words are more than adequate and yes, it makes sense. I was somehow thinking God would make me forget the pain of my past. But you make me consider that maybe I can't forget, shouldn't even try. I can only let God cover it with His love." An awesome truth filled her heart. "God's love is bigger than my pain."

He gently caught her upper arms. "You say it much better than I do but that's exactly what I meant." He studied her, with her face toward the sky, seeing her better than she saw him. "Cassie, I am so sorry about your babies. I can't imagine your pain."

And yet the way his voice deepened, she felt he understood better than George had. "I've never before admitted to anyone how much it hurt." She pressed her palm to his cheek. "Thank you."

He captured her hand, turned to press his lips to her palm.

She saw he meant to kiss her. She hesitated half a beat and then she lifted her face toward him. It was only a kiss. A thank-you for his comfort. The final act of releasing her sorrow.

His lips caught hers, warm, gentle and yet...

Her heart lifted on gossamer wings and fluttered gently, soothingly, sweetly.

He hesitated as if he meant to end the kiss but she clung to him, not ready for it to be over. She'd been kissed many times. After all, she'd been married. But nothing before this had reached into a hitherto unknown corner of her heart and made her aware of a deep, bottomless longing.

Summoning every bit of strength, she forced herself to pull away. The kiss made something between them real. She didn't know what to call it. Friendship? Understanding? Acknowledgment of shared emotions?

For now she was content to remain cradled against his side.

That thought didn't seem quite right but she lacked the energy to examine it.

Half an hour later, they decided the meteorite shower had ended.

"I should go." Cassie scrambled to her feet.

Roper bounded up and caught her hand. "Thank you for a nice evening."

It was she who should thank him but how did one thank another for being allowed to soak the front of his shirt? Instead, she said, "It was nice." And with a hurried good-night she headed away.

But Roper would have none of that. "I'll see you safely back to the shack." Again he caught her hand and guided her up the hill. They paused outside the shack. He pulled her close and she willing went back into his arms. A harbor for her pain. She pressed her cheek to his chest and heard the steady beat of his heart.

When he caught her chin in his fingers and lifted her face to him, she again welcomed his kiss.

And then he turned her toward the door. "Good night, Cassie."

It wasn't until she was safely inside the shack that she realized she hadn't told him he wasn't obligated to stay. Did she really need to do so? Did she even want to?

She wouldn't answer the question. Not tonight.

Chapter Nine

Roper grinned up at the star-filled sky. *Thank You, Jesus, that I was able to offer comfort to Cassie.*

Back at his camp, he bent over his knees and groaned as pain chewed through him. Poor Cassie, losing her babies, then her husband. Oh, if only he could have spared her the pain. Or help her get past it.

But he couldn't. He had to accept and trust that God would use it to create something special in her life.

He settled down on his blanket, remembering how Cassie snuggled close to watch the stars, then turned into his arms. He'd offered his kisses as comfort and understood she'd welcomed them as such.

Only it wasn't comfort he felt in his heart. It was far more intense than sympathy.

He had nothing to offer Cassie except his two hands to build her house, his strength to drive in nails…

And his arms to offer comfort.

If only…

But he'd long ago accepted his reality. A man with no name. No past. And a lonely future. He'd learned to find satisfaction in making others happy. It was enough. His words to her echoed in his head. Did he truly let God fill the missing pieces in his heart? He had to. Nothing—no one—else could.

The next morning he climbed the bank with re-newed determination to build Cassie's house as quickly and sturdily as he could.

But when she glanced up, a shy smile trembling on her lips, he faltered. All his fine intentions did not erase the emotions he'd felt last night. He had to fight his way back to his objective of expecting nothing more than the chance to help her.

"Morning," he called. "Everyone sleep well?"

He managed to act normal over the meal though his insides jumped every time Cassie moved, and holding her hand to say grace made his mouth run dry.

He took up her Bible, paused as he thought about the entries in the front. Of their own accord, his eyes sought hers.

They shared a silent memory of last night.

Realizing four youngsters watched him, Roper forced his attention back to the Bible. He opened to the bookmark and read, skipping over the names he couldn't pronounce.

Then he again reached for her hand so he could pray for God's safety and protection over them this day. Feeling her hand so firm in his own, gripping back as if she needed his strength, made him realize how much he wanted to be able to do this for her—and the children—day after day.

Don't put down roots. You'll only have them ripped out. He knew the pain of such uprooting. He meant to avoid it.

He said amen, and jumped to his feet. "Time to get to work."

Neil followed him over to the house and they set to sawing and hammering.

This was one thing he could do for her and one thing she would allow.

He bent his back to the task and worked with fervor. Only when Daisy called them for the noon meal did he realize Neil looked exhausted. Guilt blared through him. He'd worked the boy too hard. "After we've eaten we'll rest."

Neil almost folded with relief.

"Let's all go down to the river," he said as he sat down to eat.

"You and the children go ahead. I'll see to the dishes." Cassie looked hot and bothered as if she had worked at a frenzied pace all morning, as well.

"Seems we could all stand to cool off a bit." The sun sucked the moisture from the air and poured heat into every corner. "A break will refresh us all."

She didn't answer, simply waited for him to say grace. Even her hand felt limp. A bit of flour dusted one cheek. Her hair was damp about the edges. No doubt she'd spent the morning baking bread and biscuits. The heat from the cook stove would practically melt her bones on a day like this.

He would somehow convince her to go to the river and cool off.

As soon as they finished eating he gathered the dishes, and stuck them in the dishpan. He grabbed the kettle, and poured hot water over the lot. "Let them soak and they'll wash easier."

She didn't look convinced. "I need to get potatoes ready in case people come by for a meal."

"If the men want a meal they'll wait."

She considered the idea.

"It's not like they can go across the street to a competitor." He could see her begin to relent. "'Sides, everyone knows your meals are worth waiting for."

His praise accomplished its purpose and she nodded. "I wouldn't mind cooling off."

"Great." He led them to the river. The children took off their shoes and stockings and played in the water. He scooted out of his boots and rolled up his jeans so he could keep a hand on Pansy and protect her. "Come on." He waved toward Cassie. "This will cool you off."

She remained on the shore.

The youngsters called her to join them.

"How can I resist?"

The question teased Roper into wondering exactly what she meant. Resist the invitation to paddle in the river? Or resist all the things he wanted to give her?

She dipped her hand into the water and shivered at the cold shock.

Daisy giggled. "It feels good once you get used to it."

Neil splashed water on his face. "That sure cools me off." He cupped a handful and poured it over his head.

Billy and Daisy followed his example, and laughed.

Roper and Cassie looked at each other, the silvery water between them, Pansy at his side dragging her hands through the water. Roper held out his other hand to Cassie. "Come on in. The water's fine."

Her gaze darted to his hand then his face, searching his eyes as if the invitation held a hidden message.

Perhaps it did.

He wanted her to learn to trust him. Realize he would always protect her and take care of her if she would let him. She slipped off her shoes and slowly, hesitantly, she lifted her hand to him.

He pulled her closer, laughing when she squealed as the cold water covered her feet and then rose to her ankles. She stopped inches away, her hand still resting in his. He smiled. "You're safe."

She nodded.

Neil flicked water at Daisy and soon the three older youngsters were soaked and laughing.

Pansy jumped up and down and squealed. She tugged at Roper's hand trying to escape to join the others but Roper held on, knowing she would fall down in the water.

Suddenly the trio turned toward Cassie and Roper. He saw the mischief in their eyes in time to jerk about and plant himself between Cassie and the spray of water the children sent their way. He pulled her to his chest. She drew close, hiding from the splashes. Pansy gasped then screamed.

The water attack stopped. Roper turned to stare down at the little girl. Her eyes were wide. Had she been hurt?

Daisy plowed through the water and snatched up her sister. "You boys stop spraying. You've frightened her." She pushed to dry ground and sat down, Pansy in her wet lap, crooning comfort.

The boys followed, and sat on either side of Daisy. "Sorry, Pansy," Neil murmured. "We didn't mean to scare you."

Billy stuck his face close to Pansy's. "I'm sorry, too. Please don't cry."

Cassie remained pressed to Roper's chest. He held her close, wanting to protect her from more than a spray of cold water. She clutched his shirtfront and her cheek pressed to his shoulder as if she found welcoming shelter.

Suddenly she jerked away, darted him a red-cheeked glance then headed toward the children.

He followed, making no effort to hide his grin. He'd seen the flash of awareness before embarrassment burned it away. And he knew without a doubt that she had enjoyed being protected in his arms.

It was enough for now.

Again, warning words flashed across his brain. *What happens later?* He'd have to leave. But he'd always known that. At least he could be at peace as he moved on, knowing he'd helped her.

His mental argument failed to provide the comfort he sought.

He joined them, knelt beside Daisy and stroked Pansy's head. "You okay, little one?"

She sobbed, and leaned out for him to take her.

His heart tightened as he cradled the child to his shoulder, shushing her and patting her back. Cassie watched. Was she remembering being comforted in the same way?

He shifted Pansy to one side and reached out a hand for Cassie.

Ignoring his outstretched arm, she said, "Guess it's time to get back to work." She sat down to put on her shoes. He realized he stood barefoot and scrubbed his feet on his pant legs and sat down to put on his own footwear.

Pansy scrambled away to retrieve her shoes and stockings, and handed them to Roper.

A few minutes later they climbed the hill. Roper, with Neil at his side, returned to work on the house. Billy trailed after them.

Roper hummed as he worked, satisfied Cassie had allowed him to comfort her.

The aroma of stewing meat and cooking potatoes filled the air with pleasant thoughts. A man should enjoy such comforts all the days of his life.

He straightened so fast he sent a board skidding away.

Here he was—a nobody—dreaming of a future that he couldn't own. Forbidden dreams and hopes pushed at the barred door in the back of his heart. Not only were they forbidden, they were impossible. His humming silenced. He bent his back and heart into doing for Cassie what he could—build her a house.

If he hadn't been so intent on driving away senseless dreams with every hammer blow he might have noticed the arrival of company before Neil said, "Lane is here."

Roper spun around. Yup. It was Lane. With a bouquet of wildflowers stuck in a tin can that still wore a label indicating the contents had been tomatoes.

Lane stood with the flowers in one hand, his hat in the other.

Roper eyed the hat. Black. Looked to be all new and fancy. What happened to the battered gray thing he wore the other day?

Cassie, in the shack, had not seen the man standing awkwardly in her yard.

Daisy came out with potato peelings and saw him. Her eyes narrowed and she backed into the shack. "You got company."

Cassie stepped out, drying her hands on her apron. "Lane?"

Roper tried to decide if it was only surprise that made her word sound breathless.

"Thought you might like some flowers." Lane took a step closer and held out the bouquet.

Cassie darted a glance at Roper as if silently asking him what this meant. He crossed his arms over his chest and watched without letting any of his emotions show in his face. He should be happy if a man wanted to court her. Didn't she deserve every bit of happiness she could find? But an emotion totally opposed to gratitude raged through his veins.

Cassie took the flowers and buried her nose in them. "Umm. They smell good. Thank you." She set the tin can in the middle of the table.

"F'owers." Pansy rushed forward.

Daisy lifted her, and let her sniff them.

"Like f'owers," Pansy declared.

Roper studied the flowers. Purple bells. Pink roses. White something or other. Yellow ones. Lots of them. Did the man spend his entire life gathering flowers? "Some of us have work to do." He grabbed his hammer and pounded a nail into place. What good were flowers? Except he'd seen the pleasure in Cassie's eyes as she admired them.

He kept his back to the others as he drove home nail after nail. He tried not to hear the murmur of their voices. Forced himself not to imagine Cassie smiling at Lane.

And faced a harsh truth.

He wanted to give her more than help and safety. And he didn't want Lane giving her anything. Somehow, without his notice, and certainly without his permission, his feelings had shifted beyond simply wanting to help. They had developed deeper than wanting only to make her happy. As if he could even dream of anything more.

Neil slipped away to join the conversation around the table leaving Roper alone to face his mental struggle.

He resented not knowing who he was. More than that, he abhorred his weakness in not following his own rules.

What had he told Cassie last night? That God provided wholeness and healing? But did God provide an identity? Because Roper felt like nobody at the moment. A nameless child with no past.

No future.

Nothing he could share.

Flowers? Cassie alternately looked from them to the face of the cowboy who brought them. Sure, flowers were nice. The bouquet brightened the table. But what did he want?

Roper continued pounding away on her house, the noise blasting against the inside of her skull. Lane sat with his elbows on the table telling her about his oat crop. His words rushed through her head with the insistence of raging water.

She glanced at Roper. If he would join them she'd feel she could go back to the shack without being rude. How was she to get the meal cooked if she had to entertain Lane?

But Roper hammered relentlessly. Her eyes bored into him. He so often went on about how he wanted to help her. Well, here was his chance. He could march himself over here and visit with Lane.

But her scowl landed on his back without causing him to flinch. Certainly without making him turn to see what she needed.

Fine. She'd manage without his help. Just as she meant to from the start. "You'll have to excuse me. I have work." She waved toward the shack.

Lane leaped to his feet. "Don't mean to be in your way. I'll just hang about until the meal is ready, if you don't mind."

"No. That's fine." Feeding people was what she did. She glanced at the flowers before she hurried to the shack.

Lane was still at the table when she heard others arrive and she hustled out to take count.

Six paying customers even though she knew the two drovers would each eat enough for three ordinary men.

Her business was growing. A glow of satisfaction warmed her insides.

She left Daisy to set the table while she went inside to get the food. As she turned, she came up short, almost slamming the pot of potatoes into Roper. She staggered, caught her balance and favored him with a narrow-eyed look she hoped conveyed more than surprise. She wanted him to know how annoyed she was with him.

He grinned unrepentantly as if pleased at getting her attention, even in a negative fashion. "I'll help you."

She hesitated, wanting to prove she didn't need help. The pot grew heavy in her arms as she mentally argued with her pride. But pride mattered little when there was work to be done and men to be fed. His assistance would mean half as many trips back and forth in the heat. She didn't have the strength to say no. Truth be told she was glad to see him after being ignored for the past hour. She would have scolded herself for such foolishness but she didn't have the time. The men wolfed down food as fast as it appeared. She'd held back enough to feed Roper and the children later or they would likely have cleaned her out. The children and Roper could have eaten with the men. Probably would have been simpler. But there was something cozy about the six of them eating alone, without these hungry men sharing their table.

Anxious to fill their stomachs and get on with their business, the men washed the food down with copious amounts of coffee that Roper kept pouring.

Except for Lane. He ate leisurely. Like a real gentleman. Every time Cassie's glance slid by him he watched her. Each time she jerked away, resisting an urge to run her hands over her hair. She tried not to let his attention unsettle her, but it did.

Almost as much as the way Roper studied him. His expression gave away little but she couldn't help wonder why he was so interested in the man.

"How's that crop of yours?" Roper's question

seemed sincere but Cassie watched to see if he had something else in mind.

"Good. Going to produce a bumper crop. I'm pleased with the way this new land has produced. Shows lots of promise. I'll have a good supply of feed for the winter."

Roper considered the comment. "A man can go far in this part of the country. Good grass. Good water. Good soil."

Lane leaned back, nursing his coffee cup. "Great place for a man to start his own place. Raise a family." His gaze brushed Cassie before he brought his full attention back to Roper.

Her cheeks burned. Did he think she would be part of his dream?

She spun away.

She had no intention of belonging to any man. Ever again.

Even if she had found sweet comfort in Roper's arms and from his kiss.

It had been a momentary lapse and it wouldn't happen again.

The men finished and departed, Lane at the tail, saluting a goodbye and promising to come again.

She wanted to tell him not to bother but he was a customer. She couldn't afford to turn him away so she smiled and waved, then started cleaning up the meal. She washed plates and forks so fast Daisy couldn't keep up then attacked the pots with vigor.

Daisy giggled. "You're going to wear a hole in it."

Cassie stopped scrubbing and straightened. "Guess I'm taking out my frustration on the pot."

"Don't you like Lane? I think he's handsome." She blushed and ducked away.

"I suppose he is." Though not exactly to her liking. She preferred—

Roper's face sprang to her imagination and she closed her eyes and willed it away. How had he wriggled so far into her thoughts? "I just don't care to belong to any man."

Daisy twisted the tea towel and considered Cassie's words. Finally she spoke. "My ma said she and Pa were one. Neither was more important than the other. They were equal and stronger for being together. She didn't seem to mind belonging to Pa."

"Your parents had a special relationship." Or else they hid their problems from the children.

"I thought all married people were like them." She looked toward her brothers. Slowly she hung the towel, picked up Pansy and went to join them.

Cassie put away the last pot and turned to see Roper standing nearby watching. "What?"

"Did you love him?"

"Who?" She knew he meant George, and when he waited, letting her know he knew, she mumbled, "We weren't like the children's ma and pa."

"What were you like?"

"Why?" She remembered his understanding and comfort about her babies and longed to feel it again. But her feelings regarding George were different than her feelings about her babies. More confused. Filled with a thousand different things. Anger. Guilt. Disappointment. Shattered hope.

He didn't move in close, forcing her to confront his

gentle gaze. Instead, she felt it slip past the barricade her feelings formed.

"I married George to get away from my grandfather. George was never unkind." She tried to rein in her feelings. Stop the rush of words pushing at her tongue. "He just didn't take my feelings into account. Nor consider my wants or needs."

His gaze never faltered. Neither did it judge.

More words rushed uncensored to her mouth. "I don't know if I even understood what love was when I married George."

He waited, his eyes darkening with a deep emotion. She didn't try and analyze what it was.

"I thought we shared the same dreams."

"But you didn't?" he probed gently.

"Turns out no. I wanted only to settle in a safe home. George wanted to move West, try his hand at homesteading. Free land. Acres of it. We needed only to earn a little more money to buy machinery and supplies." She forced herself to take in a deep breath. Tried to calm the harsh words that revealed a truth she had never before confronted. "I tried to explain that I didn't want to move or start a farm in a new land but he said I was his wife and had no choice but to follow him."

His gentle smile contained sadness. "No wonder you vow not to belong to a man again."

She nodded. "There are many ways of owning and controlling a person."

He didn't speak for a moment. "What happened to him?"

"He got a job working in the woods to earn some money before our final leg of the trip out here. Got soaking wet one day." She stared straight ahead, seeing nothing as she relived those dreadful days. "His raging fever frightened me. We were in a new and strange country where I heard more French than English. I couldn't make anyone understand my need for medical help. In the end I was helpless to do anything except hold him as he gasped his final breath."

Her chest filled with a merciless weight. She thought she was in desperate straits under her grandfather's harshness. Thought things were bad when George dragged her to Canada. But when she sat beside his cold, dead body she realized that was nothing compared to being abandoned in a foreign land.

She shuddered as wave after wave of remembering pounded through her.

Roper's eyes filled with sorrow. Oh, how she ached to go into those comforting arms.

She hadn't realized he'd moved until he opened his arms and pulled her to his chest.

"Oh, Cassie. If only I'd been there to help."

She clung to his shirtfront as stored-up fear and sorrow washed through her.

"How did you manage?" His voice rumbled beneath her ear.

She sniffed back her tears. "I was all alone with no money. No home. I ended up sleeping in the train station, avoiding the conductors and station master who would have driven me out." Safe in his arms, she could almost smile at her predicament. "That's where Linette found me and practically forced me to come with her. I fought the idea, not wanting to be under another person's control again."

He laughed, the sound a gentle murmur inside his chest. "Good thing she did, otherwise what would have happened?"

"Turns out it was a move in the right direction. Out here in the West I can start my own business and stand on my own two feet with some hope of success without depending on a man...or woman, for that matter." She understood the irony of saying she had to stand on her own two feet while leaning against Roper, safe in his arms. But it was only for a moment while she gathered together her resolve. Then she pushed back and put a step between them.

"I learned a valuable lesson. I would never again be so dependent on another." She met Roper's gaze with determination. "I accept help only when I can pay for it in a businesslike fashion."

Roper crossed his arms and gave her a gentle smile. She knew he was thinking of last night. She'd accepted something from him that could not be bought or paid for.

And she could not bring herself to regret it.

Suddenly she remembered her own parents when her father was still alive. They honored each other without any obligation.

Except to love each other.

Where had those words come from? She must have heard them somewhere but she couldn't recall where. Perhaps a sermon at church. Or...

She shrugged.

Did it mean love was an obligation? A debt she had to pay? It made love sound petty and controlling.

She wished she could believe it was otherwise but she had no proof it was. Unless she counted her parents.

Roper shook his head. "Cassie, prickly Cassie."

She wanted to take offense at his words but they were spoken so softly she couldn't.

"Someday you will learn you can't reduce life to a balance statement of debts owed and debts paid. Some things are given freely. To try and repay a gift is an insult to the giver."

"Isn't there always an unspoken expectation?"

"I don't think so."

She tore her gaze from him only to see the flowers in the middle of the table. A gift. But certainly with expectations. If she wasn't mistaken Lane wanted to pursue a relationship. "My experience says otherwise."

He didn't move, causing her to look at him to see why. He watched her with a gentle, chiding expression on his face. "If you are completely honest with yourself you will know that isn't true."

No doubt he meant last night. And he was right. She couldn't deny she had nothing to give him in return and knew he didn't expect it. But she didn't know what to make of it.

She searched for an escape from his relentless look…from her confused thoughts. Her eyes scanned the site and lit on the basin full of water. "I need to finish my chores." Turning away, she lifted the pan, not caring that water sloshed over the sides and soaked her skirts.

"I'll do it." Roper reached for the basin but she jerked away, sloshing even more water over the sides.

At this rate there'd be nothing to pitch out by the time she had gone three steps.

"I've got it." *Hear me, Roper Jones. I can do this on my own.*

He wisely stepped back.

Roper grinned as she stomped away, her wet skirts clinging to her legs. She could protest all she wanted but he hadn't forgotten how she'd allowed him to hold her and give her comfort last night. Nor would he ever forget it. His smile melted away as he thought of her words to Daisy, how she'd been alone with a dying husband, hiding in a train station. No wonder she'd been so prickly those first few months at Eden Valley Ranch.

Avoiding the muddy spot where she'd slopped water, he took six strides that brought him to her side.

She stubbornly kept her back to him, shaking lingering drops from the basin as if each silvery tear must water the ground.

He ached to pull her into his arms and comfort her as he had last night. "Cassie?" Would she hear the unexpressed invitation in his voice?

A shudder crept across her shoulders, and then they settled in a slight hunch. "Guess it's true what they say."

"What's that?"

"What doesn't kill you makes you stronger." She turned, the fierce look in her eyes almost blinding him. "I know I'm stronger for my experiences."

"Strong, yes. No one could deny it. But still a mite prickly." He grinned, hoping to convey a teasing tone even though he was deadly serious.

She spared him a defiant look. "Guess maybe the two go together." And she stomped away.

He knew strong and prickly didn't belong hand in hand unless a person chose to let them, but he reckoned now was not the time to argue with her. His gaze lighted on the flowers wilting in the tomato can and he figured his expression might match Cassie's. What did Lane want? As if it wasn't as obvious as the nose on his face.

The man would no doubt hang about courting Cassie, growing more and more open about his intentions. 'Course he had to tend to his work at least part of the time. Cutting his crop. Feeding his livestock. Gathering wood for the winter. Why, Roper figured, the man should be busy most every day of the week. Perhaps a little nudge reminding Lane of the upcoming winter would be in order.

His tension fled as quickly as it came.

Lane might bring flowers that died within hours but Roper was building Cassie a house. He figured the house to be more important than flowers any day of the week.

Whistling under his breath he sauntered back to the building site. He was satisfied with his work.

Still his gaze returned over and over to the wilted flowers. And his thoughts circled back to an endless regret.

He had nothing to offer Cassie, or anyone, apart from his help.

Cassie left the washbasin on the grass, and followed the sound of the children to the riverbank. Her conscience warned her she should be working—or was it only Grandfather's persistent voice? But she didn't want to return to the home site and see Roper. Even if she couldn't see him, she heard him working and was acutely aware of his presence nearby.

Prickly Cassie. He'd said it a number of times. She saw it as determination.

Some things are given freely. Like what? It hadn't been so in her experience.

She caught up to the children.

The boys picked through a pile of rocks.

Daisy sat on the sand, piling it into a heap for Pansy. She glanced up at Cassie's approach. "Do you need me?"

"No. Supper is ready. We'll eat a little later. Enjoy your play."

Daisy got to her feet. "I'll help if you need something done. It's the least I can do seeing as you're feeding the four of us."

"Oh, Daisy, I don't mind." She rather enjoyed wiping little faces after each meal, checking that there were clothes for them each morning. She liked baking things the children enjoyed. "I don't expect repayment."

The words echoed what Roper had said.

If Cassie could give without thought of repayment, was it possible others did?

She waggled her hand at Daisy. "You play with your little sister." She sat with her back to a nearby tree and watched the children. They were a sweet bunch and deserved a home where they were loved and allowed to be children. Their uncle better be a more appropriate guardian than her grandfather had been.

Pansy joined the boys examining rocks, ever under the watchful eye of Daisy who sat close by guarding her younger siblings.

Pansy picked up a rock and headed toward Cassie.

"Stay here," Daisy said.

Pansy shook her head. "I show her." She nodded at Cassie.

Daisy hesitated a heartbeat before saying, "Okay."

Cassie held her breath as Pansy walked to her, the rock cupped in her hands. The little one had never warmed up to her like she had to Roper. Or perhaps Cassie hadn't invited it, reminding her as she did of her own babies. But now she ached to be friends with Pansy and smiled encouragement.

"What do you have there?" she asked as Pansy stood before her.

"Treasure." She held out her rock.

Cassie took it and examined it carefully. "It's very pretty. See the pink here?"

"Pink."

Cassie held it out for Pansy to take.

"It for you."

"Me? Why thank you." She tucked it into her apron pocket.

Pansy edged closer until she stood at Cassie's shoulder. She patted Cassie's cheeks, her little hands soft and gentle. "I like you."

"I like you, too." The words caught in Cassie's throat.

Pansy plopped into Cassie's lap.

Daisy, watching the whole thing, smiled and turned back to her brothers.

Little Pansy snuggled close.

Cassie closed her eyes. She pressed her cheek to the sun-drenched hair, breathed in the smell of damp sand and baby skin. She held Pansy close, and let the feel of the warm little body fill her empty heart.

They sat quietly for several minutes, Pansy wrapped in Cassie's arms, then Pansy squirmed. "I go play."

Cassie reluctantly released her to run back to the others.

Daisy turned and smiled.

Cassie's answering smile came from deep inside, from a place that had been lonely and afraid a long time.

After a while Neil left, saying he needed to help Roper. The rest of them stayed longer as the children played happily.

Cassie was reluctant to leave this peaceful place and return to the realities of her life.

Eventually the children would go to their uncle. Roper would return to the ranch. Cassie would run a successful business. It was what she wanted, what she'd planned, but she'd miss them more than she dared contemplate.

Roper was still assessing the construction of the house, planning his work when an unfamiliar voice called, "Hello, the house."

He jerked about. "Constable Allen." The Mountie had crossed silently from Macpherson's. No doubt the ability to sneak about served him well in his job but it only made Roper wish he'd seen the man coming so he wouldn't have been caught dreaming.

"I said I'd be back to check on the children."

Neil had returned a moment ago and stood at Roper's side. He could feel the nervous tension vibrating from the boy.

"What's to check? Me and Cassie are doing just fine by them. Isn't that right, Neil?"

"Sure is."

The constable held up his hands in a no-need-to-get-fussed gesture. "I expect you are. However, my duty is to make sure these orphaned children are properly provided for." He glanced about. "Where's the rest of them?"

Roper tipped his head in the general direction of the river. At that moment, Daisy climbed the bank with a pail of water, Billy at her heels. Cassie followed, carrying Pansy.

That was a first. Roper wished he had more time to appreciate the sight.

Constable Allen had ears to match his footsteps and heard the others. "Good. I need to talk to all of you." He sniffed. "Are you about to have supper?"

Joining them, Cassie said, "You're free to join us."

"That would be ideal. Give me a chance to see how things are going."

Things are going well, Roper muttered silently. *Just like I said.*

Neil echoed the words in a faint grumble that likely the Mountie heard although he gave no indication.

Cassie put Pansy down. Daisy and Billy rushed to set the table for seven. Roper and Neil headed to the washbasin, Allen on their heels.

Normally Roper would let a guest wash up first but

he was in no mood for common courtesy and took his time scrubbing his hands even though he knew he only delayed the inevitable.

Somehow he'd forgotten the Mountie had said he would come back and decide if the youngsters could stay.

He dried his face and hands and handed the towel to Neil. Cassie stood in the doorway of the shack, a bowl of potatoes in her hands. He hustled over to take it.

"Is he going to take the children?" she whispered.

"Guess he has the right but I don't see any reason he should. Aren't we doing a fine job taking care of them?"

"I think so but he might see things he doesn't like."

"Such as?" He glanced around. Seemed everything was perfectly adequate.

"For one thing, we're pretty crowded at night. And the house isn't finished." She rocked her head back and forth. "I don't know what he might take objection to."

The Mountie dried his hands, and sauntered toward the table.

With a sigh that seemed endless, Cassie got the meat from the shack and carried it out. Roper helped her with the rest of the food.

"It's ready," Cassie announced. Her words were unnecessary as everyone sat around the table.

Roper made sure he took a spot across from Cassie and as far from the Mountie as he could. Though perhaps, on second thought, he should have positioned himself between Neil and the constable.

Out of habit and a need to feel connected to Cassie and helped by a power beyond himself, he reached for Billy's hand on one side and Cassie's on the other. "Let's say grace." After he muttered his simple, customary words, he added, "Help us be able to stay together and help each other. Amen."

Cassie slowly released his hand. He held her gaze long after their hands parted. Her eyes seemed to tell him she needed assurance, and he did his best to offer it even though the Mountie had the authority to do whatever he decided.

Constable Allen cleared his throat, making Roper realize how long he and Cassie had been sending silent messages to each other.

Roper glanced away and passed the food.

Chapter Ten

Cassie could hardly swallow her food. Why had the Mountie come now when she'd finally won Pansy's affection?

What would he see?

She'd done her best to provide properly for the children. They ate well. They had a dry place to sleep, though, as she worried to Roper, it was crowded. They were reasonably clean, more thanks to Daisy than to herself.

But when had her best ever been good enough?

This time more was at stake than her own concerns. These four children depended on each other and cared for each other yet they couldn't be allowed to live on their own. They needed adults to help them. *God in heaven, I don't know if I've done a good enough job but please make it appear so to the Mountie so the children can stay together with us.*

The Mountie paused from eating. "I saw Red Fox. He said to say hello to Mrs. Gardiner."

Cassie allowed a portion of her brain to slip back to the Indian woman and her children that Linette had taken into the cabin and fed. "How are Bright Moon and the baby?"

Constable Allen chuckled. "The baby is still wearing the little sweater Mrs. Gardiner gave him. They call him Little Shirt." The Mountie sobered. "The tribe had a tough winter. Not enough food." He shook his head sadly. "With the buffalo almost gone they're dependent on what the government provides for them to eat. They must learn to become farmers, but they don't understand the concept. For them, food is acquired by hunting. It's a hard lot for them. I fear many will suffer."

Cassie momentarily forgot her own worries and cares. "Red Fox and his family are okay, though, aren't they?" She hadn't shown them much kindness when they'd been at the ranch even though she understood they were starving. Now she wondered how she could have been so selfish and bitter.

"They're surviving."

She didn't much care for the hopelessness of the Mountie's words. "Did you see their older son?"

The Mountie nodded. "You mean Little Bear?"

"Yes. I first saw him hanging around the Fort when we arrived last fall. He was helping a man. And being treated cruelly." She should have done something then. But all she could think was how her grandfather had grown even more vicious if anyone intervened in even the slightest way. So she'd backed away. Not like Linette. "Linette found the freighter who had abandoned him and gave him a slicing with her tongue." She laughed as she recalled how the big man looked so angry. "She asked if he would starve his mules and still expect them to pull a load. He as much as told her to mind her own business." She smiled in Roper's direction, sharing a common knowledge that Linette didn't mind her own business if she saw someone needing help. Cassie returned her gaze to the Mountie. Linette wouldn't allow anyone to take these children and parcel them out to homes or a foundling home. But then Linette had a big house and the Gardiner money to back her up.

What could Cassie do? Besides pray again. Which she did.

The Mountie paused to enjoy some meat and potatoes before speaking again. "We could do with more people like Mrs. Gardiner." He shifted his gaze from Cassie to Roper and back again. "People willing to help those less fortunate." He turned back to his food.

Cassie thought the meal took an extraordinarily long time but finally everyone finished, the Mountie being the last to put his fork down and lean back. He cradled a cup of coffee. "You're a good cook, Mrs. Godfrey."

"Thank you."

"Macpherson tells me you are feeding travelers."

Uncertain how to answer, she stole a quick glance at Roper. Did the Mountie see her job as a good thing or a bad thing?

The Mountie continued. "It will be nice for people to be able to get a hot meal on their travels."

"I hope so." What was she supposed to say? Couldn't he simply let them know his decision and relieve the tension that crawled up her spine and dug talons into her neck?

Daisy excused herself, took Pansy and started washing dishes. Cassie went to help.

"What's he going to do?" Daisy whispered as they did dishes together.

"I don't know. We have to wait for him to say."

But the Mountie said nothing. Nor did he leave. He sat at the table, refusing a refill of coffee when Roper offered. Thank goodness Roper hung about. Her limbs felt like fragile sticks. She worried she might fall on her face if she took more than two steps in any direction.

The chores were done yet the children hung about near the washstand. Normally they would have gone to play in the lengthening shadows.

Roper slapped his hands on his thighs. "Sorry, Constable, but the youngsters like to have some fun about now. I see no reason to disappoint them." He pushed to his feet. "You make your decision and let us know." With a courtesy nod to the man, he turned to the children. "Who wants a game of tag?"

Daisy scooped up Pansy, and followed her brothers in Roper's wake as he headed toward the river where they often played.

Cassie hung back, uncertain what she should do.

Roper paused and looked over his shoulder. Like a chain reaction each child did the same. "You coming?" he asked.

She felt their silent pull on her. She stole a glance at the Mountie. Would he think it inappropriate for her to join in the fun? She tried to weigh her choices. Grandfather would have disapproved, but then there wasn't much he approved of. Linette, on the other hand, would have little concern about what the Mountie or anyone would say. If she thought it was the right thing to do, she'd do it without fear of consequences. Cassie couldn't be like that.

Neither did she want to let her grandfather continue to have so much influence on her decisions.

She tilted her chin, straightened her spine and marched over to the others who, seeing she was coming, filed down to the river.

Roper led them to the level ground by the river. As soon as he stopped, the children gathered around him.

"What's he going to say?" Daisy demanded.

"He can't make us go away." Neil crossed his arms over his chest and silently dared anyone to try.

Roper studied the worried faces before him. Pansy wasn't sure what was going on but she picked up on the concern of the others and stuck out her bottom lip.

Cassie did her best to hide her fears but her gaze begged support from him. If they were alone he would have pulled her into his arms and assured her he wouldn't let anything bad happen. Instead, he addressed them all. "There's no point in worrying about a future we can't control or a past we can't change. Better to make the most of the moment." He danced away, grinning. "Can't catch me."

Neil churned after him.

Billy yelled a battle cry and raced toward Roper. He tripped and fell facedown in the sand.

Roper paused, waiting to see if he would have to dry a pair of eyes, but Billy popped up, brushed himself off and continued pursuit.

Daisy and Cassie grinned at each other, gave some sort of signal then hurried to flank him. They had all somehow conspired to force him to the edge of the water, circling him so there was no escape. Daisy handed Pansy to Cassie. That should have been warning enough.

In less time than it took for him to go from "Nah-

nah can't catch me," to "Oomph," the three young-sters tackled him, knocking him to the ground, the air whooshing from his lungs. He gasped but couldn't fill his lungs as all three planted themselves on top of him. He tried to hold them off but there were too many legs and arms flailing at once, tickling him all over. "Uncle," he rasped from his starving lungs.

They stopped tickling but remained on top of him in a warm heap. He finally sucked in air. But no one moved.

Neil finally spoke. "Can he really make us go away?"

"Of course he can, silly. He's a Mountie. They can do anything." Daisy's voice alternated between annoy-ance and admiration.

Roper had to admit he had similar feelings. The man had authority and, like all Mounties, used it wisely. But right now Roper resented it.

Pansy demanded to be put down and flopped on top of Roper.

He grunted. "Always room for one more." He grinned at Cassie letting her know it was an invitation.

She shook her head but not before she looked long-ingly at the spot next to his heart that he indicated.

Billy twisted and looked about. "He's watching us."

The Mountie stood at the top of the riverbank. He waved for them to join him.

Roper pushed the children to their feet then pulled himself upright. He scooped Pansy into one arm and took Cassie's hand on the other side. "Let's go see what he wants."

The morose bunch climbed the riverbank and marched over to the table where the Mountie sat waiting. They plunked down in unison and planted their elbows on the table, all except Cassie who folded her hands in her lap. She looked about as defensive as he could remember seeing her.

Roper looked about the table. "Where's Billy?"

They all turned toward the river. No sign of the boy.

Roper pushed to his feet. "I'll go see what's keeping him." He hurried back along the trail, reached the river without seeing him. He must have climbed by a different path. He rushed back to the waiting group. "He's not here?"

Cassie's eyes rounded then narrowed as if afraid the Mountie would see her concern.

"He's hiding." Daisy grabbed Neil. "We'll find him." She perched Pansy on her hip, and they spread out calling Billy's name.

"I'll help." Cassie made to dash after the children.

Constable Allen lifted his hand. "Wait a minute."

Roper sensed a warning in the man's voice and stepped to Cassie's side. At the worried glance she darted his way he would have taken her hand except he wasn't sure how the Mountie would take the gesture.

The Mountie studied them, a look of concern and knowing in his face. "This happen often?"

The way Cassie wrapped her arms about herself, Roper knew she'd heard the judgmental tone in the Mountie's voice.

Roper jammed his fingers into the pockets of his trousers. "If you're referring to Billy disappearing, it's never happened before." He made no effort to keep blame from his voice. "I promised the boy—all the children—they were safe with us."

"Then I suggest you make sure they are." The

Mountie tipped his head toward the children who had disappeared from sight.

"Exactly what we had in mind until you called us back." He stalked away, Cassie so close to his heels he wondered how he didn't kick her. He didn't slow until he knew they were out of sight of the constable then he turned and reached for Cassie's hand.

"He's hiding somewhere. Thinks the Mountie will get discouraged and go away. Unfortunately, we both know that isn't going to happen so let's find him, and then we'll fight for them to remain here."

She nodded, her expression fierce. "I wish I could believe he'll let them stay."

"Billy's just given the Mountie a good reason to think he shouldn't leave them with us."

They reached the sandy riverbank. Neil and Daisy ran to them.

"He's hiding pretty good," Neil said.

Roper signaled them to silence. "Billy," he called as loud as he could. "Come out. You're only making things worse by hiding."

The only sound came from birds protesting at the noise.

Cassie nudged him, and nodded toward the campsite.

He jerked about. Eagerness gave way to disappointment as the Mountie watched them. "Let's spread out and find him."

They did so, looking behind every tree, beneath every bush and even going so far as to ask Macpherson to look in his store.

Then they gathered back at the campsite, defeated and discouraged.

Roper couldn't find a cheerful word anywhere as the Mountie plunked down at the table and indicated they should join him. "It seems we have a problem. One missing child."

Neil refused to sit. He poked Daisy. "This is your fault. You're supposed to make sure he's safe."

Daisy scowled at him. "So are you."

"You're the oldest. Ma said you had to be in charge."

At Neil's accusation, Daisy started to sob. Pansy gave her sister one look and wailed.

Roper and Cassie got up as one. He took Pansy and tried to console her. Cassie wrapped her arms about Daisy.

"It isn't your fault," she told the child. "You've done a fine job of watching out for your younger brothers and sister."

Neil glowered at them all.

Roper caught him by the shoulder and pulled him close. "It's not anybody's fault." Though he wondered if the Mountie believed that.

Pansy would not be comforted and flung herself at Daisy. Daisy jostled her and made comforting noises.

"She's tired," Daisy explained to the Mountie.

"Then perhaps someone should put her to bed."

"I'll help." Neil and Daisy headed for the shack.

Roper wanted to follow, too. So much for showing the Mountie how well they coped. The man signaled for them to sit but neither Cassie nor Roper made any move to do so.

"Whatever you've got to say will have to wait. We have to find Billy." Roper looked at Cassie. "Any idea where he'd go?"

"Did anyone look in the cellar?"

No one had. Roper lit a lantern and raced over to the partially constructed house. He lifted the trapdoor in the floor and hung his head into the hole, shining the light into every corner. "Billy?" He couldn't believe the boy wasn't there.

He replaced the trapdoor and sat hunched forward on the floor. "Where could he be?"

"We need to get a search party organized," the Mountie said. "I'll go to the store and enlist any help I can find. Tell the children to stay here while we look."

Cassie already headed for the shack. Neil stood at the door.

"I heard him. We'll stay here in case he comes back."

Ten minutes later a group of men had assembled.

"I'm going, too," Cassie said.

The Mountie nodded. "Then stay with Roper." He gave each man a direction to search. "If you find him signal with three shots. Otherwise return in an hour."

Cassie waited for the others to disperse. "Then what happens?"

Roper squeezed her hand. "We'll find him."

They searched to the north. Calling. Listening. Looking. But they found nothing.

Cassie sat down and sobbed. "What's happened to him?"

Roper sat beside her, and pulled her to his chest. "We'll find him." But his words were hollow. A thousand scenarios raced through his mind. The cold waters of the river. A body being carried along by the stream, bashed against rocks. Or a bear interrupted at her fishing expedition. A band of marauding men...

He slammed the door to such terrors.

"The Mountie will never let us keep the children now," Cassie wailed.

"Probably not. But what matters is they are all safe." He put a slight emphasis on the word *all*.

Her tears dried instantly. "Yes. We must find him." She leaped to her feet. "Maybe someone else has." She reached for his hand to help him to his feet.

He would never admit holding her hand made getting to his feet more awkward than if he'd done it on his own. Any more than he'd point out that if someone had found Billy they would have heard gunshots. Instead, hand in hand, they ran back toward the campsite, pausing often to make sure they didn't overlook any place Billy might hide…or fall.

The rest of the men had assembled—only a handful but every bit of help was appreciated.

The Mountie remained in charge. "At this point we must assume Billy has found an ally to help him get farther away. Macpherson, who's been by in the past couple of hours?"

"A freighter headed to Fort Edmonton. And a cowboy from the OK Ranch."

Two men were sent after them.

"The rest of you continue looking around here. The boy might be avoiding us." The Mountie headed for his horse. "I'm going to ride out toward a group of Indians that were hunting west of here. They might help us."

Cassie and Roper were alone. He realized they still held hands. She sent him a look full of desperate fear and he pulled her close and pressed her head to the hollow of his shoulder.

"Pray," she murmured against his shirtfront. "Pray he is safe and we'll find him before dark."

The shadows grew long and leggy. They didn't have much daylight left. Glad of the practice he'd had in praying aloud, Roper lifted his face toward heaven.

"Our Father in heaven. You see everything. You see Billy right now. Keep him safe and help us to find him. Please. Amen."

Cassie sighed softly and slowly straightened. "I'll let the kids know we're still trying to find him." She seemed reluctant to leave the shelter of his arms. A trembling smile caught her lips before she ducked her head and hurried to the shack.

Ten seconds later a cry rent the air. "Roper."

They were all gone. Cassie couldn't believe it. "How could four children vanish into thin air?" She hung on to Roper's arms afraid if she let go she would collapse into a sobbing pile of bones and flesh.

"They can't." Roper had lifted every blanket, moved every box as if they had shrunk enough to hide in such tiny places. "I need to think."

"They have no place to go." Every word tore from her throat leaving behind an aching trail.

"They'd go back to where they came from."

"Back to where their ma died?"

"I found them on their way to find their pa."

She reared back and stared at him. "He's dead."

"But he had a house of some sort. A bit of land. They might try and get there."

She shuddered to think of them alone. "Do they even know where it is?"

"They might. Or at least think they do." He broke from her grasp and headed for the door. "I'm going to hitch up the wagon."

"I'm coming."

A few minutes later they were driving from town.

Cassie perched on the edge of the seat, alert for any sign of them. "Wouldn't someone have spotted them?"

His laugh was mirthless. "Not if they didn't want them to."

She tipped her head in acknowledgment. "How are they keeping Pansy quiet, though?"

"Maybe they aren't." He stopped the wagon and they strained to catch any sound above the creak of wood and leather and the huff of the horse.

"Nothing." Roper flicked the reins and they continued on. He stopped twice more and they listened intently. "This is where I picked them up." He pointed toward a grassy spot. They listened.

They heard the sound at the same time. His eyes glowed with victory. "If I'm not mistaken that is Miss Pansy protesting."

He turned the wagon from the trail.

She kept her eyes wide for a glimpse of them. "There." She pointed at a flash of blue in some nearby trees.

And then they saw the children dashing from tree to tree, trying to get away.

"They're all there." She could finally get a full breath for the first time since Billy disappeared.

"This is just like last time." Roper pulled the wagon to a halt, set the brake and took off after the children, Cassie on his heels.

As he gained on them, the children split up. He veered after Neil, snagged the boy and dragged him after Billy.

Billy darted behind a tree, waited for Roper to approach, then sped off in a different direction.

Roper had his hands full holding on to Neil who yelled and tried to pull away.

Roper turned to Cassie. "Go find the girls."

Cassie went in the opposite direction and in short order she found them huddled behind a bush, Pansy pressed to Daisy's shoulder. Both of them sobbed so hard it threatened to tear Cassie's heart from her chest. She pulled them into her arms. "Shush. Don't cry." From somewhere came a lullaby and she sang it softly.

Daisy stopped crying. Pansy fell asleep. Poor baby was so tired.

"We aren't going back." Daisy hiccuped the words. "We won't let him take us."

"We were so worried about you. What if something happened to one of you?" The words stuck in her throat. "What if you run away and hide from everyone and something happens?" She recalled Roper's words. "Isn't it better to know that everyone is safe?"

Daisy sat up and dried her eyes. "You're saying it's better to let them take us away?" She hung her head.

Cassie stroked her head. "Honey, I don't want him to take you. But it might be a little hard to prove we can take care of you after you ran away."

Daisy gave a shaky smile. "But we don't want to run away from you."

"Then let's go back and tell the Mountie." Their only hope was to convince him of the fact.

She helped Daisy to her feet, little Pansy still asleep on her sister's shoulder. Daisy covered the baby's ears and called, "Billy, Neil. It's okay. We're going back."

"I'm not." Billy's voice came from deep in the grove of trees. And then a little squeal.

"Yes, he is," Roper called.

A short time later they were back at the campsite. Dusk filled in the hollows and stole the green from the leaves.

Roper had fired off three shots at the wagon and he did it again. "I expect everyone is too far away to hear but just in case."

The children trooped to bed without comment but could be heard whispering inside the shack.

Cassie sank to the bench. "I am suddenly exhausted."

Roper sat across from her and took her hands, cradling them between his. "Go to bed. I'll keep watch."

To make sure they don't run away again. He didn't have to say the words; she knew. "We have to convince the Mountie to let them stay."

"We can try."

His words provided little comfort and she stifled a cry.

"It's late. Nothing will be decided tonight. Go to bed and get some rest." But he held her hands as if he didn't really want her to go.

She knew she wouldn't sleep. Not until she knew the children's future. Would they be allowed to stay? But there was no point in sitting in the growing darkness wishing things could be different.

"Good night, then." She eased her hands free and stood.

Roper stood, too. He came to her side, caught her by the shoulder. "We'll do our best."

"That's never been enough."

"It is for me. It should be for you."

She stared at him. Did he really mean it? Could she believe it? She always seemed to measure herself by her grandfather's standards. How foolish. She knew now it was time to stop it.

He lowered his head, caught her lips with his before she had time to think. Or protest. Would she have protested given the chance?

No, she wouldn't have.

She welcomed Roper's kiss. Found comfort and encouragement in it.

And more.

She wasn't prepared to deal with anything more. Not right now. The children were what mattered now.

She hurried to the shack.

"I'll be right outside the door," he murmured just before she ducked inside to crawl into bed fully dressed. She didn't sleep, aware that Daisy and Neil lay awake as if waiting for a chance to run again.

"Roper is right outside the door," she whispered. "You'll never get past him if that's what you have in mind."

No one answered but covers rustled as if they adjusted themselves. A few minutes later she heard deep breathing and wondered if they'd fallen asleep.

Or were they only pretending?

Roper jerked away at first light. He'd slept in front of the shack door. No one would have left without waking him.

Hoof beats sounded on the nearby road. Likely that's what had wakened him.

He sat up, stretched and scratched his head.

The Mountie rode up to the place and dismounted.

Roper hurried to his side. "The kids are all here. Safe and sound."

"So Billy returned?"

That's right. The Mountie didn't know the others had run away, too. Perhaps Roper wouldn't tell him and give him any more reason to judge them inadequate to care for the children.

"Found him in some trees down the road a spell."

"I see." The Mountie gave Roper a hard look but Roper was prepared and held his gaze without blinking.

Cassie stepped from the shack, the children at her heels. They all skidded to a halt and stared at the Mountie.

Cassie's expression grew hard. "Come along, children. Let's get breakfast ready."

The meal was strained. Roper almost decided to forego the usual Bible reading but the children waited, so he pulled out the Bible and read a chapter then prayed, though it felt awkward with the Mountie sitting next to Neil. Neil refused to extend his hand to the man. Instead, he reached across the table to take Daisy's.

As soon as Roper said, "Amen," the Mountie cleared his throat.

"I think it's time to think about the future."

Was he aware of three rebellious expressions turned toward him? Five counting Roper and Cassie?

The Mountie turned to Daisy. "Are you happy here?"

She nodded.

He turned to Neil. "And you?"

Neil pursed his lips and glowered at the man.

The Mountie smiled. "Is that yes or no? I can't tell."

"Yes." It was plain Neil didn't intend to say more.

"Billy, you ran away. That doesn't sound like you want to stay here."

The look on Billy's face should have made the Mountie cringe but the man looked unimpressed.

"You can't make me leave. I won't go."

The Mountie turned to Roper and Cassie. "Are you two prepared to continue doing this until the uncle comes?"

They both nodded.

"Very well. You two obviously know how to create a family environment." He pushed to his feet and leaned close to Billy. "If I say you can stay, will you promise not to run away?"

Billy glowered at the man then gave a slight nod.

"Then I'll be on my way. I'll let you know as soon as I contact the uncle." He turned to the children. "You kids be good."

"Yes, sir," three voice chorused.

As a postscript, Pansy echoed them.

He clamped his wide-brimmed Stetson on his head and returned to Macpherson's store.

Silence followed his departure until he was out of sight then Neil whooped. "Yahoo!"

Billy raced away to run mindless circles. The others headed toward the river and Billy followed. Happy sounds came from the direction they'd gone.

Cassie rose and gathered up the dirty dishes.

Roper didn't move.

"Roper? Is something wrong?"

He shook himself. "Did you hear what the Mountie said?"

"Of course. I was right here. He said the children could stay until their uncle comes for them."

"He said we knew how to be a family. How can that be? I've never been in a family. Not once."

Chuckling softly, she sat down beside him and patted his arm. "You seem to know how to be a family better than I do. Maybe because you've never seen the unfortunate side of family life."

In her words there were a thousand sad stories. Would she ever tell him any of them? He turned to study her face in the bright morning light. Regrets mingled with joy. He expected the regrets were from her memories, her joy from knowing the children could stay together.

Then she swallowed hard, and worry filled her eyes. "Roper," she whispered. "What if the uncle doesn't want the children? What if he refuses to come?"

It wasn't something he'd considered. "It's not possible. He's family. He'll come."

"See how you view family as an ideal? I can tell you that being family doesn't guarantee love."

He stroked her cheek. "Oh, sweet Cassie. Who has hurt you? Will you ever tell me?"

Her eyes grew so wide, filled with such longing that he thought the crackling of his heart would break the silence. He wanted to kiss away her pain. He lowered his head, paused in anticipation then claimed her lips. He felt her little sigh of relief and his heart righted itself. All that mattered was easing her distress, making her happy.

She leaned into him. Her hand crept up his arm, halted at his shoulder.

He lingered on the kiss, hoping she would put her

arms about him but she continued to cling to his arm. It was enough. For now. But he wanted more. He wanted her to hold him like he'd never been held before.

She broke away, withdrew her hand but stayed in the shelter of his arms. "If the uncle doesn't want them, will they end up in a foundling home...or worse, as servant—slaves—in someone's house?"

"We won't let that happen."

"The Mountie won't let them stay here indefinitely. It wouldn't be right."

He knew what she meant. They weren't married. Come winter he couldn't continue camping by the river. But there was a solution. "There is a way we can keep the children."

She searched his face for clues to his meaning.

His first thought was to kiss her again but he had to explain his idea before he forgot all his good arguments. "We can make this arrangement between us permanent."

She searched deeper. "I don't understand."

Lost in the delight of her open look, wanting to see even deeper, he almost forgot what he meant to say. "We could get married and provide the children with a home."

She pressed a hand to her chest as if trying to still turmoil. "I told you. I don't intend to be owned again by any man."

"Hang on a minute. You aren't listening to what I said. It would only be a business agreement, a continuation of what we have already. You'd run your business. I could help where needed. Hunt for food. Maybe get some land nearby and run a few cows. It could work, Cassie."

"A business arrangement." She rubbed her chest with the flat of her hand. "No strings attached? Equal partners?"

"Only if the uncle doesn't want the youngsters." Of course he would. No man in his right mind would turn down a ready-made family.

And if he did take them, Roper and Cassie would have no reason to go ahead with a marriage.

He tried to make himself believe it would be okay.

"I could handle a business arrangement."

Did her voice sound hopeful, as if she welcomed the idea and not just to ensure the children were kept together? As if she secretly longed to maintain what they had here? He couldn't tell and didn't ask, not sure he wanted to hear the truth.

It was enough that she agreed. But he had to make sure she truly understood. "If the uncle won't take the children then we will marry and keep them?"

She nodded slowly, her gaze watchful, guarded. "A business arrangement." She ducked her head. "I agree."

He must see her face, read her expression. He caught her chin with his finger and tipped it toward him, waiting until she brought her gaze to him. "We'll be good together."

They looked deep into each other's eyes, plumbing for truth and on his behalf, something more, something he couldn't—wouldn't—name because he hadn't forgotten who he was.

A nameless orphan.

Could he learn to be a family with her and the youngsters? According to the Mountie they already had. The idea wound through his thoughts, caught hold of his heart and rooted there like an old oak tree. Family. With Cassie. He sighed.

He bent and caught her mouth with his own, silently sealing their agreement, giving an unspoken promise he meant to uphold.

I will show you what I believe about family.

He would do his best to care for them all, protect them and make them happy. A distant bell tolled in the depths of his brain. *This can't last.* But he ignored the warning, lost as he was in the warmth of her kiss.

He took her response as her own silent promise though he couldn't guess what words she would put to hers.

Cassie tried to concentrate on her tasks.

Marriage as a business arrangement. Was it possible?

He'd kissed her again. Not once but twice. Surely only to mark their agreement. But something inside her shifted a little more with each kiss. To be honest she found sweet comfort in the touch of his lips.

Suddenly she realized why. He demanded nothing from her when he kissed her. He simply gave. Was it possible…?

Of course not. This was only about the children.

And if they didn't need her, she would be free to pursue her original plan. But rather than make her feel better, the realization filled her with an acute sense of loss.

She would miss the children but it was best they go to family. Her insides warred. The loss would be more painful than she dared contemplate.

She shouldn't have let herself care so much. She

smiled. She'd tried to protect her heart but what chance did she have against them? Daisy, so helpful with a sense of responsibility Cassie understood so well. Neil, determined to imitate everything Roper did. He'd even begun to walk like Roper—a rolling cowboy gait. Billy, so innocent, so mischievous. And Pansy—sweet, little Pansy.

Carrie pressed her palm against her chest where Pansy's head had rested. She'd thought she would never enjoy the feel of a warm little one in her arms.

Now that she'd enjoyed it she couldn't bear the thought of losing it.

But the children's future was not in her hands.

Whatever happened, Cassie would survive. Battered and bruised but as she told Roper, what didn't destroy her made her stronger. She'd grow stronger.

That night she fell into an exhausted sleep only to be jerked awake by a noise. Her heart kicked into a gallop. Were the children running away again? She lay motionless waiting for the sound to recur so she could identify it.

"Daisy, are you asleep?" Neil's hoarse whisper was barely audible.

"Yes. Shh. Be quiet."

The covers rustled. Cassie guessed Neil crawled to Daisy's side.

"I miss Ma and Pa." Neil's whispered words reached her ears.

"Me, too."

One of them sobbed, the sound muffled as if they tried to cover it with their hand or bury it in the covers.

"Mama." Billy's voice joined the others, louder, more intense.

Daisy scolded, "Now you woke up Billy."

"I miss Mama and Papa," Billy wailed.

More rustling and Cassie guessed Daisy drew the younger boy close. She knew it for certain when she heard Daisy hushing Billy.

"I miss them, too." Daisy's voice was full of unshed tears.

Cassie lay quiet, wide awake now. Crying in Roper's arms had healed something inside her. Something she didn't even know was broken. Nor could she say if it was the tears or the comfort of his arms that accomplished it.

All she knew for certain was the children needed someone to hold and comfort them while they cried. She turned toward them. They heard her move and sucked back sobs.

"It's okay to cry," she murmured as she moved to Daisy's bedroll. She reached for Neil and pulled him to her arms. Billy climbed to her lap and pressed her face to her shoulder—the same place where she had found such sweet comfort with Roper. "Of course you miss your mama and papa. Shh. Shh." She patted and stroked and made comforting noises until, one by one, the children lay quiet and spent in her arms.

"I think Billy has fallen asleep," she said.

Daisy eased the boy back to his sleeping mat.

Neil shifted away, too. "How long before Uncle Jack sends for us?"

He and Daisy waited for her answer. "I purely can't say. But you've no need to worry. You're safe here with Roper and me. I promise we'll take care of you until your uncle makes arrangements." Silently she added to the promise. *Even if he doesn't want you.* She would not say the words aloud, though. The children did not need to worry about such things.

Neil seemed satisfied and returned to his bed.

Daisy hugged Cassie then settled under her covers.

Cassie slipped over to her own mat and relaxed once she heard all the children breathing deeply.

Was she wrong to offer them assurances about the uncle? Even if he did come, who could guess at what he would expect in return for taking four children. Likely instant obedience, willing hard work and more. More than a child could be expected to know to do unless someone told them. It was in their best interests to be warned of what they might expect.

And who better to do it than someone who knew as well as she did.

She would speak to them in the morning.

Chapter Eleven

Roper whistled as he climbed the hill for breakfast. Cassie had agreed to marry him. Of course, there were certain conditions but somehow that didn't dampen his spirit. A wife. A family. A home. It was more than he'd ever dared hope or dream since he was nineteen years old and full of blind optimism.

He ignored the persistent warning bell in the back of his brain. Ignored the words of his rules. *Don't put down roots.*

He heard her speaking and silenced his whistle. The children sat at the table facing outward. Cassie stood before them, her back to him. The expression on the three older children's faces let him know this was a serious discussion. He drew to one side, not wanting to disturb them.

Cassie twisted her apron as she spoke. "Expect nothing for free. No matter what your uncle might say."

Poor little Billy looked confused but from the wide-eyed horror on Neil's face and the way Daisy pursed her lips, he guessed this was the tail end of a little speech and could almost guess what it involved—insistence that every kindness had a price tag. He ached for whatever experience had led her to believe this way.

"You're sure you understand?"

Three heads nodded. Pansy watched curiously.

"Good. It's best you be prepared."

Roper stepped into sight. "You youngsters go play for a moment. Cassie and I need to talk."

They scampered away as quickly as frightened fawns.

Cassie watched Roper, alerted by something in his voice he hadn't tried to conceal.

He shook his head as he studied her, reading the hurt in her eyes, the defensive way she crossed her arms over her chest. "Cassie, Cassie, who taught you there is a price tag to love?"

He expected she would deny it, refuse to answer but her face crumpled and tears clung to her lashes. With a muffled groan, he reached for her. She hesitated but a moment.

"Tell me who, sweet Cassie."

She choked back a sob. "My grandfather."

He'd expected as much. He edged her toward the bench and gently pulled her down to sit beside him. "He made you pay for love?"

She kept her head down but rested it on his shoulder as if the contact kept her from drowning. "He made us pay for the privilege of having a roof over our heads. He made it clear he owned us in exchange for every begrudging bit of charity."

"You and who?"

"My mother. When Father died—Grandfather's son—the old man took us in but he made us pay. Every day and every way. I married George against his will. He knew he was losing a slave."

The bitterness in her voice drew knife-sharp gouges in his heart. "What happened to your mother?"

"I tried to get her to come with me but she was afraid. I wrote her but she's never written back. I doubt she's even got my letters."

"Oh, Cassie, my sweet Cassie. No wonder you are prickly sometimes."

"When the children cried about missing their ma, I couldn't bear it. I miss my mother. She could be dead for all I know."

"Can you not contact a neighbor and ask about her?"

She didn't answer at first. "I suppose I could send a letter to Mrs. Ellertson. She was always kind to us at the market. She'd know."

"Then you should do that."

She nodded.

He turned her so they faced each other and waited until she lifted her face to him. "But love does not have a price tag."

"How can you be sure? You've never had a family."

The truth of the words scraped the inside of his heart. He used to dream of belonging. Had learned he couldn't. Only being part of a pretend family unit with Cassie and the children had made him forget it wasn't possible for him. "I remember a passage I memorized many years ago in which Jesus said to love your neighbor as yourself. Seems to me that means there is no charge, no expectation other than to wish the best for others."

She clung to him with her eyes, as if wanting to believe what he said.

"There's nothing better than to love others and make them happy."

Her eyelids fluttered. "I understand that's your philosophy. Mine is 'Owe no man anything,' which I know is in the Bible, too."

"Someday, sweet Cassie, you will learn not everyone exacts a price like your grandfather did."

For a moment he thought she believed him, and then she shook her head.

He pressed her to his shoulder again and kissed her hair. "Someday."

Neil poked his head over the bank. "Can we eat yet?"

Cassie sprang from Roper's arms and bolted for the shack. "Call the others. The food will be right up."

Roper moseyed over to the shack. "I'll take the coffee." He reached for the coffeepot and she jerked back a good two feet.

"No need to be all jumpy around me."

She squinted at him. "I'm not. You're imagining things."

He studied her a long, hard minute wondering if she would turn away but she admirably held his gaze. Sheer determination, he figured. But then Cassie was good at holding her own. Even when it wasn't called for. He took the coffeepot and headed for the door. "Someday, sweet Cassie. Someday."

Her defiant snort made him chuckle.

"What's so funny?" Neil asked.

"Oh, nothing."

Daisy giggled behind her hand. "He and Cassie are arguing. A lovers' quarrel."

Neil grimaced. "Yuck."

"'Fraid it's no such thing." What he wouldn't give to have a lovers' quarrel. It would never happen, though. He'd lived without love all his life. He immediately corrected himself. He'd learned to count only on God's love. He figured he could continue to do so. Though never before had his heart twisted at the idea.

The day passed in fits and starts. Pansy cried for no reason and clung to Roper. Daisy and Neil argued reducing Daisy to tears. Billy threw a temper tantrum because the fence he had built for his pretend cows crashed down in the wind. He blamed Neil even though everyone knew Neil had been helping Roper on the house.

Several times Roper caught Cassie with a distant look on her face, her hands idle, her task forgotten.

So much for knowing how to be a family.

He must do something before they were all reduced to a pile of misery. He knew just the thing to remind them that life should be enjoyed.

Over supper he outlined his plan. "Let's go see a buffalo jump. It's not far. We could leave early in the morning and be back by evening."

"What about feeding the men?" Cassie's look informed him he must be missing a few brain cells to even suggest it.

"You're the boss. You can decide if you want to work or not." He said it knowing what her reaction would be, and chuckled when she got all huffy.

"Seems if you want to succeed, people need to be able to count on you." Her scowl matched his grin for intensity.

"I knew you'd object so here's what I figured out.

You leave something cooking real slow in the oven and Macpherson could check on it for you…" He held up a hand as she opened her mouth to protest. "If that doesn't sit well with you then have a meal already cooked. We'll leave real early, spend most of the day and be back to serve the food. Might be a little later but you can leave a note informing the men they can come back after we return."

Cassie shook her head but Billy bounced up and down on the bench eagerly. "We can see buffalo skulls?"

"You sure can."

Neil didn't bounce but he was equally as eager. "I've never seen buffalo bones. Heard they were really big."

Daisy watched Cassie. "I'd help you get things ready. A picnic sounds real nice. And you've been working awfully hard. You deserve to take some time off."

"I'll help, too," Neil added.

"Me, too." Billy jumped from the table all set to start immediately. Cassie shifted her gaze from child to child, over to the half-built house and then to Roper. "Very well. So long as we're back in time for supper."

The children had convinced Cassie when he couldn't. He admitted a bit of resentment that she didn't jump at the chance to spend the day with him. Which didn't make a lick of sense. They spent every day together.

She'd agreed to go. That's all that mattered.

They cleaned up in short order then Roper got the youngsters making sandwiches while Cassie prepared and cooked meat and potatoes. He built a wooden safe, put the pots safely in it then set the box in the river and secured it. "The food will stay cool while we're gone."

* * *

The next morning Roper was up before dawn and hitched the horse to the wagon. The noise must have wakened the others for they soon clambered from the shack.

Cassie fried up breakfast and made a pot of coffee. They sat in the cool air of the purple dawn to eat. Roper read from the Bible, then took Cassie's hand as he prayed for safety, adding silently a request for a refreshing time.

As he prayed, he built memories in his head. The morning greetings of the wakening birds sang the melody of creation. The whisper of the river added a duet voice. He inserted his own words for this moment—*pleasure, satisfaction, anticipation*. In the future he'd rejoice over this day.

They were soon in the wagon, the lunch tucked safely away, the children singing in the back.

They left behind the trees and hills and meandered over deceptively flat prairie. The breadth of the land quieted the children's voices and they crept forward to watch the trail ahead.

Roper pointed to the right. "Antelope." The golden-colored animals lifted their heads and watched.

"Why don't they run away? Aren't they afraid?" Neil asked.

"They can outrun a horse so they aren't too worried."

The animals watched them pass then resumed grazing.

A jackrabbit skittered away in front of them. Overhead a hawk circled with a whistling cry.

Cassie let out a long sigh. "It's so peaceful."

Far to the right he saw a twist of smoke and made out a rock chimney. "Looks like another homesteader. Soon they'll be breaking the sod and ruining the land for cattle." He didn't welcome the notion. "Seems to me some of this land should be left as it is."

"People need to be able to provide for their family." Cassie continued to stare at the wisp of smoke as they continued along the trail.

Did he see longing in her gaze? It made him wonder what Cassie really wanted—a business so she could support herself or a real home? Like the one Lane had built? The idea soured in his stomach.

Sometimes he wondered if *she* knew what she wanted.

Did he? He couldn't say. But he would make the best of this day.

The children leaned forward, eagerly pointing out one thing or another and he focused his attention on them.

A few minutes later, Roper turned the horse from the trail and they bounced across the prairie for a bit then he pulled on the reins. "We're here." The children tumbled from the wagon. Roper held out a hand to assist Cassie. When she would have ignored him he caught her around the waist and lifted her as easily as he did Pansy.

She giggled a little, surprised and perhaps a bit uncertain at his boldness, especially when he didn't immediately release her. She glanced up at him. Her lashes fluttered and she lowered her gaze.

Good. She understood he intended this to be more than a business trip. He leaned close and whispered,

"If we are to be married we should practice acting like a couple about to get married."

She pushed his hands away and drew back. "Roper Jones, you know very well that isn't the kind of marriage we discussed."

He chuckled. "A marriage is a marriage, don't you think?" Undeterred by her dismissive sniff he took her hand. "Better let me help you. The ground is pretty rough."

Indeed it was, but he wondered if she tripped over a clump of grass or if his attention unsettled her.

The children, arms out like wings, ran shrieking across the prairie.

Cassie stopped to watch them, easing away from him and crossing her arms at her waist so he couldn't take her hand again.

"They look so free and happy." She sounded wistful and he moved closer until their shoulders touched.

"It's good for them to be unfettered for a day."

She sucked in air preparing to say something but he didn't want to hear how they might never be free again, how they would owe their very lives, perhaps their souls, to their uncle. "Come on. I'll show you the jump." He reached for her hand and she pretended not to notice.

"Come on, kids." The four roared toward him and fell in at his side, eager to accompany him.

They walked to the rim of the cliff, revealing a deep gulley. "Stay back from the edge." He showed them how the Indians drove the buffalo up the incline to this spot leaving them no escape.

"Can we go down there and look for bones?" Neil asked, leaning forward.

"Neil, stay back." Cassie's voice rang out in warning.

"We'll go in a bit. Now you kids stay away from the edge. We don't want to look for your bones down there."

Billy giggled. "Our bones are covered with skin."

"Let's keep it that way." He led them away. "Play for a while."

They resumed racing about.

Roper had plans. If Cassie wanted flowers he would show her some in full bloom. He'd spotted several bright displays on their arrival. "Got something to show you."

She hesitated.

"What? You think I have something sneaky up my sleeve?"

"Do you?" One eyebrow quirked. Something he'd never seen her do before, and he liked it. But her playful mood caught him off guard. He'd expected resistance. Prickliness. "You do manage to surprise me again and again." He couldn't tell if she was annoyed or pleased at this observation.

"In a good way. Right?" She quirked her eyebrow again making him chuckle.

"You'll like it. I promise." He held his hand out in invitation.

She studied it for several heartbeats, then put her hand in his.

He tucked his satisfied grin into a corner of his heart and led her to a patch of wild roses.

"Oh, they're beautiful." She leaned close to smell the full-bodied scent.

"There are more flowers over here." He took her to

another area with bluebells and unusual purple, white and yellow flowers.

"Oh." Her exclamation of wonder was all the satisfaction he needed. "What are they called?"

He pushed his hat back. "I don't know. Never gave it much thought."

She knelt in the midst of the flowers, her hands brushing the blossoms.

He stood back and admired her. She was so beautiful when she relaxed like this. She practically glowed with happiness.

Finally she turned to him, her uplifted face alight with pleasure. "This is wonderful. Like a refreshing drink to my soul." She pushed to her feet and faced him, separated by no more than six inches. "Thank you."

He caught her shoulders and pulled her to his chest. "You are most welcome. God has put the flowers here for everyone's enjoyment. No charge. No obligation."

She eased back. "We better check on the children."

She'd withdrawn at his comment but she allowed him to take her hand as they returned to the shrieking, racing youngsters. And she seemed lost in thought.

He hoped and prayed she was beginning to see how many things were freely given. He shepherded the youngsters into the wagon and drove to the bottom of the cliff. He barely stopped before they jumped out and raced over to the spot where hundreds, perhaps thousands, of buffalo had met their death. He'd never seen a herd coming over the cliff, or watched the Indians skinning the animals and preparing the meat and hides. But an old cowpoke who'd seen it had told him what happened and he explained it to Cassie.

"This is where the women cut the meat into strips and hung it on racks to dry. It provided plenty of food for the winter months."

She looked about. "Yet they are now starving to death. Forced to steal cattle to keep their families alive."

He knew they both remembered how Red Fox had almost been hanged for trying to rustle one of Eddie's cows because his family was starving. "Eddie did right to give him part of the cow."

"You do know it was Linette's idea, don't you?"

He shrugged. "It was still his decision."

"T'would no doubt be a shame to give the credit where it's due."

"I don't expect Eddie would object to giving the credit to his wife."

"They weren't man and wife at that point."

"Eddie wouldn't object even then. He's a fair and reasonable man."

She shrugged. "He's also a hard, demanding man."

For a spoonful of dirt Roper would argue but he figured Cassie was just itching for a chance to point out all the follies of marriage. "He's a good boss. Never had better. What are Billy and Neil up to?" he asked as he noticed the boys.

She switched her attention to the boys and he let out a relieved sigh.

"Looks like they'd found something."

The boys tugged and pulled at an object.

Cassie and Roper sauntered over to see.

"We found a skull and horns." Neil leaned back, using his weight to try and get the skull from the overgrown grass.

"Let's have a look." Roper squatted to examine it. "That's a good one." Both horns were still attached and the skull was not even cracked. He wriggled it free and stood it up.

"Can we keep it?" Neil begged.

"Please, please," Billy added, bouncing up and down.

"It's up to Cassie." They all looked at her. Roper expected his eyes were as pleading as the little boys'.

She studied the skull. "I've never seen such a big head." She rubbed the ragged, rough horns. "It's quite a treasure."

The boys rocked back and forth, impatiently waiting for her answer.

She smiled. "Certainly you can take it back."

The boys whooped and Neil grabbed one horn, directed Billy to take the other and they carried it to the wagon and loaded it carefully.

"That was very generous of you." Did she realize she'd given a gift without expecting repayment? But she looked worried. Why?

"What if the uncle comes and won't let them take it? Won't they be disappointed?"

"Who knows what will happen with the uncle? We can only take one day at a time and leave the rest in God's care."

"I know I should but sometimes—" She shrugged. "God is good and loving but people aren't always."

"Nor are they always unkind and begrudging."

She considered his statement, her gaze following the two boys. Slowly she turned toward him, her eyes round. "Trouble is," she whispered, "how can you tell who and when? Seems best to prepare for the worst. Then anything else is a happy surprise."

"Am I a happy surprise?" His throat tightened around the words.

Her study of him went on and on. He wanted her to see that he gave freely, expecting nothing in returning, wanting only to make others happy. "I guess maybe you are." She spoke so softly he wasn't sure he heard her correctly.

He read fledgling trust in her eyes and wanted to whoop with joy just as Neil had. He wanted to dance across the prairie like the girls did. Instead, he leaned close and planted a quick kiss on her nose. "It's a beginning, sweet Cassie, a very good beginning." He tucked her arm through his. "Let's have our picnic."

He had never tasted such good syrup sandwiches in his life. Or better oatmeal cookies. Even the water had a sweet taste to it.

Cassie had given him her approval. It meant more to him than a gold mine. Dare he hope he could gain with her the very thing he didn't believe he deserved? Him, a nobody? Could he have a forever family? For today he would let himself believe it possible.

The children wolfed down their food and raced back to explore but he took his time, wanting this afternoon to last forever. He couldn't stop grinning at Cassie for no apparent reason and knew he was making her nervous.

Finally she leaned close, her eyes challenging. "What is so amusing?"

He sat up straight and pressed his hand to his chest in mock surprise. "Are you addressing me? Because if you are, you mistake my being pleased for amusement."

She almost managed to hide her confusion. "You aren't laughing at me?"

He touched her chin. "Cassie, I don't laugh at people."

She lowered her lashes. "What are you pleased about, then?"

Laughter bubbled up from his heart. "Because, sweet Cassie, you admitted I was a happy surprise. That means you are starting to see that what I do for you, how what I feel about you is given without a price tag."

Her gaze dipped deep into his as if she sought something more. She pressed her lips together. "What do you feel about me?"

"I—" He sat back as a rush of emotion raced up his insides and grabbed his throat. "I—" His throat tightened and he couldn't speak. *Don't put down roots.* The words blasted through his brain.

"Never mind. It was a stupid question." She grabbed the tea towel and box that had once held sandwiches.

"I care about you." The totally inadequate words burst from his lips. It was all he could offer her. And it was not enough. She deserved so much more. The heart of a man with a past and a future.

He had neither and his insides burned with regret.

She continued to grab at things and needlessly arrange and rearrange them.

He would not hurt her by word or action. Not for all the water in the ocean. "Cassie, let me continue to be a happy surprise. Know my friendship has no price attached to it. I only want to see you happy."

A couple of hours later Cassie sat on the wagon seat beside Roper as they headed home. It had been a fine day. The children had played freely and were thrilled at the skull they brought back.

She'd enjoyed the flowers and a day with nothing to do but take pleasure in the sunshine. But her delight was tinged by unsettling thoughts. He kissed her, then offered friendship. He grinned foolishly and endlessly because she admitted he was a good surprise and then he declared he only wanted to make her happy.

What would it take for her to be happy? Not so long ago she thought she knew. Have her own business, be independent. Now she wasn't sure. Her uncertainty left her unsettled. And when had she gone from prickly Cassie to sweet Cassie? Prickly sounded strong and independent. Sweet sounded weak and—

Heaven help her. She seemed to have lost the ability to control her thoughts. All she could think was sweet sounded exactly like something she'd secretly wished for most of her life. She clamped down on her teeth and reminded herself how vulnerable it made her to let people inside her boundaries. She must keep Roper outside them.

Was it already too late to barricade every opening?

The squat buildings of Edendale came into view. She leaned forward welcoming the diversion. Had men come by expecting to be fed? Would they return or decide if they couldn't count on her they'd stop coming? They passed Macpherson's. Several men perched on the hitching rail, and a couple squatted with their backs against the wall. All of them turned as the wagon approached.

"Supper be ready soon, Miss?" Rufus, the smithy, called.

"Give me half an hour." Her thoughts slid into place. All she needed to do was keep her eyes on her goal.

Momentarily her heart resisted. Was there more to life than she allowed?

Over the following days, the question repeated itself, becoming especially loud and demanding at unexpected times. Like when Roper reached for the coffeepot to carry it out to the men and his arm brushed her shoulder. Or when he took her hand as he prayed at the table, his grasp so solid. So steady.

Her thoughts were so tangled.

Yet he seemed content to continue their normal routine. Surely it was only her imagination that made her think he grinned at her more frequently or that his gaze lingered on her just a fraction of a second beyond ordinary when they talked.

Evenings were the most confusing for her.

He liked to remain after the children had gone to bed. Sometimes he suggested they go for a walk and she agreed. Out of curiosity about what he wanted, she reasoned. Not because she longed for his company. They would saunter up the short street of Edendale and back. Or they'd follow the road from town until the deepening dusk forced them to return.

Other times he invited her to the river and they would look at the stars or listen to the murmur of the water.

She discovered he liked to talk. He had many stories about the places he'd been and the people he'd worked with.

"I was left on the step of the orphanage when I was very tiny," he said as they sat in the same spot where they'd watched the falling stars and she'd found comfort in his arms.

Her attention intensified because he seldom talked about himself.

"A tiny baby wrapped in a piece of flannel. No basket. No note. But my blanket had been secured by a bit of rope." His laugh lacked bitterness. But it also lacked humor.

"The maid who found me named me Roper because of that bit of rope. Jones was the last name of the month, I guess."

She reached for his hand. "Seems a perfectly good name. Better than Muddbottom."

They both laughed a little though she wondered if either of them was amused. "I lost two babies. I can't imagine having to give up one. I wonder what happened."

He shrugged. "I used to make up stories. But I will never know the truth. I'm not complaining. Life wasn't unpleasant in the orphanage, especially if a person tried to make it pleasant."

"And you, being Roper Jones, tried to make it pleasant for everyone." A thought began to take root. "You might not have a past but everyone who knows Roper Jones knows who he is and what he stands for. Seems to me that's a pretty good heritage."

He gave no indication that he heard or understood except for a telltale twitch of the muscles in his arm.

She squeezed his hand, hoping he would acknowledge the value of what she'd said.

"I liked to take care of the other children."

So he was going to ignore her comment. That was

all right. Sooner or later she would convince him his lack of family history did not detract from who he was.

"Most times I could cheer them up no matter how sad they were."

She understood it had become his mission in life to make others happy. Was she only a mission for him?

"Who makes sure you're happy?" she asked as the stars draped the night.

"You do." And then, as if he'd said too much—or was it too little?—he quickly added, "So do the children."

"Happy enough to marry in order to give them a home?"

"You made the same agreement. Is giving them a home enough to make you happy?"

She said it was. But it was yet another question to echo through her head in the quiet of the night when she couldn't escape her thoughts.

Her plans had seemed so complete and satisfying at one time.

Why did they now feel fractured and disintegrated?

The question rattled about in her brain so she couldn't sleep.

Chapter Twelve

The next morning, the rattle of a wagon drew her attention to the ever-deepening trail at the edge of her property. Early customers? Her worries disappeared at the sight of her company. "Linette. Eddie. And Grady. Why it's about time you came to see me." She ran to greet them.

Eddie helped Linette to the ground and Grady scrambled down on his own.

"We would have been here sooner but it's been busy. I finally told Eddie if I didn't see you soon I would simply die of loneliness." Linette laughed merrily. "Cookie sent cinnamon rolls and a few supplies."

Cassie glanced into the wagon and groaned. "You can't keep sending me so much stuff."

Linette hugged her. "Why not? We can afford it. Can't we, Eddie?"

Eddie pulled his wife to his side. "We have more than enough. But I'd have more than I deserve if I lived in a tiny cabin with two women and a child."

They shared a laugh. That's exactly how they'd spent last winter when Linette and Cassie had first arrived.

Eddie planted a kiss on Linette's nose. "I'll be back after I pick up the mail and supplies." He turned to Roper who had come from the house to see who it was. "Come and give me a hand," Eddie called and Roper jogged over to join his boss. They unloaded the supplies, stacking them in the shack where there was a little more room now seeing she had used up much of what Roper had brought previously. Then they headed for the store.

Eddie waved at Linette. "Enjoy your visit."

Linette watched him go, her eyes brimming with love.

Cassie wondered what it would be like to know such love, to be so certain of it. She thought of Roper but he offered only friendship. Besides, she didn't trust love. *Obligation to love.* The words again sprang from her memory. If she could remember the source maybe they would make sense.

She shook troubling thoughts from her mind. "Grady." She held out her arms and the boy threw himself into a hug. "How are you?"

"Papa gave me a horse." The boy had called Eddie papa ever since he and Linette married. "I can ride it."

"Good for you." Not so long ago the boy had been afraid of horses and Eddie.

"Come and meet the children." She introduced Linette and Grady to the children, and they immediately included Grady in their play.

"I want to show you my house." But as soon as they were alone she turned to her friends. "Roper informed me you have a little one on the way. Congratulations."

Linette considered her, her palm pressed to her stomach. "I wasn't sure how you'd feel about it."

"Why, I'm happy for you."

"I'm sorry my joy reminds you of your sorrow."

Cassie did not want to rob her friend of any of her deserved joy. "My sorrow is in the past. Your joy is present. I'm nothing but happy." She drew Linette into the building. Roper had put up the walls with the help of the men who came by to eat. A roof stood overhead. The rooms inside were marked out.

Linette wandered through with Cassie pointing out where the big table would go and where the stove would stand, and showed her the trapdoor to the cellar. "This room will be mine." The far end of the house would be her bedroom.

"I'll build a solid door," Roper had said, giving her a look she could only describe as possessive.

How could she think it might be such? He certainly gave her no reason.

Suddenly the house, her pride and joy, seemed so primitive and inadequate compared to the beautiful, big house on the hill where Linette and Eddie lived. "I know it's not much but I can feed men here. I can bake bread and other goods. I can support myself."

Linette linked arms with her. "It's going to be lovely. What kind of curtains are you going to make?"

"I thought red gingham. I want to make tablecloths to match. Though I'll likely use oilcloth most of the time." The men wouldn't care what she covered the table with, only what she served, but on the rare occasions a woman visited she planned to set a nicer table.

She edged Linette toward her quarters. "Maybe something a little finer in here." In truth she hadn't thought too much about how she'd outfit her room, her main concern being the eating area. "I think I'll do a quilt during the winter."

"I have some fabric scraps you can have."

For a bit they talked about sewing and decorating. Cassie caught up on news of happenings at the ranch.

"Have you had any news from Grady's father?" Linette had vowed to get the man to acknowledge his son. She'd acquired the child on her trip across the ocean when his mother died. Her task had been to deliver him to his father in Montreal but the man had turned his back on the boy, saying a four-year-old child was of no use to him.

"I have sent several letters. Last time I drew a likeness of Grady and sent it along. I pray that someday he'll realize what a gift he has in a healthy son."

Cassie crossed her arms across her middle and pressed tight. A living healthy child, boy or girl, was a gift not offered to everyone. How could the man be so ungrateful?

Linette noticed her reaction. "Cassie, I'm sorry. I shouldn't have said it like that and reminded you of your loss."

"No. You're absolutely right. The man doesn't deserve what he has."

"I hoped Grady would forget the scene with his father but he hasn't. The other day he asked if he was an orphan. When I said he has a father he got all sad. Said his father didn't like him." Linette shook her head. "I am determined to get the two of them together, appreciating each other." She glanced toward the store. "Maybe there will be a letter from him today."

"Maybe I'll have a letter soon, too." She warned herself there might never be a reply. Her grandfather would prevent it if he could. "I wrote to a lady back home asking about my mother. I would like to at least know if she is dead or alive."

Linette sighed heavily. "I can't imagine not knowing. I will add to my prayers a request for you to hear from your mother."

"I don't expect to hear from her directly. My grandfather would never allow it."

Linette turned toward the sound of the children screaming with laughter. "What's to happen to them?"

She meant the four Locke children. Cassie explained the Mountie was trying to contact their uncle. "I guess their future depends on whether or not he is prepared to take them on."

"I guess we've seen how it doesn't always work out that way. Then what?"

"Roper and I have agreed to a businesslike marriage so we can care for them."

Linette grinned widely. "I'm guessing you'll marry him whether the uncle comes or not."

"Oh, no, it's only a business agreement for the children's sake."

"Your eyes say otherwise."

Cassie squinted, hiding anything Linette thought she saw. "What could you possibly think they say?"

"That you care about the man." Linette sounded terribly pleased about her observation.

"Certainly I do. He's a good man and a good help."

"I agree, but be honest. Don't you have deeper feelings for him than that?"

Cassie shook her head. She couldn't admit it. Even to herself. "You know I am not about to chain myself to a man ever again." But it wasn't chains she pictured when she thought of Roper. It wasn't obligation and owing. What she saw was his wish to make her happy. She chomped on her back teeth. She dare not trust such thoughts.

"Raising children is a lot of responsibility," Linette continued. "Sure you want to take it on?"

"I'm sure." She could give these children what her grandfather had withheld from her—care without cost. Kindness without strings attached.

Linette seemed to be considering something. "Even without adding four children to the community we desperately need a church and a school. They only make it more imperative. I will speak to Eddie about it again."

Suddenly Cassie realized how many things four children required…schooling, clothing, room to sleep. She could conceivably outgrow her little house before she even moved in. Linette was right. Four children was a lot of responsibility. Good thing she and Roper would be caring for them together should it turn out that way.

Eddie called out a greeting. Linette turned eagerly and picked up her skirts to rush to his side. "Did we get a letter?"

"Several but not the one you're looking for." Eddie handed her a stack of correspondence.

Linette checked through it as if Eddie might have made a mistake.

Roper had paused to rearrange the supplies in the wagon box and now sauntered over to join them. His gaze sought and found Cassie and a smile brightened his face.

As if he were glad to see her.

She smiled back automatically, barely recognizing

this strange feeling in her heart. Once, in a time almost beyond her ability to recall, she'd been glad to see a man return. Welcomed it. Understood it meant she would receive love and attention…when her father was still alive. Before she'd learned there was a cost to attention. A payment due for everything given.

Linette announced they must leave, pulling her away from her dark thoughts.

Cassie hugged her friend. "It was nice to see you."

"I'll be back. We need to work together on getting a church. I think that's most important. Depending on how things work out—" Her gaze flitted to the nearby children. "We'll have to set our sights on a school, as well."

"At least you have your Sunday services at the ranch." She couldn't believe how much she missed Cookie and the others and the time of worship they conducted in the cookhouse every Sunday.

"You're welcome to join us any time you want."

Eddie lifted Grady to the wagon and helped Linette up. Cassie hated to see them go. They left behind a hollowness.

She wished Roper would move closer.

As the wagon rumbled away, she pushed such foolishness out of her mind. She had a business to run. Children to care for. And she headed to the shack to prepare a meal.

A few days later, minutes before mealtime, Lane appeared for the dinner. This was his first appearance in nigh unto a week.

"I've been putting up firewood. Got a good supply for the winter." He slid into place at the table but bounced back up before his jeans touched the wooden bench. "My oat crop is beyond expectations. See for yourself." He handed her a small bundle of green oats, tied with a bit of twine.

She examined the offering and made what she hoped were appropriate comments. Truth be known, she had little knowledge about farming and crops as she'd tried to explain to George when he was so keen to head west and stake a claim on free land. She wondered how much he knew having been raised in town and having always lived in town. His response had been to dismiss her concerns. Say it was the very reason he was determined to get a piece of land with his name on it.

When she handed the oat cluster back to Lane he waved it away.

"Keep it. Have a look at it every so often and think what promise this land has."

"Thank you." She stuck it in an empty Mason jar, not knowing whether she should water it.

"The land is rich and generous," Lane said.

His raving gave Cassie an idea. "Do you have a garden?"

His enthusiasm waned slightly as he watched her. "I put in a few root vegetables. Enough for a single man like me." He grew more intense. "I would think a man could raise enough garden produce to feed a whole family."

Cassie ignored the way Lane looked at her. She had no intention of being part of his plans no matter how wonderful he made them sound. Besides, she had a tentative agreement with Roper.

Several others joined them for the meal. As she dished stew into each man's dish, she stole a look at

Roper. His eyebrows thundered together and his eyes shot silent arrows at Lane. What on earth was the matter with him?

She ignored him and returned to the conversation about gardens. "It's too late in the season for me to plant this year but next year I'll raise my own vegetables. I wouldn't mind getting some hens, as well. Does anyone around here have some to spare?" She looked about the table for an answer.

Rufus wiped his chin. "Petey could bring some from the Fort on the stagecoach."

"I'll speak to him and I'll get Macpherson to order me some chicken wire." Satisfied with her plans, she served the rest of the meal.

Lane lingered after the others left, sitting at the table, drinking cup after cup of coffee while Cassie and Daisy did dishes.

Roper went back to work on the house. A few minutes after he'd left, he returned. "Need a drink." He guzzled a dipper full of water and stared at Lane hard enough that Cassie wondered if the man wore armor under his shirt to protect him from the heat of Roper's displeasure. Then Roper stalked off.

Again she wondered what Roper was upset about. Seems she should be the one bothered about a man occupying space without lifting a finger to help.

"My family has a dairy farm back in Toronto," Lane said. "Big place. There are four sons. I'm the second youngest. I could have stayed and worked but it seemed there were more opportunities out here. With my parents' blessing here I am."

Yes. Here you are. Drinking a pot of coffee and in-

terrupting my work. "I'm sure they're pleased with what you've accomplished."

"Yes, indeedy."

Indeedy? What kind of English is that? She scrubbed the table right up to his elbows, forcing him to lift his arms. "I suppose you'll be going back East soon to spend time with them."

"Oh, no. I'm here to stay."

Seems like it.

Roper rushed to the water bucket. "Thirsty again," he muttered, and downed another dipperful. Neil stood at the house watching, looking startled by Roper's sudden and intense thirst.

Roper swiped at the water dribbling from his chin, rocked his gaze from Cassie to Lane and back to Cassie then loped over to the house, muttering under his breath about something.

Cassie looked longingly at the little shack where she might find some peace and quiet. She'd endure the heat from the stove in order to escape these crazy men. "Excuse me," she said to no one in particular. "I have to tend to supper for the children."

Daisy looked about, obviously confused by all the coming and going. "Do you need me?"

"Not for a little time. Go play with Billy and Pansy."

She scurried away.

Lane didn't move. Cassie began to wonder if the man was glued to the bench. Suddenly it dawned on him he was about to be left alone and he finally found his feet. "I'll be back tomorrow. Say, maybe you'd like to see some pictures of my family. I could bring some when I visit."

Visit? Is that how he saw it? But if agreeing would get him moving…

"That would be nice." She ducked inside the over-heated shack before he left and leaned against the wall exhaling a loud sigh. Apparently Lane considered himself a good catch. Somehow she had to convey to him she wasn't interested in any man. Good catch or otherwise.

Besides, she and Roper had an agreement.

One dependent on the actions of one unknown Uncle Jack.

Roper pounded the nail so hard it dented the wood. He stepped away, grabbed a board and measured it, sawed it in record time and carried it to the wall.

Neil held the other end.

"Bring it this way." Roper tugged it into place.

"It's too short."

"Shoot. I measured wrong." He tossed the board to the shrinking pile of wood.

"Why didn't you just tell him to leave?" Neil asked.

"Who?" As if there were anyone other than Lane who lingered as though he didn't have anything else he should be doing. Like weeding his garden or admiring his oats. "What are you talking about?" His voice was sharper than he intended.

Neil snorted. "I ain't getting in your road." He turned to examine something on the ground.

Roper sucked in air. "Sorry." He had no call to be so cranky. But why was Cassie encouraging Lane? She'd promised to marry *him*.

Only if the kids' uncle didn't show up. Otherwise there was no obligation on either side.

But even so, Lane was not her sort of man. He was a dandy. Used to a fine lifestyle. Cassie would never be happy living the life of a fancy lady. He ought to warn her.

No, that would only make her angry. She would not welcome any interference from him.

Besides, how could he be so certain she wouldn't welcome the sort of life Lane would offer? A fine lady in a fine house.

Because, he told himself with utmost conviction, it would remind her too much of her grandfather. He knew Lane would expect her to keep up certain standards. How he knew this he couldn't say. But he would not admit he might have misjudged the man.

There had to be another way to make Cassie see the truth.

He recalled the recent conversation. She wanted a garden and some chickens. He could help her with that.

"Supper is ready," Daisy called.

Roper and Neil headed for the table. Roper squeezed Neil's shoulder to let him know he wasn't angry and was relieved to feel the boy relax beneath his palm.

At the table, he reached for Cassie's hand to say grace. After his amen, he continued to hold her hand for a beat. Two. Then he released it without once looking at her. He knew if he looked at her, she'd see in his eyes more than he wanted to reveal. More than he understood. More than he could promise.

"Is Grady an orphan like us?" Billy asked.

Cassie answered. "No, he has a father."

"Then why is he with the Gardiners?" Billy asked the question but Neil and Daisy watched Cassie with wide eyes, as interested in the reasons as Billy.

Cassie sent Roper a look that begged for help.

His smile of reassurance seemed to help her relax.

She turned back to the children. "Grady's father wasn't able to care for the little boy on his own."

There was more to it than that but Roper hoped the answer would satisfy.

None of the three returned to their meal but sent silent messages to each other.

"What is it?" Cassie asked.

"He's only one little boy." Daisy stared at her plate as she spoke.

"That's true. Ah. And you're worried because there are four of you."

Daisy nodded. "Four is an awful lot of kids when they aren't your own."

"Not if the kids are the best in the world," Cassie said.

Roper wanted to cheer at her kind answer. "Four kids like you aren't a lot of work. In fact, I'd say anyone would be privileged to make you part of their family." He didn't say what else he thought. That he wanted them and not just so Cassie would marry him. He glanced about the table. This felt like family. Real and forever family. *He didn't know about family.* The persistent thought demanded attention. This was different, he argued.

The kids grinned at the answers they'd been given and returned to their meal.

Roper met Cassie's look. They smiled at each other, content to have eased the children's worries. Her brown eyes revealed warmth and…dare he dream he saw admiration? He was quite sure she hadn't looked at Lane in such fashion.

His good humor restored, he said, "Let's clean up real quick, and then play hide-and-seek."

The lot of them sprang into action. Daisy gathered up the dishes. Cassie filled the washbasin with hot water. Neil and Billy grabbed buckets and headed for the river. Roper brought over wood.

"We're done," Daisy called before he had the last load of wood back to the shack. "Not it."

They all called, "Not it," while Roper dropped the wood into the pile close to the shack.

He was it. He didn't mind a bit. "The shack door is 'home free.' I'm counting to fifty, and then I'm going to find you." He pressed his forehead to the door, closed his eyes and started counting out loud.

He grinned as the kids scattered, and then all was quiet.

They played until dusk, laughing and enjoying one another. Twice he inadvertently crashed into Cassie and was rewarded by having to hold her tight to keep her from being knocked over.

After a bit, Cassie said, "I think it's time for bed. Poor Pansy must be exhausted." They'd taken turns carrying her as they played.

"Aww." Billy let out a protracted protest.

Daisy tapped his shoulder and gave him a warning look, then they all trooped into the shack, Cassie at their heels. Roper would have gone in and helped but there wasn't enough room.

He circled Cassie's almost-finished house. If the children stayed he'd have to add a couple of rooms.

He heard Cassie step out of the shack and hurried to join her. "Everyone settled?"

"Pansy feel asleep almost instantly but Billy is restless."

"I guess we should have wound down a little sooner."

"He'll be fine. Daisy is singing to him. They're awfully good kids, aren't they?"

"They certainly are."

"They deserve the best."

"And we'll do everything in our power to see they get it."

She sighed, a troubled little sound.

"What's wrong?"

"First, we have nothing to say about it. If the uncle wants them it won't matter if he is mean-spirited or not. They will go with him."

"Then we'll have to pray he is kind."

"And if he doesn't want them, doesn't even come," she went on as if he hadn't spoken, "they'll be stuck with us. Do you think we can give them the best? You, who never had a family and me—" She waggled her hands.

He caught her hands and stopped their fluttering. "Oh, sweet Cassie. You are completely blind to all you have to offer, aren't you?"

"As you say, I'm prickly and overly defensive."

He'd never said the latter. "You're gentle and kind. I've seen you hug the children, heard how you encourage them. I've seen the way you watch them, your eyes full of affection. You care about them."

"I don't deny it. But is that enough?"

"I'd say caring in the shape of kindness and affection is certainly enough. Wouldn't you?" He pulled her to his chest and looked down into her uncertain eyes. "Wouldn't you have been grateful for that?"

She gave a crooked smile. "I would have thought I'd died and gone to heaven."

"There you go." He placed a gentle kiss on her forehead and, before she could react, he said, "Now, where did you think you would plant a garden?"

She showed him.

He measured off a plot and drove in four stakes. "I'll start turning over the sods tomorrow."

"It's not up to you. I'll—"

"I'm thinking of the children. If we become a permanent family we'll need to feed them. The ground should be broken this summer so the sods can break down over the winter."

She looked so uncertain, he laughed.

"We're in this together."

Finally she nodded. "For the children."

Roper allowed himself a moment of joy at what the future offered.

Several times the next day, Cassie glanced at the stakes Roper had driven into the ground. He'd be a good father, always making sure the children were well taken care of. He'd do the same for her.

If she let him.

Part of her welcomed his gentle concern.

Another part feared she would turn out like her mother—selling her soul, forfeiting her freedom for someone to take care of her. She sucked in her bottom lip. She'd never do that.

She was still preparing the meal when Lane headed

across from the store. One hour earlier than the posted mealtime.

Cassie groaned. "How am I to get the meal ready on time if he expects me to visit with him?"

Roper gave what passed for a grin. "If you encourage him he'll keep coming back."

"I don't encourage him. But he's a paying customer."

Roper shrugged and sauntered away. "Guess he wants to make sure he gets what he paid for."

"What do you mean? He pays for a meal. That's all I give him."

Roper glanced over his shoulder. "Seems to me you're letting someone own you for the price of a meal. Isn't that exactly what you're fighting against?" And then he ducked out of sight in the house leaving her with her mouth hanging open and Grandfather's words echoing through her head.

I provide for you. That gives me the right to say what you can and cannot do.

You plan to eat? Then you do as I say.

Truth was it wouldn't have been hard to do things for him if he was a kind man. Instead, he was cruel and seemed to delight in making sure the things he demanded were unreasonable, petty and downright objectionable. Like the time he insisted the laundry must be hung out in a bitter winter wind. He'd wanted Mother to do it on her own. It was one of the times Cassie defied him and insisted on helping. She made sure she hung three baskets to Mother's one.

But this was different. Lane was only— What? She understood there was more to his visits than a home-cooked meal. He no doubt fancied that he courted her.

But she'd never given him an ounce of encouragement. Neither had she discouraged him.

Was that what bothered Roper?

In all fairness she must make it clear to Lane she had no interest in him. Even if the children's uncle came and got them and her agreement with Roper ended, she didn't intend to give up her independence.

Lane reached her side, his face beaming. "I thought you might have time to look at these pictures before the meal."

"I'm sorry, Lane. But I must have the food ready when the men arrive."

"I'm sure they won't mind waiting."

"I'm not prepared to test them to see. They are working men who want to eat their meal and get back to work. You have to understand that I have a business to run here."

He edged closer, purposely rubbing his elbow against her arm. "You wouldn't need to if you had a husband."

She stepped back. "That's just it. I don't want a husband. I want to be independent."

He only grinned. "I think you could be persuaded to change your mind."

No doubt you think you're just the one to do so. For two seconds she considered asking him to leave but she couldn't afford to turn away customers. If word got around that she did so, others might decide to avoid taking the chance she would do the same to them. "Not today. Now if you don't mind, I must do my work." She turned away. But Lane didn't move. Cassie couldn't decide if she should invite him to sit while she worked or simply ignore him.

"Lane." Roper's soft voice scratched along Cassie's nerves. "The meal will be served in an hour. Come back then."

Lane sputtered and looked toward Cassie for direction. She found a frayed edge on her apron to examine. "Perhaps you'd like to see the pictures later?"

She nodded. "Perhaps."

Finally he headed back toward the store.

She didn't speak until he disappeared around the corner then she flung about to glower at Roper. "Don't get the idea you can start running my life. I don't intend to ever again give a man that right."

He gave her a look of pure disgust. "Well, excuse me if I thought you didn't want him bothering you while you made the meal but were too polite to say so." He dragged the final two words out as he stalked back to the house, Neil skulking at his heels.

Cassie tossed her hands upward. "Men." But she saw Daisy watching her with big eyes. And of course, Billy and Pansy played nearby and overheard the whole thing. They looked about ready to cry. "Don't worry." She did her best to inject a bit of laughter into her voice and guessed she missed by a mile. "We aren't angry. Just expressing our opinions." She couldn't vouch for Roper's feelings but it certainly wasn't a hundred percent true for her. She felt a lot of anger. She meant what she said. He had no right to think he could run her life.

A little later Roper came out to help serve the meal as he always did. But he refused to meet her eyes, which suited her just fine. So long as he understood.

When Lane remained after the others left, she smiled at him. "Just give me a few minutes to clean up and then I'll join you."

Daisy helped with the dishes though the girl seemed unwilling to talk. She dried the last dish and hung the towel to dry. "I'll take the little ones down to the river so you can be alone with him."

It wasn't what she wanted. Roper and Neil had left a few minutes earlier. She wanted to join them but she'd already promised Lane. Besides, it was time she made it clear that she stood on her own two feet.

She sat beside Lane and looked at the pictures of his home and family. He came from a seemingly well-to-do family of good breeding if he did say so himself. As she commented on the pictures and listened to his detailed description, she heard Roper's voice as he called to the children.

Yes, she echoed to herself, that's what she wanted—to be with the children…and Roper.

Chapter Thirteen

Even over the laughter and screams of the youngsters, Roper caught snatches of the conversation between Cassie and Lane. Lane had a family. A good family. He had something to offer. Cassie, smart woman that she was, no doubt recognized it.

Roper's only claim on her was on behalf of the children.

She'd made it clear she welcomed Lane's attention. And would allow no interference from Roper.

Why should he think it would be any other way? A familiar ache reared its head and squeezed his heart until he wanted to groan.

They played a rowdy, noisy, vigorous game of tag. He ended up on his back as the children tackled him. They pounced on him, tickling him unmercifully. Finally they settled down, hopefully as exhausted as he.

"Is Cassie going to marry Lane?" Billy asked.

"Of course not." Neil's voice was full of disgust.

Billy wasn't convinced. "I think she likes him."

"She's just being polite." But Daisy's voice conveyed a healthy dose of doubt.

Roper wished he could assure them Cassie was going to marry *him*. But they'd agreed it was best not to tell the children of their plan. Besides, their agreement came with no assurances.

"I don't think he would make her happy." Neil had drawn his own conclusions.

Roper grabbed the notion and clung to it. He only wanted Cassie to be happy. Seems the only thing that would make Cassie happy was being independent.

He'd never noticed before how dismissive the word sounded.

Peeling the children off him, he scrambled to his feet. His horse might welcome a flat-out ride but he couldn't walk away and leave the children.

Neil poked his head over the bank. "The man is gone."

"Let's go home." *Home is where I kick off my boots.* And yet this rough little plot of land—with the shack made half of wood and half of canvas, the table only a rough slab of wood out in the open and an almost-finished house nearby—was as close to home as anything he'd known.

The children followed him up the hill.

He'd only meant to help her. But he had no right to interfere. As soon as the children were tucked in, he approached Cassie. "I apologize. I didn't mean to suggest I had any right to order things in your life."

"Apology accepted." She said the words and yet he felt as if a great barricade of logs and rocks and dirt had been piled high between them.

Soon after, he said good-night and returned to his camp.

Over the next few days he devoted every minute to

completing her house. The only thing that kept him from putting in longer hours was consideration for Neil who tried to match Roper's efforts. He would not drive the boy that hard.

Cassie was everlastingly polite, but distant, and he missed the closeness they'd shared for a few days.

And every day Lane came by with more and more evidence that he was a fine, upstanding young man with family roots and something to offer. He brought flowers, a picture of his family that he gave to Cassie. He told of attending school. From all accounts—his own—Lane had been an excellent student.

Roper knew his cynicism was unfounded. Understood it was due to the fact that Roper had not had such opportunities. He hadn't even completed fourth grade because he was always needed to help at the orphanage, or when he was a little older, hired out to local farmers and businessmen. Schooling, after all, was not important for a nobody kid left behind when he was only a few days old.

A wagon approached. Roper looked up and recognized Linette and Eddie. He set aside his tools.

"Neil, no more work this afternoon. Run and play with the others." Roper barely waited for the wheels to stop rolling before he jogged over to the wagon. "Need a hand, boss?"

"Yup."

Roper climbed to the seat and waited as Eddie escorted Linette to Cassie's side and Grady joined the other youngsters.

Eddie returned to the wagon and took the reins. "How are things going?"

Roper almost blurted out how bad things were but

it seemed foolish to be sulking because a better man was interested in Cassie. "Be done here soon. House is almost finished."

"Good. I hope that means you're coming back to work."

"Depends on what we hear from the uncle."

"Right. Linette told me about it. It's good to know the children will be taken care of properly. I suppose then you wouldn't be coming back to the ranch?"

"Cassie has her business to run. It's important to her."

"But are you prepared to give up your life? What's important to you?"

Roper shrugged, though the question ricocheted about in his head. He hadn't let himself think that far ahead. "We work well together and more important, the youngsters seem happy enough to be with us."

"I see. Well, if you change your mind please come back. I'm thinking I might need a foreman to help run the ranch. You'd be my first choice."

"Thank you." He'd like the job. Eddie was a good man to work for, and the ranch was growing. Roper wouldn't mind having a hand in that. "I'll give it some thought but it will depend on the uncle." And if Cassie continues to show interest in Lane.

The first stop was to pick up the mail. Eddie glanced through the handful of letters, paused at one in particular. "If I'm not mistaken this will be from Grady's father. Linette has been waiting for it. I fear she will again be disappointed by the man's response."

"He still refuses to acknowledge his boy?" Cassie had said Roper didn't understand the dark side of family. This certainly proved it. He couldn't understand how a parent could abandon a child. Yet he was living proof such things happened.

The men continued to talk about ranching things, the others at the ranch and general news as they loaded up supplies. Before they headed back to Cassie's place, Eddie drove down the road to a pretty spot close to a bend in the river. "Linette is keen to see a church established in the community. At first I didn't see any need. There were too few people, too scattered about. But every time I turn around, I see more people coming in. That young fellow, Lane Brownley, and a young family over there—" He pointed in the general direction of the place Roper had seen when he took Cassie and the youngsters to the buffalo jump.

He smiled as he recalled the event. Then his smile slid away. How had he gone from the happy contentment of that day to this restless uncertainty in such a short time?

"I haven't met them but I'm told their name is Schoenings and they have four very small children. As Linette points out, we need to draw together in worship. She says this will be an ideal place."

Roper agreed it would, though he wondered about the possibility of drawing together. From what he'd seen, even in the orphanage, differing religions often caused division rather than unity.

They turned back toward Cassie's place and Eddie collected his wife and Grady then headed home.

He noticed the stark longing on Cassie's face as she watched the wagon depart. Did she miss the ranch?

A suspicion mounted in his brain. One he wished he could deny. But it refused to be ignored.

Did Cassie see the love between Eddie and Linette

and wish for the same for herself? Was she ready to forget the many cruel years under her grandfather and accept love? Believe in it?

Another unwelcome notion took root.

Perhaps what she wanted was what Linette and Eddie had—a nice home, a ranch to support them—all the things Lane could offer her.

He spun away and stalked down to the river, murmuring something about taking care of the horses.

Cassie watched Roper disappear. The man had gotten so moody the past few days she feared to talk to him. He helped when it came time to serve the men a meal but without the usual joking and teasing. And it seemed he couldn't wait to be out of sight as soon as the men finished eating. Had she offended him so badly he couldn't even bear the sight of her? Had he expected her to change her mind about who she was, what she wanted? Was that why he was angry?

Not that she could change her mind even for the sake of peace with him.

Thanks to Roper, her house was almost finished. Her dream was about to come true.

But she didn't want to be friendless. They must mend this rift. For the sake of the children who watched them warily when they were together. And if the uncle refused to take them, they must learn how to be a family.

But she didn't know how to fix things. Every time she started to bring up the idea that there seemed to be a problem between them, Roper found an excuse to leave. He couldn't seem to wait to get away from her. About all she could do was pray things would improve.

Roper returned a while later and Cassie watched for a chance to speak to him, but the afternoon slipped past without her finding an opportunity. Not that she didn't try. Roper just ducked away every time she took a step in his direction.

As usual, Lane came by early and brought something. Sometimes it was a gift. Other times it was a letter or something from home he wanted to show her. Today he had a bit of burgundy fabric. "What do you think of this for curtains for the front room?"

She sighed back her impatience at his repeated interruption of her work. "It's very nice. Do you like it?"

"It's similar to what Mother has at home so it should be appropriate."

"I expect it's fine."

"If you saw the place you could better judge. My description is very inadequate."

She refrained from saying it was more than adequate.

"Why don't you let me take you out for a visit? Say Saturday afternoon?"

"I'm sorry, Lane, but who would cook for the men?"

He studied her long and hard.

Cassie thought his look very demanding and she had to stifle a reaction. He was not her grandfather. He had no hold over her.

"Seems you could arrange something. Let the others take care of it."

She kept her voice as gentle as possible but felt the sharpness in her words. "It's *my* job. *My* responsibility."

"You should be taking care of a home and family, not feeding a bunch of strangers."

She forced herself to give a little laugh. "Most of them aren't strangers. Take yourself for example."

"You know what I mean."

"Yes, I do. Need I point out that this is what I want to be doing?"

Lane made a noise of exasperation. "You'll change your mind some day."

She thought it best not to deny it. "I need to tend to the meal." She waved her hand in the general direction of the table where he would sit and wait as she escaped into the shack. She wished Lane would take her hints and leave her alone.

She would have to be clearer with him. Somehow convince him she wasn't interested in his attention. And she had to find a way to ease the tension between herself and Roper.

The next afternoon she still sought for a way to accomplish the latter. She prayed. She contemplated a dozen different scenarios. She even approached him twice but both times he'd suddenly found something he needed to do twenty feet away. Once it was to arrange some wood in the woodpile.

"Thought I saw a snake," he explained.

The other time he held a tape measure and kept consulting it. "Sorry. I have to mark a board before I forget the measurement."

He was making it very difficult.

But when he stepped out of the house and stood back to study it she decided this was the time. She put down the basin of potato peelings and headed across the yard. She barely reached his side when she heard footsteps heading their way. *Oh, please. Let it not be Lane. Not this early in the day.* But it was Constable Allen.

Daisy had been tidying up the little yard and straightened to watch him. Billy, assisting her, jerked about as if feeling the tension in the air and stared at the Mountie. Neil stepped out of the house, holding a hammer against his chest like a shield. Only Pansy, playing nearby, seemed oblivious to the importance of this visit.

"Hello," the Mountie called out.

Cassie couldn't find her voice to respond.

Roper jerked into action and reached out to shake hands. "Howdy."

"I expect you all know why I'm here." No one answered. "Why don't we sit down?" He sat at the table, put his Stetson before him.

They slowly joined him. Cassie pressed in close to Roper needing his comfort. Thankfully he didn't slide away. The children crowded in beside Cassie and Roper, all of them sitting across from the Mountie.

Roper cleared his throat before he spoke. "I think we know why you're here but perhaps it's best if you just say."

"Very well." He directed his gaze toward the children. "I was able to contact your uncle."

None of the children appeared to breathe. Cassie twisted her hands in her lap, aching to reach for Roper, to hold tight and find courage.

He must have felt her nervousness for he wrapped a hand about hers. She flashed him a tight smile then concentrated on what the Mountie said.

"He responded immediately saying he wished to come and see you."

Cassie couldn't swallow. Her muscles clenched. It was the news she'd hoped and prayed for. The children should go to their relatives. But she'd miss them terribly. And now there would be no reason for her and Roper to marry.

The Mountie continued to speak and Cassie forced herself to focus on his words.

"He wants to meet you right away."

"Right away?" Daisy squeaked.

Cassie knew her voice would sound every bit as strained if she tried to talk.

"Yes, he's at the store waiting."

Daisy and Neil turned as one toward the store. Billy watched his brother and sister, gauging their reaction to see what his should be.

Constable Allen leaned forward. "He realizes this is scary for you. He said he doubts any of you remember him."

"I do," Daisy managed to squeeze out.

"He doesn't want to make any of you uncomfortable so he said I was to inform you. He'll wait until you are ready before he comes over."

No one spoke. Cassie knew this must be the children's decision. She must have turned her hand into Roper's at some point because they were palm to palm, their fingers intertwined. He squeezed her hand encouragingly. Despite the strain that had been like a wall between them the past few days she glanced up and held his gaze, seeking and finding a common interest in the well-being of these children.

And something more. Something that pinched the back of her heart with unspoken yearnings, impossible hopes. Something that made her wish she could be different. That she could be the person he needed her to be.

What did she mean by that? Who or what did she think he needed? She tried to make sense of her thoughts but Roper shifted his gaze back to the children and she decided she was simply confused, her equilibrium upset because of the uncle's arrival.

Daisy and Neil silently consulted each other again. Then Daisy nodded. "Tell him we're ready."

The Mountie rose and positioned his hat on his head. He didn't immediately leave. "I think you'll like the man. I know I do." With that he departed.

Cassie stared after him.

Her life was about to take a sharp turn. She couldn't imagine what lay around the corner.

A few minutes later, Cassie watched the man accompanying the Mountie across the yard. He bore a startling likeness to Billy. Or rather, she supposed, Billy looked like him. He had a gentle expression but Cassie wasn't about to trust first impressions. Sure the Mountie liked him but the Mountie wasn't a child about to be at the mercy of the man's moods. No, she would be observing him closely. If she saw even the faintest sign the uncle would be cruel and unreasonable, she would offer the children a home with her, whether or not Roper intended to continue with their plan for a businesslike marriage.

"I'll be watching him," Roper murmured close to her ear.

"Me, too," she whispered.

The pair of men drew to a halt before the table.

"Children," the Mountie said, his hat in his hands, "this is your uncle Jack."

The uncle removed a fine woolen cap. His hair was

white and thinning. His skin pale and translucent with a thousand tiny wrinkles. Cassie tried not to stare but the man looked old. And thin. Whoever provided his meals needed to be more generous.

The Mountie nodded toward Cassie and Roper. "May I present Jack Munro." Then he introduced Roper and Cassie to the man. "They've been caring for the children since they arrived in this neck of the woods."

Jack spared them a glance. "I owe you a debt of gratitude." He smiled at the children. "Daisy, I remember you when you were no bigger than this." He indicated Billy who pressed to Daisy's side. "You were much like Pansy. And Neil, you were only a baby. Billy, I've never had the pleasure of meeting you before." One by one, he greeted them and shook their hands.

The children murmured a response, obviously overwhelmed.

So far the man seemed friendly, Cassie acknowledged. Would he be so after a few days of dealing with children who needed more than a roof over their heads? And certainly more to eat than this man appeared to consume.

Cassie pushed to her feet. "I'll make tea." When Daisy rose to help, she shook her head. "You stay and visit."

Roper gave her a little nod. He wasn't going anywhere until he saw how this visit went.

She ducked into the privacy of the shack, and while the kettle boiled she put cookies on a plate and she prayed.

Oh, God. Let this man be kind. And if he isn't, help us see it before he whisks them away. Though she wondered what she could hope to do about it. It would likely prove futile to fight against the uncle's claim to the children.

She would not think how any decision either way would affect her future. She would only think of the children and what was best for them.

The kettle whistled. She poured the boiling water over the tea leaves and put the pot, the plate of cookies and cups enough for everyone on a tray and carried it out.

Uncle Jack was telling the children that he lived alone—"Apart from my housekeeper," he said—in an apartment in Toronto.

A city man. Cassie knew it shouldn't matter but she couldn't imagine the children living in such surroundings.

Jack asked each child what they liked. The children answered politely, loosening up a bit over tea and cookies.

Cassie glanced over her shoulder toward the shack. She needed to prepare a meal before half a dozen hungry men descended on them.

Roper understood why she kept fidgeting. "Why don't we go down by the river to talk so Cassie can get at her cooking?"

"I'll help," Daisy said, jumping to her feet.

"No, you go with your uncle and the others." Cassie shifted her gaze to Roper. "I'll manage on my own." She hoped he understood she wanted him to go, too. Surely he'd notice if there was anything amiss.

He nodded, and led them away to the sandy bank where they often went, and she turned her attention toward meal preparations, even though part of her followed the others down the bank. She would like to be able to observe from some hidden spot without the uncle's knowledge. Almost always, unkind, cruel things happened in secret places out of the public eye.

Memories flooded her mind. Times when she knew if she revealed the pain across her shoulders where Grandfather had strapped her, she would get more of the same when they were back home. Occasions when visitors commented on how fortunate she and Mother were to have such a kind benefactor. How she'd struggled to answer sweetly and falsely.

She didn't hear Roper return until he spoke.

"They are having a good cry in Uncle Jack's arms."

She spun toward him. "You left them alone?"

"Constable Allen is with them." He leaned closer. "Are you crying?"

"No, of course not."

"Then what is this?" He caught a tear with his fingertips.

"Nothing." She turned away as anger and sorrow and pain crowded close.

"Oh, sweet, sweet Cassie."

The compassion in his voice threatened to unlock the dam of tears. It was something she didn't want to happen. But when he caught her shoulders and turned her about, she could not refuse the invitation of his comforting arms.

"What has upset you so?"

She couldn't speak past the knot in her throat.

He patted her shoulder and rubbed her back.

Oh, how she'd missed the comfort of his friendship. "I'm afraid." She could go no further.

He waited, as if he understood there was more.

"He could pretend to be kind and good while there are others around."

Roper nodded, his chin gently bumping against the top of her head. "He said he wouldn't take the children right away. It will give us time to assess him. Besides, both Daisy and Neil are being cautious. They intend to protect the younger ones."

"Who will protect *them?*"

Roper edged her back so he could look into her face. "I think he is a good man but we will make sure they know they can contact us if they ever need to."

She nodded. "I have never heard from my mother."

"I know. Perhaps you will one day, though."

She clung to his steadying look and sucked in a cleansing breath. Then she straightened. "Maybe I worry too much."

He squeezed her shoulder. "Could be because you remember what happened to you."

"I will never forget."

"But maybe one day you'll be able to leave it behind."

She bristled. "What do you mean?"

He brushed her cheek, his touch soothing, calming. "Nothing, sweet Cassie. Nothing at all. Now what can I do to help?"

The table needed setting. The meat needed slicing. He did both while she tended the vegetables and iced a cake.

When they took the food out to the table, half a dozen men waited, including Lane. He watched Cassie's every move. He said something about the weather but she barely heard him as she tried to listen for any sound from the river. Were the children okay?

She sent Roper a desperate glance and he smiled encouragingly. As they passed each other, he murmured, "Relax, the Mountie is with them."

As soon as the meal ended, she left the dishes and hurried to the river.

The children clustered about their uncle Jack, talking eagerly. He seemed demonstrative, reaching out to touch one of the children on the head, squeeze a shoulder and smile encouragement.

Cassie's throat tightened. She was only beginning to understand how much affection such touches offered and realized how much she'd been deprived of as a child. Her gaze sought and found Roper—a man who freely offered such gestures. Roper turned, caught her look, read something in it she meant to hide and smiled softly.

She jerked away returning her attention to the children and their uncle. Jack turned toward her. He looked weary, no doubt exhausted from his travels and the emotion of seeing his orphaned nieces and nephews. She allowed herself a bit of sympathy but on the other hand, when a person was tired, they often lacked the strength to pretend. It was a good chance to observe him and gauge his true attitude toward the children.

The Mountie was sprawled out, his hat over his face. So much for someone watching the children. But the man lifted the brim of his hat, peeked out to check on their arrival then resumed his stance.

Everything appeared fine but she wasn't ready to believe appearances.

A little later, she served a family meal, the table more crowded than usual with both the Mountie and Uncle Jack in attendance.

The Mountie sauntered off after a slice of cake. Uncle Jack said he wanted to spend a few days with the children before they made any changes so Roper invited him to camp with him.

"Thank you. I'm very weary. Do you mind if I retire immediately?"

"Of course not. Come along. I'll show you." Roper led the way to his camp.

Cassie stared after them as the children clustered around her.

"He seems nice." Neil's words sounded tentative.

"He says I look like Mama." Daisy sounded as if nothing else mattered.

Pansy lifted her arms to Cassie and Cassie hugged the little one close. She'd grown to love all of them. How would she survive without them?

Why was everything she cared about snatched from her?

Daisy sighed. "I guess we might as well go to bed." She headed for the shack. The boys followed without arguing.

Cassie helped prepare Pansy for the night, delighting in the way Pansy lifted her face to be washed and how she had to unfurl each chubby finger to wash it. She wouldn't get many more opportunities to enjoy this.

Daisy wriggled between her blankets. "Cassie, did you like my uncle?"

Cassie scrambled to think how to answer. The children needed to face their future with strength and optimism, yet they also needed to know they had alternatives if things didn't turn out well. "He seems nice enough but I think it's too soon for me to make any firm assessments."

Daisy nodded. "That's kind of what I think, too." She turned to Neil and Billy. "We need to remember what Cassie told us about not giving our uncle any reason to regret giving us a home. That means no arguments, no punching each other and be quick to do whatever chores there are."

Both boys nodded.

Cassie regretted her words on the matter. If they acted naturally, being rowdy and argumentative at times, she'd get a chance to see how Jack reacted. But it was too late to change things. She kissed the children goodnight.

It was too early to go to bed and her mind was in too much turmoil for her to expect sleep to come so she went outside.

Roper sat at the table and without hesitation she went to his side. Their plans for a marriage no longer existed. She would soon be alone, but for tonight she would allow herself this bit of comfort and she rested her shoulder against him. "I wish I could keep them."

He touched her hand. "Me, too, but this is the best for them. He's their uncle. He knows their history." His voice grew soft and she saw that he stared into space. "It's important to know who you are."

"And yet I wish I could forget."

His attention jerked back to her. "Do you? Do you really want to forget your mother and father?"

She instantly repented of her words. "Never."

"Then you understand how important it is for the youngsters to hold on to what is left of their family."

She nodded slowly. Yes, she knew it was for the best. "We've done well together, though."

When Roper didn't answer she turned to study him.

Deep lines gouged his face. His mouth drew back in a fierce scowl.

She'd seldom seen him without a smile. "Roper? What's wrong? Didn't you say this was best for the children?"

He nodded, his gaze fixed on a spot in the table. "They deserve family." The words ground out as if every letter scratched his throat. He jolted to his feet like he'd been shot from a cannon. "They are fortunate to have an uncle who wants them." He headed toward the river and paused. "Good night."

She stared after him long after he disappeared. He'd never acted so strangely. Did it hurt him so much to know the children were leaving?

An ache the size of all her tomorrows grabbed her gut and she groaned. The children would leave with their uncle. Their business agreement ended, Roper would leave, too.

She would get the independence she wanted.

Shouldn't she be rejoicing?

Chapter Fourteen

Roper had done his best to reassure Cassie that Jack was to be trusted but as he lay on his bedroll under the stars he strained to make out the words as Jack tossed and turned and talked in his sleep. But he could make no sense of the mumbling.

The man was older than Roper had pictured but that didn't automatically make him unsuitable. Constable Allen assured him Jack's credentials were flawless.

"He's a well-respected businessman. My superior in Toronto says he's a fair man with a healthy bank account."

Roper had no bank account. He wasn't any sort of businessman. Most of all, he had no claim to the children. But despite his words to Cassie he wished the man had not come.

How was he to say goodbye to the children?

His plans for marriage to Cassie ended with the uncle's arrival.

He would continue on as a cowboy with no family ties—empty and alone.

It was a familiar position for him. He would make

the best of it as he'd always done. But would he be happy?

Next morning, he was up early, impatient to be at work finishing the house. He knew Cassie would refuse help once the children left so he meant to get as much as possible done in whatever time he had.

Jack staggered from the tent, pale as butter and shaking.

"Are you okay?"

Jack nodded. "I'll be fine as soon as I have coffee."

"Cassie will have it ready when we get there." He'd normally have been at breakfast before now but had waited for Jack.

The other man washed at the river, shivering at the coldness of the water then they climbed slowly to the top of the hill.

The children watched their approach, caution filling their eyes.

"Good morning, Uncle Jack," Daisy called. She nudged the boys and they added their greeting.

Jack paused, breathing hard. "Good morning, children." He made it to the table and collapsed on the bench, letting out a weak sigh. "I'm not used to sleeping on the ground."

Roper studied the man. He looked worse than when he went to bed. Cassie watched him, too, and she and Roper exchanged glances. Was the man up to caring for four children? Of course, he wouldn't have to do it personally. He could doubtlessly afford a nanny.

But after two cups of coffee, Jack seemed to revive. He asked to be shown around.

"Go ahead," Cassie said in response to Daisy's questioning glance.

"I'll be back to help with dishes," the girl promised.

Cassie waited until they were out of earshot then gathered up the dishes. "Daisy will soon enough be gone. I can manage on my own."

Roper could point out that she wouldn't be feeding and washing up after six or seven. Only herself.

It sounded mighty lonely and unnecessary.

After they'd eaten the noon meal, Jack said he'd like to have a nap. Daisy tucked Pansy into bed, then hovered about the house where Roper and Neil worked. Roper considered the girl. "You look worried."

Billy sidled up to his sister. "She doesn't want to go."

"Billy!" Daisy grabbed the boy and shook him gently.

"You can pretend you do, but I don't. I like it here." He confronted Roper. "Why can't we stay?"

Roper put his hammer down on the window frame, using the time to gather his thoughts. He must ignore his own feelings. Not let them know that he wanted them to stay as much as Billy said he did. They had a future with their uncle that was likely full of all kinds of good things. Somehow he had to convince them of it.

He sat on the doorsill and waved them to join him. They crowded together. For a minute he let himself enjoy the way they sighed and pressed tight to each other. They expected words of strength and understanding from him. He uttered a quick prayer for wisdom then began to speak.

"You all know I was raised in an orphanage. I never knew who my father and mother were. Yet I was happy. Not everyone was, though. I remember when the Trout children came to the orphanage. You kind of remind me of them. There were four of them and they were so scared. The oldest one was a girl so she had to go to the girls' side. The others were boys so they were separated from their sister. It was really hard on the girl, Judy. She told me time and again that if she could be with her brothers and keep caring for them she would feel so much better. You see, she'd promised her mama to always watch out for them."

He paused to look into each intent face.

"What happened to them?" Billy asked, worry lines furrowing his forehead.

"Well, Judy grew up. She was offered a job working for a nice family."

Daisy gasped. "She had to leave her brothers?"

"She could have. That's what was expected." Roper let the words sink in. "But Judy had never forgotten her promise to her mother and she begged the matron to let her stay. Said she would do anything—cook, clean, help teach."

All three watched him with eyes wide. He guessed they had all forgotten to breathe.

"Did the matron—" Neil couldn't complete his question.

"The matron was very understanding. She let Judy stay, and then her oldest brother was big enough to go out to work. Last I heard Judy and Mike had made a home for their two younger brothers and they were all together."

The tension eased from the three children. Daisy and Neil exchanged a look.

"We'll be together," Neil said.

"And soon we'll be grown up."

Billy jumped up. "And then you'll bring us back here and we can live with Roper and Cassie."

Daisy laughed. "We won't have to live with anyone then."

Billy plunked down again and sat with his chin in his hands. "I want to live with them."

Roper gave them a big hug. "Let's promise to keep in touch."

"We will," Daisy said, and with that they all had to be content.

Roper returned to his work, Neil at his side.

"I hope we'll be happy," Neil said.

"You can learn to be no matter what."

For the first time he didn't believe it. Not even for himself. His only hope of family gone, he would have to fight to be happy after the children left.

He crossed the floor and pretended an interest in the door frame for Cassie's room.

He couldn't imagine returning to his solitary life.

No children.

No Cassie.

A groan tore from his throat.

Neil rushed over. "Did you hurt yourself?"

"Just a pinch. I'm fine." This pinch was internal and he wondered if he'd ever be fine again.

Roper concentrated all his thoughts and energy on finishing the house. Later in the afternoon, he glanced up as a familiar voice came across the yard.

Lane.

Roper had seen how Lane resented competing with Cassie's distraction over the children yesterday and wondered if he'd return. But he was there, a look of determination branded on his face. To his credit he did not come early but neither did he leave when the meal was over. Instead, he followed Cassie around as she worked, doing everything on her own as Daisy and the children had gone to the river to visit with their uncle.

Roper was torn between accompanying them and staying behind to keep an eye on Lane.

He tipped his head toward the river but the children were quiet. No doubt Uncle Jack lacked the energy to play any sort of active game with them. The man still seemed rather peaked in Roper's opinion.

He brought his attention back to Lane's lingering presence. He wanted to tell the man to leave but Cassie had made it clear she would be the one to tell him if she so desired. Obviously she didn't mind his attention.

Roper ground about on his heel and stalked back to the house. He couldn't abide to watch them together.

Yet he seemed to find himself at the window at every turn.

Lane hovered at her side as she washed dishes. Roper stared at Lane's back. Didn't the man see the tea towel and the dishes needing to be dried? Apparently not. Instead, he constantly got under foot forcing Cassie to take extra steps.

Any minute now she would reach the end of her patience and suggest he take himself on home.

The man twisted his hat in his fingers and said something that brought Cassie up short. Roper wished he could see her face but she had her back toward him.

Lane smiled. Rather uncertainly, Roper thought. Or was it just hope? And then as he watched, Lane lowered his head.

Roper lurched closer to the window. It looked for all the world like Lane meant to kiss Cassie. Surely now she would step back. Tell him to be on his way.

But she didn't move so much as an inch. She allowed

Lane to kiss her right on the mouth. Did Lane linger? Sure seemed like he did.

Roper ground his teeth together. He should never have left the pair alone. Should have been there to protect Cassie.

He narrowed his eyes. Cassie didn't slap the man. Didn't even seem upset. She sort of hung her head, all shy and uncertain.

The wind felt as if it were sucked from his insides, leaving him weak as a newborn kitten. He leaned against the wall.

Seems Cassie didn't need or want his protection.

He grabbed his forgotten hammer and returned to his work. He'd constructed a frame for her bed, built a table and benches for the house. The heavier table and benches they'd been using he meant to leave outside to use in pleasant weather. He'd also put shelves up for her to store things on, built bins and more shelves in the cellar. Tomorrow, as soon as the stove cooled, he'd get it moved inside. That left him time to do a couple of extra things that he'd been planning.

He would do them for Cassie and expect nothing in return but her happiness, and if that meant giving Lane the right to kiss her...

He had nothing to offer her but the work of his hands. No fine home. No parents and brothers. No history. Not even a name. He'd always known he could never be part of a family. It shouldn't surprise him that this attempt was no different.

That night, for the first time since he and Cassie had started this business agreement, he could hardly wait for the evening to come to an end so he could retire to his camp.

Jack accompanied him. The man was full of talk about his plans for the future with the children. "I know how much my sister loved them. Even as I loved her. I'll do everything in my power, God helping me, to raise them like she would want." The man choked and couldn't go on.

Cassie needn't worry about the children. They were going to a good home. He'd give her this last bit of assurance tomorrow.

The next day was a repeat of the previous one except Jack looked even more worn out and chose to spend most of the day sitting. Cassie suggested the children play near their uncle.

Roper followed her to the shack, helping return the food and dishes.

Cassie planted her hands on the worktable and leaned over as if consumed by pain. "I'm going to miss them," she said, her voice thick.

"Me, too." He wanted to take her in his arms and comfort her. But shouldn't he leave that to Lane?

"I hope and pray they'll be okay." A sob ripped from her throat.

Lane wasn't here and he was, so he opened his arms and pulled her to his chest. "Jack is a good man. I believe he'll give them the sort of home that neither you nor I knew."

She eased back to look into his face. "I never thought of it before but we do share that."

And so many other things. Long talks in the dusk. Laughter and play with the children. The work they'd both contributed to getting this house and business built. And a few hugs and kisses. He couldn't say what they'd meant to Cassie—and he wouldn't admit they meant the world to him.

He withdrew his arms and backed away. "Let the stove cool so I can get it moved." Without one glance backward, he returned to the house where he put the final touches in place. He'd added an unnecessary detail he hoped would give her sweet enjoyment.

He stood back to assess his work. The place was pleasant. He hoped she'd enjoy many hours of happiness here.

He had only two things left to do—dig the garden, which he would do before he left, and put in the stove. By noon he had that in place.

Only then did he open the door and wave Cassie inside. He'd asked Jack and the children to give them a moment alone.

She stepped across the threshold and her eyes and mouth widened with pleasure. "My own place." The way she clasped her hands together at her throat was enough thanks for Roper. Walking around the house, she examined each detail. Her gaze lighted on the little extra he'd added, a tiny shelf next to the stove and the pretty vase he'd found in the depths of Macpherson's store. He couldn't help wonder what she thought of the meager collection of wildflowers he'd stuck in the vase but if she liked flowers so much, he thought she should at least have a nice place and a nice vase for them. Even if, after this, he wasn't to be the one to bring them to her.

He planted a hand to his chest to stop the pain and sucked in air to calm his inner turmoil. It hurt to give up his plans even to a fine dude like Lane.

She continued her inspection of the house. She tried

the door to her bedroom. Then came full circle back to face him. "Thank you so much. I feel like I owe you something for this."

"It was part of our agreement. There is no owing." *No owing for my work or my friendship.*

She nodded, uncertainty erasing her pleasure.

He heard her silent question. Now what?

"We did well together, didn't we?" He wondered if she heard the uncertainty and longing in his voice or did it exist only in his heart?

She smiled into his eyes. "I'd say we did."

Her agreement eased his tension. "Seems a shame to end a good thing."

Her smile disappeared and sorrow filled her gaze. "But the children will be leaving soon."

He hadn't meant the children. He knew one way to test whether or not she had any interest in continuing their arrangement. "I figure to dig the garden this afternoon."

She jerked to full attention. "I know you planned to do it for the children's sake. But that's no longer necessary. They're leaving. Our agreement is over."

"It doesn't need to be." He looked intently into her eyes hoping she would see all he meant. That she would understand he didn't want this to end.

She marched to the window and stared out, her shoulders drawn up with tension.

He waited, hoping to see the tension soften. "Cassie, I—"

She spun around, her features iron-hard. "I only let you help because of the children. Don't get me wrong, I appreciate all you've done but I think I've made it clear that I don't need or want anything more. This—"

Her hand circled to indicate the room. "Is all I need. My own business. Independence."

The back of Roper's eyes burned. His throat tightened so he knew he couldn't force out a word. Not that he had anything more to say. She'd left no doubt about what the future held for them.

All he could do was nod and stride from the house. His steps didn't slow until he found escape and solitude by the river. He sat on the damp sand, his legs out before him like poles clad in denim. He stared at his boots and slowly his mind began to function.

The boots said it all. He was a cowboy. He belonged in a saddle behind a herd of cows. And Eddie could use his help. It was time to return to what he did best.

Cassie closed her eyes and held on to the window frame as wave after wave of shock lapped through her. Roper had offered to stay—to continue their business arrangement.

Like he said, they had done well together.

But to continue without the children made her heart clench until it hurt to even breathe. She guessed he meant they would marry as they had discussed. But wasn't marriage the ultimate form of control?

It wasn't for Linette and Eddie. Surely they were the rare exception. They loved each other enough to sacrifice, to allow the other to follow their heart.

On further consideration, marriage wasn't the ultimate form of control.

Love was.

Or was it the ultimate form of surrender?

What was the difference?

She moaned as her thoughts twisted and knotted with questions she couldn't answer.

Why was she even thinking such foolishness? It wasn't as if Roper had suggested he loved her. And she wasn't ready to make that ultimate sacrifice. No, sir. She finally had her freedom and meant to keep it.

Her mind was made up, but rather than peace she knew only the sensation of her insides rushing out the soles of her feet, leaving her painfully empty.

"Cassie, Cassie." The shrillness of Neil's cry jerked her from the quagmire of her musings and she rushed outside.

Neil grabbed her hand. "Come quick. Something's wrong with Uncle Jack."

Forgetting all else, she lifted her skirts and raced across the yard to where Jack lay on the ground, the children clustered around him. She knelt beside the man who was curled into a fetal position, his teeth chattering.

"I'm so cold," he choked out.

"Daisy, get a blanket. Neil, bring a drink of water. Billy, take Pansy over to the table and keep her occupied."

The children scattered to obey.

"Now tell me what happened," she said to Jack.

"I tried to stand but my legs refused to work." Saying those few words left him panting.

"Have you been sick before?"

He shook his head.

Daisy returned with the blanket and they helped Jack sit up. He drank the water Neil brought.

"I'm feeling better now." He smiled weakly, but he made no attempt to get to his feet.

"Where's Roper?" She regretted the words as soon as she spoke them. Hadn't she assured him she could manage on her own? And yet the first time she had a problem she looked for him.

"I'll find him," Neil said, and he took off before Cassie could say not to bother.

Not that she would have. Jack's weakness worried her.

Would it mean the children stayed longer? Wouldn't Roper then stay, as well?

Angry with herself for such selfish thoughts she turned back to Jack.

"I'm hot." He tossed aside the blanket and his face grew bright pink.

"What's going on?"

She'd never been so happy to hear Roper's voice.

"He's sick." Her answer was unnecessary considering the way Jack mumbled and plucked at the edge of the blanket.

Roper knelt beside her. "We need to get his fever down. Get some tepid water and a cloth. We'll sponge him."

She rushed to do his bidding. Daisy shepherded the children to the table where they sat watching. Their fear was palpable. Cassie paused in her haste to get water and cloths.

"We'll do everything we can to help him," she assured the children.

"If he dies we have no one," Billy said.

Daisy took his hand. "We have each other."

"And you have us," Cassie added, then returned to Jack's side with the supplies.

It didn't take any effort to put aside her selfish

thoughts and concentrate on Jack for the next few hours.

His fever broke and he was able to sit up, though obviously weak and shaken.

Roper pulled her aside. "He's not well. Sleeping on the ground, living like this is not doing him any good. I'm taking him to the ranch to recover."

"I expect that's for the best."

"I'll take the kids, too."

"But—"

"They need to be with him and no doubt he'll rest better if they are nearby. I'll be leaving as soon as I hitch up the wagon."

She nodded, feeling the blood drain from her face.

"Of course. I'll help the children get ready." Her voice sounded like she'd ground the words with shards of glass. How long would he be gone? She spun around and announced Roper's decision to the anxious children hovering nearby.

Roper soon drove the wagon to the side of the house, his horse tied at the back. He helped Jack into the back where he'd made a pallet of his bedding.

Cassie stood beside the children. "Your uncle will be well cared for at the ranch." The words she wanted to say stuck in her throat. *I don't want you to leave. I thought we'd have a few more days together. Please don't go back with your uncle without a proper goodbye.*

Roper carefully arranged the children's belongings beside his own. "Ready?"

No one moved.

"Your uncle is waiting."

Daisy turned to Cassie. "We have to go." A sob escaped and she threw herself into Cassie's arms.

Cassie blinked back tears as she hugged Daisy and wished her all the best. "I'll be here if you need me."

Daisy nodded as she stepped back.

Cassie hugged each of the boys, then scooped Pansy into her arms. It took every ounce of self-control not to hug the child hard enough to make her squirm. She kissed the chubby cheeks several times, then handed the little one to Daisy who waited, teary eyed, in the wagon.

Cassie swallowed hard and turned to Roper.

He twisted his hat round and round in his hands. "I'm going back to my job with Eddie."

Each word dropped into Cassie's heart like a heavy river rock. Then the meaning of them grew clear. "You're not coming back?"

"Like you said, our agreement is over."

She'd said the words without truly understanding the full consequence of them. He was leaving. She crossed her arms across her chest and pulled them tight. "I guess this is goodbye, then."

He nodded. "It's time to move on."

She groped from one heartbeat to the next. Tried to recall how to breathe in and out. Forced words from her starved lungs. "Goodbye and again, thank you."

He touched the brim of his hat. "Goodbye, Cassie. If you ever need anything—"

"I'll be fine."

She didn't move as he drove away. Long after the wagon disappeared from sight down the long, dusty trail she stared after them.

Then she shook herself into motion and headed for

the house. Yes, she'd be fine. She'd stand alone and independent.

She stood in the middle of her new house. She hadn't expected them to leave so soon, hadn't expected him to go so quickly, but there was nothing to make him consider staying. She'd seen to that.

She forced her attention back to her surroundings. Everything was perfect. He'd added a few special touches. He'd built a platform for her bed.

Her gaze lighted on the little shelf with the vase of pretty flowers. What kind of business agreement involved flowers? She grabbed the vase and headed to the door intent on pitching the contents into the woods, but she made only three steps before she stopped and slowly retraced her steps. No point in throwing the flowers out while they were still so bright and cheerful.

She set the vase back on the shelf and considered the room again. She had the fabric for curtains. Time to get them made.

Work would put her thoughts to right again. Work was the antidote to foolish emotions.

Chapter Fifteen

$\sim$

Roper concentrated on the road ahead of him. He needed to get Jack to a proper bed and proper care as soon as possible. The man looked ready to pack it in. What would the children do if their uncle died?

He and Cassie would give them a home.

But he would never wish ill on anyone for his own benefit.

He ached at the idea of leaving Cassie. But it was for the best. The sooner he left the easier it would be for them both. With the children gone, Lane would no longer see Roper's presence as a necessary evil.

He couldn't even think it without his insides churning.

If she'd given him even a hint that she wished to continue this agreement—

But her dismay over his suggestion to do so couldn't have been plainer.

Thankfully they reached the ranch and his thoughts were consumed with getting Jack into bed. Linette took over immediately, ordering Eddie and Roper about as they settled Jack and got the children moved into two nearby bedrooms.

"I'll take the kids out and show them around," Roper said when Linette seemed satisfied that everyone was organized.

"We'll talk later," Linette warned.

Roper didn't answer. He had no desire to face a bunch of questions about Cassie and guessed that's what Linette had in mind.

He took the children down the hill. The first place he stopped was the little log cabin. "That's where Cassie and Mrs. Gardiner and Grady spent the winter." He opened the door. Daisy and Neil stepped inside.

"It's nice," Neil decided. "We could live here."

Daisy looked about. "Uncle Jack lives in Toronto." She sighed heavily. "We'll make the best of things."

"Good choice." Roper drew them outside and turned them toward the cookhouse. "Cookie will want to meet you."

She'd have his hide and skimp on his share of the cinnamon rolls if he passed by without taking the children in.

He led them into the cookhouse. "Cookie, these are the Locke children Cassie and I have been looking after."

Cookie lifted her hands in a jubilant gesture. "Well, just look at you. It's a joy to have more children on the ranch."

He introduced each child, relieved when Cookie spared them her normal hearty slap on the back.

"Good to see you." She sent him forward with her pat. "But where's Cassie?"

"Back in Edendale. She's got a business to run."

Cookie scowled at him. "And you just left her there? By herself? Roper Jones, you're about as dumb as a hammer."

"You got no call to judge me."

Cookie sighed loudly. "That's the saddest part of all. You don't even know what you've done."

"I ain't done nothing but help her. Help these kids and bring their sick uncle here so he can get better." He'd lived up to his personal expectations, making sure everyone was happy and taken care of.

Cookie planted her hands on her hips and gave him a look fit to scald him. "Humph. Where does Cassie figure in all this?"

"Cassie is doing exactly what she wants to do."

"Men are so blind. Except for my Bertie, and he's one in a million." She leaned close. Roper dared not back up or show the least fear. "Have you ever taken a real good look at Cassie?"

"Of course I have." He could describe her in great detail if Cookie cared to hear it. From her shiny black hair that never quite stayed tidy to her brown eyes that could be so warm and yet sometimes so cold, to the way she hustled about, her hands and feet flying as she worked.

"I beg to differ. If you ever looked close you would see a woman aching to be loved. You don't deserve tea and treats but the children do." Her gruff voice grew cheery only as she served the children.

By the time they'd enjoyed milk, tea and Cookie's famous cinnamon rolls, Cookie acted as if she'd forgiven Roper for being so blind and stupid.

He stood. "Come on, kids. I'll show you the barns

and pens. You might even catch sight of some baby kittens."

Cookie followed him to the door and grabbed his arm to hold him back. "If you hurt my friend Cassie you will answer to me."

He held up his hands in surrender. "I've done nothing."

"Likely that's the problem." She pushed him out the door.

Roper hurried away, taking the children on a tour of the barn, letting them explore the hayloft in a fruitless search for kittens. They visited the pigs, watched the colts romping and stood on the bridge catching flashes of silver minnows in the water of the creek. He talked to the children, answered their questions, pointed out things for them to look at and tried to forget Cookie's words.

Likely that was the problem. But he had spoken to Cassie, had said it all.

Or had he? Had he been honest about all that was in his heart?

Would it have made a difference except to scare her even more?

Over the next few days Cassie moved everything from the shack to the house. She decided to leave the shack as it was. Perhaps with what she'd learned from watching Roper she could build solid walls and a roof and use it for storage or a chicken house. She would ask Petey about getting hens from the fort.

She made meals for the men, serving them at her new table indoors. She fashioned curtains for the window.

And she congratulated herself on being an independent young woman. She ignored the inner restlessness that made her feel she worked for a task master as unkind as her grandfather had been.

Lane came by every evening, even though she had been less than welcoming since he'd the gall to steal a kiss right in front of the washstand as she did dishes. It had taken every ounce of her self-control to keep from slapping his face.

She shouldn't have curtailed her instincts because he now seemed to think he'd gained some sort of favor with that stolen, unwelcome kiss.

"Cassie, leave the dishes and sit with me."

"I like to get them done before the food hardens on them." She continued to wash each plate and set it in a pan to drain.

Lane failed to hear the hint in her voice. "Aw, come on, Cassie. I don't enjoy watching you work all the time."

She handed him a towel. "If it bothers you so much then dry the dishes."

He looked like she'd suggested his mother was evil. "That's not what I meant."

She guessed as much. "Who washes and dries dishes at your place?"

"I do." It obviously pained him to admit it. "But when I get married, my wife will."

She practically boiled at the way he studied her, all possessive as if he already had her in the kitchen with a towel in hand. "Sooner or later the dishes have to be done. I prefer to make it sooner."

He tossed the towel aside and crossed his arms. His disfavor was evident. "They can wait."

Her temperature climbed dangerously. What right

did he have to expect anything from her? None whatsoever. And if he thought stealing a kiss gave him the right... Well, he had better give the idea another thought.

Each dish bore the brunt of her anger. By the time they were washed and dried, she was about ready to blow a cork.

Lane stood up from his impatient wait. "Finally. Now let's go for a walk."

She faced him, keeping a safe distance away lest she smack him, as she was so tempted to do. "Lane, you are a good customer and I appreciate that."

He reached for her arm, grinning widely. "I hope to be more."

She sidestepped him. "I know you do. But you are mistaken in thinking that's what I want."

"But of course—"

Her eyelids flashed red. How dare he assume he knew what she wanted? "This is my life." She waved her arm about the room. "The one I want. It's what I've dreamed of for a very long time."

Clearly the idea didn't suit him. His lip curled. "You can't be serious. My house is far better."

"Lane, I'm not interested in running your house. Or any man's." Unless it was Roper's, an insistent voice protested. She pushed aside the idea. Roper wasn't interested in anything but a business agreement. And she didn't want a continuing business deal.

Then what did she want?

"I want nothing more than to be independent."

His mouth tightened in disapproval. "You will live to regret this decision." He grabbed his hat and reached the door in three strides, slamming it after him.

"I guess I lost a paying customer," Cassie murmured but she felt not one hint of regret.

She turned full circle, examining the room. It was empty. So empty.

And she was alone. So alone.

The walls crowded her. With a cry of protest she raced to her room and sank to the bed. *Oh, God, help me. I have my heart's desire so why am I so unsettled?*

Her Bible sat on the nearby shelf. She hadn't read it since Roper and the children left. With desperate fingers she picked it up, stroked the cover, remembering Roper's strong hands on the leather. She opened the cover to the page with her babies' deaths. A familiar pain snaked up her insides but it lacked the deadly power of the past. She'd been at peace about her loss since Roper held her and comforted her. She flipped the pages to Genesis and could hear Roper's voice reading the words. Guilt flowed through her veins that it was Roper she saw in each line …not God. Utter loneliness consumed her. This Holy Bible was her only companion, her only comfort. She turned the pages past Genesis, unable to bear the memory of Roper reading, Roper holding her hand as he prayed, Roper—

She flipped the pages to the Psalms. She'd heard them read at funerals. Seemed a fitting place to rest her eyes. Psalm 1. *Blessed is the man.* Guess that didn't fit her. She was neither man nor blessed. *He shall be like a tree planted by the rivers of water.* She sighed. She had all she wanted yet she felt neither blessed nor planted. But because she had nothing else she wanted to do and because doing so brought Roper closer, she continued reading the Bible.

As the days passed, she spent more and more time

pursuing that activity. Her soul found healing and peace, even though a constant loneliness caused her heart to ache.

The days passed woodenly as Cassie fed a growing number of men. Some were passing through to the north in search of land. Others came to scout homestead possibilities close to Edendale. But mostly they were men conducting business with the local ranchers. All of them were happy to pay for a hot meal.

As usual, one morning several days later, Cassie headed to Macpherson's with her latest batch of bread. It sold well, as did her biscuits. All in all, she had a very successful business venture.

A wagon stood in front of the store. A very tired-looking young woman slumped on the seat. Cassie watched a moment wondering if the woman would fall forward but she rocked back with a groan, her eyes closed so she didn't see Cassie.

Cassie hurried onward and slipped into the store. A young man spoke to Macpherson, pacing before the counter as he talked. Not wanting to interrupt, she hung back.

"I don't think my customers would like having a sick woman here," Macpherson said, turning to see who had entered. "This is Mrs. Godfrey. She might be able to assist you."

Cassie waited, not about to commit herself to anything until she knew what it was.

"This young man says his wife is too ill to travel any farther. Wants to find a place where she can rest." He turned to the young man. "Mrs. Godfrey operates a dining place. She has a nice little house."

Both men turned toward her.

"Ma'am, I'm Claude Morton. My wife, Bonnie, is unable to continue. She's deathly ill. If you could help?"

Cassie had seen the woman and knew it to be true. But she wasn't certain she wanted to share her quarters. Not with strangers. She thought of how crowded she and the children had been in the shack—

The shack. "I can offer primitive accommodations. If you don't mind them, you're welcome to bunk there."

"Ma'am, any place dry where my wife could rest."

She turned the bread over to Mr. Macpherson then led the man outside. "Drive around the store. You'll see the place."

The man wasted no time in following her directions and stopped near the shack as she indicated. She showed him inside the little building.

"This is fine. Just fine. Hang on, Bonnie, dear. I'll have you settled in a moment." He trotted to the back of the wagon and pulled a bedroll from under the canvas tarpaulin. With barely a nod as he passed Cassie, he spread the blankets on the floor, then dashed back. "Come, Bonnie."

She tumbled into his arms.

He staggered under her weight, then carried her gingerly to the shack and made sure she was comfortable.

Cassie's eyes stung at the tenderness between them. She wanted that kind of caring. Her mind hearkened back to the comfort Roper had offered her again and again.

She spun away. She had her independence. It had to be enough. "There's lots of wood in the stack. And you're more than welcome to join the others for a meal."

Bonnie tried to raise her head. "Thank you so much

for your kindness." She panted by the time she finished the few words.

The poor woman. "You rest. Get strong." She spoke to Claude. "If you need anything just holler." He barely acknowledged her, his attention focused on his wife, his face wreathed in such concern Cassie's eyes stung. She slipped away.

For three days, Bonnie lay on her blankets. Cassie began to fear she would die. Claude walked around in a cloud of misery yet he kept her wood box filled, took out ashes, carried in water and after the second day began to help serve the meal. Just as Roper had done.

Cassie appreciated the help but it made her miss Roper with an ache that tempted her to lie down beside Bonnie and wallow in misery.

On the fourth day, Bonnie got up. She struggled into the house and Cassie made her tea.

"It's good to see you feeling stronger."

"I'm ashamed of how weak I was. Poor Claude was so worried yet he never once complained. Even though it means we still haven't found a place to settle."

Cassie hoped they'd find a place soon and get a solid cabin built before the snow came. How would Bonnie survive the winter?

Bonnie gave a weak smile. "I know you're thinking I'm not very sturdy to be going homesteading but it's what Claude wants. I'll get stronger with time."

"Claude is a farmer?"

"No. He just wants to own his own land and be independent."

It was too sharp a reminder of George's quest. If he hadn't died before he could claim a piece of land she wondered if he would have survived the first winter.

Bonnie looked about. "This is nice."

"It's a solid house." Thanks to Roper. Again, pain grabbed her breath. She missed him. She missed his company, their conversations, his understanding—

Stop! There was no point in wishing for things that couldn't be.

Claude and Bonnie stayed a few more days before they moved on.

Cassie missed them but she told herself she enjoyed the daily work. Told herself she was content. But she could not persuade herself she was happy.

At the end of the week she took her earnings over to Macpherson as payment on her bill.

"You're making quite a dent in your account," the storekeeper said. "What with your baked goods and the money from the meals you serve." As he spoke he checked the mail. "Something came for you in the latest mail bag."

Her heart skipped a beat. A letter from home? She took it, saw the return address bore Mrs. Ellertson's name and with a hurried "thank you" headed back to her house to read it in private. Her fingers shook as she opened the envelope.

Dear Mrs. Godfrey,
It's a surprise to think of you as a married woman and now a widow. I was some surprised to hear from you, I can say. I recall, I do, how you and your mother scurried about getting your things at the market. Always so quiet and cautious as if ye thought we'd bite. I've since put it all together and realize it's your grandfather you's afraid of. He's a hard man but I guess you already know that.

You ask if I've had any contact with your mother. I'm pleased to be able to say she still comes to the market and I took the opportunity to mention your letter to her. She was some surprised, I could tell, and teared right up. She says to tell you she is fine. Just fine. Your grandfather has suffered a mild stroke. She didn't say anything more about that but I can guess it likely hasn't improved the man's state of mind but perhaps he's weaker so she finds it easier to put up with him. Your mother said to say she would write if she got a chance and please take care of yourself and be happy. It's all that matters to her. I hope this message has cheered you. I will be glad to receive another letter with news to pass to your mother. Your servant,

Mrs. Ellertson

Cassie read the letter twice trying to picture the changes. Was Grandfather confined to bed? If so she didn't want to think how cantankerous it would make him, but if he was, at least her mother would be able to escape his constant supervision.

Take care of yourself and be happy.

She was doing the first reasonably well. The other? Perhaps happiness was too much to expect or hope for.

Except as she read the Psalms she got the impression God wanted His people to be happy with life.

She folded the letter and slipped it into the Bible for safekeeping. *Thank you, God, that my mother is alive and well.*

A knock startled her and she went to answer the door. "Linette. Come in." She reached out to grab her friend and drag her inside, then thought how desperate it made her look. She hadn't realized until now that she was that eager for a friendly face. The men she fed were friendly but it wasn't at all the same.

"Eddie and Grady are still at the store but I couldn't wait." She waved an envelope. "I got a letter from Grady's father." She closed the door and ripped open the letter, then read it quickly. "He says the child looks like his side of the family. Thanks me for caring for the boy."

Cassie waved Linette to the table.

"Not a word about coming for Grady. Not even an inquiry about how his son is doing." She shook the pages in disgust.

Cassie shook her head in disbelief. "How can some men be so unfeeling?"

"He just needs to get to know Grady but how will he if he never sees him? There must be a way to get him to come out West." Linette mused about what she could do as Cassie made and served tea.

Finally she gave a heavy sigh. "About all I can do is keep writing him and pray God will change his mind." She gave a short laugh. "Sorry to rattle on so. How are you?"

Finally Cassie could ask the questions burning her tongue. "How are the children? How is their uncle Jack?" But she didn't voice the most pressing question. How is Roper?

"Jack is improving but still weak. He does his best to spend time with the children but admitted to me that he's happy they are able to amuse themselves. Grady is really enjoying having some children to play with.

The children are so lovable." She launched into an accounting of everything the children did and said.

Cassie took it all in but wished for some news on Roper.

Linette pushed her empty teacup away and looked about. "Your place looks nice. How are you doing?" She rested her gaze on Cassie, waiting for her to answer.

"My business is going well. Macpherson is pleased with how quickly I'm paying off my bill at the store."

"And Lane?"

"Lane? What about him?" She couldn't understand how he deserved mention.

Linette studied her and Cassie met her look openly.

"Roper told me that Lane was courting you. Figured he'd be asking for your hand any day."

Cassie gave a short, mirthless laugh. "Lane thought the same thing but I told him I wasn't interested. Haven't seen him since."

"So you aren't encouraging his attention?"

"No and I never have."

"Ahh, I see."

"There is nothing to see."

Linette took her time answering as if considering her choice of words. "Roper seemed to think otherwise. He's been morose since he came back. I think he misses you."

"He's worried about the children. So am I."

"Strange. He seems at peace about the children but the minute your name comes up, he clams up tight."

Cassie assessed this information, trying to think what it meant.

"Cassie, he's lonely and hurting, and I think you're the only one who can fix it."

Hope hummed through her veins. Did this mean he cared about her? Reality set in. "He never mentioned anything but continuing our business arrangement."

"He's afraid you'll reject him because he has nothing to offer."

"He said that?"

Linette waggled her hands. "Not in so many words but I'm good at reading between the lines."

So it was only Linette's opinion. Linette, the eternal optimist, the dreamer.

She reached out for the post from Mrs. Ellertson. "I got a letter, too." She read it aloud to Linette.

"Isn't that good news?" Linette asked when she'd finished.

Cassie nodded.

"God answers prayer."

"Not always."

"He gives what's best." Her eyes resting on Cassie, she added, "I'm going to pray that you and Roper get together."

Cassie laughed. "Don't we have anything to say about it?"

"I'm expecting you will both come to your senses. It's plain as the nose on your face that you're lonely and missing him. It's equally plain that Roper is lonely, too, and missing you."

"Seems to me you're reading a lot into innocent expressions on a person's face."

Linette only smiled and nodded as if she had a secret.

Cassie decided it was time to change the subject. "What brings you to town?"

"Oh, I almost forgot. Eddie is arranging a meeting to discuss starting a church. Everyone is invited to the ranch next Saturday for it. You should come."

Before Cassie could reply, Eddie came to the door. "Sorry to rush your visit but we have several other stops to make before we go home."

Linette hurried to his side, pausing to thank Cassie and to press her point. "Come to the meeting about the church."

"I have no transportation."

"I'm sure Macpherson will be coming. You can accompany him."

She murmured something noncommittal and hugged her friend goodbye.

The room echoed with emptiness as the wagon drove away.

Why did Roper think he had nothing to offer her? If he thought she wanted a big house and fancy clothes, he hadn't learned much about her.

Had she misinterpreted his offer of a marriage based on business interests? *An obligation to love.* Why did those words again blare through her head? What did they mean? Where had she heard or read them? Would she find the answers to her confusion in the Bible? She'd learned it offered comfort and she opened the pages seeking something but not knowing what it was or where to find it. Then her eyes lighted on Romans 13:8. "Owe no man anything, but to love one another."

She sat back. The words that mocked her were from the Bible. How could love be a debt? Or was that what it meant? Slowly another thought worked its way into her mind. Perhaps loving wasn't a debt or obligation, perhaps it was a gift. She recalled where she had heard the words. At a sermon in her grandfather's church. It had been an admonition to put people ahead of possessions. Ahead of duty or profit. To give and accept love. She had rejected the words at the time because her grandfather was exactly the opposite.

Was she becoming like him? Putting work and obligation and money and her own interests ahead of all else? And in doing so denying her own needs? She finally admitted she wasn't joyful even though she had achieved her goal.

She did not want to end up unhappy and mean-spirited like her grandfather.

What did she really want? She knew the answer but wondered if it was possible.

She wanted to love and be loved. And she wanted it all with Roper.

She fell on her knees. *Dear God, I have been driven by the wrong motives. Forgive me. And help me plan my next move.*

Roper saw Linette headed across the yard to him. She and Eddie had been driving around the country announcing the meeting about starting a church. He knew they had gone to Edendale. No doubt they'd visited Cassie. Likely Linette was on her way to tell Roper that Lane and Cassie were growing more and more fond of each other.

He veered away to avoid her.

"Roper, hold up," she called.

He thought of ignoring her but she was the boss's wife. And he liked his job enough not to give Eddie cause to dismiss him so he ground to a halt and waited for her. "Howdy. What can I do for you?"

"I don't want anything except to tell you I saw Cassie. Thought you'd like to know she told Lane not to bother coming anymore."

His heart clawed up his throat and stuck there. She had dismissed Lane? After kissing him? Had they argued? Or had she finally realized how controlling he was, how he was not her kind of man at all?

He knew what sort of man she needed.

His heart settled into place with a thud. At least Lane had provided some company. "She'll be a mite lonely, I 'spect."

"Maybe so but the trouble is, she has eyes for no one but you."

He wondered how words had the power to make him suck in his breath like he'd been punched. "She said that, did she?"

"Not in so many words but I'm good at reading between the lines." She waved and headed back toward the house.

He stared after her, his boots rooted to the ground. Eyes for him? Oh, he missed her. With every beat of his heart, with every breath he drew, with every move he made. If only she had accepted his offer to continue their plans.

But he didn't want a business arrangement.

He loved her and wanted a real marriage.

He wanted to protect her, help her, comfort her, be at her side every step of her future. But what did he have to offer her?

Only love with no strings attached.

He'd never spoken words of love because he didn't think he had the right to offer his heart. He was nobody.

Nobody but a man in love with her.

Was it enough?

Chapter Sixteen

Cassie heard a wagon approach and went to the door to see who had come. "Claude and Bonnie, how nice to see you. Come in and visit." She studied the pair as they climbed down. Both looked healthy enough but sent quick little looks from one to the other.

She waited until they were seated at the table enjoying tea and cake before she asked the question begging to be asked. "Is something wrong?"

Another secretive glance passed between them. Then Claude spoke. "We've been talking."

Bonnie edged forward on her chair. "Remember I said neither of us knows anything about farming?"

"I remember."

"Then perhaps you also remember that I said we only wanted to own our own little piece of land."

Cassie's curiosity grew as the pair continued to dart looks at each other.

"We have something we want to discuss with you." Claude swallowed nervously. "Don't answer right away. Hear us out, and then think about it."

"And pray about it," Bonnie half begged.

"Okay."

Claude sucked in air. "We thought about how alone you are here. We could see you missed your former partner and the children." He held up a hand to stop Cassie's protests. "You keep awfully busy and all. Our idea is we could become your partners." The last words rushed out.

Cassie couldn't believe her ears. "But this is mine. I've worked hard for it."

Claude deflated. "I thought you might say that but we thought we had to try."

"Won't you at least think about it overnight?" Bonnie asked. "We need to plan what we want to do next. Maybe we could rent the little shack again. Spend the night."

Cassie nodded. "You're welcome to its use."

The pair beamed at each other. Then Bonnie spoke again. "We'll help with the chores as payment."

Cassie couldn't refuse. The afternoon sped past as the pair regaled her with stories of the people they'd met, the places they'd seen and a particularly entertaining tale of encountering an old man in a tiny shack up in the hills.

"At first he ordered us off the place, then he changed his mind and insisted we sit down. Hard to refuse when he aimed his rifle at us." Claude chuckled. "I think he was lonely for someone to talk to. Said he had moved out there three years ago to get away from people. By the end of our visit he confessed he was getting a little weary of no one but himself to talk to. Then he laughed loud and long, and showed us that his gun wasn't even loaded. Said he'd never hurt anyone."

"Poor man," Bonnie said. "So lonesome. I told him he should leave his isolated cabin and move closer to people. He got all serious and said he didn't trust people." She sighed again. "I tried to tell him there were more good people in the world than bad. You just have to be ready to take the risk of meeting both but he isn't ready to believe it."

Travelers began to arrive then, and the conversation ended. But Cassie kept thinking of what Bonnie said. *You just have to be ready to take the risk.* It seemed the words could apply to Cassie's life, too. She had to believe not everyone was like her grandfather. She had to be willing to take a risk.

The words still circled her brain hours later after she'd bid good-night to Claude and Bonnie and retired to her room.

Some risks were worth taking. Like starting her own business. Like Linette coming from England expecting Eddie to marry her.

Was letting herself admit she loved Roper an acceptable risk? Her heart jolted with hot fear.

Fear of being controlled. Fear of disappointment. Fear of the unknown.

She examined each fear. Would Roper try and control her if they married? A smile tugged her lips. If so, he'd soon learn she wouldn't accept having his will imposed on her.

Would he disappoint her? She didn't even have to think about that answer. Never. Because she would be happy simply to have him sharing her life.

The unknown remained scary simply because it was exactly that. She couldn't control it. But reading the

Psalms had filled her soul with deep conviction. God held the future. She could trust Him.

That left her one question to answer.

Did she have the courage to confront her fears?

Roper watched the buggies and horses drive in for the meeting about getting a church. He figured Linette and Eddie must have visited everyone within forty miles, judging by the number of people arriving. Seems only a year ago that there was no one but a few scattered ranchers and the people working there.

Guess it was inevitable that things would change.

He leaned against the corner post of the corral fence and watched. No doubt Cassie would come. He'd told himself he'd speak to her. He'd even practiced a countless number of speeches but he still had no idea what he would say. Only that he must tell her how he felt and see if he had a chance.

It scared him to think of confessing his love but anything was better than this endless misery of wishing, hoping, telling himself not to hope and going straight back to wishing.

The Mountie rode up to the house and dismounted. Roper hadn't expected him to attend the meeting but then he hadn't thought about much except Cassie.

Macpherson's wagon rumbled up and Roper pushed away from the post, unable to breathe. The man jumped down but rather than reach up to help a lady down, he headed straight for the house.

Roper stared. Where was Cassie? Was she ill? What else would keep her from attending?

He intended to find out. He jogged toward the barn

as fast as his bowed legs and riding boots allowed. In minutes he had a horse saddled and raced from the yard.

If something had happened to Cassie—

He should have never left her there alone. It was his stupid pride that had made him walk away.

The horse was doing all the work but Roper sweated like he did the running.

Down the road came a tail of dust indicating another wagon headed for the ranch. Whoever it was should slow down. The meeting wasn't important enough to risk an upset.

He reined the horse off the trail to let it pass, caught a twinkle of a dark blue dress and a surprised expression as it flashed by. He blinked. Cassie? Why was she driving like that? The wagon rattled to a halt.

Cassie stood up looking as surprised as he felt. "Roper, what are you doing out here?"

He edged closer. "I could ask you the same thing." He saw what appeared to be all her worldly goods piled in the back. She was going somewhere? In a hurry? Without a word to anyone? Not even him? His heart threatened to leak out the bottom of his boots. "You planning on leaving the country?" Or had she changed her mind and was headed to join her life with Lane Brownley? He grabbed the top of his boots and tugged in a vain attempt to stop the way his insides sank.

"Not leaving. Going back." She watched him closely as if her words should mean something special to him.

How far back did she mean? "Back to Montreal?" His words were cautious. Maybe she was going back to England.

Her smile seemed a little crooked. "No, back to the ranch."

Her answer made no sense. "Eden Valley?"

She nodded.

What reason did she have to go to the ranch? "What's back there?"

She lifted one shoulder. "I thought you were."

The words wound their way through his head with maddening slowness. He couldn't grasp her meaning. "Me?"

She nodded, her gaze watchful, intent.

Understanding crept closer. "You were coming to see me?" He squeaked like a twelve-year-old boy. "Why?"

She looked away. "Maybe I missed you."

A visit? But the wagon was full. He swallowed hard. "How much did you miss me?"

"Enough to sell half my business to a young couple who are prepared to run it for me. Enough to pack all my belongings in a borrowed wagon. Enough—"

He leaped from his horse into the wagon, sending it rocking, and grabbed Cassie's shoulders. "Are you saying—"

"Roper, I'm not saying anything more. I think it's up to you now."

He squinted his eyes at the goods in the wagon box. "Just exactly what did you have in mind?" It tickled him to think she might have planned to ride up to the ranch and propose to him.

She looked away. "I knew Linette would always welcome me. I could work for her."

He choked back his disappointment. Where did he fit into the picture?

Then she smiled at him, tipping his world sideways with her blinding intensity. Was it only his hoping that made him think he saw love and acceptance?

"Did you—" His tongue couldn't seem to find the right shape for the words he wanted to say and he tried again. "Did you see me in your plans?"

"I guess that's up to you."

It was all the encouragement he needed and yet his mouth was so dry he couldn't speak. He couldn't make his brain work. He could only stare at a face full of hope and promise. A face he saw in his thoughts day and night. A face he'd missed beyond measure. "But I have no name."

"Roper Jones is a very nice name."

"I have no past."

She smiled and touched his cheek with fingers that soothed him like cool water. "Sometimes the past is best forgotten."

"I don't know who my family is. Maybe they're idiots or insane."

"Or maybe they're kings and scholars."

He chuckled at that. "What happened to being independent?"

"I think love doesn't mean owning, but honoring."

She'd thought of everything. So had he. He took her hands and studied her face, cherishing each feature. "Cassie Godfrey, I love you and if you'll have a nobody cowboy, I'd like to marry you." His lungs locked up tight and he couldn't continue. Maybe he'd misunderstood her. His heart ticked out the seconds as he waited for her answer.

She lifted their joined hands and smiled. "It would be my honor to marry you and share your life. I love you, Roper Jones."

His heart blasted into action, sending relief humming through his veins. It was beyond belief that she could love him but he wasn't about to argue and he pulled her into his arms and hugged her, wanting to keep her next to his heart forever. But he wanted even more than that.

He lowered his head and kissed her, his love flooding his heart until he had to step back and whoop his joy. The horses both snorted a protest but Cassie laughed.

He kissed her again, love pouring from his heart in a gushing waterfall.

A little later, she sighed. "I meant to attend the meeting."

"We can still go. Might be a bit late, though." He tied his horse to the back of the wagon and they returned to the ranch.

As they stepped into the big room at the ranch house, Linette glanced toward them. Her eyes grew wide and she started to grin.

The others in the room followed her gaze and saw Roper with his arm around Cassie.

"About time you two came to your senses," Eddie said.

"Now we really need to get the church built so we can have a wedding." Linette would have it all planned out in a minute.

Roper murmured to Cassie. "Not sure I want to wait until they build a church and find a preacher."

"Me, either."

But they said nothing and slipped into two chairs at the back of the room.

Cassie had a hard time concentrating on the meeting. She could not think past the joy of the moment. Roper loved her and she loved him. Together they would create a new family. She would not let herself think of the four children she had grown to love. They'd been a family, but now the children had a new family of their own.

The meeting ended and Linette insisted Roper and Cassie come to the house. Cassie needed no persuasion. The children and their uncle had remained there, and she was anxious to see them again.

The children saw them coming and screamed her name as they raced down the hill. Only Roper's protective arm about her kept her on her feet as the children flung themselves into her embrace. She hugged and kissed them all and lifted Pansy to her arms. The little girl patted Cassie's cheeks and gave a watery smile.

"Oh, I've missed you all," Cassie said.

Daisy tucked her arm through Cassie's. "We've missed you."

"How is your uncle?"

The three older children all answered at once. From what Cassie could make out Jack was feeling better but wasn't strong.

Cassie stopped and drew them all close. "Roper and I are going to get married." Her heart overflowed, and she hugged them all close. Roper wrapped his arms around them as best he could, trying to include them all.

"I wish—" Billy started but Daisy's jab cut him short.

Me, too, Cassie agreed, feeling exactly as Billy. She reached for Roper's hand and strength, seeing in his expression the same regret none of them voiced.

They reached the house and Linette drew them into the family sitting room where Jack sat so he could see out the window.

Cassie hurried to greet him. "You look much better than last time I saw you."

He gave a wry smile. "I'm feeling much better, thank you." He eyed her and Roper. "Seems you two have finally allowed yourself to see what the rest of us saw from the beginning."

Cassie laughed. She didn't mind knowing others had seen their love before they did…or at least before either of them willingly admitted it.

"Children," Jack said, "would you run and play for a few minutes? I want to talk to Roper and Cassie in private."

Billy complained he hardly got a chance to see Cassie but Daisy shushed him and pulled him out of the room.

Jack seemed to consider his words before he began to speak. "I'm glad to see the two of you together. It makes it possible for me to make a rather large request of you." He stopped for a moment.

Cassie darted a glance at Roper. What was this all about? But Roper quirked an eyebrow, letting her know he didn't know.

"I love the children and would be glad to give them a home but I've discovered I am not strong enough. I guess I knew it before I even left Toronto but I wasn't about to let my sister's children be put in a home. Or given to begrudging people. But with you—"

Cassie held her breath not daring to believe he meant what she thought. What she hoped.

Jack studied each of them carefully. "I know it's a lot but I'm asking if you would be willing to care for my nieces and nephews."

Cassie heard Roper swallow. He gripped her hand tightly.

"Are you asking us to take the children?" he said, his voice full of uncertainty.

Cassie nodded, filled with the same doubts as to the meaning of what Jack said.

"If you would?"

Roper pulled Cassie around to face him. He grinned. "I don't even have to ask what you want. I can see it on your face as plain as day." As a pair they faced Jack. "Yes, we'll gladly give them a home."

"It will be our joy," Cassie said.

"Thank you. Now go tell the children. I think I know what their reaction will be."

Roper called the children back indoors. "I have an announcement to make." He waited until Billy stopped dancing about. "Your uncle Jack asked us to keep you and we agreed."

Neil understood first and whooped. The others followed suit, even Pansy. The noise of the joyous celebration brought Linette from the kitchen and Eddie from the yard where he visited the neighbors.

"This is wonderful news," Linette said.

Roper pulled Cassie into his arms, uncaring about the audience about him. "This is a day of good news. I am the happiest man on earth."

And in front of all those present he kissed her and their kiss brought a roar of cheers and clapping.

Epilogue

Roper drew Cassie into the crook of his arm and rested his chin on the top of her head.

"I wonder how many couples get married and adopt four children on the same day."

"Only a fortunate few, I venture to say." Cassie sighed her contentment. "Isn't that right, children?" she called over her shoulder.

"Yes," they chorused in unison.

Jack had wanted to sign the papers before he returned to Toronto so they had made the trek to Fort Macleod where they were married. With promises to write and Uncle Jack's assurance he would return to visit, they'd said goodbye to him as he began his journey back to Toronto.

The children stared after their uncle as he departed on the stagecoach.

"I wish he didn't have to go," Daisy said.

"Me, too, but I'm glad we don't have to go with him." Billy's comment made them all smile.

They were soon homeward bound. A little later,

the children recognized landmarks and pressed close to watch.

"Are we almost there?" Neil asked.

"Almost. Look. You can see the ranch in the distance."

Suddenly the children sat back.

Cassie gave Roper a questioning look. He shrugged as he turned to consider the huddle of children.

"What's wrong?"

The children silently consulted each other then Daisy spoke for them all. "You adopted us. You're giving us a home. We have nothing to give you."

Cassie shifted and signaled them to come close. She hugged them. "You have given us the best gift anyone can give. Your love."

"Amen," Roper said. Then he turned the wagon up the trail toward home. Eddie had appointed him foreman before they left and promised him the little cabin. It would be crowded until they could build on a couple of rooms but they'd been crowded before and managed just fine.

Eddie and a bunch of the cowboys came from the barn.

Roper wondered at the way they all grinned, then he turned the wagon toward the cabin.

"Hold up," Eddie called.

"What's up, boss?"

"Here comes Linette."

Linette trotted down the hill, Grady at her side, and when she reached Eddie she laughed.

Roper thought it rather odd.

"Hop down."

"You're the boss." He jumped down and helped Cassie to her feet. The kids scrambled out on their own.

"Let's go."

Cassie raised her eyebrows and looked from one grinning face to another. "Where are we going?"

Linette grabbed her arm. "You'll have to come see."

En masse they marched down the trail, past the storage sheds, past the barn, past the corrals. They kept going and drew to a halt before a new building.

"That wasn't there when I left," Roper pointed out.

"We built it while you were gone."

Linette laughed again. "It's your new house."

Cassie stared. "You built this while we were gone?"

"We had it all planned and the material ordered. As soon as you left the yard we got to work." Eddie waved them ahead. "Have a look."

Roper let Cassie go ahead of him. There was a nice big kitchen, furnished and ready to use. Beyond that, a small sitting room with two rocking chairs.

"Jack provided them," Linette said.

Roper opened the doors off the sitting room to find two smaller rooms.

"Bedrooms for you and the girls," Linette explained. "There's a loft for the boys."

Roper stared at Cassie, saw the shock in her face and knew she was as surprised as he. "I never expected—"

Eddie chucked him on the arm. "I want my foreman to be happy."

"I couldn't be happier but it's not because of the house. Don't get me wrong. I appreciate the room. But it's Cassie—" He pulled her to his chest. "And the kids." He opened his arms and drew them all close. "They provide my happiness."

"We know that." Linette signaled to her husband, and they all withdrew, leaving Roper alone with his new family.

He kissed Cassie. "I love you."

"And I love you."

"Us, too," the children chorused.

Roper knew he had never before known such joy. Joys shared were joys doubled, and he meant to double his over and over.

* * * * *

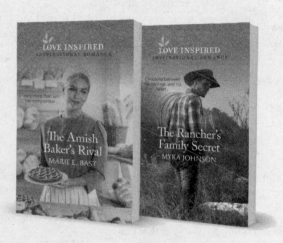

SPECIAL EXCERPT FROM

❧

LOVE INSPIRED
INSPIRATIONAL ROMANCE

Rescuing a single mom and her triplets during a snowstorm lands rancher Finn Brightwood with temporary tenants in his vacation rental. But with his past experiences, Finn's reluctant to get too involved in Ivy Darling's chaotic life. So why does he find himself wishing this family would stick around for good?

Read on for a sneak preview of
Choosing His Family, *the final book in*
Jill Lynn's Colorado Grooms *miniseries.*

In high school, Finn had dated a girl for about six months. Once, when they'd been watching a movie, she'd fallen asleep tucked against his arm. His arm had also fallen asleep. It had been a painfully good place to be, and he hadn't moved even though he'd suffered through the end of that movie.

This time it was three little monkeys who'd taken over his personal space, and once again he was incredibly uncomfortable and strangely content at the same time.

Reese, the most cautious of the three, had snuggled against his side. She'd fallen asleep first, and her little features were so peaceful that his grinch's heart had grown three sizes.

Lola had been trying to make it to the end of the movie, fighting back heavy eyelids and extended yawns, but eventually she'd conked out.

Sage was the only one still standing, though her fidgeting from the back of the couch had lessened considerably.

Ivy returned from the bunkhouse. She'd taken a couple of trips over with laundry as the movie finished and now returned the basket to his laundry room. She walked into the living room as the movie credits rolled and turned off the TV.

"Guess I let them stay up too late." She moved to sit on the coffee table, facing him. "I'll carry Lola and Reese back. Sage, you can walk, can't you, love?"

Sage's weighted lids said the battle to stay awake had been hard fought. "I hold you, too, Mommy."

Cute. Finn wouldn't mind following that rabbit trail. Wouldn't mind making the same request of Ivy. Despite his determination not to let her burrow under his skin, tonight she'd done exactly that. He'd found himself attending the school of Ivy when she was otherwise distracted. Did she know that she made the tiniest sound popping her lips when she was lost in thought? Or that she tilted her head to the right and only the right when she was listening—and studied the speaker with so much interest that it made them feel like the most important human on the planet?

Stay on track, Brightwood. This isn't your circus. Finn had already bought a ticket to a circus back in North Dakota, and things hadn't ended well. No need to attend that show again. Especially when the price of admission had cost him so much.

"I'll help carry. I can take two if you take one."

"Thank you. That would be really great. I'd prefer to move them into their beds and keep them asleep if at all possible. If Reese gets woken up, she'll start crying, and I'm not sure I have the bandwidth for that tonight."

Ivy gathered the girls' movie and sweatshirts, then slipped Sage from the back of the couch.

Finn scooped up Reese and caught Lola with his other arm. He stood and held still, waiting for complaints. Lola fidgeted and then settled back to peaceful. Reese was so far gone that she didn't even flinch.

These girls. His dry, brittle heart cracked and healed all at the same time. They were good for the soul.

Don't miss
Choosing His Family *by Jill Lynn,*
available February 2021 wherever
Love Inspired books and ebooks are sold.

LoveInspired.com

LOVE INSPIRED

INSPIRATIONAL ROMANCE

UPLIFTING STORIES OF FAITH, FORGIVENESS AND HOPE.

Join our social communities to connect with other readers who share your love!

Sign up for the Love Inspired newsletter at **LoveInspired.com** to be the first to find out about upcoming titles, special promotions and exclusive content.

CONNECT WITH US AT:

Facebook.com/LoveInspiredBooks

Twitter.com/LoveInspiredBks

Facebook.com/groups/HarlequinConnection

HARLEQUIN

Heartfelt or suspenseful, inspiring or passionate, Harlequin has your happily-ever-after.

With new books published
every month, you are sure to find the
satisfying escape you know you deserve.

SIGN UP FOR THE HARLEQUIN NEWSLETTER

Be the first to hear about great new
reads and exciting offers!

Harlequin.com/newsletters